# REKINDLE THE FIRE

As Annie collapsed next to Quinn, thin sheets of ice fell off her hat and collar. He touched his fingers to her cheeks, then her neck. Forgetting the aching in his shoulder, he pulled off her hat.

"You have to get out of these freezing clothes," he told her as he began unbuttoning the wet coat.

He tried not to notice how her hips moved against his nakedness as she wriggled out of the wet denim.

"Jesus, Annie," Quinn muttered.

He drew her body against him and tried to ignore the confusing emotions that swirled about him like fresh snow. The simple human horror of seeing another in such straits. The selfish concern that if she died, he might well die too, from lack of care. The revulsion at her flesh, not much warmer than a cadaver's against him. Bare flesh against bare flesh. The dim tickle of lust that he felt looking on that graceful, slender body.

Quickly, he pulled the blanket over them, amazed especially by his last thought. Amazed that he could feel anything now, just a few short days after being shot down, and that he could still see beauty in this woman who had wreaked such havoc in his life.

# BOOK YOUR PLACE ON OUR WEBSITE AND MAKE THE READING CONNECTION!

We've created a customized website just for our very special readers, where you can get the inside scoop on everything that's going on with Zebra, Pinnacle and Kensington books.

When you come online, you'll have the exciting opportunity to:

- View covers of upcoming books
- Read sample chapters
- Learn about our future publishing schedule (listed by publication month *and author*)
- Find out when your favorite authors will be visiting a city near you
- Search for and order backlist books from our online catalog
- Check out author bios and background information
- Send e-mail to your favorite authors
- Meet the Kensington staff online
- Join us in weekly chats with authors, readers and other guests
- Get writing guidelines
- AND MUCH MORE!

**Visit our website at
http://www.zebrabooks.com**

# CANYON SONG

## Gwyneth Atlee

ZEBRA BOOKS
KENSINGTON PUBLISHING CORP.
http://www.zebrabooks.com

ZEBRA BOOKS are published by

Kensington Publishing Corp.
850 Third Avenue
New York, NY 10022

Copyright © 2000 by Colleen Thompson

All rights reserved. No part of this book may be reproduced in any form or by any means without the prior written consent of the Publisher, excepting brief quotes used in reviews.

If you purchased this book without a cover you should be aware that this book is stolen property. It was reported as "unsold and destroyed" to the Publisher and neither the Author nor the Publisher has received any payment for this "stripped book."

All Kensington titles, imprints and distributed lines are available at special quantity discounts for bulk purchases for sales promotion, premiums, fund raising, educational or institutional use.

Special book excerpts or customized printings can also be created to fit specific needs. For details, write or phone the office of the Kensington Special Sales Manager: Kensington Publishing Corp., 850 Third Avenue, New York, NY,10022. Attn. Special Sales Department. Phone: 1-800-221-2647.

Zebra and the Z logo Reg. U.S. Pat. & TM Off.

First Printing: December, 2000
10  9  8  7  6  5  4  3  2  1

Printed in the United States of America

*This one is for Connie:*
*Your star is rising, Sis...*

*"And ruin'd love, when it is built anew,*
*Grows fairer than at first, more strong, far greater."*
—William Shakespeare,
*Sonnet 119* :1.11

## ACKNOWLEDGMENTS

I'd like to thank my husband, Mike, and son, Andrew, for their support and encouragement throughout this project. I couldn't do it without you, guys.

Thanks also to my agent, Meredith Bernstein, and my editor, Tomasita Ortiz, for everything they do to make a manuscript a book.

As always, I'd like to acknowledge the best little critique group in Texas, the Midwives: Wanda Dionne, Betty Joffrion, Bobbi Sissel, and Linda Helman. I consider your sharp eyes and kind words to be among my greatest assets.

Thanks also to friend and fearless reader, Kathleen Y'Barbo, as well as to the members of the Northwest Houston Chapter of the Romance Writers of America, Guida Jackson, Bill Laufer and the Friday Nighters, and the Woodlands Writers' Guild. I appreciate your enthusiasm and friendship.

Rosa Lockwood was especially helpful in researching herbs and the Mexican-American healing and spiritual arts known as *curanderismo*. Marie Schwarz helped with the Spanish. Thanks to both for your assistance.

And finally, thank you to the readers who take the time to let me know that what I'm doing matters. It's always a pleasure to write with you in mind.

# Chapter One

*Cañon de Sangre de Cristo, Arizona Territory*
*March 20, 1884*

Anna frowned at the dead man lying on her doorstep in the snow. The Navajo were always dragging hurt things to her, as if they thought her years spent with the curing woman had conferred upon her the same ability to heal.

Sometimes the dead woman's training did work. Last spring someone had left a skinny dog with a hugely swollen leg and less hair than it took to guess the creature's color. Against her better judgment Anna tended the dog and nursed it through what appeared to be a dose of rattler venom.

Notion, as Anna had named him, stepped out of the cabin and gave the man's corpse a thorough sniff. The dog, which had filled out and grown a thick gold coat, looked up expectantly and fanned a fringy tail.

"Not even a growl," Anna commented, surprised. Notion's deep bark usually alerted her whenever anyone came near either the cabin or corral. That service, in addition to his company, was worth the trouble of feeding the big mongrel.

Anna wrinkled her nose in distaste and stepped carefully around the pile of bloody rags that made up the prone man. She wished he hadn't been left there, for the task of digging even a shallow grave in the frozen soil was nearly impossible. First she'd have to build a cairn of stones to cover the fellow until the spring. Otherwise the coyotes or perhaps a bear would come to gnaw and scatter the remains.

Cursing softly, she stooped to drag her pail through the snow that had drifted up against the cabin's north side. After she melted it to make fresh coffee, she needed to saddle Canto and go check on Catalina and the infant daughter Anna had helped deliver two nights back. The child's cry had sounded weak, so Anna had brewed a tonic to enrich the mother's milk.

The strains of the infant's squalling sliced through Anna's memory. Nothing fragile about that. Anna shook her head in wonder. What made her think that Catalina's daughter's cries sounded different from any healthy newborn's? By now she should have banished the specter of this place, should have refused to let it taint the present.

Yet she hadn't, and something in that child's cries still troubled her. Just as they had in the last babe she'd delivered months before. And the child before that too. Both boys were fat and healthy the last time she had seen them.

Anna sighed, knowing that she'd have to ride out to check the infant or she wouldn't sleep that night. After all, it was a girl that she'd delivered.

She glanced to the east, toward a red cliff clothed only in juniper and desolation. Peering beneath a pall of silver, the rising sun limned the scraggly evergreens in gold. If she set out within the hour, she'd reach the Rodríguez rancho just past noon. After a short visit she could turn back and make it home before dark.

But if instead she stopped to cover up this stranger's body . . .

She thought again about coyotes and black bears, about the burden they could spare her if she but dragged the carcass from her doorstep. But she wouldn't want to trip over any gnawed, dismembered parts, nor would she want to encourage predators who'd come back later to finish off the last survivors of November's chicken massacre.

As if he'd read her mind, Notion whined and pawed the dead man.

"Don't even *think* of eating that!" she warned the dog.

The dog lay down beside the corpse and rested his head on the man's shoulder. Anna couldn't be sure, but she thought Notion looked insulted.

For the first time, Anna noticed the unfortunate victim's pale skin and light brown hair. Fairly young, too, from what she could make out of the bloody profile. She scowled at the corpse and shook her head.

"You're right, Notion. I can't leave him."

She'd been left for dead once, six long years earlier. The man who did it hadn't given a damn what beast scattered her bones or how she'd suffer in the dying. He'd just left her after he'd been done. As if she were nothing more than refuse. As if the secret she carried meant nothing at all.

She closed her eyes against the painful blur of memory. Even all these years later, she still glanced toward a tiny mound of red soil well hidden by the snow. Then she reached reflexively to touch the part of her coat that covered the thick scar on her belly. As if she needed some reminder of how he'd tried to gut her like a deer.

No, she couldn't leave this man's corpse to scavengers. Even if covering it would take her several hours.

Out of exasperation at the delay more than malice, she kicked the corpse's boot.

The dead man groaned, unmistakably, and old Notion whined once more, then stared at Anna, his great brown eyes beseeching.

*"Reina del cielo!"* Anna cried. She dropped the pan of snow on her own foot and fell onto her knees beside the man.

With a great effort she managed to roll the half-frozen creature to his back. She sucked in her breath so sharply that the cold air hurt her lungs.

She recognized the man's face. And worse yet, he knew her.

When Quinn Ryan relived the attack, he dreamed it differently. In one less painful version he ignored the smoke rising in the distance and never saw the flaming hogan. Or else, he decided sensibly enough, a burning Navajo dwelling was strictly an Indian matter, not his business. Instead of riding toward the black plume, he continued his journey to Copper Ridge, where he visited the bathhouse in honor of the completion of a weeks-long prisoner transport. He ate a thick steak in the Cattleman's Club and chatted amiably with Stark and Ramsey about the days when he'd lived in fear of being sent to Yuma Territorial instead of accompanying thieves there to begin their terms of incarceration.

In another version of his dream, he did investigate the smoke but remained mounted and coolly ignored Ned Hamby's provocation. Quinn pictured himself skewering Hamby with the law-and-order glare he'd reluctantly perfected, then turning his horse toward town. He rounded up a posse and his able deputy and later returned to arrest Hamby and his fellow raiders.

After a brief but satisfactory gunfight, Ned was duly perforated by the bullets from Quinn's Colt Peacemaker. The men who'd come with Quinn rounded up the other murderous thieves and later bore witness to their sheriff's courage. The territory sent him a reward so generous that he turned in his badge and bought a ticket on the Santa Fe Railroad. First class, all the way to New York, where his family lived.

Sometimes his dreams took him all the way home, to air redolent with the scents of his Irish mother's rich lamb stew, her dark soda bread. All the way to those streets, where he'd scabbed his knees playing stickball and his knuckles playing man.

*Home is years gone, and everyone that mattered there long dead . . . because I was too late. Too late.* With the numbing jolt of that realization, his rational mind took hold, then began to tally all the hard ways his dreams differed from the truth.

First of all, he had no loyal followers. His only deputy, Max Wilson, was twice as likely to crawl out of a saloon as to police one ever since his mail order bride had received a better offer en route to Copper Ridge. And Quinn couldn't think of any of the good citizens who would risk their lives chasing after Hamby in the canyons. Not for murdering a bunch of Navajo or even the rumor they'd killed white strangers.

Then there was the part about ignoring Hamby when he'd waved those little scalps.

"Once I pick the nits off, scrape the hair, and stretch 'em, might make a decent pair of winter moccasins, I 'magine."

Ned Hamby had leered as he spoke, his grin repulsive with both his brown teeth and his meaning. One of his brown eyes stared at Quinn, while the other gazed vacantly across the clearing. There, another filthy white man and what looked like a half-breed wrestled to pull back a ewe's neck and slit its throat. They laughed as the doomed creature staggered madly and then dropped, its bright blood splashing the trampled, muddy snow.

They cornered yet another sheep in the corral, and Quinn knew they meant to kill the whole lot simply so the Navajo wouldn't have them. Hamby and the others with him lived this way, stealing where they could, raping and killing where they wanted. The territorial judge, Ward Cameron, made it clear Quinn ought to turn a blind eye when Indians were murdered, but the men were now also suspected in the killings of white and Mexican settlers. Indiscriminate predators, Hamby and his men did not deserve to live.

So Quinn thought, and he planned sensibly to at least try to gather up some men and track the killers. Until Hamby swung those dripping scalps, spat out his vile words, and grinned.

Quinn had remembered at that moment his nights spent fighting on the Bowery years before, the feeling of his heart pumping, his fists slamming into bone and flesh. He'd been small as a boy, wiry and terrier-quick. He'd hit hard too, hard enough that he'd made the leap from fighting with his gang for turf to fighting in a makeshift ring for money, the first step toward a career in gambling.

He wasn't so small now, but he was still quick. And he longed to see if he could still hit hard. He ached to feel Ned Hamby's teeth collapse beneath his fist.

Yet Quinn wasn't stupid either. He knew he was impossibly outnumbered, so he tried to console himself with the thought that the Navajo would eventually catch these outlaws and deal them justice. But as he thought it, he knew the Navajo's other troubles had them hamstrung. Nervous about the latest Apache uprisings to the south, the United States government might use any provocation to try to move them back to the reservation. Even the killings of a pack of mad-dog white men such as these.

Yet those thoughts still hadn't propelled Quinn from

the saddle. He had years before drifted from the wager-driven world of prizefighting to less bruising forms of gambling. He'd made a decent living with his uncanny ability to judge and act upon the odds. And odds were he would die if he did anything to try to stop this now.

Though that instinct had been right, a thin, weak wail unhinged him. Rising among the bleats of panicked sheep, it was a child's dying cry.

Quinn realized that at least one Indian child had been scalped alive, then left to perish in agony alone.

He remembered little after that, for the knowledge launched him from the saddle and sent his fists flying toward Hamby's face. He would have killed the bastard too. Would have beaten him to death if he'd ever reached the man.

Beyond that he recalled only scattered fragments: a deafening boom from an unexpected angle, a boyish-sounding shout. "Sheriff didn't see that comin', did he?" Last of all, he heard harsh laughter, which abruptly spiraled into a blackness far too painful for oblivion.

Some son of a bitch had shot him in the back.

A chill wind whistled through the narrow canyon. Its passage rattled the bare fingers of the trees. Yet the cold did nothing to dissuade those thin, stick hands from reaching desperately toward their share of the scant light.

The same wind stole beneath the leather brim of Anna's hat as if seeking out her ears, her nose, her lips, for stinging vengeance. Fine snowflakes rode the icy blast, then alighted on the prostrate form that still lay near her feet. She looked up from the face that had so long haunted her, up past the bare trunks of the aspen that lined the frozen creek, past even the red cliffs high above her, and wondered vaguely if this was a true snowfall. Here, in the bottom of the narrow canyon, or *cañoncito* as the healer,

Señora Valdez, had called it, drifts collected, spun into this shadowed realm by the winds that scoured the more open lands above.

Here, where only narrow shafts of sunlight followed, the snow and cold would quickly blanket anything exposed. Here, a wounded man would quickly die.

All she had to do was go and boil her coffee. All she had to do was tend to Canto as if she'd never seen the man.

*I'd be leaving him for dead.* Her conscience breathed the words more quietly than the rustling of the wind. If she concentrated on the noises around her: the faint rattle of branches, the horse's throaty nicker from the direction of the corral, the dog's unending whine, she could ignore the murmur of those words.

She glanced down once more at the man. Blood soaked the back of his sheepskin coat, up near the left shoulder. More blood matted his brown hair. She forced herself to look toward the horse, an ancient speckled gelding who stretched his thin neck toward her. If she left the man there and he died, he'd never recognize her. If he died, he'd never set the law on her.

Tears stung in her eyes, then shimmered as the wind grew brisker. All she had to do was go and feed the horse or walk into the cabin.

*I'd be leaving him for dead.*

Without conscious volition her hand left its warm pocket, then glided to the spot at her belly where her clothing hid her scar. Her gaze drifted from the old horse and slid lower, lower, until it reached the visible portion of the gambler's bleeding face.

Notion raised himself onto his haunches and stared at her, then howled. He might have been her conscience given form and fur and lungs.

This time its voice was too loud to do anything but heed. She'd try. From the looks of the gambler, he'd probably die anyway and resolve her dilemma. If she did what little she could, at least she wouldn't have to add his death to her guilt.

Though she was quite tall, Anna had never been particularly strong before she came to live with the old woman. Her life had been hard in many ways, but not in those that conferred power. When she'd come there, badly wounded, she'd been weaker still. Yet as soon as she was able, the curing woman had demanded she adapt to the rigors of this place to help earn her food.

Gradually Anna grew into the work as if she had been born to it. She chopped wood throughout the year for heat and cooking. In the winter, she chopped holes too, in the creek ice to draw water. She planted corn and beans and squash. She tended these throughout the growing season, along with chickens, when she could keep the foolish creatures safe. She had a few goats, which were smarter than the chickens and at times required milking. Along with these responsibilities she had been expected to dig the various roots, scrape bark, and gather leaves for the old woman's potions.

All of this made Anna stronger than she'd ever been before. Even so, she struggled to drag the wounded man inside the cabin.

Groaning at her aching right knee and her cramping muscles, she cursed the Navajo who'd brought him. They could have saved time and the strain on her muscles by bringing him just this much farther. But the idea of Indians knocking at her door was almost beyond imagining. The Navajo might have a grudging admiration for the skills of Señora Valdez, but they still avoided her as an outsider, a non-person in the terms of their beliefs. She rarely caught a glimpse of a foraging squaw or child or hunting warrior. In lieu of either attacks or friendship, they sometimes left strange tokens of acceptance: a clay pot filled with honey, a pair of moccasins. In accordance with the curing woman's wishes, she left a skin of Señora's smelly goat's-milk unguent upon a certain split rock on the plateau twice a year at intervals marked by the moon and season. Anna had left her strange offering only twice since the old woman died in her sleep last spring.

She'd have to use the unguent now to try to help this man. Notion watched expectantly as she pushed the limp form closer to the fire. The gambler's flesh felt cold beneath her hand, but he'd groaned several more times as she'd moved him, enough to let her know that he yet lived.

Funny, how she didn't find that reassuring.

She thought of bringing him her blanket but decided instead to check his wounds. First she retrieved the pan. After refilling it with snow, she hung it on a rack beside the fire, which she had just rekindled. Though she'd prefer to cook her coffee, just then she'd need warm water to bathe the half-congealed blood from his injured body.

Next she slowly, carefully, removed his bloody clothes.

She had to be a nightmare, Quinn decided, some phantasm brought on by his body's desperate struggle against pain, blood loss, and cold. She couldn't be real, couldn't, for if she were, he must be dead.

If she were, he must now be in hell.

Curled up on his side, he watched her furtively through slitted eyes. Because he suspected his wounds of playing havoc with his reason, he catalogued her features: the tall, slim build, the sun-streaked, straight blond hair that fell loose well past her shoulders, the broad cheekbones and straight nose, and the pale eyes that looked smoky inside the dimness of this cabin. She looked no less beautiful, but she had changed in many ways. The bright blue silk dress had given way to a rough shirt and what looked like miners' Levis, which molded to her body in a manner he found surprisingly provocative. But beyond that, her merry smile had vanished; the flirtatious gleam had fled her eye. Instead, she now looked chiseled by hardship or the elements, or perhaps by her own sins.

As she withdrew a long and vicious-looking knife, he decided that this must be hell indeed, for she clearly meant to add more mischief to all she'd wrought already, years before. Did the demon mean to flay the flesh from him, too, now that she'd stripped him of all else he had owned?

Though he swore to remain still, feigning death, the memory of the last time he'd lain helpless while she worked drew forth a shudder, excruciating in intensity. He groaned against his will.

*"Paz, mi amigo."*

The honeyed richness of her voice convinced him beyond all doubt that this was really Annie Faith, despite her use of Spanish. Her words flowed as sweetly in that tongue as in the English she had spoken years before.

*"En el nombre de Cristo, te voy a ayudar,"* she continued, promising he knew not what. No matter, for even when he'd understood her, her words had all been lies.

She pulled something on a long cord over her head and placed it in his right hand. *"Por valor,"* she offered.

He thought back to his own scant store of Spanish phrases. Didn't that last mean "for courage"? Yes, he needed that just then. He pressed the crucifix into his palm while she cut away his outer coat, his jacket, and his shirt. She peeled back the sodden layers, and he squeezed the silver cross more firmly so he would not cry out with the pain.

*"¡Dios mío!"* she swore a moment after he felt cool air against his back.

"Speak English, please," Quinn grunted. "I know that you can."

Her gaze met his, the gray-blue of her eyes for a moment a cold fire. He realized his mistake then. Before that moment she probably hadn't known he recognized her. Perhaps she did not remember him at all. In the six years since she'd robbed him, she could have had many victims.

Her expression said she hated him for remembering who—and what—she was. The steely flame of her eyes promised he would die soon, most likely at her hand, if the bullet couldn't kill him fast enough.

Silently he called upon the power behind the tiny cross to come to a sinner's aid.

Anna wrung the damp cloth. The warm water that dripped into the pan blushed deeply with an infusion of Quinn's blood.

Such a lot of blood. Even more than Catalina Rodríguez lost the night that she gave birth. And the Mexican woman had been delivered of the growing child within her. Quinn, in stark contrast, had been invaded by a smaller and infinitely more hostile body.

She thought again of Catalina's newborn daughter, tried to reassure herself that this infant, like the last two, would be fine. She would have to be, for Anna couldn't leave her home. Maybe not for a long time if Quinn survived.

Anna dug the bullet from his left shoulder as if she were a prospector extricating a rare nugget. She only hoped her mining expedition didn't kill him. Weak from blood loss and exposure, he might easily succumb to an infection from her makeshift surgery.

Anna wished the curing woman were alive to help her. Born Hattie Forster in the Appalachian Mountains of central Pennsylvania, the scrappy, blue-eyed woman told Anna she'd learned healing at her own grandmother's elbow. But Hattie's father, a trapper, had moved the family ever westward, in search of better furs and wider spaces. Somehow, during the clan's travels, Hattie met and married a Mexican soldier named Carlos Valdez just outside Santa

Fe. While her husband fought Indians across the region, Hattie lived with his *familia*. By necessity, she picked up Spanish. As the years passed, she blended what she learned of *curanderismo*, the local healing art, with her own folk healing. For every ailing or wounded creature she encountered, the old woman had an opinion, some herb or unguent or prayer ceremony that would fix it, if only it were carried through with solid faith and a good heart.

Señora Valdez would have known just what to do, thought Anna grimly, but her own experience with gunshot wounds consisted only of butchering a couple of deer and a jackrabbit. She hadn't even been completely certain the man had been shot until he started muttering about it before he'd passed out.

Quinn's breath rattled more loudly than the mumbled words, more noisily than the popping of the fresh log she had placed on the fire. He swore again about the bastard who'd back-shot him.

Judging from his breathing, blood loss and a bullet wound were not his only problems. Time spent lying on the cold ground had touched his lungs with death. Anna half expected every exhalation to be his last. Yet he had obviously been a man in the prime of his vigor, so he had strength to draw on as he slept.

She washed his face next to uncover the handsome features she remembered: the wide-set eyes, now closed and shadowed, the generous mouth, its good-natured grin now vanquished, the slightly crooked nose, a memento of a prizefight gone far wrong. She nearly smiled at the memory of Quinn telling her the story. His self-deprecating humor as he spun a half-truth into tall tale to amuse the saloon's singer, a woman he'd been surprised to learn was not a whore.

*Annie Faith.* She could almost hear the way it sounded when he said it, though six years had passed since anyone had called her by that name.

Not long after she'd gone west, Anna had received the sobriquet courtesy of a love-struck cowboy. He'd claimed she reminded him of a long-lost sweetheart out Kansas way. The name had been as good as any, better by far than her own, too formal appellation. For the thought of strange, drunken men calling her Anna Bennett overwhelmed her with memories of others who had once spoken her name. First her mother, who had died so many years before that Anna didn't know if her voice was remembered or imagined. Next, Grandmother, whose stern, relentless love had been so difficult to bear. And last of all, her father, who had wounded her more deeply than she'd imagined possible.

For a long time she'd been Annie Faith, even to herself. Annie Faith could still smile and sing. Annie Faith could even dream. Anna Bennett had lost all those gifts that day when she'd returned for Papa with a handful of stolen coins. And found him—but that didn't bear thinking of just then.

Only when she'd come to the canyon had she realized that false identity had been her armor, as thin and brittle as a wasp's carapace. And like a wasp, it had a sting. The smile had been illusory, an enticement for those whose gold might take her from this raw, rough town. The songs had ignited false hopes for a future forever beyond the likes of her. The dreams had been the cruelest though, for these had convinced her that there was no price too high to achieve them.

She had sold her talent to survive, but she had sunk even further to pursue her foolish dreams. She cursed them now, realizing that her only chance at peace had been to turn her back on them, to live alone inside her canyon, where she'd somehow found the strength to go on living despite losing self and song. The canyon that was now her universe.

She hated sharing it. The presence in this canyon was

all the company she wanted. Her infrequent sojourns to visit the curing woman's Spanish-speaking patients gave her all the purpose she required. She didn't need a man, and most especially not this one.

Yet, she had him as long as he survived. So she put on her coat and went outside to gather what she needed for the poultice she would make to try to cure him.

*Estiércol de vaca.* She needed cow manure, according to what the old woman taught her. But Anna had no cow, and in a pinch she knew the fresh droppings of any plant-eater would do. At first, used to the ministrations of the eastern physicians from her youth, Anna had been horrified at Señora's suggestion. But she had seen the reeking concoction prevent infection more than once.

The goats baaed a reminder of their late breakfast. Anna threw them an armload of the bundled dried grasses she stored in the crude feed shed. In return, the spotted billy goat provided her with the most important component for her poultice.

Carefully Anna scooped the still-steaming offering onto a shovel and carried it indoors.


"Good God," Quinn moaned. "Are you trying to kill me?"

He said the words as he was waking, before he had the chance to recall to whom he spoke. Before pain buried him like a landslide. He felt crushed beneath the weight of it: the pounding in his head, the burning in his left shoulder. His first reaction was to gasp in shock and outrage, but his lungs felt choked with mud, his nose with something worse.

As he fought for breath, he heard her siren's voice, the voice that once had lured him to the rocks.

"If I wanted you to die, all I'd have to do is give up

trying," Annie told him. "Instead, I cooked a poultice for your wound."

His cough sounded like rattling leaves and racked him with fresh agony.

"As long as you don't make me any food," he said when he recovered.

"Why not? Are you in too much pain to eat?"

Since he was lying on his stomach, he had to turn his head to see her. "It's not that. It's just that . . . well, your cooking smells like shit."

Anna felt a cool ripple deep within her first, like the creek at spring's thaw. The current intensified, then found its voice, her laughter.

She could not recall the last time she had laughed. The explosion of sound surprised her, and she would have stopped, except it felt so right.

Notion, who had been lying beside Quinn, leapt to his feet and cocked his head at the strange noise. For some reason the dog's reaction made her suddenly self-conscious. She fell silent.

"You always made me do that," she accused Quinn.

"Women have—" His speech was interrupted by harsh coughing.

She knew she should wish him dead, but still she loathed the painful sound. She helped him raise his head, then held a cup of water for him to sip.

Afterward, he continued. "Women have laughed at me my whole life. It's a curse."

His voice sounded just as amiable as she remembered, but his green eyes glittered with suspicion. She knew for certain then that he had not forgotten what she'd done, nor would he have trusted her now, had he any other choice.

She wondered what, if anything, she should say to ease

his fear. Any apology she could think of seemed inadequate. Blushing, she turned her gaze away from him, into the fire. *Madre de Jesús*. The events of six years past were as clear as if they'd been part of a play she'd seen just last evening or a book she'd read only the day before.

She recalled how a pillow had partly muffled the gambler's groggy voice.

"I can do better. I swear it." His words had moved so slowly, like sorghum dripping down the sides of thick, brown bread.

Annie Faith checked the rope that bound his hands behind him. She didn't want to hurt him, but she couldn't risk him getting loose too quickly. Not when so much was at stake.

"Come here, sweetheart. I believe I'd enjoy another chance t'prove m'self in your bed," he called.

The slurring in his words reassured her that he'd remember little when he woke. At least that was what she told herself, since she so desperately needed that much to be true.

She paused a few moments, until the laudanum she'd mixed into his drink set him snoring. Then she resumed her search through the pockets of the gambler's trousers and jacket, which had been neatly draped over a straight-backed chair.

Quinn's rattling cough returned Anna to the present and to the certain knowledge that no apology could ever be enough. Not for him, not for her, not even for the God whose strength and goodness she drew upon to heal.

# Chapter Two

*Copper Ridge, Arizona Territory*
*March 21, 1884*

Judge Ward Cameron's dark-haired housekeeper, Elena, smiled at him as she ushered Horace Singletary into the elegantly appointed office. Ward frowned, certain that whatever news the county land clerk brought him would be nothing to smile about at all.

"I'm terribly sorry to trouble you, Mr. Cameron—" The young man spoke as cordially as always.

"That's *Judge* Cameron," Ward corrected Horace, as he did each time the two conversed. He would have liked to correct Horace's other words as well, for both of them knew the clerk was never sorry to inconvenience Cameron. One might even say he lived for such occasions, since the day the judge bought his family's property at a tax auction.

Horace nodded swiftly, putting to mind Judge Cameron of a weasel, a skulking little creature that nosed around Ward's business deals.

"Of course, *Judge* Cameron." He passed Ward an envelope, then waited for the older man to tear it open and remove the sheet inside. Before Cameron could read it, he continued. "As you see, I was unable to process your mining claim. On further research, I discovered the land you specified already has an owner. Very unusual situation for so remote an area, but I thought I remembered filing a change of ownership for the tax office."

Cameron felt heat rising to his face. That worthless Frenchman who'd given him the sample and the map must have known about this! The bastard tricked him and was laughing from his place in hell! Or maybe not. Maybe Luc-Pierre would have been just as surprised as he, had he survived.

Still furious, Ward scanned the letter.

"Who the hell's this woman, the owner?" he asked after a moment. *Anna Louise Bennett.* That name rang a bell, but he couldn't place it.

Singletary interrupted the act of polishing his glasses with a handkerchief to nod. "About four years ago she was named the legal heir of a Señora Hattie Valdez, a white woman widowed by Pedro Calderón Valdez, a former *capitán* in the Mexican army. The entire canyon was a Mexican land grant, properly registered for transfer after the territory was established."

Something in the clerk's expression convinced Ward he was enjoying every moment of this conversation. The short, slightly built young man had asked too many questions about Cameron's previous land dealings. He definitely had suspicions about how Cameron had come to be the only bidder for his father's ranch. Fortunately, young Horace couldn't seem to find the proof he needed to act against him.

Ward frowned at the letter. Singletary would have neat copies in case something unfolded. He was obviously too green to understand how men of standing were sometimes forced to grease the wheels of justice.

Ward had hinted earlier that he could be quite generous if Singletary chose to "expedite" his arrangements. But Horace couldn't do that, he'd explained, not while he intended eventually to start up the first newspaper in Agua Fresca County.

Ward swore at the young man more than at the situation.

Were Horace Singletary anyone else, they might have come to some mutually beneficial agreement. The land grant registration record might have been destroyed, or the will naming the white woman might have turned up missing.

But Cameron could almost hear the little weasel planning the front page of the first issue of his newspaper. Nothing would sell it better than a little homegrown corruption. Especially the kind that involved a presidentially appointed local judge.

"A Mexican land grant," Cameron thundered, pounding on his massive desk. "Goddamn it all. This is a territory of the United States, not Mexico. Did we whip them in that war or not?"

"I presume a man of your position has at some time read the law," Singletary told him, his blue eyes glittering as if that weasel nose had scented blood. As always, he withdrew his fangs after just a taste. "Excuse me, I meant the territorial law regarding prior land grants. As I am sure you know, they are quite valid once properly registered and proved. All this is in order. Miss Anna Bennett, a United States citizen, now owns the land."

"And she's paid taxes?"

He slipped on his glasses. "They've been paid in advance."

Once again the judge's gaze dropped to the annoyingly precise handwriting on the letter. Hattie Valdez, widow of

Pedro Calderón Valdez, had bequeathed the land to Anna Louise Bennett on March 14, 1883.

He could easily envision how the names would look typeset on a weekly paper should Anna Bennett suddenly be found dead. He could picture his new bride, on seeing Singletary's printed accusations, rushing back home to her father, consigning him forever to this hell.

*Anna Bennett.* Why did that name nag him so? His disappointment—and Singletary's presence—made Cameron's head pound with frustration, for he felt certain some crucial fact eluded him, something that could ruin all his plans.

Perhaps if he took his leave of the land clerk and attended to a few last-minute arrangements for his future bride's comfort, he would think of it. But he already had in mind a solution to his problem.

The quiet disappearance of this Bennett woman from *his* land.

*En el nombre de Cristo, te voy a ayudar.* In the name of Christ, I will help you.

How many times had Anna used the words the curing woman taught her? She had spoken them to Quinn that day. Did she really mean them? Did she truly draw upon their power when she helped bring forth a child or lanced an old man's abscessed gum? Did she believe them now?

Her gaze rose to the dark, weathered wood of the carved cross hanging on the wall above her table. From the time she had arrived, that cross had been the cabin's sole adornment. She'd been beaten, bled, and nearly emptied when she got there, only to be refilled by an old woman's skill and faith.

Anna absently grasped the worn silver of the matching cross that once more hung around her neck. She shuddered with a memory of her first lucid thoughts inside this cabin, near the very spot where Quinn now lay. The pain and, almost worse, the stark humiliation. Even the scant comfort of her songs had been denied her. How she had cursed Señora Valdez for prolonging her suffering. Didn't the old crone know she wasn't worth the effort of a poultice, the blessing of a prayer?

But throughout those first weeks of healing, the old woman had scorned her patient's self-pity. Anna well remembered the withered little healer's deep scowl of displeasure.

Drawing her striped serape's worn wool tight around her arms, the señora spoke, this time in English. "You feel bad about what you did and what you were? Then make it up to God, whose power saved you. He has replaced your emptiness with *el don,* the curing touch. I can see it in you as if you were born to it as I was. Learn with me now. Learn to heal his children, the sinners and the saints. And chop more firewood. God likes a cabin warm too."

*Heal them.* So simple, so succinct. A way to pay back God for her existence. But even more important, it was a ladder to start climbing, a passageway to peace.

Perhaps *el don* would serve her now as well. For Quinn's suspicion, his knowledge of her theft, had her feeling as unsettled as she had been in years. Old fears and recriminations had returned like ghosts to haunt her, and she knew that only the ways she had learned within this canyon would banish them again.

Because she could do nothing to repay her debt to Quinn, she would do her best to help him now. He might die anyway, and if he lived, he might try to hurt her or have her arrested, but those possibilities were as far from her control as the seasons or the phases of the moon. She could never make amends; she could only heal now. Anna could almost hear the old woman grunt approval at the thought.

The poultice should be warm now, ready to be put on

Quinn's shoulder. The heat of it might do his lungs good too. If she could only get him past the smell.

She soaked flannel strips in the reeking liquid and then wrung out the excess moisture. Quinn peered at her, his bloodless face the picture of distrust.

"You're not putting that on me," he growled. "I can't let you do . . . more."

Now that she regarded him more closely, she saw something else, the vulnerability of one near death. She spoke only to that part of him, for the other was too painful.

"I'm not who you remember, Quinn. I'm not Annie Faith. I'm Anna." Her words dropped into the calming rhythm of ancient incantation. "I heal you in the name of *el Hijo de Dios*, the Christ—"

"No! Keep that—that mess away. I was helpless last time, but not now. I can't let you."

"What do you intend? To crawl out of that door into the snow? You'll die without my help."

"I can't let you. Not this time," Quinn repeated.

"Fine." She dropped the steaming poultice back into the iron pot to keep it warm. A flash of anger rolled over her like thunder. Why hadn't she cooked coffee, instead of wasting time and effort on a man who preyed on those afflicted with her father's weakness?

She grabbed a rag and wiped her hands. So he wouldn't let her heal him. She shouldn't care at all. If he died, he'd never have her imprisoned for taking his gold or, even worse, hung as a horse thief.

She bit back a curse, confused by the strength of her reaction. Why had his refusal prompted fury? Had it been his lack of faith in her or his interference with her plan to buy herself redemption? Did she really believe that God hovered over her with a slate of her sins in one hand and an eraser in the other? She tried to laugh off the idea, but this time her laughter was a whisper, dried leaves in the wind.

*En el nombre de Cristo, te voy a ayudar.*

She'd promised that to him and to herself when she first found him. And she *did* believe the words the curing woman taught her.

She would have to win him over gradually, just as Señora had won her. Until that time she would simply do her work against his will.

Through his haze of bone-deep weakness, Quinn tried over and over to remind himself of what Annie Faith was, of what she'd done to him.

She repositioned him with strong and gentle hands, then placed the stinking poultice on his shoulder. As dead set as he'd been against it, he felt the warmth of it radiating downward into his chest to ease the deep ache that accompanied his breathing. As she worked, she spoke in flowing Spanish, a prayer of some sort, he imagined, or perhaps a chant.

"Can't forget," he told himself, but his whispered words did nothing to ease the suspicion that a stranger now inhabited her body, a woman he had never known before.

Her face and voice might be familiar, but her actions and her words conspired to compel him—*him,* of all people in the world—to trust.

"*De las doce verdades del mundo, dime nueve,*" she intoned as she lit candles arranged atop a wooden chest. "*Los nueve meses de María.*"

Her voice continued, soft, melodic, as her fingers touched his forehead, then massaged his scalp with something cool and wet. Stubbornly he fought the spell, his mind lurching from the rhythm of her words, carrying him backward to another place and time.

She'd thought him unconscious then too, and he'd been equally helpless against whatever she might do. That time there had been no bullet to rob him of his strength. Then she must have drugged him before the two of them made love. Unable to move, he'd peered through slitted eyes while she had fumbled hurriedly through his belongings. He'd wanted to throttle her for her betrayal, but instead, he could do no more than watch.

With each item she yanked out of his pockets, she had whispered "San Francisco," her voice shaking over the two words like a sinner's deathbed prayer. First she pulled out a deck of cards and riffled through them, running her fingertips along the edges he had shaved.

He could tell she'd detected the system he had used to mark the deck, for she turned her head to glare. The hostility that burned in her eyes had made him realize for the first time that she might prove to be a danger and not just a thief.

"You cheating louse," she'd muttered.

Next she pulled out a pair of loaded dice and an ivory-handled derringer, which she tossed into the corner without comment. The last item from his pockets was a small leather-bound book, worn from frequent use. Quinn gritted his teeth as he watched her flip through its onionskin pages. He breathed a prayer she would not tear any of them out.

Instead, she glanced at him, her expression perplexed. "Shakespeare. Hunh, Ryan . . . you cheat somebody out of this, or what?"

He'd groaned quietly as he watched her push it into her reticule. But still, she wasn't done.

And the next thing she had stolen had changed his life forever. Or perhaps destroyed it would be the more accurate description.

He'd thought he'd known her in the weeks before she'd robbed him, thought he'd understood the sad sweetness that lay behind her dazzling beauty and her dulcet songs. That time he'd learned too late that Annie Faith was nothing but a scheming opportunist.

He'd be damned if he let her steal her way into his heart again.

"Can't forget," he once more told himself hoarsely.

She leaned close to pull the blanket up to cover him completely and whispered to him, "No one is asking you to do that."

He felt the warmth of her breath, soft against his ear, and his mind held on to the memories.

Including those most painful, of the last time they'd made love.

The moment Ned Hamby finished chuckling over the tale of Quinn Ryan's shooting, the territorial judge erupted in a fury.

"Idiot!" Ward Cameron spat out the word as though it were the vilest of profanities. For him it truly was. He could abide sons of bitches, bastards, perhaps even those who fornicated with their female forebears, but as for idiots, he had no tolerance at all.

Hamby started visibly, and his good eye's gaze slid dangerously downward. The lazy one, as usual, stared off in some indeterminate direction. He'd be thinking of going for his revolver about then, Ward guessed. Hamby might be the idiot that Ward had named him, he might stink like an old skunk carcass, and he would certainly kill with no more compunction than a rabid dog. But even so, the man still had some crude sense of pride. Ward decided he'd better defuse the lunatic right then. After all, despite his vile nature, Hamby was more useful than one dead sheriff.

"Sit down. Have a drink of something better than that poison you boys swill." Ward gestured toward a well-padded leather chair in the office of his grand home. His hand glided over his luxuriant brown mustache, smoothing both the whiskers and his lingering misgivings about Ned Hamby's temper.

Clearly there was no cause to worry. He'd proven to Hamby long ago that he was the superior man, the one who had risen above base origins instead of sinking to their depths. Cameron's books, his education, even the cut and cloth of his suit, marked his mastery over Hamby's sort as indelibly as a brand of ownership.

Ward took special pride in the fineness of both this office and his respectable frame home, an anomaly better suited to an elm-lined avenue in Connecticut than a pine-studded hill in northern Arizona. Certainly his abode was beyond his means as a simple territorial circuit judge. But Ward had no intention of remaining stuck in this backwater post much longer. The home he'd built and the trappings of wealth that he'd acquired only served as portents of the future for which he was destined.

His gaze swept across the room, and he tried to imagine how intimidating it would be to filth like Hamby. A stark memory rippled through him like a sick chill. Himself as a young boy, invited into the home of his Connecticut burg's mayor and his wife, the parents of a schoolmate. The stunning realization that not every house had floorboards gnawed by rats or walls lined with newspaper advertising. Not every mother reeked of cheap liquor, sour sweat, and vomit. Not every father's fists swung whenever a son ventured into reach. Even then, though years had passed and he'd come so very far, the old shame rose, a bitter shade.

He vanquished it, as always, by surveying the elegant paintings of racehorses that graced his paneled walls. In addition to the expensive chairs, a huge black walnut desk gleamed, polished to a luster by his housekeeper, Elena. Nearby, a long, matching table held an engraved silver tray. Atop it stood a crystal decanter of smooth Tennessee whiskey and a sextet of crystal glasses.

Ward felt pleased at Hamby's look of confusion, as if

the offer of a rare boon after the insult had thrown him off balance. Ned nodded and dropped into the chair.

Ward smiled as he turned toward the table. He could almost picture his civilized offer extinguishing Hamby's anger like a heavy snowfall smothering the flame of a lit fuse.

His outstretched hand had nearly reached the decanter, when he heard a sound that froze the breath inside his lungs. The sound of boot heels striking precious wood. He wheeled around and glared at Hamby, whose feet now rested atop the dark river of the desktop. A small, moist clot of horse manure clung to the right sole.

"Were you sired by a boar hog and dammed by a burro, boy? That's *furniture* right there." God in heaven, he didn't need to deal with this oaf now, not after the mess he'd unearthed earlier that afternoon. His head was still reeling with the news that his claim had been denied because the land already had an owner.

Something in Hamby's face tightened. With studied nonchalance he removed his feet one at a time. Crumbs of droppings remained atop the desk, but he ignored them. "I didn't ride out here to be chawed on, Cameron. I come to tell you 'bout your sheriff. Thought you'd want to know you got to get a new one. Maybe a blind one what won't stick his nose in where it ain't wanted. Ever since he took that horse off me in town that time, he's been forgettin' what you told him."

Ward shook his head. "Ryan minded my warnings for five years. Until you provoked him. Jesus wept, man! Did you think he wouldn't recognize his own horse when you rode it into town?"

"Hell, I didn't even know the horse was his. I took it off that beanpole blond slut, as I 'spect you remember."

"You were lucky I was in town to smooth things over. That's the second time I saved your neck, as I expect that *you'll* remember too." Every now and then Cameron felt the need to remind his people not to bite the hand that banged the gavel, the hand that stayed the noose.

But Ned only looked resentful, so Ward sighed his exasperation and grumbled, "What'd you boys do this time to provoke him?"

Hamby shrugged. "Just a squaw too dried up to be much entertainment and a couple of Indian brats. Nothin' special. Just them ones that live too close to our claim, like you said."

"*My* claim. Never thought he'd be the type to worry about the Navajo," Ward said. But maybe after six years on the job, Ryan had fancied himself a real lawman instead of a hard-luck gambler who owed his job to Judge Cameron's influence. Now the damned fool had gone and gotten himself killed, just when Ward especially needed Copper Ridge's lawmen to turn their backs. By God, Miss Lucy Worthington would be arriving in a matter of a few days, and he needed to convince her he was the man of substance he had claimed to be.

He thought about the lies he'd told the senator, her father. Though he'd acquired a number of items extravagant by territorial standards, his efforts would look laughable to a bride from such a prominent family. He had to do more to prove himself an up-and-comer if he wanted to convince the senator to recommend him for the position he deserved. His future depended on her letters home.

Hamby licked his lips.

Ward, distracted from his worries, poured each of them three fingers of the whiskey. He sipped his and watched, revolted, while Ned gulped his glassful like the swine he was.

Instead, he took a deep breath. "Have you run them all off yet?"

Hamby shook his head. "Them Injuns? It ain't that easy, and you know it. 'Specially since they got nowhere else to go. There's still a mess of 'em living around that canyon."

"Run 'em off or kill 'em. Either way." No one would worry about some missing Navajo.

Hamby shook his head. "They're watchin' for us now. Desperate folk's dangerous, 'specially Injuns. It ain't hardly worth the risk to keep goin' back to that one area."

Again Cameron sipped his whiskey. Hamby stared at him and licked his lips.

"What's the matter. You boys lose your taste for the killing and the women? You get whatever you can haul off from your raids."

"Damn Navajo got nothin'. We're tired of eatin' goddamn mutton and sick of pokin' Injun snatch. Them white settlers east of there got better . . . not that we would ever—"

"Save your protestations of innocence. If you were in my court, I'd string up your whole lot on hearsay."

As Hamby turned his cockeyed gaze on Ward, Cameron felt a twinge of apprehension in his gut. A certain coldness in his expression seemed to hunger for the warmth of flowing blood. Cameron wondered how long he could play on promises to keep the beast at bay.

Hamby narrowed his dark and crooked eyes and grimaced, showing teeth no straighter or less brown. Years of frustration and hard living shook his voice. "I want you to know I could add your hair to my collection. I want you to know that I could kill you anytime I want. You're nothin' to me, Cameron, nothin' but a greedy bastard no better than the boys I ride with, leastways if they was to clean up decent. If it wasn't for my mama, you wouldn't last a minute in a room with me."

Only sheer determination prevented the judge from tossing down his whiskey, just as Hamby had before him. He wondered how many of the dark stains on Ned's filthy clothing were from blood.

A thin trickle of sweat rolled down Cameron's back between his shoulder blades. Had he overestimated his hold on Hamby? Would this reeking, ignorant pawn pull out some hidden weapon and cut him down just as he was about to clear the way to a fortune beyond anything the senator would expect?

Hamby's lethal expression softened, transforming his face into one that could have belonged to a feed store clerk or a young wrangler. "But that ain't all I want. I want somethin' fine like you have, somethin' I can take back home and show what I've done with my life. Maybe I'll just take that fancy pocket watch you're wearin'."

Cameron placed a protective hand over his gold watch. Strange, how Hamby had settled on it just the way that Cameron had first noticed the mayor's gold watch long ago. Ward's watch had been the first thing he had saved for when he'd started making money. Despite his concern about Ned's threat, he'd be damned if he gave it up. But he understood Hamby's longing. He understood it well.

"I'll order you a brand-new pocket watch," he offered.

"A gold one. I want a gold one just like yours."

"I'll even have your initials engraved inside the cover."

"That ain't all, Judge. I wanna hear that promise again." The threat of violence once more edged Hamby's voice.

"I've given you my word already." If he showed his fear now, he would lose control. At all costs, he mustn't lose control.

"Say it, Cameron . . . say it," said Hamby.

With those final words the balance shifted, and Ward knew the prestige of position and possessions had retained their magic touch. He smiled his condescension on the younger man. "Certainly. You have my word, Ned, that once my situation becomes stable, you'll be financially rewarded—"

"—The rest. Tell me the rest."

Cameron nodded and settled himself into the padded chair. His words sounded as magnanimous as if he really meant them. "Patience. As I've told you, I'll arrange your amnesty. You can return to Texas, see your mother. No one will ever come for you. Her slumber will never be disturbed by lawmen pounding on her door or the news that you've been gunned down by a bounty hunter. You'll receive the second chance that you deserve."

Hamby released a pent-up breath in a sigh that gusted like a cold wind through the treetops. "I'm gonna prove to her I ain't no no-'count after all."

"All you have to do is help me with those Navajo ... and one more small thing."

Suspicion hardened Hamby's features once again. "No tricks. No tricks or I swear I'll—"

Ward's hand waved dismissively. "It's nothing, nothing really. Listen, Ned. I can see you have a fondness for good whiskey. I had this shipped at great expense from Tennessee. How about I send you along with a full bottle? Just for checking to see if there's a white woman living up in Canyon Sangre de Cristo."

"And if we find her?"

"Then I'll send whoever makes her disappear five hundred dollars—and a case of this fine whiskey so you can celebrate in style."

Hamby secured the bottle of fine whiskey inside his brand new bedroll. New to him anyway. He'd gotten it, along with the tack and the horse beneath it, from the late Sheriff Ryan.

Thinking of the way the judge had treated him, he wished he had the dead sheriff's scalp to drop on top of Cameron's precious "furniture." But moments after Hop shot Ryan, Ned spotted Indians approaching, and the whole gang had gone in pursuit. Never did catch up with those Indians, and he never did bother going back for Ryan's hair.

That was fine by Ned though. He had something far

better in the sheriff's mare. Despite the bitter-cold grayness that had crept over the hill while he'd been inside with Judge Cameron, Ned grinned at the thought of riding there on the stolen horse. The judge would have wanted to hang him for stupidity, but Hamby had fond memories of the animal from the last time he'd taken her. A more willing, spirited horse he'd never ridden before or since.

Yesterday he'd nearly had to kill Hop to reclaim the chestnut mare.

"I shot the bastard. I got his horse. It ain't right if you take her." Hop tapped his pistol's grip for emphasis.

The youngest of Ned's gang, Hop was barely old enough to shave. He hadn't grown into his spindly legs yet, making him look more insectlike than human. The bulging gray eyes emphasized the effect and had the others calling him Grasshopper within days. But the men were shortcutters by nature, so he soon became Hop. Hamby couldn't even remember his real name.

"This horse was mine before. She's mine now." Ned grabbed the mare's reins, causing her to toss her head back. "You ask these other fellas. Ain't this Ginger?"

The other two examined her white star and the rim of white above her far back hoof. Both agreed she was the same horse he'd called Ginger before the sheriff reclaimed her in Copper Ridge.

"That ain't right," Hop insisted. His voice dropped to a fair imitation of a man's, as if to remind them all he'd packed a lot of bloodshed into his brief years. "I earned her."

"She's already mine. But tell you what. You can have old Ark here instead, for bringing her back to her rightful owner."

Hop spat on the half-frozen ground and glared at Hamby's fleabag roan gelding. "Hell, Ark's ugly as homemade sin, and he kicks like a Missouri mule. He damn near busted your leg last month out near—"

Ned used the horse's reins to whip Hop's face. The kid grabbed for his pistol, but by then it was too late. Hamby hadn't made it to twenty-six by being a slow draw. The mare, now loose, trotted away until the brush fence of the Indian sheep pen blocked her progress.

Ned watched two stripes redden Hop's left cheek where the leather reins had bitten. The boy stared down the barrel of Ned's drawn revolver, his eyes wide with shock. It took only a moment for his astonishment to harden into something sullen, something that promised trouble in the not-too-distant future.

But there was always trouble waiting, biding its time in Black Eagle's hostile stare or Pete's surly remarks. The kind of trouble that eventually caught up with a man if he didn't know when to back away and cut his losses.

Just as Ned was going to, soon as he ran off those Navajo and maybe killed some woman for the judge. At the thought, he licked his lips. A white woman, Cameron told him. He hoped she had a pretty scalp.

Grinning in anticipation, he swung up on the mare's back and thought how anybody might ride a horse this fine. Could be a banker's horse, a lawyer's even. When he showed up back home riding Ginger, folks would look up from their business and say *Ned Hamby's done all right*. His ma might even smile. She'd probably bust her jaw grinning when she heard the bright clink of Cameron's gold inside his pockets.

He patted the horse's sleek red-brown neck and nudged her into a smooth trot. As the first fat snowflakes swirled past, he resolved to brush the muck and blood spots from his Ginger every day, to keep her looking fine.

*Cañon de Sangre de Cristo, March 23, 1884*

At first Anna had been glad of Quinn Ryan's long silence. His unconsciousness made it far easier to treat him. But more than two days had passed since he had spoken, and although his breathing sounded easier, she began to doubt he ever would again.

The hen squawked indignantly as Anna grasped her scaly legs and lifted her off her nest. Her wings beat frantically, setting puffs of inky feathers adrift inside the storage shed where she had sheltered.

Anna frowned. Her last black hen. Were the gambler's need or her own guilt less pressing, she would spare the chicken's life.

One of Señora's patients might require a black hen later. To those people the chicken's customary color would likely matter more.

If she had some branches of sweet basil or even lemons, she might use them instead. If her bedraggled chickens had not quit laying, she would have some choice.

The black hen cackled, as if asking Anna for another chance. The chicken's pleas availed it nothing, but something else sufficed: a brown curve Anna glimpsed beneath the straw.

Releasing the hen, which clucked furious complaints, she took the half-hidden egg instead. Her stomach growled as the warm shape filled her palm. She would have welcomed an egg to supplement the pinto beans and bacon she had eaten earlier, but instead she focused her attention on the current of *el don* that would sweep through her as she sought to heal Quinn Ryan. Curling her fingers around the light brown shell, she imagined it as a spring flowing through a fissure in the stark face of a canyon wall. Life bursting through the cold rock, touching the stream's edges with the tender greens of new growth.

She thought again of Quinn, lying still as death inside her cabin. Neither the curing woman's poultices nor her herbs had opened the closed door of his consciousness. Only faith suggested that a simple egg and prayer might be the keys.

Anna closed the shed door and stepped outside. She shuddered against the deepening cold. Glancing up beyond the canyon's red walls, she studied the perfect stillness of the junipers' upper branches, the flat blue-gray of the sky beyond. She smelled snow coming, a frigid moisture that weighed down the odors of evergreens and animals, of dried grasses and cold earth. A bad day for travel, she decided. Maybe she'd been right to stay with Quinn instead of riding to check on the Rodríguez child. Burdened as she was by the injured gambler, she could only offer prayers for the young babe.

Quinn, too, needed words now even more than he needed herb lore. Sometimes the soul required more attention than the body's wounds. During her apprenticeship Anna had seen many people relieved by healing rituals. Their faith helped to restore them because they had been brought up to believe. Yet hadn't the old woman made her believe as well? Hadn't Anna been saved by the strange cleansings and whispered prayers every bit as much as herbal treatments?

In their common log corral, the horse and goats munched noisily on their feed as she walked past them toward the cabin. Perhaps she could pass on Señora's favor to this man that she had wronged. Perhaps in doing so, she could restore peace to her own troubled soul.

"Shit. If there was a white woman within twenty miles of here, we'd of heard tell of it," Pete growled. He hadn't stirred out of his bunk all day that Hamby knew of.

Hamby grabbed the whiskey bottle from Pete's hand. One thing he could always count on. Pete wasn't going to leave a warm cabin or a bottle without whining like a babe pulled off the tit. The miners' shack they'd taken over wasn't much by anybody's standards, but that morning, when Ned had stumbled outside to relieve himself and tend to Ginger, the air felt cold and oddly heavy. Rheumatism weather, his mama always called it.

He wondered how she was faring in the harsh dregs of winter of the Texas Panhandle. The thought set him to worrying, as always. Worrying that his mama wouldn't be alive when he got back. Worrying almost as much that not even his fine mare and gold watch would be enough to buy him his family's welcome.

*You always was a no-'count. Always was and always will be too.* The words stung like scorpions when Mama said them and only a bit less when his younger brothers took them up as well. It was up to him to prove they'd all been wrong. Ned Hamby was going to make his mark on this world, show them all.

Ned took a slug out of the inch or so remaining in Pete's bottle, then roared with anger at the especially smooth taste.

"We was savin' this, you idiot! We was savin' this for goin'-home time." He glared at his men and realized that although they were as likely to kill each other as ever, the three had passed around his bottle while he'd been asleep. Sorry bastards.

"If any one of you was worth the bullets, I'd shoot the whole damned lot," Ned said. "But as it happens, you ain't, and besides, I got a thing we need to do."

"Trackin' down some imaginary white woman in the canyon?" Hop laughed. "Hell, Ned, that's half a day's ride, not to mention whatever it'll take to find her. Why not just tell Cameron she's dead and be done with it?"

"Judge's got them puppet's strings too tight," Pete said.

Hamby's revolver was clear of its holster in an instant. Unlike the others, who had slept late on his whiskey, Ned had gotten up and around at a decent hour that morning. And he never dressed without strapping on the Navy Colt.

"Didn't mean nothin' by it, Hamby," Pete murmured. "Just don't none of us like runnin' Cameron's errands."

The silence stretched out, long and brittle. Ned wondered if he'd have to shoot Pete sometime soon if he were to keep the other two in line. The tension made him tired, as well as the thought of hunting that white woman in the canyon. He wanted to be done, done with this bunch of idiots, done with the woman so he could get on home.

"You mean to tell me you got no use for Cameron's gold?" Black Eagle asked. He spooned some beans onto a tin plate. Raised by his white mother, he bore the strong Apache features of the man who'd raped her. He'd once told Ned he'd had a proper Christian name when he was younger, but around the time he'd turned to stealing cattle and horses, he'd decided Black Eagle more fitting for an outlaw.

If Black Eagle was trying to keep the peace, he must have some reason. Damned half-breed never did anything out of the goodness of his heart. Of the three men Ned rode with, he was by far the most dangerous, Hamby had long ago decided. A fellow who was smart enough to learn to write his name and cipher when no schoolhouse in the country'd take an Indian. A fellow who was mean enough to skin a man alive, then tan his hide for leather.

If Black Eagle wanted to ride on out to the canyon, he must have his own reasons. And they probably involved killing the woman on his own and claiming all the profit instead of sharing, as they'd earlier agreed. 'Course, the half-breed didn't know that the reward Ned had promised was only half what Cameron offered, but what use was being leader if Ned couldn't claim a bigger cut?

And Black Eagle better never find out either, or Ned figured he wouldn't survive to see his mama, much less live to make her proud.

Quinn jerked awake at the warm moisture on his shoulder. If she had put that stinking poultice on him again—

He sniffed. It didn't smell the same now. Instead, the odor was sour, almost cheesy.

"Don't you make any medicines that smell *good?*" he turned his head to ask.

The blasted dog licked his mouth. He swore. Being shot was one damned humiliation after another. It wasn't enough that Annie had plastered that disgusting mess all over his shoulder while he slept, he also had to endure the affections of this overgrown mongrel. He shooed the cur away, only to have it circle around and slather him with damp affection once again.

If he could get up, he would boot it out the door into the nearest snowdrift.

"Annie!"

She didn't answer, so carefully he moved his head to look around and for the first time noticed his surroundings. The walls were made of peeling logs with mud and dried grass daubed between the cracks to keep the wind out. Judging from the draft, the effort wasn't entirely effective. Still, the crude stone chimney drew well, so no smoke hazed his vision.

Where the hell had Annie gone? With his luck she'd be out collecting dung for her demented idea of a treatment.

Strangely enough though, his breathing had eased, and he did feel better. Maybe there was something to her ideas after all.

"Annie!" he called again, though the effort set him coughing. As if in sympathy, the dog stopped licking and lay its head down on its paws.

Uncomfortable on his belly, Quinn decided to try turning on his side. That was when he noticed someone had undressed him.

"Shit," he muttered. That lovesick dog must have taken advantage of him in his sleep.

Actually, the only possible truth didn't sit much better.

Annie's hands had touched more than his wounded shoulder; no part of him remained a mystery to her smoky gaze.

What in God's name had she done with his clothing? Feeling more vulnerable than ever, he hoped she'd merely washed the mud and blood away and they were hanging somewhere close to dry.

Carefully he eased himself over to the left but not quite carefully enough. The movement sent expanding shafts of bright pain into his shoulder and clouded his vision.

He lay still for a time, willing himself to outwait the discomfort. After a few seconds, his gaze focused on a pair of battered pans hanging on pegs, then took in the remainder of the room. A thick woolen serape had been tossed carelessly over a crude table. Nearby, a pair of flimsy-looking stools stood close at hand, and a wooden chest took up the space along one wall. Atop it sat a clay bowl, a small painting that might be the Holy Virgin, and a half-dozen candles, all unlit.

A ladder pointed toward a narrow loft, more a shelf than a true room. He wondered if Annie slept there, if she might be asleep there now. At least one mystery was solved though. His shirt and jeans dangled from the overhang, reminding him uncomfortably of a hanging man.

Hating to do it, he called her name again. His mouth felt bone dry, and this mongrel's slobber was a poor substitute for a cup of water.

Above the loft, bunches of brittle-looking twigs and roots hung from the ceiling, making strange shadows in the amber firelight. But aside from his drying clothing, none of the shadows looked remotely human.

Had she abandoned him?

He hated the fear that permeated the thought, his overwhelming need for her. Physical needs, for water, sustenance, and someone to tend his wounds. His body did not care that she'd once robbed him and, worse yet, delayed him in Mud Wasp and then Copper Ridge until it was too late. His body only needed what there was no one else to give.

His sense soon overtook his terror. Of course she hadn't left. The fire still burned brightly. The dog was by his side. She might just be outside, tending to the needs of nature or bringing in some wood.

Might be. Must be.

*Must be.*


Cañon de Sangre de Cristo may have been named for Christ's blood, but Ned Hamby thought it looked more like the devil's lair. A mile wide at one end, it snaked for what seemed an eternity, ever thinner, along the narrow creek that carved it. In some spots, openings honeycombed the rock, doorways to the dwellings from some long-forgotten Indian past.

Hamby had always hated those caves that seemed to stare like empty sockets, even though he and his boys had holed up in them more than once. The hard, cold rooms, though sheltered from the elements, set him to mind of tombs and all the crawly things that gnawed a body when it lay inside one.

Astride his stolen horse, Ned gazed down into the canyon. If there really was some white woman down there, she might have a cabin tucked up in the trees or partly hidden by a rock outcropping. Possibly, she was crazy enough to live inside one of the caves.

He'd be damned if he wanted to spend the next six months looking for her. He had something easier in mind. This far from civilization, the folks that lived around this canyon were likely to rely on one another now and then. Hamby thought back to his family's Texas ranch, how even distant neighbors might help sink new post holes for a fence line or maybe castrate calves.

Among those who weren't Indian, that might be true

here too. And he'd remembered one small family of Mexicans they'd mostly ignored so far, except for stealing stock from time to time. Hamby was glad they'd let them be, for he felt sure that they could be convinced to tell him what they knew. And if they resisted, hell, he and the boys were always in need of entertainment.

Hoofbeats marked the approach of a horse even before it neighed a greeting to the animals it knew. Black Eagle, who liked to brag that he was a better scout than any fullblood, was returning.

"Find them Mezcans?" Pete asked eagerly. He wasn't much for work, but the idea of a raid always got his blood up.

"They ain't moved. Guess they thought we'd ride on past that sorry little hut of theirs forever," Black Eagle responded with a shake of his lank hair.

Hop turned from his task of picking a stone from one of Ark's huge feet. The gelding's hooves were magnets for horse cripplers. "They see you?"

Black Eagle's face froze. "You think I'm so clumsy I'd let 'em know that I was there?"

The boy grinned. "Way you *tell* it, you move like the wind. Way I *hear* it, sounds more like a tornado."

The half-breed pulled an evil-looking bowie knife from his right boot. The same knife he'd used to teach the bunch of them the art of scalping.

Ned gritted his teeth. He didn't know which was worse, Black Eagle's mean streak or Hop's attempts to prove himself a tougher outlaw than the others. Fortunately Ark chose that moment to bite Hop on the hand.

Pete, who'd always liked Hop, laughed extra hard to defuse the situation. Black Eagle glared for a long while, then finally put away his knife. For then.

One of these days, that half-breed was going to cut up Hop. Ned peered at Hop's red-brown thatch, trying to imagine how it would look in his collection.

Even though Black Eagle was the half-breed, it was Ned who'd started the collecting. He liked to take those scalps out and rub his fingers through them. Made his skin prickle with accomplishment at the thought of those he'd killed.

Ned thought again of killing, so he urged his mount in the direction of the Cortez place. One way or another, they were going to learn the whereabouts of a lone white woman in this hell.

It didn't take much time to find out what they wanted. An hour later they were riding toward the canyon's mouth. Ned didn't like the low gray ceiling of the sky, the quick transition from a few white flakes to what looked like serious snowfall.

He reined in Ginger and imagined the others admiring the smart way the mare pulled up, nearly sitting on her haunches. Their sorry mounts' gaits dribbled to a halt.

"If Cortez told the truth, it could take us half a day to ride to where she lives," Ned said. He brushed snow off his coat and wished he'd grabbed the pair of leather gloves that Pete had taken from the sheriff's saddlebags.

"He wasn't lyin'," Black Eagle insisted. "Not with his brat's hair in my left hand and my toothpick in the right."

Ned wouldn't have been surprised if Black Eagle had killed the child anyway, just to hear its mama scream. Hamby nearly grinned to think of it.

"I don't see as why we had to leave them Mezcans livin'," Pete complained.

Ned shook his head. "We'll pick them off later. Prob'ly catch them on their way someplace else. Somethin' tells me after today they'll be wantin' to move on."

"Aw, Pete just wanted a go at that boy's mama," Hop said. "Man don't got no discipline at all. Me, I'm savin' myself for one genuine white woman. Hope she ain't plug-ugly."

Pete spat, and stared after the glob, which sank through the thin layer of new snow. "What kind of woman holes up way back in some canyon by her lonesome? Curin' folks, for Christ's sake. Probably wrinkled up and senile to boot. Let's go get this done, boys. I wanna see what this crazy woman's got for us that we couldn't of took off them Mezcans with a lot less ridin'."

Ned adjusted his hat and glared at Pete. His hunger for blood and a woman faltered against the bitter realities of cold and snow. He shivered, longing for the few comforts of the miner's shack they'd taken over, the warm fire they'd left behind. He must be losing his edge, because he didn't want to ride down the canyon in a blizzard. Didn't want to do it in the least. But if he wanted to live long enough to get home, he couldn't give these boys the slightest inkling that he was going soft.

If the boys were hell-bent on killing the woman today, he'd best make them think that it had been his idea all along.

# Chapter Three

Miss Lucy Worthington drew a clean white pair of gloves out of her dust-grimed reticule. It was essential that her appearance and demeanor remind her future husband of her station despite the fact that she was clearly meeting him in hell.

She gazed once more out the window of the bone-jarring stagecoach and thought she'd never seen such a wretched, empty place in all her life. She'd been thrilled to finally disembark from the Santa Fe train, whose motion had sickened her from Washington to northern Arizona. At least she was thrilled until she recovered sufficiently to look around.

Where she was from, the collection of raw-looking huts wouldn't have qualified as an eyesore, much less dared to call itself a town. Thankfully one of the vile mud huts, adobe, according to the locals, proved to be the station where she would begin the last leg of her journey. The round, suspiciously swarthy-looking woman who ran the place offered her some sort of bean gruel that stank of rancid grease and unfamiliar spices. Lucy declined as quickly as was politely possible.

She'd begun to think of the whole trip as a desperate struggle with starvation. Only the respite of the Harvey House meal stops had saved her from perishing from hunger, for she'd been unable to eat a bite during the ride.

The stagecoach was far worse. She'd been incapable of keeping down her meager bites of food, and she was forced to share the cramped space with the most uncouth of travelers, a pair of the shadiest-looking creatures that ever dared call themselves "businessmen."

They were persistently, inappropriately friendly. Were it not for the dour expression of Miss Rathbone, her companion, she would have feared for her honor. Fortunately the old woman had a face that was the envy of all bulldogs. When Lucy's silence failed to convince them she had no desire to speak with them, Lucy could almost hear the starched Bostonian woman's protective growl. Finally the two men took the hint and apologized, muttering excuses about the appalling lack of decent females in these parts.

Although the air outside was freezing, Lucy insisted on opening the window against the sour odors of the unwashed bodies in the coach. At first the others had protested, until she added to the stench with her own vomit. Now, when she stared out the window, she wondered if there could be anything but hardship waiting in this harsh land. Mile after mile of wilderness rolled past them: distant snow-capped mountains; rugged red-rock earth. Even the trees looked bent and stunted by the cold wind. She cursed her father once more for sending her out here against her wishes.

He'd explained the situation again and again. "Ward Cameron wants the Worthington name and all it can bring him. He's a man of ambition but not a man of breeding. He'll accept whatever he must to further his career. And realistically, my dear, he's your only choice. If you'd wanted better, you should have . . ."

Lucy pressed her delicate, gloved hands against her ears, as if they could blot out the memory of her father's cruel words. Words that reminded her of the shameful thing she had done. Words that whispered that despite her grand name and her white gloves, Ward Cameron might still abandon her to whatever demons lurked in this harsh land.

As Anna walked from the feed shed to the cabin, thick snowflakes began to spiral down toward the ground. She glanced up, past the bare creek willows toward the cliffs. The trembling whiteness leached the canyon walls of redness, robbed the junipers of green.

Something in the shimmer of the gray air, the ache of the old injury at her right knee, hinted that this snowfall would be heavy, a true blizzard, though spring was close at hand. But the seasons were often unpredictable, and she was glad of the good store of firewood Javier Cortez had cut for her in payment for setting his son's broken arm last fall. It would be one less thing to worry about as she worked to cure the unconscious gambler.

She paused a moment inside the cabin's doorway to allow her eyes to adjust to the dim light. One luxury she truly missed from her earlier life was glass. One clear window would make such a difference in the lighting of this cabin, but even if she had the money, bringing such a thing unbroken to this canyon would be nearly impossible.

Even so, the fire's amber light lent comfort as well as warmth. The only sounds she heard were the low rumbles of Notion's snores, and the burning logs, which shifted amid a shower of quickly fading sparks. She'd have to light the wall lamp, or she'd soon be lulled to sleep herself. Something about a snowfall, even when she couldn't see it through the tiny, shuttered windows, always made her feel content to be inside the cabin, decently fed and comfortably warm.

Cupping the egg inside her hand, she slipped off her coat and reached up to hang it on a peg. Then she placed her broad-brimmed leather hat beside it.

"How 'bout some water here?"

Quinn's voice, so unexpected, startled her so badly that Anna dropped the egg onto the hard dirt floor. The yellow dog, instantly alerted by the thin crack of the shell, bounded over in two steps and began lapping the rare treat with his broad pink tongue.

*"Madre de Dios!"* Anna cursed, then told Quinn, "I was going to cure you with that egg."

"Must have worked. I'm feeling better, or at least I might be once I get some water and my clothes back." His voice sounded weak and parched.

Anna brought him a tin cup of the tea she'd brewed that morning in case the gambler roused.

As she helped him tilt his head to drink, she noticed he'd removed the poultice. She glanced around the pallet, wondering what he could have done with it.

Quinn gulped the still-warm liquid, then made a face like a tiny child force-fed turnip greens.

"Gads, woman. Is this juice from that stinking poultice?"

"It's only spikenard tea. It tastes just fine, Ryan." She marveled that the man complained more about what she did to help him than the bullet that had slammed into his shoulder. "What did you do with the poultice? It should still be on your back."

"It smelled even worse when I tossed it on the fire. And you've been living in the sticks too long if you think this tastes decent."

"I don't brew it for the taste."

"Then for what? Torture?"

"The curing woman who lived here claimed the Indians use it for a lot of things. It makes babies come easier."

"So that's what's wrong with me. I shoulda listened to my mama and kept my legs crossed."

She bit her lip to keep from smiling. "In your case I had more in mind its respiratory uses. Your breathing's worried me. That and the fact that you've slept for two straight days."

"I've slept—two days?"

His voice stretched taut, and his smile twisted into a grimace.

"Are you in pain? What's wrong?" she asked.

"Two days . . ." He closed his eyes and shook his head. "The last time, back in Mud Wasp, I was out two days."

*Dios mío.* Anna wished he hadn't brought up the incident that lay between them like a coiled copperhead. She poured herself a cup of spikenard. Sweetened with a little honey, its mild flavor suited her. She sat down on one of the stools and sipped, as if for strength.

Since Quinn had been dropped off into her life, she'd thought of little else besides the need to talk to him about what happened. Still, the words that she'd rehearsed turned cold and sticky in her throat, as if the honey in her tea had congealed.

She hesitated, her thoughts returning to the little book of Shakespeare she had taken from him. Then to the greed and desperation she had felt to learn where on earth the swindler had secreted his money.

Once more she'd picked up his jacket, though her earlier search through its pockets had yielded nothing in the way of cash. This time, however, she noticed its surprising weight. Ah, yes. She'd known he'd keep it somewhere nearby. Smiling at her victory, she set to work ripping apart the well-made garment.

"You're quite the tailor, Ryan," she told the snoring man.

The gold coins had been sewn into it, cleverly distributed inside the hem and seams. While the gambler slept, she robbed him of his hoard. There was enough there to take her far from little Mud Wasp, enough perhaps to finally reach her goal.

"San Francisco," she had whispered once again. As they always had, the two words soothed her, promising riches for an attractive young woman who knew how to entertain a man. And she didn't mean to do that entertaining at third-rate hellholes any longer either. No, sir. God had given her a fine voice, as if for consolation, and she was going to use it to start a brand-new life. A new life with a new name, Miranda Flynn.

Miranda Flynn had style, élan. Miranda Flynn was a star's name, like Jenny Lind or Lillie Langtry. Miranda Flynn had never been some two-bit singer who allowed a bullying bartender to rough her up, demanding favors she was not prepared to give. Favors she wouldn't be able to protect from him much longer.

She closed her eyes, but nothing dammed the flow of tears. Miranda Flynn had never been gullible, like Anna, nor a thief, like Annie Faith.

"I'm sorry," she told the sleeping gambler. She picked up the carpetbag that contained the few items she would take and headed for the door. Pausing, she gazed down at the young man's tousled, sandy-brown hair and barely resisted the temptation to stroke it, as she had so many times these past two weeks. Despite his vile profession, he hadn't seemed such a bad sort. Though he'd bought her pretty gifts, he hadn't considered that a license to ill-use her. If he hadn't been a gambler, she might have chosen someone else to rob. Or at least she would have thought of it if she felt she had more time. Putting down her bag for a moment, she covered him with the worn gray blanket. There was no need to let Miss Frieda find him lying there, trussed up like a Christmas goose and bare-assed to boot. No need to do more than steal his money and his horse.

Anna's face burned with shame at the memory of how

she'd allowed fear and ambition to cloud her sense of right and wrong. And the agonizing lessons it had taken to clear her vision of those flaws.

She sipped the cooling liquid and forced herself to speak past the painful lump that prevented her from swallowing. "There's nothing I can say that won't sound like an excuse for what I did in that hotel room. And there is no excuse. I had my reasons, but they were all wrong. I can see that now. Back then I was a petty thief, and I robbed you for a petty dream. I'm sorrier than I could ever tell you."

He said nothing, only opened his green eyes and stared with an expression so full of raw hatred, it nearly took her breath away.

After a brief pause she steeled herself to say the rest, though the words threatened to dislodge a private store of tears inside her. "If it makes you feel any better, I was punished for my crimes—"

"Punished?" His voice sounded shockingly strong now, considering his condition. "You want to hear about punishment, Annie Faith? Let me tell you about what happened when I woke up two days later. How the kind and caring citizens of Mud Wasp threw me in the hoosegow because I couldn't pay for the hotel or the livery on the horse that you ran off with. Let me tell you about how your two days turned into two *weeks* while I waited for the circuit judge to come to town. And how those two weeks turned into two *years* before I saved the money I needed. And how by that time it was too late. Too late because of you."

Tears burned in Anna's eyes, but she couldn't bear to let him see them. Instead, she shoved a thick log into the fireplace.

"I told you, I'm not Annie anymore. I'm Anna," she insisted. He said nothing, and she knew that in his mind she'd always be a thief.

She had not expected his forgiveness, but she'd still thought herself at peace with what she'd been. But the moment she had seen the anger etched in his expression, her own self-loathing rushed back at her, inevitable as winter on the bright heels of the fall.

Barely had the flames begun to lick around the loose bark, when she grabbed her hat and stalked back outside into the nearly blinding snow. She found the storm no colder than the darkness in her heart.

---

"Have some more soup, Papa." Horace Singletary thrust out the spoon. Exhausted from a ten-hour day spent processing claims, the clerk tried to will his hand to steadiness so he would not spill every drop. Despite his effort, fatigue made the curved bowl quiver, and he felt the patience draining from his soul.

Outside the cramped wood structure, a wintry dusk had long since robbed the sky of color, and Horace had been up before the dawn. He was cold in the ramshackle bunkhouse, cold and tired to his bones. Tired as his father now looked, despite the fact that Horace was only twenty-four years old.

His father's blue eyes appeared to focus briefly on the spoon before growing soft and distant once again. Enveloped in an old wool blanket, the old man nodded, eyelids drooping like a pair of setting suns.

"Papa, please, you have to eat." Horace hated begging. How he wished Laurel would come back. She had always been so much more patient, and their father seemed to listen more attentively to her. But a week earlier, his sister's husband had grown impatient at her long absences. Fearing that her three-year marriage would unravel, she'd finally returned home to their ranch, two days' ride from there.

Horace felt a small surge of victory as Papa reluctantly accepted the spoon. Until a moment later, when his eyes closed once again and the contents dribbled from the old man's mouth.

"Please stay awake so we can do this!" Horace shouted in frustration.

The old man's eyes shot open with an expression of clear terror. "Sorry . . . sorry . . . sorry . . ." he began. Tears rolled unchecked down his hollow cheeks.

"Oh, Papa, no." Horace used a worn kerchief to blot the moisture on his father's face. The skin felt more like paper than the flesh Horace remembered. It seemed as if, since he'd lost his land, the old man had withered into weightless shadow, a fragile husk of the giant he'd once been.

Watching Papa's slow decline was pure hell. Horace felt impotent against it, as powerless as he had been a thousand miles away at college. More than anything, Horace hated his father's now-frequent tears. They reminded him too sharply of how proud Papa had been. And they made Horace feel so guilty that he nearly wept himself.

He should be more patient. And he should have done something to stop Judge Cameron years before.

It took nearly another hour's effort to feed his father half the bowl of lukewarm bean-and-ham soup. Afterward, Horace threw two more split logs into the bunkhouse stove and rubbed his own cold hands amid the sparks. A chill wind whistled through the gaps between loose boards.

He supposed they had been lucky that Judge Cameron had left them this. An old bunkhouse on the nearest section of what once had been their ranch. The rest had been sold for back taxes two years after the attack. So close to Copper Ridge, the land's value had risen. Horace shouldn't have been shocked when Judge Cameron bought it, shouldn't have been outraged when Cameron tore down the comfortable house where he and Laurel had been raised and replaced it with a newer, grander residence.

The only vestige the judge kept of the old place was the ranch house's name, The Pines.

Yet Horace couldn't help but think about how neatly it had worked out for the bastard. How after Hamby's raiders had come and beaten his father, then driven off the herd, Judge Cameron had been so harsh about the tax bill. How suddenly, the bank—even family friends—wouldn't lend Papa so much as a Yankee dime. How amazingly, when the ranch at last came up for auction, the judge had been the only bidder.

Not surprisingly, he had bought it for a song.

All this had occurred while Horace had been away, working on his education. He had to return home, his degree unfinished, but not his long-held dream.

Oh, no. Never his dream. If he couldn't find work with one of the big newspapers in the States, as he had planned, then he would start one of his own. And with it Horace would ruin Judge Ward Cameron for all the neat coincidences that had worked like deadly poison against Papa's will to live.

Ward Cameron nearly choked on the *cuernito* his housekeeper had baked when the realization struck him. *Anna Bennett*. There was a damned good reason that name stuck in his craw. Already it had prompted him to take out Singletary's letter more times than he cared to admit, even to himself.

He brushed off his hands, showering the gleaming walnut desktop with crumbs of sugary cinnamon. Not noticing the mess, he scooted back his chair and pulled out a journal, one hidden in his desk's bottom drawer. Unlike the dime novels that currently popularized an outlandish version of the West, his writings told the true tales, stories he could not afford to share. Yet he documented them religiously, for the pure joy of seeing his true exploits on paper, the feeling of power that it gave him to read of how he'd gone from nothing to a position where he decided whether men should live or die.

Guessing at the year it happened, Cameron flipped through his journal to the section written in 1878. He chuckled in appreciation of his cunning as he revisited the story of how he'd fined a drunken rancher into ruin as a result of a spree in Three Cow Crossing. When the man grew sufficiently desperate to sell his ranch, Cameron had stepped in as the "sympathetic" buyer—and then resold the property at a terrific profit. In another case he'd shown mercy to a copper miner's son accused of stealing horses. In exchange, the grateful father had cut him in as a part owner of that mine. And then there'd been that larcenous blond singer who'd been brought to him for justice. What was it she'd gone by? There it was. It had been Annie Faith, but later he'd learned her real name was Anna Bennett.

He smiled, recalling how the sheriff caught her mere steps out of Mud Wasp. Riding a stolen horse, she'd been carrying a reticule of gold coins. The little fool.

She'd made a halfhearted attempt to seduce him out of hanging her, but her shoulders slumped in defeat, as if she knew she'd swing. Damned eager sheriff had made it difficult to do otherwise. Ward had had to do some fancy footwork to make it look like she'd escaped and taken off with the gold as well.

That gold had helped Cameron build this house, and the gift of the woman and the horse had helped establish his relationship with Ned Hamby. He could take her, Cameron told Ned, provided that she never again turned up alive to talk.

Remembering Hamby's reputation, Cameron could barely imagine how the blonde had managed to escape alive. But she must have. There couldn't be two women in these parts by that name.

God help him if she reappeared and met up with Singletary and the real story ever saw the light of day.

He sighed and tried to take some comfort in the memory of his recent request that Hamby kill her. This time they'd both better pray that Anna Bennett would *stay* dead.

As if he sensed her tears, Padre Joaquín nuzzled against Anna's leg. She scratched the shaggy brown-and-white head and wondered once again what had possessed Señora Valdez to name a randy billy goat for a Catholic priest the old woman had once known. The moment Anna quit scratching to stroke Canto's thin neck, the goat butted her leg for more attention.

"Ow!" Anna jerked away from the sharp horns and glared at Padre, who stood on his hind legs as if to meet her gaze. "Do that again and you're *cabrito* dinner."

Despite her threat she could neither resist another scratch nor think of anything much tougher than old goat. One of the nannies wandered out of the open shed for her share of attention, but Anna instead led Canto from the pen. She needed to ride, to check her traps, but more importantly, she wished to get away from what Quinn Ryan had told her.

*Two days . . .* Had they really led to weeks in jail, then to years to replace what she had stolen? Maybe he'd been lying to punish her. Maybe it hadn't been as bad as he'd made out.

She was a fool if she believed that. No, he hadn't lied. She had only to recall the anguish in his voice to know his words had been the truth, or part of it. She didn't think she could bear to hear the rest.

She led Canto by his rope halter. The speckled horse followed quietly, swatting his tail at thick snowflakes as if they were fat flies. After closing the gate, she stopped by the feed shed and saddled the old gelding.

*If it makes you feel any better, I was punished for my crimes.* She couldn't imagine why she'd tried to tell that to Quinn Ryan, why she'd thought the little mound of red gravel might make a difference to him. Did she really think her suffering would somehow diminish what he'd endured because of her?

She lowered herself slowly onto Canto's sunken back and touched his side with gentle heels. Heaven alone knew how old the poor beast had been when he'd stumbled into the clearing two years earlier and started munching on her beans. Anna thought light work and good care kept him going. Señora Valdez swore it was the howling of coyotes, the black silhouettes of buzzards against the brittle winter sky. The fear of dying, she claimed, proved a powerful incentive for those of her age to continue. Not the being-dead part, but the painful crossing over into the next life.

Anna imagined that was true, for she'd experienced the pain part the day that slack-eyed demon had plunged a long steel blade into her gut. She'd surprised him by fighting harder than he imagined any saloon slut should against his attempts to rip her clothes off, and he lost his temper with her. Not that it mattered much. If she hadn't fought, the filthy beast and his drunken friends all would have taken their turns, perhaps for days on end, and then they would have tried to kill her all the same.

Thankfully her memories of the incident were fragmented and few. Sometimes the crack of her ax blade against wood brought back the blows of fists. Sometimes the sun glinting off the summer creek returned her to the flashing knife. Now and then the ache of her right knee sent her mind reeling, tumbling down the rock-strewn hillside where she'd been thrown to die.

She wiped tears from her eyes and nudged Canto's sides once more. Talking to Quinn had brought back far too much at once, and she sensed more bitter memories looming just beyond her consciousness.

The gelding shuffled through the accumulating snowfall, his broad hooves sending sprays of white ahead. With indignant snorts he shook his head from time to time at the thick flakes that alighted on his ears.

Gradually she let the quiet sounds of creaking leather and muffled hoofbeats loosen the tension in her chest. As she rode toward the trail where she had set her snares, her worries faded into the whiteness falling all around her. She imagined snow blanketing old pain with thick and frozen layers.

All too soon her peace was punctuated by an intermittent patter. A shower of icy raindrops plummeted past the feathery snowflakes. Anna shrugged deeper into her leather coat and pulled the hat farther down over her ears. Her breath and the horse's formed plumes in the still air. Surely it was far too cold to rain.

Apparently no one told the raindrops, for they continued to drill small, icy holes through the snow's surface. Gradually their rhythm grew staccato as the frigid shower pelted both Anna and the horse. Despite both hat and coat, the moisture quickly found her flesh and chilled her, making her wish for the shelter of the cabin.

She shivered. Snow was one thing, but this was dangerous weather for walking and especially for riding. The rain that punctured the new snow would quickly freeze against the cold ground, creating a treacherous layer of hidden ice.

She nearly turned the horse's head before the possibility of a jackrabbit or a fat grouse gave her pause. Something other than beans and bacon with cornbread sounded too tempting to leave to hungry scavengers. She would quickly check the snares, and then she'd turn around.

The first snare hung, an empty wire loop beneath a low tree branch. She picked it up, not wanting to kill an animal that the weather would prevent her from retrieving.

She had barely dismounted to check the second trap, when a strange noise startled her, the sound of a heavy step on underbrush. The nearest pine tree shuddered, and its branches spilled a mist of snow, but she couldn't see past the thick boughs. Her heart thumped hard against her chest wall, and her right hand shot instinctively toward the knife she carried in her pocket. Meant to gut and skin small prey, its blade was also sharp enough to wound, perhaps to kill, a larger beast.

Even if that beast turned out to be a man.

The dog rose from his place beside Quinn Ryan and padded toward the door. He scratched, then turned to gaze at Quinn with a sorrowful expression.

"We're both going to have to wait till she comes back," Quinn said.

He was feeling pretty sorrowful himself. Though the tea had eased his parched throat, he could barely move without setting his shoulder to throbbing mercilessly. That was just as well, however, for his ordeal had left him weak.

He'd expected worse as soon as he had realized he'd been shot. He'd seen shot folks before, and those who hadn't been hit in some appendage the local sawbones could lop off mostly died. Most of those who didn't cash in quickly burned with the fevers of infection like kerosene-soaked haystacks. Others rotted like apples going bad from the core out. Back when he'd been a young pup, he'd thought the ones that died fast lucky, but now the Bard's words sang in his memory, "Fight till the last gasp."

He remembered his red-haired uncle's grin as he'd shared that line, along with so many of Shakespeare's finest. His uncle Ferris, a bright, self-educated immigrant, had dreamed of being a great actor, but his Irish brogue consigned him to the brutal life of a day laborer. When he could find work at all, that is. When he could talk his way past the hand-scrawled signs NO IRISH NEED APPLY.

Still, Ferris's smile had lit the shared family apartment. His dream might not have been his future, but it somehow sustained him even more than the few coins he'd brought home.

Quinn knew his uncle had fought to the last gasp inside that fiery tenement. He knew that Ferris would want his sister's son to fight just as hard for his life now.

Quinn surprised himself with the fierceness of his desire to comply. What was *he* but a ruined gambler and a failed lawman? Who was he to wish to live? Since his family's death, he lacked even a dream like his dead uncle's to sustain him.

Still, he meant to live, if only to find Hamby and his gang and do what he should have years before. For with this shooting he felt his ties to Cameron severed. He would make damned sure no other child was scalped and left to die, no other lawman back-shot. Not by Ned Hamby's men, at least, for they would all be dead.

Strange, how it had been the scalps that sent him flying from his saddle when nothing else in six years had convinced him to care enough to risk bucking Cameron's orders. He closed his eyes, trying not to see the blood-caked black hair held tight in Hamby's fist, trying not to see the filthy smoke that marked the burning hogan.

And then, suddenly he knew. Though his two younger sisters' hair had been sandy-blond, not black, though the home that burned around them had been a tenement and not the round hut built by the Navajo, that child's dying whimpers had merged the two events inside his mind. Perhaps because, as with his mother's apartment back in New York, his help hadn't been in time.

*Too late, Annie. Too late because of you,* he'd told the thief. But he'd been wrong, or lying, because his own greed had been responsible. He could have gone back long before she'd robbed him, but his fine horse had too well pleased him, as did his flashy clothes and the pretty company his generous gifts could buy. Annie Faith had been the prettiest of all, always ready with a saucy smile to encourage or a song so soulful that it made him long to hold her tight. But she was only one of many beguiling, heartless creatures who waylaid the unwary on the road of sin.

If Annie hadn't robbed or shot him, someone else would have, for he'd grown greedy, cheating more and more boldly, cutting corners in his grasping desperation to accumulate more money. He didn't just want to go back to help his family. He'd wanted to return a dapper hero, and in the end that vain desire had cost him everything.

He would never forgive himself for that, no more than he would forgive the woman who had robbed him, even though he knew that with her herbs and unguents, Annie Faith had saved his life.

When Canto sidestepped nervously, Anna wondered if he, too, sensed something, or if his restlessness was only her apprehension communicating itself to the old horse. A chill breeze stirred to blow the damp ends of her hair into her face. Another tree nearby shook off a portion of its load of snow.

Of course. The rain had caused some of the snow to melt and shift. And that cracking in the underbrush? It could have been a loose branch settling, or even her imagination. Thinking about the horrors of the past had made her suspect the present. There was nothing here beyond the possibility of her next meal.

The gelding quieted, then stretched out his scrawny neck to grab a mouthful of winter grasses. Only a few feet beyond him, a cottontail hung beneath a low limb, a wire snare around its neck.

Anna dismounted, then stooped to retrieve the dead

rabbit, her knife still in her right hand. Barely had her back bent, when something huge and tawny flashed above her head. Two screams rent the air, one like that of a furious woman, the other of the horse.

Anna's legs loosened with the unexpected sound, and she dropped, knees first, onto the hard ground. Twisting her head, she saw a cougar atop the gelding, which plunged and bucked against his clawing rider.

The mountain lion screamed frustration, once again sounding more like a human female than a beast. But the horse stumbled in its panic, and within moments the big cat brought it down. Anna stared in fascinated horror as the cougar fitted its jaws around the larger horse's throat and held on tight.

The gelding's legs flailed violently, and Anna gripped her small knife tightly. The cougar's green-eyed gaze caught hers and held it. Despite its full mouth, it managed a deep growl.

The big cat might easily weigh one hundred fifty pounds, and its every claw outmatched her puny weapon. Yet how could she sit there and watch it kill her only horse?

Anna forced herself to stop staring and grabbed up sticks, then hurled them. One bounced off the gelding's haunch. Another struck the cougar's back, but it barely flinched, intent only on its prey.

Gradually the spasmodic thrashing of Canto's legs slowed to a stop. Anna watched the life fade from the old gelding's eyes.

She scrambled for more sticks but let them drop without bothering to throw them. The big cat had clearly won its prize, so she would be foolish to risk an injury. Still watching the beast cautiously, she retrieved her hat, which had fallen into the wet snow. Cold rain continued to patter through the pine boughs, onto her head, and into her neckline. Yet Anna felt flushed with the sudden warmth that fear brought, an unexpected boon.

And she would need it, she decided, for the long, cold walk back home.

Just ahead of Ned, Pete whipped his bay horse in an attempt to force it to jump a fallen tree that blocked the trail. It tried to drop its head to buck, but Pete yanked the reins up hard. Finally the animal had had enough. After an awkward lurch forward it leapt the three-foot barrier.

As it landed, its front hooves struck earth glazed with ice. The horse's forelegs slid, and its body twisted. With an audible grunt it fell onto its side.

Pete's scream followed. "Christ—oh, Christ! My God, my God!"

With a terrified whinny the bay scrambled to its feet and trampled its fallen rider before galloping down the trail. Black Eagle and Hop, who were riding just ahead, both tried to catch the horse's reins, but it charged past them, deeper into the rocky canyon. Both spurred their own mounts after the runaway.

Ned dismounted and then squatted down beside Pete, who lay screaming on the cold ground, clutching a contorted upper leg. Blood soaked his jeans at thigh level, and Ned could easily see the white splinters of bone.

Icy raindrops chased the snow, turning the rocky surfaces steadily slicker. They were hours away from either riding or climbing to any sort of decent shelter, even the damned caves. It would take forever with a man this badly wounded. Ned swore at both the weather and Pete's ear-splitting shrieks and howls.

"Shut your damned mouth," Ned warned the downed man. He didn't want to stand around freezing his balls off and baby-sitting this bellyacher. All he really wanted was to get back to a warm cabin and maybe some coffee if they had any left from their last raid. He glanced once more at Pete's ruined leg and then made his decision.

Pete's eyes appeared to focus, and something he saw in Ned's expression made his screams stop abruptly. No sooner had he stopped wailing than his teeth began to chatter with the cold, or maybe fear. His gaze flicked to his gun, which had been flung just a few feet out of reach.

Ned scooped up the revolver and stuck it in his own belt, then peered down at the spreading bloodstain. "That leg's busted real good. Be a hell of a job to carry you out of here. Real painful too, I 'magine. Then you'd probably go and die on us anyway. Fever'd get you even if the move didn't kill ya right off. Lot of noise and trouble to be goin' to for nothin'."

Pete's voice rose on a tide of panic. "I'm strong, and I can keep my mouth shut. I swear I ain't dyin'. Maybe if the leg came off, I'd heal up. . . . Please, Ned. You and me, we been together, how many years is it?"

Just before he answered, Ned thought about the stolen whiskey. "Long enough, Pete. Plenty long enough."

Pete's eyes popped open so wide, Ned could see thin rims of white all the way around the dark brown centers. The injured man's lips drew back into something that might have resembled a grin, except for the missing teeth and the gagging smell of terror that rose from him.

Ned whipped out his gun and fired so fast, Pete didn't have a chance to scream. Instead, the young man's head flopped back into the snow, blood welling from the wound above and between his still-wide eyes.

Ned stared down at the man he'd ridden with for four long years and wondered what emotions other folks might experience at a time like this. As for him, he felt just like he did when he killed anybody, completely empty of all but physical sensations, in this case exhaustion and cold. His hands especially were freezing. That must be the reason they shook as he holstered his gun.

His hands warmed a little when he used his knife to hack off Pete's scalp. Maybe he oughtn't to have done that to old Pete, he thought, in light of everything they'd been through. But by then the action had become a habit, one he didn't know if he could break. Besides, Pete hardly looked the same with a chunk of that hair missing. A wet mask of crimson made his face seem almost like a stranger's.

His grisly task completed, Ned began to shiver once again. He stooped to pull Sheriff Ryan's leather gloves off the corpse's stiffening hands.

As he turned away to put them on, he offered his old partner a few final words. "Sorry, Pete, but the way I figure it, you'll have the fires of hell to warm you now."

With hands so cold she could barely feel them, Anna turned up her wool coat's collar and once more adjusted her broad-brimmed leather hat. Neither action helped much. The collar had acquired a thin layer of frozen moisture. Now against her neck, it melted, sending freezing rivulets into her shirt. Though it offered more protection than a bare head, her hat had been transformed into a crown of ice.

The rain continued, still mingled with thick white snowflakes. A chill breeze stirred the gray-sky cauldron with the cruelty of the devil's hand. As it increased, Anna heard a mysterious sound, like the most delicate chiming. She held her chattering teeth still, and for several moments her fogged brain thought the sound was the tinkling of coins as they struck one another, the evening's take at the last saloon where she had worked.

She struggled onward, keeping beneath the pine trees' limbs for whatever scant protection they might offer. Another gust gave her an answer to the mystery of the chimes. It was the treetops, covered as they were with glassy layers, striking one another whenever the breeze stirred. The beauty of it awed her, as did the crystalline sculpture of the icy limbs. If the clouds lifted and the sunlight touched the treetops, it would look as if the canyon bottom were afire.

How strange for her thoughts to linger on the splendor of this canyon even as its wild beauty killed her. Though she felt oddly separate from that hard fact, she knew it was true, that while her numb, wet feet yet staggered forward, she was quickly losing her race against the cold.

So cold she ached with it. So cold that her body gave up its futile shivering and struggled to drag its own dead weight. Though some part of her knew she was close to home now, she suspected she wasn't close enough. With that realization came a misstep into snow much deeper than it first appeared. In an instant she spun downhill to strike the base of an oak tree.

She lay there, stunned and outstretched like a child making angels in the snow. And as she did, she heard the thudding steps of something heavy on the frozen ground above, on the opposite side of the screen of bushes she'd slid past.

*The cougar!* Panic flooded her veins, once more offering the unexpected blessing of its warmth. For while she might freeze to death, she wasn't going to just lie there as she was eaten. She dug her hand into a pocket, but her fingers were too cold to grasp her hunting knife.

No matter. It wasn't the mountain lion at all, she realized, for the muffled thumps were hoofbeats in the snow, not broad, soft paws. Something uphill charged past her, and she caught a glimpse of the dark brown neck of a horse. She saw no one aboard it, but she couldn't be completely sure.

She had to catch that horse. If it was halfway tame, she could ride it back to her cabin. If there was a rider, she could flag him down and persuade him to take her the short distance home.

But the horse was long gone now; she'd never catch it.

Not in her condition. Not even, probably, if she weren't half covered in ice. Tears welled in her eyes as she struggled up the slope. Yet, as she continued, she heard more hoofbeats—two horses this time, she guessed.

The thrumming pounded to a stop.

One man swore, "Goddamm it! You think old Pete would run halfway to Texas chasing one of *our* nags through this blizzard?"

Something in that voice formed razor-edged shards of memory in Anna's mind. The sound of her own blood in her ears rose to a deep whoosh, like the rushing of the creek in early summer after the snow melt. She could no more continue moving uphill past the intervening bushes than she could will the storm to stop.

The second rider's voice sounded younger, as high-pitched as a boy's. "Let him catch his own horse—if he ain't dead already."

Those words provoked no reaction in her memory, but the first speaker boomed cruel laughter, a sound that resonated in her core. "Yeah. Ned ain't the safest nanny for a hurt man. I thought I heard a gunshot a while back."

"Then why didn't you stop us?" The younger voice brimmed with impatience.

"That bay's a better horse than this used-up mustang I been ridin'."

"Maybe he'll go back to the cabin. Horses usually run home."

"If nothin' kills him first. It's been a hard winter. There's hungry critters all over these parts."

The jingle of a horse's tack, or perhaps the tinkling of the breeze-touched treetops, did nothing to soften the harsh sound of the man's voice in Anna's ears.

"I ain't goin' one more step to chase him. Old Ark here's about done in, and I'm colder than a whore's heart."

"Yeah. Let's collect Hamby, then get back to the cabin.

If that woman's 'round these parts, she'll still be here once this storm's over."

*Hamby*. The name made Anna's world careen crazily, as if her feet had just flown out from under her. She'd been right about that voice. It was one of Hamby's men, perhaps one who'd helped toss her down a hillside, leaving her to die.

The horses' hoofbeats receded into the distance. Anna once more found herself shivering, but this time with fear, not just the cold.

*Madre de Dios!* If the blizzard didn't kill her, it sounded as if those beasts meant to do the job.

She set her jaw and started walking. If they came back, they would find her at her cabin, but this time she would not cower helplessly and beg them to go. This time, with God's help, she would destroy them before they could kill her.

# Chapter Four

Quinn sensed Annie's continued absence almost before his shivering fully woke him. The fire had burned to red-gold embers despite the thick log she had placed on it before she left the cabin. How long had he slept? Had she come back at all during that time? Looking around the cabin, he saw nothing that indicated she had been there recently. The dog still sat beside the door and gazed at it expectantly.

*I'm sorrier than I could ever tell you.*

Her apology returned to him even though she hadn't. The simple earnestness of her words sounded nothing like the captivating singer who'd caught his eye so long ago. This time she sounded like she meant what she said.

Could six years have really changed her as much as it changed him?

*If it makes you feel any better, I was punished for my crimes.*

What the devil had she meant? Certainly the law had never caught up to her, or she would have been hung, or at least imprisoned. Since he'd been a sheriff, he would have learned about it, maybe even recovered his gold as he had finally gotten back his mare, Titania.

He wondered anew about how he'd come to reclaim the horse from Ned Hamby the day the outlaw rode her into town. Quinn had always suspected that Annie had a lover among the ruffians, though the idea had both amazed him and made him surprisingly uneasy. She'd never seemed the type to admire outlaws, though she'd never seemed the type to rob him either. Perhaps, after she'd turned over her ill-gotten treasures, her man had turned on her.

Some part of him hoped the man had beaten her black and blue. Quinn had dreamed about doing the same thing a time or two, at least. But another part of him wondered if it had been Annie's "punishment" that had dampened all her spark.

He'd be an idiot to care what happened after she had robbed him, after she'd caused him to lose everything that really mattered. He was a fool to worry now, yet he did.

She'd been gone for hours if the fire was any indication. He wrapped the blanket around himself more snugly, but both worry and the growing cold kept him from drifting back to sleep. His stomach, roused from its rest by the sweet tea he'd drunk earlier, now demanded sustenance.

It was only natural, then, that he was worried. Not for the thief, of course, but for himself. He was still too weak to tend to all his needs without her.

He peered at the dying fire a few short feet away. Beside it lay a neat pyramid of logs. If he could scoot that far and put more wood on the fire, the cabin would warm quickly. And when Annie returned, she would see he wasn't completely helpless.

He groaned at the idea of moving after lying still for so long. The memory of his shoulder's throbbing pain was still fresh in his mind, and he hated like hell to rouse it from its almost pleasant stupor. Yet every minute the cabin grew a little colder. If he let the fire burn down completely, he'd have the devil's own time starting it again.

He hated himself for needing her, wondering when she would return. He envisioned how he would look to her naked, with his teeth chattering, just a few feet from the wood. Absolutely helpless.

Damned if he would let her find him that way. He steeled himself and slowly began to edge his body closer to the fireplace. As he pushed himself nearer, he felt sweat beading on his forehead, and he had to grit his teeth against the ache. He must have made some sound, for the gold dog leapt to its feet and trotted over.

"Don't you dare," Quinn threatened.

The mongrel licked his face anyway, until Quinn pushed him away. He couldn't allow himself to be distracted from his goal. Just a few more inches . . .

He reached out and grabbed a log, then began to lift it toward the pile of glowing embers.

The dog barked and grabbed the log's other end in his mouth. With a playful growl he began to pull. Quinn tried to hold on to his prize, but the damned cur tore it from his grasp. Wagging his tail in victory, the dog bounded around the small cabin.

Quinn called him repeatedly, but to no avail.

"If I could get up now," he threatened, "I'd beat you with that log."

He reached for a second log and hoped the dog wouldn't initiate round two of the tug-of-war. Fortunately it seemed content to chew its trophy. This time Quinn quickly shoved a log into the embers and was rewarded with the satisfying crackle of new flames. He put on another log for good measure before he began to push himself carefully back to the pile of blankets where he had been resting earlier. To warm his back, he rolled onto his opposite side, so it would face the heat.

The cabin door banged open, nearly startling him out

of his skin. In a blur of motion Annie staggered into the room. She groaned and kicked the door shut against the howling wind. A host of snowflakes settled to the floor to melt into the dirt.

"Son of a—" he started to say, just as she fell to her knees. "What's wrong? What happened to you? You were gone so long. I was—"

He couldn't make himself say that he'd been worried. Couldn't let her think he'd cared about anything but getting fed and keeping warm.

She was shaking, shaking as violently as a drunk in deep withdrawal. The firelight glittered off her hat, her coat, her flesh—ice. She was iced over, he realized in another instant.

"Can you make it over here, closer to the fire? Then you can get warmer. I'll help if you come here."

She did not respond at first, but the dog sprang to life once more, pawing at her and whining loudly. It licked at her face until she roused, then began crawling toward the fire. At one point it grabbed her sleeve in its strong jaws and pulled her in that direction, as if it understood her need and meant to help.

As Annie collapsed next to Quinn, thin sheets of ice fell off her hat and collar. He touched his fingers to her cheeks, then her neck. Her flesh felt cold as a corpse's. He couldn't imagine how she'd gotten here.

Forgetting the aching in his shoulder, he pulled off her hat, which caused a small avalanche of icy snow.

"You have to get out of these freezing clothes," he told her as he began unbuttoning the wet coat.

She flailed her arms and tossed her head back and forth, as if she meant to deny him. But her trembling robbed her of coordination, and he managed to remove the coat and then her shirt.

"Jesus, Annie," Quinn muttered. Nothing else seemed adequate to what he saw and felt. The cold pallor of her skin, even in the firelight's orange glow. The thin sheets of ice that slid off her clothes and melted, making chill mud of the dirt floor. The bluish tint of her lips, even the nipples of her small, round breasts.

He drew her body against him and tried to ignore the confusing emotions that swirled about him like fresh snow. The simple human horror of seeing another in such straits. The selfish concern that if she died, he might well die too, from lack of care. The revulsion at her flesh, not much warmer than a cadaver's against him. The dim tickle of lust that he felt looking on that graceful, slender body, with its high, firm breasts exposed. Quickly, he pulled the blanket over both of them, amazed especially by his last thought. Amazed that he could feel anything now, just a few short days after being shot down, and that he could still see beauty in this woman who had wreaked such havoc in his life.

As if she read his mind, she spoke, her voice rumbling with the rhythm of her chattering jaws. "You—you b-better not be enjoying this, Ryan. El-else I'm gonna m-make you a—a nice pot of goat-t-turd tea."

"Oh, come on. You're about as entertaining as cuddling up to an icicle. Now, help me with those jeans."

"No!"

"You're dripping ice water all over, and as much as I hate to admit it, I can't strip you by myself."

"F-first time for everything . . ." She fumbled at the buttons on her jeans, but her fingers shook too hard to be effective.

"On a better day I'd charm you out of those." He pushed away her hands and attended to the buttons himself, feeling awkward as a schoolboy.

He tried not to notice how her hips moved against his nakedness as she wriggled out of the wet denim. But memories overwhelmed him anyway: the sweet floral scent of the powder she had worn, the wheat-gold gleam of her hair, the silken sweep of it against his skin. Then. When he had been a whole man and she had been a pretty saloon singer.

What was wrong with him, remembering? She was nothing to him now, nothing but a lifeline, a thin thread of bad memories that kept him suspended between recovery and death. Certainly nothing to remember fondly, nothing to nudge an old attraction into wakefulness. Just bare flesh against bare flesh, a reaction as natural as a sneeze.

All in all, this felt more pleasant, though her chill flesh robbed him of needed warmth. A sneeze just then would probably feel like something detonated inside his wounded body. This explosion was far gentler and slower and after a time wrapped him in a sweet, dark blanket.

He became aware of her breaths lengthening, then matching his own. Of her body, which began to warm degree by slow degree. Of her muscles, which loosened just as slowly. Until she slept, and then he, too, could finally rest.

Even though the stage was still a distant silhouette against the snowy sky, Ward Cameron rose from the hard pine bench where he'd been sitting. He'd been waiting for this moment for twenty-five minutes and twenty-five years—ever since that fateful visit to then Mayor Worthington's fine home. Despite his youth and his appalling ignorance, he'd known then what he wanted, what he needed. To blend into that group of people who knew things and who owned things. To someday overcome his awful origins, to be one of *them*.

He had studied the rich as if they were some unknown species. Then he adopted their exotic ways, mastered each and every one. Yet still, there must have been some invisible difference, some taint of poverty that clung to him like the hint of an old stench.

He suspected as much while still studying law. In groups

with his classmates, he sometimes met lovely young ladies, even made them laugh with his studiously witty bon mots. Yet when he tried to call upon them privately, a knowing servant always said, "How sad. You've just missed her" or "Miss B. is not receiving visitors this afternoon."

Later his suspicions were confirmed. When the time came to take his place in his profession, all the choice positions went to young men with family connections, even young men with the charm and perspicuity of parsnips. Still, he'd hammered out a career in law from the scraps left to him, and finally he'd managed to turn his idol, Worthington, into a benefactor. The former mayor had parlayed shrewdness, ruthlessness, and an uncanny ability to say the right things to the right people into a seat in the United States Senate. Thanks to the senator's influence, Cameron received a presidential appointment as a territorial judge out west, where ancestry mattered far less than a man's skill and ambition. Where no one would whisper about how his mother had died drunk in a pool of her own vomit, how his father had turned as mean as a mad dog.

As the stagecoach drew nearer, Cameron snatched the expensive bowler from his head and promptly crushed it in his nervousness. Noticing the damage, he smoothed the brim and brushed furiously at the stiff brown felt.

When Ward had returned home in the wake of his father's funeral, he'd been grateful for Senator Worthington's kindness. Although sorting out his old man's laughable "estate" had been Ward's excuse to go home, he had really come to renew his acquaintance with the man who'd become quite influential during his tenure in the Senate.

The senator had fond memories of Cameron too. From the start he'd appeared to recognize the young boy's awe for what it was. Jonas Worthington was a man who fed on admiration like a half-starved grizzly on an elk carcass. But this time he'd seemed interested in more than praise and envy. After Ward impressed him with a few broad hints about his growing wealth, the old man had done everything but drop his twenty-year-old daughter into Cameron's lap.

Ward tried to remember Miss Lucy's features, but all that came to mind was her slight, short stature and fashionable coil of dark brown hair. He couldn't even say for certain the color of her eyes or if her nose was long and thin or short and snub. He remembered almost nothing except the senator's encouragement and her nearly wordless acquiescence to his wishes. They were engaged in no time, since Ward had to leave town soon. Stranger still, Worthington suggested that Ward marry her out west, instead of going through the unnecessary delay and travel involved in a Connecticut ceremony. He'd hinted that he would not forget his son-in-law when it came time to put in his two cents about federal judgeships in more civilized realms.

Ward had the distinct impression that Worthington was eager to rid himself of this daughter—and quickly—for some reason. But he didn't give a damn what it might be. The carrot of a federal judgeship close to home filled him with grand visions of lording his influence over those who'd snubbed him. The host of opportunities he'd enjoy back east were worth learning later that quiet little Miss Lucy had six toes on each foot or the temper of an agitated rattler. He'd be married to a Worthington, so he'd be one of *them*.

And if he didn't like Lucy, he still had his lovely, raven-haired housekeeper, Elena. Elena might be furious that he was marrying an eastern *gringa*, but he knew she'd come around. She'd do what she must to ensure her special gifts would not cease now.

He couldn't let Miss Lucy see how nervous he felt, couldn't let her guess the reason that her presence meant so very much to him. As the coach drew nearer, he willed his hands to cease their trembling, willed his flesh to absorb the beads of sweat that belied the frosty air. Still, his body made a fool of him.

Let it, he decided stubbornly. Let her think he was trembling with his desire for her. Women read these things through lenses fogged with hope, or so his dealings with Elena had assured him. Lucy would be nervous about leaving family and friends for a fiancé she barely knew, for a territory so remote. Though she might well suspect her family name had induced him to propose marriage so quickly, she would hope for evidence of something far more flattering, of a love that sprang from Cameron full-grown as Athena had sprung from Zeus's skull.

Cameron only hoped Lucy would be somewhat less a headache.

Horace slid off his buckskin mare's back and adjusted a cinch that felt too loose. He'd ridden out to see Edgar Renfro, but the old miner was just like all the others, too scared to speak out against the corrupt judge.

"He already done me harm enough, the way I see it," he'd told Horace, referring to the copper mine whose profits he had been compelled to "share." "And he didn't have nothin' personal agin' me then. What say that fella had a ax to grind?"

The stoop-shouldered man had gone back to cooking fry bread then, letting his question end the conversation. Horace hadn't bothered to try to dissuade him. He feared too much that Renfro might be right.

Judge Cameron had hurt people just because it was convenient and he wanted what they owned. How much worse might he be if he were protecting himself from harm?

If Horace had anything at all to lose, he would not have bothered. But Papa seemed so frail now and their tiny house so desolate, Horace had already given up nearly everything he had that passed for hope.

He remounted his horse and turned its nose toward the old bunkhouse. Riding past the mission and the pair of tumbledown saloons that flanked it, he continued down Main Street, passing the tiny station where a stage had just come in.

His jaw clenched at the sight of Judge Ward Cameron helping a delicate-looking young woman step down to the ground. That must be the bride from back east. He pretended to adjust his glasses so he would not appear to stare. Naturally Cameron hadn't told Horace about his upcoming nuptials, but in a town the size of Copper Ridge, the news had spread faster than the sweep of a winter wind.

Injustice made Horace's throat close and his stomach churn. With so few women in these parts, it didn't seem right that this one should go to a man so vile. It especially seemed wrong on a day when he felt so alone.

Horace thought of returning to his papa to spend another evening coaxing the old man to eat just one more bite. His stomach roiled with the coming struggle, and he thought of taking his buckskin and riding past that bunkhouse, riding past and on and on. To a new life, where he'd be free to chase his dream of the newspaper. To a new life, and perhaps, someday, a woman and a family of his own.

With a sigh he nudged the mare toward home with his heels. Guilt rode with Horace at the thought of his temptation, for he dearly loved his father and would die before he abandoned him in his time of need. No matter what the cost, he meant to take care of Papa.

And no matter what the cost, he'd find someone to help him ruin the bastard who had built his own house on suffering, the bastard who would now share it with a pretty eastern bride.

* * *

Vomiting would make a poor impression, Lucy realized. So she swallowed back the sour taste and grasped Miss Rathbone's elbow as soon as her fiancé helped her down from the coach. She tried to stare her questions at Ward Cameron: Was this mockery of a village really Copper Ridge? Would she truly be expected to abide here?

She grimaced to imagine whatever hovel he would have. Would it be one of those crude "adobe" mud huts such as the natives used? Despite her father's anger about her indiscretion, she'd believed that at least he would be certain her perdition wasn't too unpleasant. Now she wondered if her father hadn't found her a new home so remote that it would be left open to the wanderings of chickens, the scavenging of scrawny pigs.

As if on cue, a loose cow trotted down the raw red trail that appeared to serve the town as Main Street. Two poorly dressed black-haired boys chased it. She couldn't tell if they were savages or Mexicans. Not that there was much of a difference to her way of thinking, except the latter, at least, were Christians of a sort.

The stage driver, a gangly young rogue, picked up a stone and grinned, then hurled it at the cow's backside. Bellowing complaints, the animal mooed and bolted, leaving the children yelling curses in its wake.

After sneaking a glance, she decided Judge Cameron didn't look like the sort of man who would abide livestock in his dwelling. Ignoring the youngsters and the cow, he stood ramrod straight before her. With his suit freshly brushed and every bristle of his mustache expertly subdued, he looked the very picture of a Washington official, as out of place in this rough land as she.

Yet there was something else in his bearing, some hard edge she had previously been too demoralized to notice, that suggested she was wrong. Perhaps it was the squareness of his jaw, the angle of his shoulders, or even the broadness of his stance. He looked confident, as if he knew this place and ruled it. Just as her father ruled in his.

Her heart sank at the thought. Despite their eighteen-year age difference, she'd hoped for an indulgent husband. Papa said he'd be in awe of her family background, and she'd spun those words into wishes that he'd consider her above reproach. Heaven only knew she would need that in a husband. She would need it very soon.

Two details lent her hope that Father had been correct in his assessment. The first was Ward's brown bowler, which he was nervously attempting to smooth out. The second was his slight bow, the gentle way he reached to take her hand.

Her gloved fingers looked tiny in Cameron's palm, felt so fragile as he lifted her hand and kissed it politely.

"My dear Lucy, welcome."

His gaze made her feel like a goddess, though she knew that she must look—and smell—of travel.

Releasing her hand, Cameron reached to take Miss Rathbone's, but the thick-set older woman snatched it away from him with an indignant sniff.

"I would happily dispense with such niceties to determine whether this outpost offers any hospitality to two very weary lady travelers."

Lucy blinked in surprise. This pronouncement from the sulking Miss Rathbone nearly qualified as oratory. Lucy hadn't heard her string together so many words at one time since their exile from Connecticut—and civilization.

The woman's irritable words prompted Cameron to action. With a sweep of his arm he gestured toward a waiting covered phaeton drawn by a span of handsome sorrel horses. It was a finer-looking turnout than Lucy had expected at this frayed hem of the world.

She shot a smug smile at Miss Rathbone, whose tight-lipped disapproval she'd endured for weeks on end. Ward

Cameron, despite his humble origins and the setting, must be a man of substance. A man whose wealth would insulate her from this wretched land and the rashness of her youthful errors.

Despite the shameful circumstances of her exile, she was nearly certain she had landed on her feet.

Warm fur lay along the length of Anna's back. A breathing coat of fur. Notion must have crept onto her pallet again, as he sometimes did when it grew cold inside the cabin. Anna's irritation flared briefly, then dissolved at a memory of a skin of ice across the holy water she kept atop a chest. On such a frigid night it was hard to blame even a smelly dog for taking whatever comfort it might find.

But she felt other warmth beside the dog's. Another body lay beside her—she was sure of it. Anna cried out and jerked suddenly beneath the blanket. Despite the chill in the air, she felt a nauseating rush of heat. As her mind lurched toward consciousness, she first felt sure that this was just another nightmare. Even years after the events that had provoked them, vivid flashes jarred her out of sleep several times each month. She shuddered as a solid voice rose out of that memory:

*Sing somethin' pretty, Annie Faith. Sing for us, you stinkin' bitch!*

She flinched against a phantom kick, then realized she was alone.

"Whaa—?"

The groggy voice catapulted her toward panic, until she remembered. It was Quinn who lay beside her.

She felt his breath against her cheek, felt the warmth and weight of his arm draped across her rib cage. As she wriggled beneath the scratchy woolen blanket, another fact came into focus. Neither of them wore a stitch of clothing. With a start, she tried to pull away.

But his strong arms held her close, until she felt his scratchy whiskers tickling her ear. "Annie ... you all right?" His voice was clearer now, more present.

Her heartbeat pounded like the raindrops beating on the cabin walls. *"Dios mío ..."* she breathed, "I thought you were *them* ... coming back to hurt me."

His eyes reflected firelight. "Who?"

"Them—the men ... but it's over. Over long ago," she reassured herself more than she did him.

"Did it happen after you left me?"

She nodded but offered him no more. The rude awakening left her feeling jittery and unexpectedly weak.

"You're warmer now, at least."

She was relieved he'd changed the subject. The flashing memories of her attack scattered like marbles from a child's pouch emptied onto hardwood.

"I thought you'd never thaw." He gently brushed her hair out of her eyes.

She flinched at even that small movement, then willed her limbs to stop their violent quivering. "Warmer?"

Almost before she asked, she recognized the tapping at the rooftop, tapping on the cabin's north wall. Icy raindrops clicked against the wood, bringing a snow slide of recent memory: the mountain lion's attack on the old horse, the long walk in the freezing rain toward home, her fall down the slick slope and the harsh words she'd heard above her. But most of all, the aching struggle of her body against its frozen shell of death.

Dimly she recalled reaching the cabin, recalled how Quinn had helped strip the icy clothes that sheathed her. How, despite the awkwardness and weakness of his wounded body, he'd pulled her close to him beneath the blanket and shared his warmth.

Just as he still shared it.

Notion rose from his place behind Anna's back and stretched with a wide yawn. He ambled to his more customary spot against the old chest and turned precisely three tight circles before lying down once more.

Without the dog's presence Anna became uncomfortably aware of the body that still lay against her, which, despite its injured shoulder, was all too obviously a man's. Though sleep and warmth left him relaxed, she noticed the firm contours of strong upper arms, the long-forgotten coarseness of his sparse chest hair against her breasts, the breathing that timed itself precisely to match hers. Or had it been vice versa? Had her sleeping body betrayed her by merging with his rhythms?

Then other realizations struck her, nearly as disturbing as any dream. The invitation of their nakednesss, their isolation, what had passed between them other times when they had lain alone together. Her body ached with emptiness and, unexpectedly, with longing.

She had shunned male companionship for six long years. But she had known much of it before. So much of what men could do: their roughness, their demands, even their violence. In a saloon, men often assumed she sold her body like the soiled doves that worked the upstairs rooms. Many times she'd had to use her derringer or knife to carve out a night alone. Until Quinn.

In those two weeks they'd had together, he'd taught her that a man could give pleasure, not just take it, and that pleasing her could increase his joy. She well remembered the awakening of her senses, his introduction to a secret, unimagined world. For the first time in her life she went to a man willingly. He'd paid Miss Hilda a god-awful pile of coins to guarantee the two of them her boardinghouse's finest private room—with no intrusions. The money he had spent made Anna feel special, and she had tried to pretend for those two weeks she was the gambler's woman, not just a diversion on the road.

Yet in the end she knew he'd leave her. A man like Ryan couldn't shear the same sheep for too long. Already he had overstayed his welcome, returning to her bed night after night. And without a string of other men to harass her, she began to look forward to his visits, to fall prey to his gentle, expert touch.

Of course, he'd meant to leave her. They all did, even the ones who seemed to fall in love. A singer in a cheap saloon, she was little better than a prostitute, she realized, and all he'd bought was the illusion of something that was real. So she steeled her soul against his kindness and remembered only the ease with which he spent money on an expensive new felt hat, the fortune he had squandered on a fine silk dress for her. He must have so much more. He might even have enough . . .

Her own delicate shiver brought her to the present. Quinn pulled the blanket higher. Protectively, as might a lover, though she realized that with his injury, with her near freezing, they had not made love, as she had begun to imagine.

Mixed up in her relief, she felt a bright stain of regret, which took her by surprise, like a spot of blood in a fresh egg yolk.

She forced her mind to turn back to what she'd overheard, then forced herself to speak. "I fell when I was walking. I've never been so cold. Then I heard men's voices—saying they'd come back to find a woman. I think—I think they might have been the ones who—ones who . . ."

"The ones who hurt you? Who, Annie? You have to tell me who."

"They'll come back, and God forgive me, I'll kill them before I let them lay a hand on me again."

"Who are they?" he insisted.

"I don't know their names except for one. There was a man named Hamby. I can't let him—"

Quinn swore softly, interrupting her descent into panic. "Hamby. That makes sense. I caught him with my mare. And don't worry. You won't have to kill him. I'd be glad to do the honors for you. One of his boys put that bullet in me."

"I have to get up now," Anna whispered, her mind swirling with old horror. "I won't let them catch me here like this."

He pulled her toward him. "Calm down and relax. How can you be sure of what you heard? You were half frozen when you stumbled in here, ice all over you. People hear things, even see things when they're cold like that. Hell, I thought I was having lamb stew with my mother when I was lying in the snow."

"I heard them . . . at least I *think* . . . maybe . . ." She pulled away, more appalled by the comfort she was drawing from Quinn's nearness than a possible attack. Her skin tingled with a whisper of old pleasure where it grazed his.

Surely Quinn must feel it too, the way their bodies remembered what they both would disavow. He must, or else he wouldn't pull her even nearer, wouldn't touch his lips so cautiously to hers.

Anna felt an almost painful spark where their mouths met, almost like a shock that sometimes leapt from metal to flesh on a dry, cold winter's day. Yet unlike that sensation, this one drew her forward like a lodestone drew a compass needle, giving her direction, a new path to point out.

His kiss grew less tentative, more questing. As if he sought some treasure he would know only once it was found. As if he'd somehow forgotten what she had done to him.

Their mouths together formed a moist warmth so inviting, she could barely force herself to pull away. Yet finally she did, for she remembered things that he would not acknowledge, and other things that he would never know.

"Don't go," he whispered. "No one's coming after you.

Even if what you heard was real, no one's coming now, not in this weather. Please don't go."

She liked the way desire rumbled in those words. Though she had no intention of opening the sealed chambers of her passion, it felt good to hear him knocking at the door.

"Don't be foolish," Anna told him. "You've already made your feelings for me clear."

"This isn't about feelings."

"At least not any that are *north* of your navel. Come on, Ryan. I told you I'm not that kind of woman anymore. Haven't been since . . . well, since you."

"Sorry I soured you for all those others," he grumbled. "Hey, you leave that blanket. It's nippy in here."

"But I'm—"

"Naked too. I noticed." A lopsided grin lit his face, which the firelight bathed in golden flickers.

She grabbed the blanket firmly. "I'll need it for only a minute, so I can find dry clothes and make us something hot to eat."

He held on to it like a shred of dignity, even though she thought she heard his stomach growl at the mention of warm food. "From what I remember before you drugged my drink, it's a little late for you to go developing a sense of modesty, Annie Faith."

"I *told* you, I'm not Annie anymore."

"What's in a name? 'That which we call a rose, by any other name would still have thorns.' "

"I thought the line ended '. . . would smell as sweet.' "

He grimaced. "How should I remember? Somebody stole my book of Shakespeare—Annie Faith."

"*Sangre de Cristo*, you're such a—" Biting back another curse, she ripped the blanket from his grasp.

He groaned, and laid his right hand atop his wounded shoulder. Strips of torn cotton surrounded it to bind his wound. Otherwise, nothing concealed the masculine contours of his upper body, the taut muscles, thicker than she recalled, the— She forced her gaze from straying southward, suddenly ashamed. She had no interest in looking at him that way. She hadn't earlier, when she had worked at curing him. A fluttering beneath her stomach suggested she was lying to herself.

How foolish she was to even think of his man's body. She loved the stark isolation of her canyon life. She needed nothing, no man, most especially the one who had the most cause to hate her. Yet she remembered, only moments earlier, how good it felt when he had held her, how warm and safe and . . . whole.

A flash of memory nearly overwhelmed her. Hammering a cross into the stony soil. A reddish pile of loose gravel that made a tiny mound over the grave. Though she'd been so weak with grief she could barely stand, she'd dug the hole herself. Deep, so scavengers could not unearth it. Deep, as if by doing so she could hide it from herself.

Tears made the hearth's flames sparkle in her vision. Tears that she had never shed in the six years beyond that cross.

Now, as if his body's heat had thawed what might have been, she looked back toward Quinn. His gaze sparked against hers, cold and angry at his weakness and perhaps the memory of what she had done before.

Like an offering, she tossed him back the blanket. The floor was cold, and she would soon pull on her other pair of worn jeans, another coarsely woven shirt.

She turned her back on him and felt him glaring as she dressed.


God help him, he couldn't pull his gaze away from her. Sore and weak as he was, Quinn watched the way she moved as fluidly as melt-water trickling downhill in the spring. Reaching for a pair of jeans hung from a peg, she pulled them on to cover nothing but her bare flesh. Flesh that had lain against his moments before.

He groaned at this impossible arousal, the staggering realization that she was doing it again. She was making him want her with her firm, lean body, which had felt so right against his. She was ensnaring him, though her silken words now whispered psalms of healing, not of sin. She was convincing him, a little at a time, that though her beauty and her voice remained, Annie Faith had changed to Anna, and Anna might be someone he'd like to know.

Or else he was, despite his wound, a healthy man, just shy of thirty, who hadn't had a woman in so long, he couldn't say. The reaction he had as he watched her dress could be nothing more, nothing but his basest instincts, trying to distract him from cold truth.

After what she had done, he couldn't trust another woman, much less her. After what she'd cost him, he ought to want her dead.

Yet he had to admit, at least to himself, that he no longer did. Though he had told himself before that he was warming her so she could tend him, he realized now he couldn't bear to watch her die. Not even if he'd been strong enough to ride out of there today.

Her obvious fear and loathing for Hamby and his men spun his long-held hatred for her on its axis. She hadn't turned his mare and goods over to them as he had so long suspected. Instead, as strange as it might seem, the thief must have fallen prey to an even greater evil.

Did that make her any less a thief? Did it make her any less guilty for her part in his family's deaths? And most important, did he betray their memories by wanting her the way he did?

\* \* \*

They would be married in a week's time, Ward had told her. Though for her it was an answer, the thought made Lucy's soul quiver like a hummingbird's frail wings.

Still, she felt the need to keep up appearances with Miss Rathbone, who had helped to guide her in the five years since her mother had passed on.

Lucy chattered quickly, half starved for some scrap of approval. "Why, if one didn't go outside, one would almost suspect we'd never left the States. The house is so much finer than what I'd expected. Don't you think so?"

Miss Rathbone looked up slowly from unpacking one of Lucy's bags. Her fathomless brown eyes surveyed the surroundings, as if she hadn't deigned to take them in before.

The judge had shown them to the pair of bedrooms, which someone had decorated thoughtfully. Someone who understood a woman's tastes. The bedding had been trimmed with expensive eyelet lace. The chamber sets were painted with delicate violet flowers.

Nervously Lucy drew back the heavy green and violet curtains of her room to gaze out over the thick pines outside. Snowflakes filled the air like a host of wintry moths. She could feel their cold radiating through the windowpane, so she quickly closed the draperies once again.

Miss Rathbone lit an oil lamp against the resulting gloom. "I suppose it could be worse."

Lucy had nearly forgotten her question to the older woman. But that was typical of her recent conversations with Miss Rathbone: fits and starts, long pauses, terse replies, while all along, her every deliberate gesture, every brooding glare, blamed Lucy for their change in circumstances.

As well she might.

Lucy swallowed back her guilt and swelled her chest with an almost painfully deep breath. She was here now, in this place, destined for marriage, and she would make the best of it. After she wed Cameron, she could send Miss Rathbone packing, sever every tie she had with what had happened in Connecticut that winter.

And then there would be no one there who might too soon guess her secret. No one to hold up a mirror and reflect at her those dark-eyed glimpses of her shame, and of her pleasure most sublime.

In an economy so ingrained that it was second nature, Anna had tucked the cottontail's small carcass deep inside her coat. Despite the shock of her horse's death and her own near freezing, she had carried the rabbit home. It remained inside her coat, so she recovered it after she dressed, happy for at least that small bit of fortune on this luckless day.

She draped the coat across a stool near the fire so it could dry. Then she and Quinn shared tea and corn bread left over from that morning. Anna ate in wary silence, thinking about how she had lost her balance in the few days since he'd arrived. Before, everything had seemed simple, sterile, just the way she liked it. Now her emotions, which she thought trapped in amber, had bubbled to the surface and threatened to overwhelm her.

Afterward, she took the rabbit by the back feet and retrieved the knife from her coat pocket. She threw the old serape over her shoulders, then took the rabbit out the door, beneath the roof's narrow overhang. The dog pranced eagerly, awaiting the viscera that were loosed by her quick blade. She left Notion outside to enjoy his bloody meal, then returned indoors to skin the cottontail over a shallow pan.

From his pallet near the hearth, Quinn watched her cautiously. He sat cross-legged, the blanket draped around his frame. "When I first got here, I figured you might do that to me."

Expertly she peeled off the soft pelt, turning it inside out as she worked. "What makes you think I've ruled out the idea?"

He shook his head. "You were right before. You didn't go through all this trouble just to kill me. But I'm still wondering why."

"It's what I do, heal people." She cut through joints and tossed the meaty chunks into a pan she'd filled with snow. Blood droplets bloomed into pink petals against the field of white.

"But why heal me? Didn't you realize who I was?"

"The Navajo brought you here. I trusted their wisdom. And I trusted the curing woman's teaching." Anna paused to add some spices from her precious store into the pan. She measured out a double portion of dried corn she'd soaked that morning and poured it in as well.

He said nothing, but his moss-colored eyes seemed to flicker in the firelight, to weigh her every word.

She decided it would be best, this time, to answer him completely. "The only other voices that spoke to me were those of fear and of what I once was. I trust neither of those voices anymore."

His words dropped into a husky whisper. "What happened to change you? What did they do to you, Annie Faith—no, Anna?"

She hooked the pot's handle over a metal arm and swung it into place to cook above the fire. She watched the snow inside the pan melt gradually over the heat, just as she sensed herself dissolving with Quinn's question and the emotion in his words.

She turned to look at him and saw his shape sparkling with the tears trapped in her eyes. "I owe you a great deal, Quinn Ryan. But I don't owe you that story."

He paused as if to consider, then continued. "It's all right. I've decided. I won't try to take you when I go."

"Take me where?"

"To Copper Ridge, to face what you did to me six years ago. You might not believe this, but I'm the sheriff there. Guess old Hamby took a fancy to my badge, or I would show you."

She blinked at him, unable to comprehend what he had said. When she recovered, she asked, "Since when do they put cardsharps in charge of law and order?"

"I suppose about the same time they cast a thieving saloon singer in the role of angel of mercy. I don't gamble anymore. Haven't since . . . well, you."

His words hurt, but she supposed she deserved them. "You mean you weren't shot by someone you had cheated?"

"It was one of Hamby's boys, like I said before. I caught the bastards burning out some Navajo. I meant to ride back into town, get help. But they—they were—good Lord . . ." He closed his eyes tightly, as if by doing so he might stop reliving something far too awful to describe.

As she watched him, she could feel the dark echo of his pain. She imagined him being overwhelmed by lurid images, much like those that had touched her when he'd asked what Hamby's men had done. She tried to clamp down on her compassion, bring it under tight control, but instead it grew as wild as the creek with the melting winter snows.

As if she'd never broken with music, Anna felt a tattered fragment of a song rise. The first song since that terrible attack six years before. A Spanish *corrido*, its simple melody might soothe Quinn. But even more compelling was the feel of it inside her mind, the weight and texture of each note.

She had to try to sing it, not only to console Quinn but

to assure herself she still could. She had to give voice to this bright mirage of music lest it dissolve into old pain.

She'd never sung the words before, had only heard them in the old woman's creaking voice. Yet her mouth gently curved around each word, each note, as if she'd sung it all her life.

> *Se ve vagar la misteriosa sombra*
> *que se detiene al pie de una ventana,*
> *y murmura: "No llores angel mío,*
> *que volveré mañana . . .*

Before she'd never thought much of the words, a soldier's lament at his leave taking, a soldier's promise to his angel to return. She thought of Quinn's return to her, though there had been no heartfelt promise, and the only angel in their story lay long shrouded in a cold and stony grave.

Quinn lifted his head to look at her. She heard, as she continued, his exhalation of surrender. She felt rather than saw his own sharp-toothed memories loose their choke hold on his soul.

When she finished, he spared her a weak smile. "You sound even nicer singing sad tunes than you did belting bar songs back in Mud Wasp. Ever consider going back to that—to the singing?"

She gave the pot over the fire a stir, thinking of the music she had lost. Whatever had it earned her but trouble anyway? She shook her head. "Do you think of returning to your wicked ways, Quinn Ryan?"

His stare sent a shiver rippling up her spine. "Only to the one that's tempting me right now. Aside from that, I'm mainly thinking of going back to get my spare gun and a couple of deputies to fix Hamby and his boys for good."

"It could be weeks until you're strong enough to walk out of this canyon."

"I was hoping you might have an extra horse that you could lend me."

"I had only the one. He's gone."

Quinn shifted the blanket to cover both his shoulders. "Gone? Where is he?"

"Just where this poor rabbit's going," Anna answered, "to satisfy the hunger of a beast."

---

Though Lucy lay sleeping in a bedroom designed to insulate her from the wildness of Arizona, the blue-gray expanse she dreamed of appeared no more civilized. Neither the hoofprints of the horse in harness nor the runners of the sleigh yet marred the moonlit surface of a snow-covered cornfield. She glimpsed that unsullied scene from beneath the poor cover of bare elm trees and the sheltering dark boughs of a holly. Brilliant berries dotted the leaves' bases, like small globules of blood.

There had been blood inside too, in that sleigh tucked in the shadows. Blood beneath the rug that warmed them. Blood amid the plumes of steam that rose from breathy exhalations, faster, harder . . . all so enticingly forbidden.

Lucy's breaths grew quicker as she dreamed of David's hands, his mouth . . . dear, God!

She'd told Miss Rathbone she was going to a sleighing frolic with Edward Harris and his sisters. Miss Rathbone, acting in her father's stead while he finished his Washington business, had allowed her. But what Miss Rathbone hadn't guessed was that a second young man met her just outside the gate when the Harris siblings brought her home. He'd convinced Edward he would be happy to escort Miss Worthington inside, where he had business.

And why shouldn't Edward, steady Edward, have believed them? Lucy, his fiancée, had always conducted herself honorably. His young sisters both complained of the icy clear cold of the night. And David Tanner, the Worthingtons' assistant coachman, had always presented himself as one who knew his place.

But Edward had never seen the flirtatious glances that passed between his fiancée and the fellow, nor heard the shocking words he whispered when she chanced to cross his path. He never would have guessed how his decorous Miss Lucy, instead of having the impertinent young man fired, had gone out of her way to come upon him with increasing frequency, had even sent to him one of her embroidered handkerchiefs on Christmas Eve. He had no reason to suspect that David had a horse in harness in the barn, that handsome, dark-haired David had been waiting for his chance.

How many times had Lucy dreamed that evening? She had known, as if by instinct, how the secret touch would be the one that would ignite her, just as David's daring whispered words had sparked her soul. And oh, how those sparks had caught, how they'd leapt into a roaring blaze in those few minutes. . . .

At least until that awful instant when Edward returned to find her. Until he dragged her home and saw—even Miss Rathbone had seen it—that damning splotch of blood upon her skirt.

The rush of shame that wakened her made Lucy sob aloud. And yet, and yet . . . she wiped tears from her eyes, then closed them, trying to recapture the exhilaration of what had happened in those lustrous moments before she had been caught.

*Cañon de Sangre de Cristo, March 31, 1884*

"Here, Ryan, why don't you make yourself useful?" Anna leaned over to pass Quinn the damp bundle she had brought in from the cold, even though he'd just awakened.

Notion roused himself to walk over and sniff her smelly burden.

Quinn sat up, yawning, and quickly coughed. His face screwed up, apparently at the odor. Shaking his head, he reminded her, "You said yourself last night the wound was healing nicely. No more of those stinking poultices."

She unceremoniously dumped the slimy burden, which was far bigger than a poultice anyway, into his lap. The newborn goat squirmed and weakly bleated, "Maaah."

She fought a smile at the confused expression on his face. For the love of *Dios*, he looked as sleep-tousled as a boy when he awakened.

"It's a tiny cabin, no room for deadwood. Come on," she urged. "Take that rag and rub down the little fellow before he freezes. He came a few weeks too early for spring weather."

Her memory took her back to the mornings during her recovery, when Señora Valdez had first awakened her at dawn to demand she help with simple chores. Anna had cursed the old woman at the time, unable to make sense of the *curandera*'s methods.

It was doubly important now, thought Anna, to recast herself into the role of healer. Since her own near freezing last week, though she and Quinn had kept as far apart as possible, she sometimes caught him watching her intently. She tried to avoid eye contact, but several times a day their gazes locked with an almost audible click, and she knew beyond all doubt that he was remembering when he'd held her, the sensation of her bare flesh against his. He was recalling other times, too, when their bodies twined toward ecstasy, as if they'd had forever, not two weeks.

She knew it because she, too, was reliving those lost hours . . . as well as imagining things she had no right to dream of, things that would only serve to hurt them both.

To distract herself, she ordered, "Rub briskly—and use both hands. You're favoring the left."

"That's because this shoulder's sore as hell," he snapped.

She felt the corners of her mouth twitch. "I know your little friend there's small, but maybe he could still provide us with the crucial ingredient to make another poultice."

"I'm rubbing already. *There*— satisfied?"

The gold-and-white kid's hair now stuck up in all directions. Notion cocked his head at the small intruder and whined in canine confusion.

Anna quirked an eyebrow. "That goat's looking more like you every minute. Think I'll call him Ryan."

Quinn chuckled, an easy sound that reminded Anna of other times they'd laughed together, six years earlier. The moment choked down to silence as he looked into her face. The warmth in his green eyes made her wonder if he'd forgotten for the moment what she'd done to him . . . and if he'd lost sight of how much hatred he still carried.

The newborn kid broke the silence with a hungry bleat. Gratefully Anna scooped him back into her arms and told Quinn, "Thank—thank you for drying your new namesake. His *mamacita* will be worried, and her milk will warm him from the inside out. I'm—I'm going to put the two of them in the feed shed until the weather warms a bit."

Without waiting for an answer, she stepped back outside and leaned against the door to shut it. For a long time she remained there, eyes closed against the icy wind, a bitter wind that chilled the farthest reaches of her canyon but not the glowing embers resurrected in her heart.

# Chapter Five

*Copper Ridge, Arizona Territory*
*April 6, 1884*

Ward stared out his window and glowered at the icicles. Damned incessant winter had delayed all his plans. He would have been married by this time were it not for the late ice storm that prevented Judge Clancy's arrival. Travel all over the northern territory had come to a standstill, not just for days but for weeks. At least the sky had cleared that morning, its blue as bright as a jay's feather.

The closest fang of ice began to drip, slowly at first, then with a steady plop, plop, plop onto the slushy snow beneath the eaves.

*Finally*. He poured a shot into his morning coffee just to help settle the foreboding that gnawed at him like termites at an old log cabin.

Maybe the worst of the snow would melt today. Maybe Clancy would perform the marriage before his housekeeper lost her mind and Miss Lucy lost all patience.

"Why do we have to wait?" the girl asked time after time.

She seemed not to hear his explanation, that there wasn't another local white man who could do the honors. For a while he half expected her to insist on a local padre, even if the ceremony must be held in Spanish—or in Latin.

Ward could imagine the senator's reaction if he learned a Mexican papist officiated for his Protestant daughter's wedding vows. The old man had insisted that the ceremony be both proper and expeditious.

Once again the eagerness of both Lucy and her father nagged at him. Once again he wondered why both seemed to desire such haste.

Ward sipped the coffee. Whatever could be wrong with Worthington's youngest daughter? He'd watched her carefully these past two weeks, but he saw no signs of either physical or mental defects. She seemed pleased, almost *too* pleased, with everything about their impending marriage. Except for the delays.

Could she truly love him? He dismissed the wild idea. The two of them barely knew each other. What, then? What would he find out once they were married?

Cameron added a touch more whiskey to his brew.

In addition to his wedding, other important business had also been held up by the weather. Ned Hamby had not yet informed him of the outcome of his search for Anna Bennett. Perhaps the snow and ice had only delayed the message. Surely one woman would be powerless to stop the outlaw and his men, just as she could do nothing to delay his plans to mine the narrow canyon.

He sat behind his huge desk and pulled open the top drawer, where he kept his finest silver nugget. He'd had the other analyzed to see if Luc-Pierre's wild tale would prove true. Ah, that had been a story for his journal, a tale of luck too late, of love and avarice.

For years Luc-Pierre had prospected among the mountains of the Arizona Territory, accompanied by a beautiful Paiute bride he'd picked up in his travels. Though he never had much luck, he possessed a generous soul. So when he met a fever-stricken trapper, he and his squaw nursed the fellow back to health. The trapper, a fellow by the name of Jake Chambers, was a charmer, always ready with a wild tale of his reckless youth and daring. He drank Luc-Pierre's whiskey and flirted with Luc-Pierre's long-suffering squaw, hinting that he could offer plenty more than an old prospector with pockets full of sand.

Luc-Pierre was elated when the assay on his last samples came back showing high-grade silver. All he could think of was getting back to his woman to celebrate the news. What he came home to, however, was an empty camp. The recovered miner had lured the squaw to follow him.

They hadn't gotten far. Luc-Pierre shot both of them dead a few days later, in Bottom Dollar, just outside the blacksmith's shop.

When the Frenchman used his knowledge of the rich location where he meant to stake his claim to bargain for his life, Cameron had listened carefully, imagining the profits from the mine. The Frenchman, encouraged by the judge's attention, even drew a map and produced ore samples. Cameron smiled at the thought. People fearing for their lives could be so very careless. In the end, that carelessness more than the murders cost Luc-Pierre his life.

The hanging had been well attended, Ward remembered, nearly as festive as a Fourth of July gathering.

But lately Cameron suspected that the prospector had gotten the last laugh. If he'd known the canyon had an owner, he had certainly kept it to himself.

The judge frowned at the tap at his door. After putting away the silver, he took out some papers and pretended he'd been reading.

"Come in," he called, his voice gruff at the interruption.

Elena stormed into the room. She carried his customary *cuernito* on a plate. He noted the fire in her dark eyes just in time to duck to avoid being struck. The hurled plate shattered against the edge of his desk.

"If you do not send Señorita Holy White Daughter of the Senator and her complaining *duenna* from this house this instant, I swear to you I will kill them both—and maybe you as well!"

Ward feigned calm long enough to pour an extra shot of whiskey into his coffee. He gazed miserably out at the dripping icicles and wondered if he stood in exactly the right spot, one could fall down and impale him so he wouldn't have to face this day.

*Near Cañon de Sangre de Cristo*
*April 7, 1884*

Ned Hamby's revolver cleared leather before either of his men could strike the other. "Stick to fists—and outside," he warned. "I ain't scrapin' either of your guts off my boot leather."

Black Eagle and Hop glared at each other, still furious over their escalating war of words, which had begun over Hop's unwillingness to take more than two steps out the cabin door to relieve himself. Tired of fighting with each other, both then turned resentful gazes toward their leader. Really, they ought to thank him, Ned thought. If he hadn't insisted on keeping their guns in his possession, they'd both be dead, killed by the endless days they'd spent holed up inside this miner's shack. Way he figured it, those two owed him their sorry lives.

"Today's the day, boys," Ned announced. If he had to stay there one more hour, he'd likely give in to temptation and shoot both of them himself.

They blinked at him sullenly, angry that only he could

give the word to move yet too eager to escape this hell hole to argue.

"We're gonna go find us that woman and take care of our business so I can go home."

Black Eagle glowered at the crusted-over bean pot. "Maybe she's got good food."

"And whiskey," Ned added.

"And an appreciation for male companionship," Hop said.

For the first time in many days, the three men shared a smile, a smile that darkened into laughter that would chill the marrow of an honest man.

Anna tried to chase the melodies from her mind the same way she'd once chased a pair of swallows from the cabin after they flew down the chimney. Dolorous as tears, the Mexican *corridos* sang of longing, of the sweet pain of good-byes.

She added yet another handful of dried pinto beans to the sack and wished she had more to spare. But the food from last year's disappointing harvest must last until next season, and Quinn's unexpected presence had already strained her stores.

She watched him as he brought in another armload of firewood. He moved like a strong and sound beast now. He'd even found the energy to sharpen an old razor to shave his sandy-brown beard. Yet new seams in his mended clothing bore testimony to his hidden wound. Even so, it was difficult to imagine how close to death he'd been when he was left at her doorstep.

*Just as you were* a voice inside her sang, then shifted into Spanish to continue its dark hymn of desolation.

Clearly Ryan's presence had awakened something in her, something she almost wished to banish to the half-remembered territory of her dreams. The music licked like spicy flames around her memories from the canyon: the old woman who had found her, then cured her stubbornly despite her wish to die. The songs Señora Valdez sang as Anna healed, foreign songs that dissolved the false dreams of the *cantiña* ballads Anna had once sung. The music whose strands once trapped her in a web of silken snares.

Amid the *corridos* she heard them, the faint echoes of a nightmare far too real to be a dream.

"Sing somethin' pretty, Annie Faith," Ned Hamby demanded as he kicked her stomach. "Sing for us, you stinkin' bitch!"

Then coarse laughter . . . they'd laughed at her because she'd told them that she could not remember any words. She suddenly recalled clearly lying there, curled up against their onslaughts, wiping the blood that trickled from her mouth like crimson notes. She remembered seeing for the first time the sparkling blade in Hamby's fist and realizing that he meant to plunge it into her in some deadly parody of sex.

Anna moaned and realized that what she'd told them yet held true. Even after all these years her mind could not recall a single English song. Dried beans bounced off the tabletop and landed on the floor.

"What's wrong?" Quinn asked. "You look as if you're rubbing elbows with your granny's ghost."

"Not her ghost . . . one of mine."

He looked at her strangely, as he often had since that night when he had warmed her body close to his. She imagined he was still trying to reconcile her with the woman she'd once been, the woman who had wounded him so deeply. She wanted to laugh at how he tried to make sense of her, as if she were a puzzle to be solved but one with razor edges that could hurt him if he tried too hard. Since that evening—since their sweet and stillborn kiss—he'd kept his distance, both physically and in conversation. She wondered if he knew how happy that made her.

And yet ... that morning, as she was packing supplies for his departure, she almost wished that they had better spent their time. Instead of skittering around the edges of this tiny cabin, perhaps together at its center, they might have trod closer to forgiveness, or maybe something sweeter still. Perhaps she should have even told him about the little grave. The one beside the resting place of Señora Valdez. The one that might mean something to him too.

Quickly she dismissed the ridiculous idea. The tale was too personal, too sacred to share with anyone. Not now, six years later. Even if he cared it would never stop him from returning to his own life now that he was feeling better.

*Reina del cielo!* Is that what this was about? Was she such a fool that she'd already grown accustomed to his presence? Had isolation dimmed her senses so she didn't realize he could never fill the void that death and music had left inside her heart—a void she'd never fully realized before Quinn's reappearance?

Cursing her stupidity, she began to wrap the cornmeal tortillas she had made. She'd never make a wise old *curandera* if she didn't drive the silly girl out of her soul.

Only a few feet away, he rolled an extra blanket she had given him for his long walk. His voice, when he spoke, took her by surprise. "I saw something the day you lost your horse, when you were naked and you gave me back the blanket."

Despite her mood, she couldn't stop amusement from quirking up the corners of her mouth. "*Santa Maria*, Ryan. You mean to tell me you've been so long without a woman, you don't even recognize it anymore?"

"Not *that*. The scar. That long one on your belly. I was wondering about it."

Just like that, her gush of playfulness froze over. Slowly,

as though great age had stiffened all her joints, she turned away from him.

"Anna, tell me what they did to you, and I *will* pay them back." His voice had lost the strictly-business tone he'd kept these past two weeks, betraying what sounded strangely like affection.

"Pay back your own wounds, not mine. I don't want anybody's blood. I just want to be left alone here, *en mi querencia*, where I can heal."

"Your *what?* Either quit speaking Spanish to me or tell me what you mean. I want to understand you for a change."

"My *querencia*—the place where I belong, this canyon."

"Have you ever thought it's not a *place* where you belong, but with a person?"

*But I* am *with her here.* The canyon and the grave were inseparable within her mind, and Anna knew that she was bound to both.

He laid his hand on her shoulder. She enjoyed the solid warmth of it and wondered, once he left, when anyone would touch her next. Oh, there would be times when she would lay her hands on others in an attempt to comfort or to heal them. But who would ever lay his hands on her?

"You're not suggesting that I belong with *you?* After what happened between us?" Despite the absurdity of what she asked, she hoped he wouldn't move his hand again, not yet. His touch would have to last her for a long, long time.

"Of course not. But a beautiful young woman isn't meant to be out here alone. For one thing, it's not safe." He turned her toward him and drew her close. "I think you learned that six years back, when they gave you that scar. It's from a knife wound, isn't it?"

She wanted to pull away from his intrusions, but his strong arms held her tight. With a sigh she nodded her chin against his shoulder for an answer.

"Anna," he continued, "there are plenty of men in

these parts who came west looking for a second chance. Men who don't want anyone to ask too many questions about who they were or what they did before. They'd be so grateful for a sweet-faced woman like you, they wouldn't want to know about your past. Why, I have a deputy, Max Wilson, who'd sell his soul for a chance at meeting you."

"Your *deputy?*" She freed herself from his embrace, anger underscoring each word. "You must not like him very much."

He hesitated, as if he'd realized that he'd trod on dangerous ground. "I didn't mean him personally. I was thinking somewhere farther, where we wouldn't have to see each other. At least not very often."

She felt ridiculous for imagining he might want her for himself—her, a woman he had bought with gifts once, a woman who'd repaid his kindness with an act of utter selfishness. She should have known even a former card cheat wouldn't want a traitorous thief.

"I don't want to worry that those voices you heard were something more than hallucinations from the cold. I don't want to lie awake nights thinking of what might happen if they come back here after you." He reached out to touch her thick braid, as if he wished to stroke it.

She flipped aside the length of golden hair. "They'll be dead. That's what will happen. They won't get close enough to hurt me again. Not ever."

"You don't even have a horse to get away. Come with me instead. We'll walk out of here together."

"So you can fix me up with some nice man?" She breathed the words into his ear, intoxicated by the closeness of him, the strong, safe feeling of his arms around her.

He turned his head toward hers until their mouths were so close she could almost taste his words. "I think I have one in mind right now."

* * *

The closer they drew, the more helpless Quinn became. And feeling helpless with her left him angry. But not so angry that he couldn't smell the scent of her, clean and fragrant as spring wildflowers.

The blond siren had *had* to bathe last night, as if she knew how difficult it had been these past two weeks to keep his thoughts—and hands—off her. As if she guessed how wanting her was turning his soul inside out. Perhaps she *did* know, and behind that makeshift curtain she'd set up before the fire she was laughing at the way her vixen's tricks tormented him. Surely she must realize the effect of her shapely silhouette as the fire's glow cast it on the cloth.

"I can't wait anymore. I'm starting to smell worse than the dog," she'd called over the flimsy barrier between them. He heard the water splashing inside the washtub she'd dragged near the hearth and laboriously filled with heated snow-water.

"I can't wait much longer either," he had muttered, imagining her naked a few short steps away. When he got back to Copper Ridge, he would have to find relief.

Wrinkling his nose, he thought of Liliana and Carmen, the harlots who lived in the rooms over the Blue Streak Saloon. He'd never succumbed to either of their charms, but even at a distance it was apparent neither one was too particular about her hygiene. Come to think of it, hadn't Max complained of coming back from Carmen's bed with so many crabs he was reminded of his lost youth at the seashore?

With a shudder of revulsion, Quinn had decided he *could* wait.

But not now, not with Anna's bow-shaped lips only a fraction of an inch from his. Not with the scent of whatever herbs she'd dropped into her bathwater making him want to drink her in.

Now he leaned in close to taste that lovely mouth of hers once more. It tasted golden, with a hint of the rare treat of honey she'd allowed them for that morning's griddle cakes.

He felt the wiry tightness of her lithe body relax into his arms. His lust accelerated like a fractious horse taking the bit into its teeth. With every moment it thrummed faster, harder, wanting her ... wanting ...

He traced the angle of her jaw with his thumb, then used his tongue to separate her lips. Sweet Lord, she felt as good as he remembered, as right as he had hoped. She kissed him back, caressed his neck with her palm, not with the reluctance with which one might discharge an old debt but with the tender eagerness of an innocent toward her first lover.

Quinn couldn't wait another moment. He had to reach under her shirt to find those small breasts with his fingers. No iron-staved layers of female undergarments formed a stockade against trespass. Beneath the cotton fabric there was only soft, smooth flesh. His hand brushed past the warm silver of her necklace, on its way to finding someplace warmer still. Anna rocked back on her heels and gasped out her pleasure as he touched her hardening nipples.

Yet even as he unbuttoned her shirt, used his mouth to follow where his roving hands had led, he wondered what it was about her that sent him plunging past all reason. He felt helpless to control his actions, a river raging in futility against the ocean's pull. But instead of waves, the sweet curves of her body drew him; instead of the thunderous surf, he heard only the echo of her song. Not the unintelligible Mexican lament she'd sung two weeks before, but a sprightly saloon ditty that had once convinced him she had spirit. Annie Faith had sparkled among those world-weary fallen women he had known, so alive he couldn't help but be drawn to her, as if her light would also bestow warmth.

It hadn't. Though he'd been well on his way to offering her the moon, she had offered only treachery in return. And now what? On the day that he would leave here, what could they give each other? A ghostly afterimage of sins from the past—or only a reminder of the wreckage left from their impact?

Though he was powerless to rein in his body's urges, she pushed him away.

"I'm sorry," she told him without elaboration. She might have been apologizing for allowing him liberties or for stopping him, or even for her crime from the past.

That was one of the changes about her that annoyed him most. He felt as if she were reading him every other line of someone's letter, that her silences meant far more than the words she let him hear.

"I think we should go now, to take advantage of the light." Anna buttoned her shirt, then handed him the food to pack with his bedroll. After he had finished, she helped him tie the bundle on his lower back, beneath his still-sore shoulder. Last of all, she slung a water skin on his good arm. Quinn noticed it smelled suspiciously of goat.

"I suppose this means you won't come with me." He should have felt relieved, but the irritation in his voice was real. Although he still hadn't forgiven her for what she'd done six years ago, she was no monster—and she had saved his life. He'd sleep better if he knew she was safe. At least that's what he tried to tell himself. But his body had ideas all its own.

She smoothed the silky golden strands that had escaped her braid, then reached for her broad-brimmed leather hat to put it on. "I'll help you find the trail to Copper Ridge. That's all I ever promised."

"I know. But, Anna . . ."

She pulled open the door and let Notion bound out before her. She hesitated, turning toward him. Daylight spilled inside, casting a shadow that fell across her eyes, making her expression as cryptic as her silence.

He cleared his throat, wondering once again at the woman she'd become. "I want to thank you for helping me. You had plenty of reason to leave me in the snow. If you'd been the woman I used to know, you would have left me there to die."

She hesitated for a moment, adjusting the canteen's strap across her shoulder, then turned her shadowed gaze on him once more. "I was left for dead once, Ryan. The Navajo found me and brought me here, the same as you. Don't you see? It's just a circle. My reward is in completing it. Or maybe 'reward' is the wrong word. Maybe I'm repaying something owed."

"To me?"

She shook her head. "To this canyon, to the woman who once lived here, maybe even to the god that shaped them both. But not to you. I wouldn't presume to name the price that could repay what I took from you when I was Annie Faith."

That was when he realized it hadn't been only lust that made him want her. It was Anna herself, the woman who had grown out of the ruin of the girl he had known. Comparing Annie Faith's superficial glitter to Anna's inner light was like comparing a cheap glass bauble to a diamond.

If he stayed with her much longer, he might fall in love. The thought frightened him deeply. The last time he'd lingered with her, she had caused him so much grief. Could he ever truly forgive what she had done? Could he ever really put it from his mind? Or would it lie in wait like a drowsing monster, to spring to howling rage at the slightest provocation?

He took off her hat and let the sun illuminate her face and awaken the soft blue of her smoky eyes. He imagined her gentle features hardening into a mask of resentment, finally hatred, when he brought up her crime again, when memories of his lost family—and his own part in their deaths—pushed him beyond the brink of cruelty.

How could he do that to her? How could he do it to himself? With his fingertips he traced the angle of her cheekbone, the curve of her jawline.

Anna caught his wrist in her hand. She gazed into his eyes as if she were reading the fine print on his soul. Turning his hand, she kissed his fingers, then stepped out of the light. When she closed the door, she shut both of them inside.

Her hand still on the door's latch, Anna smiled up at Quinn and softly said, "I know now."

He squeezed her hand very gently. "You know what?"

"I know what I owe you." She paused, distressed by the pain it would bring her, yet pleased with the rightness of the idea, the simple fairness of it.

Ryan's expression shifted from confusion to discomfort. "You would . . . you would make love to pay me back? Do you really think that—"

She shushed him by touching her fingers to his lips. "I've told you, I'm not the woman you remember. I give you something far more valuable than simple favors of the body. Wait there, by the fire."

"Annie—Anna . . ." He sounded troubled, though he walked closer to the fireplace, as if to warm himself. "Don't do this. There's too much you don't know."

"Secrets separate us from the past. Maybe they keep us from the future too. Perhaps it's time that I let go of mine."

She went to the chest and opened up a small drawer built into its side. From it she pulled with trembling fingers a little book of Shakespeare. She took it to the spot where he stood near the hearth.

She spared Quinn a quick glance before she knelt, still holding the treasure.

"My uncle Ferris gave that book to me." Ryan's face softened with the memory. "You should have heard how he read *Hamlet*."

" 'From Uncle Ferris, with love, December 25, 1874.' " From long memory, Anna quoted from the book she had once stolen. " 'May the Bard's words sustain you.' They sustained me, Ryan. I liked to read them often. 'My only love sprung from my only hate! Too early seen unknown, and known too late!' "

Something long-dimmed in his green eyes quickened. *"Romeo and Juliet."*

"The very one."

"I thank you for the book's return."

"The book is not my gift. It belongs to you already."

Anna let the thin pages slide open until she found the right one.

"You don't need to do more. What happened was so long ago, and you already saved my—"

She glanced up at him, tears sliding down her cheeks. Something in her expression silenced him, allowing her to return her attention to a fine blond lock of hair. How long, how long since she'd last touched it? How long since she had dared to look?

She lifted it by the narrow strip of violet ribbon that bound it, a still-lustrous bit of trim she'd salvaged from the ruined dress that Quinn had bought her long ago. Carefully she untied the silk, then used her knife to cut the trim in half. Just as carefully, though her hands trembled, she divided the lock of hair into two smaller sections, then retied two smaller bows.

As if he sensed her pain, Quinn then knelt down beside her.

"What . . . ?" His question faded into confusion.

She took his hand and opened it, then placed one lock of fine hair on it. Her tears flowed freely now, as she had feared. "Rosalinda was her name. She was born eight months after I came here. But I'd been badly hurt. She was so small, the tiniest baby you've ever seen. Beautiful though. Pink like the desert sky gets in a winter sunrise, with eyes that pale, pale blue. I thought she was my gift, for surviving."

"How long did she live?" His voice had softened so she could barely hear it.

"Just three days. I wanted to die too."

He closed his hand around her gift. "You think she was mine."

"I know it. From our two weeks." She passed him the book, then folded her half of the lock of hair into her hand. "Let me put this away so we can leave."

She stood and walked to the chest, favoring her bad knee, which had stiffened. She never heard him come up behind her, but he must have, for he took her in his arms once she had put the lock of hair back in the drawer.

It felt so easy to lean into his strength, so good to let her tears disappear into the fabric of his shirt, as if he could absorb her pain the way the cotton soaked up moisture.

He smoothed her hair as if she were a child. "I'm sorry," he said simply. "I'm sorry for it all."

"I told you I'd been punished. Every day since I hurt you. If I hadn't robbed you back in Mud Wasp, I wouldn't have been caught. Judge Cameron couldn't have given me to Hamby. Hamby never would have hurt me. I could have had a stronger child. And Rosalinda might have lived. . . ."

She felt his muscles tense.

"Judge Cameron?" Ryan asked. "Cameron *gave* you to Ned Hamby?"

"On the condition that I never reappear."

"But why? Wait a minute. You mean to tell me Hamby's been Cameron's boy all along? The judge got rid of you so *he* could take my gold, didn't he? Sweet Jesus!"

She pulled away from Quinn. Of course this was about the gold. Not Rosalinda. Never Rosalinda. Anna pulled open the door, sick with regret for bringing up her daughter's name.

*Their* daughter's, even if she meant less to Ryan than a bag of stolen coins.

Her voice quavered as she spoke. "We'd better go now. We'll need every bit of daylight if we're to find the trail."

Back in Texas, the bluebonnets would be blooming. Ned Hamby imagined sapphire fields of white-tipped blossoms rippling with the spring breeze like the surface of a lake. Occasionally the fiery blooms of Indian paintbrushes would fleck the surface, as brilliant as the last pure shafts of sunlight before dusk.

The longhorns liked to graze among the wildflowers. Ned dreamed himself a herd, each one wearing his own brand. Each one munching blossoms in the mild spring sunshine.

"My Ned got off to such a rough start," Mama'd tell her friends. "Who'd of guessed he'd turn out to be a man of property so young?"

Ned's pride swelled with her phantom words, so he dreamed up one more line for Mama.

"Can't imagine why I ever called that boy no 'count," she told the other hens.

He smiled, though the vision made him sick with longing to go home. Home. That's what it still was, no matter how many years, how many sins had passed since he'd been back there.

Lost in his reverie, Ned never heard Black Eagle coming till the half-breed's plug loped past and splattered him with mud.

"Goddammit!" Hamby swore. Damn the slushy melt-off, damn that idiot half-breed for his impatience, and especially damn Hop for laughing so hard.

Ned wiped mud from his cheek with the rough jacket's

sleeve. Tearing his revolver from his holster, he shot at both his men. Black Eagle and Hop wrenched their mounts' heads in opposite directions and disappeared into the trees.

Christ almighty. He had to get clear of these boys, this close-walled canyon, and his debt to Cameron before he lost his mind. Ned didn't even care about the promised money now. He'd long suspected the judge would always hold the possibility of wealth like a carrot, dangled just beyond his reach.

No, the money didn't matter anymore. Only Texas mattered, that and getting back to Mama without a bounty on his head.

And he'd kill every mother's son who got between him and that goal.

# Chapter Six

Quinn mutely followed Anna as she walked, a battered canteen slung over one shoulder, her old rifle tucked comfortably beneath the other arm. That crooked bastard, Cameron, had been the one who took his gold. Quinn could barely think past that bald fact despite a good three hours' hike. The judge had stolen his gold, then employed its theft to coerce a hapless gambler into becoming a puppet lawman, his hands tied by Cameron's ever-changing demands.

"Son of a bitch," he swore, furious for all the damage Cameron had wrought, more furious still at himself for being such a fool.

Ahead of him, Anna flinched. He might have called out to her not to worry, but instead he began to wonder how he felt about her now.

Was she a victim or a thief? Surely Cameron had used her even more callously than he'd used Quinn. He'd given her away, to be abused and then disposed of. Murdered, by outlaws so violent that the rumors of their crimes made grown men shudder. Although Anna had survived, she'd clearly suffered. Yet hers had been the hand that set this debacle in motion.

Even so, he wasn't bothered by the sight of Anna carrying a gun. He didn't worry, as he once would have, that she would turn on him again. Though she was still young, the harshness of her life had weathered away her cutting edges. Only a meaty jackrabbit or a rabid coyote need fear her now.

Perhaps, he thought, more than hardship had changed her. Perhaps the life that had once grown inside her had altered her as well. That tiny life too fragile to survive beyond the warm, safe confines of her womb.

*Rosalinda was her name.*

The memory of Anna's words blazed through him, as painfully charged as tiny bolts of lightning. Bolts from the blue.

*You think she was mine,* he had told her.

She truly believed it, and he was stunned to find that he was beginning to believe it too. Had he really made a child once with Anna? He reached into the pocket of his mended coat and touched the book of Shakespeare. Secreted between its thin and precious pages was the lock of fine blond hair, a treasure beyond reckoning.

Anna's treasure. He recalled her separating the thin lock into two equal halves, then tying each one with a tiny bow of violet silk.

She had shared her treasure with him, one as sacred as a gift of her heart's blood.

*I know what I owe you,* she had told him. And though he'd first misunderstood her, she had been right about one thing. What she had given was far more valuable than the simple favors of the body, as she'd put it.

Not that he could have turned down an offer of that sort. As much as he hated to believe it, he knew if she had beckoned, he would not have left the warmth of her cabin till tomorrow. He wasn't certain that he would have ever left her bed again.

Remembering the way she'd once moved beneath him, moaning with soft cries of pleasure, broke him out in a cold sweat. Sweet Jesus. He wanted her more than he'd ever wanted any woman, including the sparkling beauty she'd once been.

"Anna," he said softly, not wanting to spook her. "I think you should come with me to Copper Ridge."

She slid down a few feet of loose and slushy scree. At the bottom she rested her back against a vertical span of red rock and glanced up at him. Weak winter sunshine glimmered off the silver crucifix depending at her throat. "The trail's just up ahead, and I need to get home. I can't go back into that world, Quinn. You and I both know that. There's nothing for me there."

Her yellow dog pushed his head beneath her hand until she scratched his ears.

Ryan half jumped, half stumbled down beside her. He came to rest too close to her, so that his face was only inches from hers. But Anna didn't step back from him. Instead, tall as she was, she looked him nearly in the eye.

"I could make a place for you there," he offered, and his next words flooded out before he could examine what they meant to him. "You—you were the mother of my child."

For several moments she merely stared at him, silent and expressionless as the wind-carved red stone around them. Then a smile warmed her features, almost as gradual as dawn.

"You believe me, then," she told him.

He nodded, wondering if she might be playing him for a fool. But only for the slightest fraction of a moment.

"Please, come with me," he whispered, surprised to realize just how much he meant it.

She shook her head, but barely, and her smile faded.

"I had a friend once, Maggie, back when I was singing out near San Miguel. She was a harlot, but she was a sweet-natured red-haired girl, looked like she belonged in the angel section of some church's Christmas pageant. A man named Cullen Rayburn, who owned the general store, fell in love with her. He came around to see her as often as he could afford it. Then he finally proposed, and unlike most, he meant it. The day he married Maggie, she became his wife. A real wife, Ryan, not a woman who'd once made her living by taking strangers to her bed. She couldn't associate with any of us after that, but we were all proud of her, especially the upstairs girls."

Anna paused, and to Quinn the blue-gray of her eyes grew darker, as if thick storm clouds gathered in her memory.

After a few moments she continued. "At first we'd hear about Maggie dressing proper and keeping her house just like something out of *Godey's Lady's Book*. I remember how we envied her. Then, after a bit, we heard how the other women, the ones who called themselves 'real ladies,' didn't like her, how they wouldn't even walk on the same side of the street when she was shopping. How they got up and left the church one Sunday when her husband brought her in."

"Hypocritical biddies," Ryan interjected. "I'm not much on religion, but isn't forgiveness what church is all about?"

"They must have missed that sermon, I suppose. Anyway, they refused to shop in Maggie's husband's store. Not everyone in town went along with it, and Cullen stood by his wife, but even so, his business began to fail. I don't know whether it was the guilt or the isolation, but a few months later Maggie Rayburn decided that she'd had enough of living. She cut her wrists while her husband was at work one day. They say she sat inside the washtub so she wouldn't leave a mess on the braid rug. Cullen found her lying in a tub of her own blood."

"Poor girl." Quinn gently took her hand. "But, Anna, you were no soiled dove."

"I might as well have been, working in the places where I did. Most of the men assumed it anyway, and no woman would believe I never sold my body."

"I could take you somewhere, where no one would know your past. I—I could go with you."

"You have a job here. What else would you do? Go back to gambling, to ruining men by using marked cards and shaved dice?" Anger tinged her words, though he could not guess why.

"I'm no more a gambler now than you're a thief. I'm a lawman. A real one since this happened." He gestured toward his shoulder. "There has to be some town that needs my services, somewhere."

Anna stepped back, away from him. "I thought Copper Ridge needed your services right now."

He nodded once. "Only till I've gotten rid of Hamby. Then they're on their own. I'm finished taking orders from Ward Cameron. He used me too Anna, and I won't be used again."

"So stop him."

"He could have me hung. Cameron dispenses the law in these parts. When he can't do that, he makes it up. I can't fight that. He's got a hand that I can't beat."

A cool wind stirred the wisps of her hair where they'd escaped her thick blond braid.

"You have said you aren't a gambler any longer." She touched his temple with the barest pressure of her fingertips. "So the only cards Cameron holds are inside here."

Her fingertips slid down his neck, leaving his chilled skin warm and tingling in their wake. Her hand stopped above his heart. The palm flattened there before she continued. "What you have that can defeat him is in here."

Before he could respond, she dropped her hand, then

began to turn away. "Do what you must, Quinn Ryan, just as I will."

He might have called after her, insisted she come with him, but an image rose up before him like a filmy barrier. An image of a scrap of worn cream lace. His mother had rescued it from someone's ash can, had laundered it and hung it in the window of the room she shared with her daughters in the tenement. "Just a spot of cheer," she'd said, "to show us where we're going."

*Going . . . going . . .*

He had *gone*—away from Mother and her forlorn scrap of lace, from Uncle Ferris and his Irish-tainted Shakespeare, from his chattering sisters, Molly and Nell. Away from poverty and toward a future twinkling with a thin veneer of gold dust and ambition.

He had gone and stayed away too long. And whether that had been his own fault or Anna's he could not say. He knew only that it had been easier to hate her. What he felt now was too complicated to sort quickly, too important to rush through.

And so for the present, he decided, he would let her go back to her *querencia*, back to that small cabin where she'd decided she belonged.


"Notion, *ven*," Anna called, but the big dog ignored her just as he had when she'd asked him to come in English. Ever since she had turned back, Notion kept lagging behind, looking, she guessed, for Ryan, even whining in the direction where they had left the gambler.

Disloyal animal couldn't remember who it was that fed him.

She turned toward home and started walking once again, remembering from the first how Notion had taken to Quinn. Maybe the dog's previous owner had been male.

Or maybe that wasn't it at all. Quinn had always had a

winning way about him. Perhaps the man's charisma affected animals as well as people. She shook her head, thinking of how hard she'd had to work to charm men, how carefully rehearsed her songs and jokes had been. But for Ryan, making people smile had seemed so effortless, so natural. She imagined he'd cashed in on that ability a hundred times in his gambling career to beggar weak men like her father, perhaps to orphan other girls and leave them to the future she'd endured.

"Don't be so gullible," she told the dog, which now had fallen far behind her. "It's just his way. He can't help it. It doesn't mean a thing."

None of it did. Not Quinn's charm or his caresses, his smiles or his pretty words.

*I think you should come with me to Copper Ridge.*

How easy it would have been to fall for his offer, to ignore the doubt that she'd heard in his words. He might truly believe her about Rosalinda, but he didn't yet believe *in* her, at least not fully. And he never would. How could he, after what she'd done? It wasn't the kind of crime a man could be expected to forget. Even after six years. Even after the long kiss that had passed between them in her cabin, the one that reminded her so painfully of making love with him.

She closed her eyes against the memory of the taste of him, the strength of their attraction. She reminded herself she had been right to let him go. She'd found a place here and a calling, and though both were lonely, she knew that there were many worse things in this world. Besides, it was only in the wake of Quinn's departure that she saw solitude as hardship. Wasn't that what she loved best about her quiet canyon home?

As she drew nearer to the creek, she heard the music of flowing water thrumming through its rocks. She approached the bare-limbed willows that grew near it and could see how it had swollen with the melting snow. Soon spring would come into the canyon. Deer would bear their fawns, coyotes their pups; tough canyon shrubs would unfurl fresh green shoots. More of her patients would be able to travel to her for treatments of both the body and the spirit. Like the cold, clear water, she'd move on past Quinn.

The echo of an old cry warned her first, the thin wails of her dying infant long ago.

A few moments later a man's voice startled her in the clearing near her cabin. Her patients had come earlier than she'd expected. Normally she'd be eager to see an old acquaintance, visit about the homely details of the canyon winter. But something was amiss. She could hear pain in the voice—and worse yet, raw terror.

"¡Por favor, no! ¡Socorro!" the man screamed.

Responding to his cry for help, Anna broke into a run and rushed headlong into the clearing. And came upon a sight that tore away her breath.

Ned Hamby had Señor Delgado on his knees before him. The seventy-year-old shepherd sometimes came to see her for a salve to treat his rheumatism. The outlaw held a fistful of the old man's silver hair in one hand, a long knife in the other. A knife that Anna recognized at once, for she had felt its bite six years before.

Nightmare visions of that day detonated in her memory. All the awful flashes that woke her screaming at least twice a month now rushed back with blinding intensity, like the white-hot face of the summer sun. But the images were not the worst. Worst were broken songs that crashed down like mammoth waves from a hell-spawned storm. Every song she'd ever heard or sung, every note and every lyric, coalesced into an incredible crescendo.

*Amazing grace, how sweet the . . . As I walked out in the streets of Laredo . . . that saved a wretch like me . . . Got shot in the breast and I am dying today . . .*

With a cry of pain and horror she clapped her hands to

her ears, barely feeling the old rifle strike her bad knee as it dropped from her grasp.

*When we are called to part ... with proudly waving starry flags and hearts that knew no fear ... it gives us inward pain ... he came to fight for freedom's rights ... and hope to meet again ... a Union volunteer ...*

A hand clamped down hard on her shoulder, shattering the spell. Hamby used his leg to sweep her feet out from under her. Anna grunted as her fall forced the air out of her lungs.

He straddled her in no time, screaming, "Son of a bitch! It's my goddamned lucky day!"

His left eye stared vacantly across the clearing, but in the right she saw his hellish glee.

Dear God, he had her, even though she'd had a gun! He had her once again!

The echo of her own words accused her: *I'll kill them before I let them lay a hand on me again.* She'd made that promise to Quinn Ryan; she had made it to herself. Yet now shock drained the strength from her limbs and terror stole away her screams like a hurricane-force wind. Last, errant snatches of old lyrics skittered through her consciousness like hungry mice.

*Met her on the mountain ... stabbed her with my knife ... hang down your head, Tom Dooley ...*

Remembered pain tore at her belly. She retched with it, flooding her mouth with bitter bile.

Hamby's breath reeked of alcohol and something more unpleasant, like decaying meat. "Scare you, don't I?" he asked.

As if he couldn't feel her shaking. As if he couldn't imagine what the sight of the knife in his right hand brought back.

"You got plenty to be scared of ... little bitch." His words hissed through his clenched and crooked teeth.

Out of the corner of her eye she saw Señor Delgado

crumpled on the ground. His blood stained a patch of snow that remained in the cooler shadow of her cabin. She turned her head, trying to see if he might still be alive. The old man was motionless as clay.

Hamby's fingers ground into her shoulder.

"You think I don't recognize you, don't you?" Hamby roared. "But I do."

She said nothing but only trembled as his fingers moved to slide along a lock of blond that had escaped her braid to hang beside her cheek. She heard the sharp, almost sexual intake of his breath.

"Take a lot for me to forget a head a hair like yours. That'll look real good in my collection. Coulda been enjoyin' it all along if I hadn't been in such a goddamn hurry." He shook his head as if disgusted by his lack of care. "Sloppy work on my part, lettin' you out here all this time like some kind of medicine squaw. You been livin' on some borrowed years, girl. But don't you worry. I'll do you right this time. Judge Cameron still wants you dead. But I'll do you for my own reasons, slow and easy like, once we have our fun."

She tried to tell him it wasn't going to be like that, that she would fight him off, that she wouldn't let him hurt her. But the paralysis that had let him catch her hadn't eased, not even enough to let her speak. Self-disgust rode over her. If she would let him do this, she did not deserve to live.

"Seems to me that cabin would be a mite more comf'table." Hamby began to yank her to her feet, but her body's limpness worked against him. He swore and stuck his knife into his belt.

The moment the blade disappeared from sight, Anna felt a jolt of strength course through her veins. Harnessing her panic, she screamed and jerked away.

Hamby fumbled for his holstered gun, and Anna

thought, almost gratefully, that he would have to shoot her now, a quicker death than he'd intended.

Before he could raise the revolver, however, Notion burst out of the woods, snarling and barking. The dog exploded toward the outlaw and leapt on him, clearly intent on tearing out the man's throat.

But Hamby had unholstered the gun, and Anna heard another man's shout in the distance.

"Ned? What the—"

Like a morning fog her inertia had burned off and coordination had returned. Anna raced toward the spot where a chestnut mare stood tied to the thick branch of a live-oak tree. The horse pranced nervously with the commotion and rolled its eyes. Anna slowed her approach and spoke soothing words. The animal sidestepped away and threw back its head, obviously unnerved by Notion's growls and Hamby's screams.

"Come away from this, girl," Anna repeated. "I'll take you where it's quiet."

The horse's dark gaze shifted to Anna's face and finally grew still enough for her to untie and mount. The familiar star Anna had glimpsed on the mare's forehead convinced her this was Quinn's horse, the same one she had taken from him back in Mud Wasp years before.

Anna scrambled aboard the animal's back and hoped like hell this would work out better than the last time she had stolen Ryan's mare.

She dug her heels into the horse's side just before she heard the gunfire erupting in her wake.

---

Although the judge had seen to it the parlor was tastefully decorated with delicate dried flowers, the ceremony's witnesses looked anything but festive.

Lucy cut her eyes toward the little Spanish señorita who had so long attended the judge's needs. Lucy had no doubts about what sorts of needs the hussy had attended. Why, even if Lucy had been the innocent the judge imagined, she would have noticed how Elena's nostrils flared each time the black-haired beauty glared at her. Repeatedly the housekeeper fisted her small hands, wadding a lace handkerchief into a ball no larger than a dove's egg.

Miss Rathbone stood in attendance beside Elena. The older woman wore her usual dour countenance, along with her stodgiest gray dress and bonnet, in honor of the occasion. Lucy imagined Miss Rathbone didn't know whether to be relieved about her upcoming departure or horrified at her charge's utter lack of scruples.

Judge Clancy's baritone voice rumbled like an ancient waterfall over the sacred words. The words that would soon wed Lucy to Ward Cameron. The words that would give Lucy's bastard child his name.

A haze of nausea swirled around her, weakening her knees. What would Cameron do once he found out? By her reckoning, she was nearly four months pregnant. Even Lucifer's accountants couldn't explain a September child out of their April wedding date. Damn all the delays! She'd be lucky if he didn't realize she was pregnant right away. With her petite frame, she couldn't hide much in the way of baby, especially not stripped of her clothing.

Words surfaced in the stream of Clancy's droning. "... Do you, Lucille Maddox Worthington, take this man ..."

Did she? Ward Cameron seemed prosperous enough, solicitous enough, respectful enough of her family background to serve as a solution to her problems, but did she truly *take him*? Could she take him across from her at breakfast every morning, beside her in bed every night? And most important, could she take him *inside* her, knowing that it was handsome David's child who grew within her womb?

"Lucy? Lucy?" Her attention focused on Judge Clancy's fleshy face, now touched with a kind smile.

It must be time to answer. Time to step off this dreadful precipice. Lucy glanced around the small room, first at Ward, who looked uncomfortable and slightly nervous, then toward Miss Rathbone, who nodded stiffly once, and lastly toward Elena, who raised her chin and smiled victoriously. The two women must think she would back out now. Miss Rathbone's nod confused Lucy, but the housekeeper's Spanish haughtiness made anger burn inside her chest. Drawing herself to her full height, a mere five feet, Lucy enunciated firmly, "Yes, I do."

She let Judge Clancy's words blend back together, let them go from drone to roar, let them merge into that other roaring in her head. Within moments the roaring darkened into blackness, and she passed out, not knowing if Judge Clancy had yet pronounced her and Ward Cameron man and wife.

*"Manos arriba!"* the man screamed hoarsely.

Quinn jerked his hands into the air, not certain he'd correctly understood the orders but positive about the gesture the man made with his gun. One thing for damned sure, he must be dead tired to let the Mexican catch him unawares like this.

The short, dark-haired man rattled off another stream of staccato Spanish, but this time Quinn couldn't guess his meaning. Behind the man stood a dappled gray horse he was leading. On its back an olive-skinned woman and her child huddled together, their brown eyes huge with fear. All three of the Mexicans were dressed in coarsely woven brown wool. In addition, the woman had a worn blue-and-dove serape wrapped around her buxom figure.

Quinn swore to himself. He'd let the whole clan sneak

up on him. He'd never imagined that a few hours' walk could have deafened him.

Even as he thought it, he knew that wasn't right. He'd been thinking about Anna, the way her voice had sounded, the way she'd felt in his arms, when the Mexican appeared as if from nowhere.

"I don't understand!" Quinn shouted at his captor. *"No comprendo."*

He hoped like hell that worked. He'd just about exhausted his entire store of Spanish with those two words.

The woman helped the boy down and then slid off the horse. Pushing her child behind her, she stepped forward, then said something to the man Ryan took to be her husband. She gestured toward Quinn and shook her head, fanning out her long black hair. The Mexican man peered at Quinn more closely, then slowly lowered the barrel of his rifle.

"He very sorry," the woman offered. Smallpox scars marred her otherwise attractive features. "He thought you very bad *hombre*, ride with outlaw."

"Outlaw?" Alarm coursed through Quinn's limbs. "You've seen outlaws lately?"

The last rays of the dying sun touched her eyes with flame. *"Sí, señor.* We try to make a rancho, but these bad men, they keep coming. They drive away our cattle, all our horses but this one. We go before they kill us too."

"My name is Quinn Ryan. I'm the sheriff of Copper Ridge. Who are they? It's important that I know so I can stop them."

To her credit, she didn't laugh, though she looked doubtful. At last she shrugged, as if she'd decided no harm could come of naming the outlaw to an unarmed, unhorsed man who didn't even have a star to support the claim that he upheld the law.

"I have heard men call him Hamby," she said. "I call him *el diablo*. The devil, in your words."

"That he is. You're wise to take your family where it's safer," Quinn said. "You've seen him recently?"

"This very morning. He came, and the Apache with him held a knife up to my son so we would talk."

"What did he want from you?"

"To know about a woman, a *curandera* of the canyon. An American, like you."

"Anna..." Quinn groaned, feeling the hair rise on the back of his neck. He'd been so quick to dismiss Anna's tale two weeks before. It sounded as if she'd been right after all. And now, when she returned to her cabin, Hamby would be there... waiting for her. Terror gripped Quinn's chest with ice-cold talons. Sweet Jesus, he had sent her home to die.

He glanced once more at the western sky, as if his need might coax the sun aloft. But even if the light were with him, he was many hours away. Many hours from Anna, who might be dead already.

If she were lucky... He closed his eyes against the lurid flashes of what Hamby and his men might do to her if she yet lived. With sickening detail he recalled the way Hamby swung those little scalps and laughed. *El diablo,* this woman had called him, but Quinn suspected his atrocities would make Old Scratch blush with shame.

The woman grasped his arm. "You know Señorita Anna?"

Quinn nodded, too miserable to waste words on an answer.

"She has helped us many times." Tears rolled down her pockmarked cheeks. "We had no wish to cause the *curandera* harm, but Juan... they would have killed our son. You would help her if you could?"

"I—I would give my soul to help her," Quinn said, his voice rough with regret, for he feared that as with his family, he would be too late.

The woman turned and spoke in Spanish with her husband. They seemed to argue, but finally they appeared to come to some agreement. The man handed the gray gelding's reins to Quinn. He unfastened several packs behind the saddle and pulled them to the ground.

"You take this horse and go to find the señorita. And you tell her *la familia de Javier Cortez* says many prayers for her."

"Thank you." Quinn swung into the saddle. "I will tell her."

And without another word he galloped off into the deepening gloom.

Anna leaned close to the mare's neck to duck beneath low-hanging branches. She knew this canyon, knew the places where a horse would slide in loose rock, where phantom pathways ended in impenetrable thorns, or, worse yet, precipitous drops. Her pursuers would have to be more cautious, unless they could keep her in clear sight, or unless they had an expert tracker in their midst.

Swallowing back her terror, she checked the horse's frantic pace, then drew the big mare to a halt. Already the shadows had grown long. Soon the light would weaken and then fade out altogether, leaving her alone and without shelter in the dark.

With a shudder at the thought Anna swept a lock of loose hair behind an ear to listen. Beyond the blowing of her tired mount, she heard the sharp caw of a raven. She listened closer still and heard the gentle sweep of a light breeze among the trees and rocks, the distant voice of melting water in the creek. And then a clattering of hooves on rocks. The hoof strikes of the horses of the men who followed her.

In the canyon it was difficult to gauge distance and direction. Sounds bounced between the red walls and echoed in the hollows, each sharp with the threat of violence. Flashes of old terror rose once more, punctuated by the chords of mangled song.

*No!* Anna nearly screamed the word aloud to stop the macabre parade of memories. She could ill afford to let them paralyze her once again. Already she'd let them cost her the advantage of her rifle. Already they had cost her what might have been her only chance to put Ned Hamby in the ground.

And surely there was no one who more deserved to die. Not after what he'd done to her. Not with what he meant to do.

Her panic once again receded as she planned what she would do. If she kept heading north, she'd come to a little draw with an entrance almost completely hidden behind an outcrop of red rock. Unless the outlaws knew the canyon intimately, they'd never dream the spot existed. She could hide there, then climb up onto the cliffs above on foot. From that vantage she would be able to overlook a large portion of the canyon. If luck were with her, she'd be able to see if Hamby and his men had left. When she thought it was safe, she could try to catch up with Quinn to warn him Hamby's men were close and to return his horse. And then the two of them could find a way to drive the outlaws from her home.

Her plan had one disadvantage she could think of. If Hamby's men, by some chance, discovered where she'd gone, all they'd have to do is cut off the narrow entrance to entrap her there. Although it seemed unlikely, the thought made her scalp prickle.

All things considered, going to the little draw seemed a better idea than pursuing Quinn right away. If she did that and was followed, she'd be leading the outlaws straight to him as well. And now neither of them had a gun.

*Sangre de Cristo,* she wished she were miles away from there. Yet even as the thought coursed through her, terror gripped her fiercely. For all its loneliness, the canyon sheltered memories, memories and a presence she was not yet ready to give up. How could she leave her home to outlaws?

*Not forever,* she swore to herself. Not even for long. Just long enough to warn Quinn. Then she'd return and somehow reclaim the place where a part of her lay buried, the only place she could feel at ease.

Anna nudged the mare's ribs with her heels and rode toward where the draw lay. The sooner she reached it, the sooner she could learn exactly where the outlaw and his men were.

Lucy sputtered and coughed with the water that was poured over her face.

"You didn't have to do that," Cameron shouted at Elena. "It's her wedding day, and you've made her look like a drowned rat."

*Wedding day.* Lucy coughed again. So it had been neither dream nor nightmare. It had happened—was still happening—right now.

"Are—are we—?"

Judge Clancy loomed above her, his jowly face smiling with the paternal amusement one reserved for a small child. "Yes, my dear. The two of you are married, but don't worry. You're not the first young bride to be overcome by happiness."

"She looks sick with fear to me," Elena offered, still brandishing the pitcher she had poured onto her rival's face.

Lucy wondered if it yet held water enough to drown a woman. If she felt stronger, she'd be tempted to hold down the housekeeper's head to see.

She shoved her sodden curls out of her eyes.

Miss Rathbone tugged her arm. "She does look pale. Let's take her to her room so I can loosen her corset."

Cameron lifted his new wife to her feet by one arm while Miss Rathbone helped support the other.

Elena rushed toward the corridor where the two eastern women had been staying.

"I will help you," she insisted.

"No!" both Miss Rathbone and Lucy said at once.

Lucy felt a rush of blood heat her face and neck. The last person she would want to learn her secret was Elena, but both men in the room had surely heard how vehemently she and her companion wished to keep the housekeeper from helping with her underthings. She couldn't bear to look at either of them—and most especially to look at that concubine who called herself a maid—to see how they'd reacted to the outburst. So she kept her gaze cast low until she realized that was exactly what a woman shamed by guilt would do.

But not a Worthington. Never a Worthington, she told herself. A Worthington must hold her head high no matter what the circumstances. Isn't that what her father had done last August when those self-righteous reporters had questioned him? Although they'd had what appeared to be solid evidence, her father blustered his way past the allegations. Recalling the valuable lessons he had taught her, she favored Elena with the haughtiest glare she could muster.

It must have been effective, for the smug expression shriveled on the woman's face.

"What I meant to say," Lucy said, her voice tight with condescension, "was that your services—in *any* regard—will no longer be required in this house."

Her pronouncement had exactly the effect she desired. Both Elena and Cameron gaped and paled. Lucy would have bet her last gold eagle any suspicions they might have had about her had evaporated with their bewilderment.

While she had both off stride, she pressed her advantage. "I'm certain my new husband will be happy to give you a glowing letter of recommendation. But since my mother passed away some years ago, I've been used to hiring my own household staff."

She glanced quickly at Miss Rathbone, as if daring her to dispute the notion. In reality her father had insisted on handling those details himself.

Miss Rathbone surprised her with a puckered smile. Clearly she found Lucy's verbal sleight of hand amusing.

"Come along, *Mrs.* Cameron," the older woman said with more cheer than Lucy had heard in months. "I'm certain you can walk now. Let me help you with that corset."

Lucy nodded once in answer and allowed Miss Rathbone to lead her. Before they left the parlor, Lucy spared her husband one last glance. And found his gaze locked with Elena's, his mouth gaping like that of a new-caught fish.

Turning her back on the pair, Lucy could not suppress a smile. Today she might have taken a new name, but the appellation did nothing to change what she was at her core, what she would be forever.

A Worthington, and with sufficient arrogance, a Worthington need apologize for nothing.

# Chapter Seven

Anna hid the horse carefully behind a shroud of rock and juniper, then tied the animal so it could graze on the sparse brown winter grass. God knew, she might need to ride fast when she next mounted, and she would need the mare to be in the best shape possible.

Afterward Anna began to climb. Above her a handful of the brightest stars already glowed against a sky bruised by the nightfall. To the west the last stains of scarlet faded into oblivion. The full disk of the moon offered thin illumination, splashing eerie shadows in the lee of every rock.

She hesitated and leaned against a cooling boulder. Climbing now was a fool's errand. Even in the best light, the Indian trail was nearly undetectable. In the dimness she might easily step off a steep slope or twist an ankle on loose gravel. Any injury in this place could easily prove fatal. And even when she reached the top, she would never see distant riders in the canyon.

Yet, after a brief rest, she pressed on as quickly as she could safely move. If she reached the top, there were some things the darkness could not hide. The light from a campfire. Or flames rising from her cabin if they burned it, or perhaps a plume of smoke to tell her they were staying there instead.

She shuddered with revulsion at that last thought. Somehow, she'd rather Hamby and his men destroy her things than use them. She thought about the lock of hair inside the chest drawer, bereft even of the dubious protection of a book's thin pages. She thought with sudden nausea of Hamby touching it.

It was all Anna had left of Rosalinda, that and the tiny grave that lay close to the cabin. Her anger smoldered, then burst into full flame. How could she leave that soulless bastard at her cabin? Even if he left it standing, the place would be defiled in her mind.

Quivering with emotion, she paused to rub her shoulder where he'd grabbed it. The memory of his threat hissed in her ear.

*You got plenty to be scared of . . . little bitch.*

A powerful spasm gripped her stomach, and she bent to vomit. Her legs shook so that they nearly buckled at the knees.

"I can't ... I can't," she whispered without knowing what it was she couldn't do. Face the threat of Hamby? Climb up to these steep cliffs in the dark?

She spat and wiped her mouth, then thought of the ancient people who'd once dwelt there. They had left scattered caves and shards of pottery all around these canyon walls. Once, she'd found bits of bone carved into what looked like game pieces. Evidence that they had raised their offspring here as well. She could almost hear those long-dead children, laughing at her fears, laughing as they scurried nimbly up these slopes.

Below her she heard a clattering of loose rock. Her knees buckled once more. Had they found her so quickly? She tasted bile once again and crouched low behind a gnarled piñon tree. Her best chance lay in stillness, like a fawn left by its mother for the night. In this poor light they'd never see her if she didn't move. Besides, she wasn't certain she could make her legs work. Once again raw fear had crippled her.

Small stones rattled their way into the lower canyon, and she heard something moving through the brush downhill from her. Something quickly moving closer. Her own blood whooshed in her ears; a band of pulsing pressure made her head ache.

*"Dios mío,"* she breathed. *My God.* This time the two words were more a desperate prayer than exclamation.

As if in answer, something whined. Almost before she recognized the familiar sound, a bark rose, sharp and joyful.

"Notion!" she called back.

Within moments the big dog found her. In his enthusiasm he knocked her on her seat.

"I thought they'd killed you, fellow," she crooned, stroking his thick fur. "I thought they'd—"

The dog yelped in pain. Anna raised her hand and peered down at the sticky, dark stain. Blood. A bullet must have grazed him, or perhaps a knife.

"Poor boy," she said. But quickly a new fear overwhelmed her. For in the morning, with the sun out, Notion's blood would lead Ned Hamby and his gang right here. Or maybe, if the outlaws had followed the dog's progress, they already waited down below.

And if they did, there would be no getting out of there alive.


"Come on with me, Ginger. I reckon ol' Ned'll pay dear for your return. Leastways, he will if he ain't too dog-chawed."

Black Eagle led the chestnut mare from the stand of

juniper where the woman he was hunting had concealed it. Hidden as it was behind an elk-sized boulder, he might have ridden by it if not for its neighed greeting to his mount.

He'd wondered how the hell that woman had disappeared so fast. He'd been almost on her heels when she ran off. Hiding here would have been a good idea if that dog of hers hadn't painted him a map with its own blood. Clearly she hadn't lost her head the way most women would have. She would have made a good Apache, or so he would guess.

If he were a full-blood, he would climb that outcropping tonight, then cut like a blade through shadow and drag her from wherever she'd holed up. And afterward he'd slice through her as well.

After he killed her, he meant to take the head to Cameron, to dump it on the judge's desk and demand the whole reward. Not just the portion that Hamby'd promised either, but what Black Eagle thought was fair. And if Judge Cameron didn't feel like dealing with an Apache whelp, Black Eagle'd start talking—to anyone who'd listen. He could damned sure spin out enough details to fix the judge's flint.

Black Eagle cocked his head and listened to the dog's bark from somewhere in the dark mass of rocks above. He'd tracked the mongrel here, following the damp trail of its blood from Hamby's desperate shot. Black Eagle grinned, thinking about the way the dog had tangled with old Ned. No telling which of the two bled more.

He wondered if Hop had gone back to the cabin to help Hamby bind his wounds. More than likely Hop had returned to loot the place while Hamby was distracted and Black Eagle was still out hunting for their prey.

Probably both thought Black Eagle would play the dutiful lackey, truss up the bitch, and bring her back to share. He'd take his turn last, of course, 'cause Ned might have taken to scalping, but he was still squeamish about poking any woman after a half-breed. Or maybe it wasn't the poking that bothered Ned, but the way Black Eagle liked to cut his women while he had them, the way he liked to hear them scream.

He remembered last time, with that skinny squaw, how he'd smeared himself in war paint made of her bright blood. He shuddered and grew hard with the thought of coating his face with this woman's still-hot blood, of having her all to himself.

Quivering with anticipation, he considered the horse's presence and the single dog bark he had heard. The mongrel must have found its owner. He thought again of climbing up to find the woman, but the darkness and the fierce animal made it too dangerous. Too dangerous for a man with only half a hunter's soul.

As he staked the mare beside his worn-out gelding, Black Eagle once more cursed the white blood flowing in his veins. He thought of his mother, the rabbit woman with her bulging, frightened eyes. He thought, too, of how Grandpa blamed him for what had happened to her.

"You goddamn little bastard," the old man swore at him, pulling off his thick leather belt. "We'll see if I can beat the savage out of you *this* time."

Black Eagle spat in disgust at how he'd cried and screamed then, just like his mama must have the day she'd been attacked. With those eerie, almost human screeches like a rabbit in a snare.

He wondered if this woman would scream much when he caught her. He imagined her terror, her weakness, his own rising hate and strength.

He wasn't going to let the rabbit get away. As he made camp near the woman's only avenue of escape, he wondered how long it would be till she came down. He wished he could build a fire, for a chill had settled in the canyon. Might as well put it from his mind. If the prey sensed his presence, she'd never come down on her own. If Hop and Hamby didn't show up and make their white man's racket, he could just wait here real quiet till she tripped over him on her way to find her horse.

Quinn peered down a trail silvered by the full moon's glow, but at this pace he relied mainly on the vision of his borrowed mount. Perhaps because it galloped in the direction of its familiar corral, the animal moved with surprising surety and speed. But even his stolen mare, Titania, would not have been quick enough.

*Too late.* He heard the two words in the hoof strikes on the ground beneath him, in the creaking of the saddle and the snorted exhalations of the gray. He would be too late for Anna, as he had been too late for his own family before.

Despite the coolness of the evening, heat rose from his collar as if it were a leather chimney. He trembled as one fevered within a layer of chill sweat.

Sweet Lord, he'd been too late for her already, hadn't he? Six years too late to piece together all the clues, and two weeks too late to come to know her as the woman she now was. A woman who had both betrayed and saved him, a woman who had glimpsed redemption in the ruins of a man.

Her walls, like his, had long since crumbled. Her rooms, like his, yet echoed with the whispers of old ghosts. For him, his family's. For her, their babe's. And if he had at least the memories of the past to make up for the lost future, she had only possibilities, which had been stamped out as cruelly as smoking cinders on a hearth rug.

She'd been so long living a life without those possibilities that she'd been unable to accept his offer to take her from this place. She might truly love her canyon home, but that wasn't the real reason she'd denied him. Something in her eyes convinced him it was fear instead. Fear he hadn't meant it. Fear of the long, slow burn against her heart of hope snuffed out.

He knew—or imagined he knew—because he'd felt that same way all those empty years while Cameron held his leash. He knew because a part of him was still afraid to think of what he'd do with Anna if she were still alive.

Black Eagle swore, wishing he had another blanket. All the warmth of afternoon had been sucked out into the blackness of an inky sky. He got up and paced awhile, then stripped the saddle from his mustang. Damn woman must've died up there—or, worse yet, spotted him. She plainly wasn't coming down that night.

He robbed the dark bay gelding of its saddle blanket, then lay it atop the quilt he always used. Mama's quilt, the only thing he had left of her—except the nightmares.

Black Eagle shifted restlessly and thought back to his mama. He'd never meant to hurt her, even if he did despise her weakness. But she had heard his eerie cry and come running to the woodshed, and that was where she'd caught him settling accounts with his grandpa—with an eight-inch bowie knife.

He didn't like to think about what he'd done next. Not to Mama, who'd at least taught him to read books. Who at least had held him on her lap and hugged him, even if she was too ashamed to take him with her into town.

Not to Mama . . .

But she'd screamed then, harder, higher, with that almost human cry. And his knife leapt in his hand just like a live thing, plunging, jabbing, until her screaming stopped.

He didn't like to think of it at all.

But every killing since then blunted the horror of that

recollection. Every woman he stabbed put that one time a little further back.

So he hoped like hell the slut climbed back down here soon. Because he couldn't wait to use his knife to dim the bloody images his mama's memory revived.

Anna glanced down at the dog, now far below her feet. Blue-tinted with the moonlight, Notion shifted his front paws and whined. His tail had wagged frantically when he'd found her, even as she'd bound his front right leg with a kerchief to stop the bleeding. But he obviously wasn't happy to be left behind. The way he was wriggling, he'd surely lose his makeshift bandage.

"Shhh, quiet, boy," Anna said, her own voice soft against the possibility of listeners. She prayed that no one had heard the single bark before; she prayed that none of Hamby's gang remained close enough to hear.

Again the dog whined, this time slightly louder. He'd been content enough limping after her on the steep trail. But now that she had nearly reached the top, she would have to use both hands and feet to climb a nearly vertical span of cliff face for about twenty feet. A deeper sound low in his throat convinced her he was going to bark again.

"Hush! I'll be only a little while." The whispered words bounced off stone, sounding louder than she had intended.

Though she felt guilty at her plan, Anna pulled a fist-sized rock from the cliff. She knew Notion had saved her by leaping at Ned Hamby, but she had no choice now except to drive him off.

She tossed the rock toward his hindquarters and was almost relieved when she heard it strike the path beside him instead. Reaching out, she grabbed a second, smaller stone. This one found its mark. Notion yipped in surprise, tucked his tail between his legs, and slunk beneath a fringe of cliffrose. Anna doubted he would go far, but he at least might think twice about crying after her for a few minutes.

She didn't think she'd need much longer. Turning her attention to the rocks above her, she felt around for handholds. Slowly she pulled herself farther up the steep face. She'd considered herself fit, but her muscles strained with the unaccustomed task. She thought uncomfortably of falling. Though a drop from this height probably wouldn't kill her, if she broke a bone, the result might well be the same.

She slipped when stony soil crumbled, but her handholds kept her safe. With a grunt she clambered to the top and panted for several minutes until she caught her breath.

Once her breaths grew more even, a wave of fatigue engulfed her. *Madre de Dios*, but she could sleep forever. She'd risen early, then walked a long way before Hamby's attack. Yet even if she'd lain abed all day, her conversations with Quinn and the mere sight of the man who'd nearly killed her were enough to leave her feeling spent.

But she could not afford to rest for long. Not with the night air cooling rapidly, not with the possibility of Hamby's men around. Brushing the dirt off her elbows, Anna stood and faced the vast emptiness that yawned before her.

The canyon, washed in moonlight, had lost its bloody hue. In its place the rock, the tops of juniper, appeared a ghostly gray. Where the cool light could not follow lay deep pools of blackness, places where a single rider or an army might lie invisible in wait.

She stared in the direction of her cabin, spotted the silvery reflection of the swollen creek. By tracing her gaze along its course, she found the correct location. Neither flames nor thick smoke drew her eye, but after staring long and hard, she made out a narrow column that hazed the stars behind it.

Smoke rising from her chimney. They were staying in

her house, probably roasting a goat or her chickens by this time. Eating her food and infesting her pallet with their vermin.

Anna's teeth ground in her anger. She'd like to ride there, nail the door shut, and set fire to the whole lot, even though she would lose everything she owned. It would be well worth it to make them pay for all the harm they had done. It would be worth it not to fear them anymore.

But her desire to kill them was but a shadow of the terror Hamby's attack still inspired. Again she cringed at the thought of how the memories had unhinged her, memories and the clashing of a hundred vanquished songs. Crushed beneath their weight, she'd waited like a lamb for him to come and get her. Blinded by old pain, she'd even dropped the rifle that she could have used to kill the demon.

Hugging her arms against the cold, she realized she would have to climb down from the outcropping to escape this nightmare. Climb down and mount Quinn's mare, then ride far from this place. With a tired sigh she let her gaze sweep across the moonlit canyon. She wished she could stay there long enough for the dawn to bring its gift of color to this land she loved. She wished she could have time to say good-bye to Rosalinda. Good-bye but for a little while, she swore to herself.

*Mi querencia.* The words made her eyes tear, and a lump of sorrow filled her throat. *The place where I belong.*

Feeling as if she'd just surrendered, she crouched on hands and knees to begin her downward climb. Downward into what? she wondered. Downward into where?

Below her the chestnut mare remained tied. Though Anna was no expert on horseflesh, she knew the animal was something special. Special enough to buy her a fresh start, once sold? Special enough to pay her way to San Francisco?

As she grasped her first handhold, her mind screamed

its outrage. It was just temptation, nothing but a lost dream calling her.

*Your music's coming back.*

*Sangre de Cristo,* how could she even think such thoughts? She was going to find Quinn, to take the horse to him. She was no longer the kind of woman who would consider larceny.

The voices whispered softly, sweetly. Quinn might have wanted her body when he made his offer, but she knew he never really wanted her. He was nothing but a smooth talker like her father, a man who'd only let her down. She'd be better off without him, maybe even singing.

*You're still young enough to have it all.*

The old fantasy beseeched her, and with it came a sound. An infant's cries, so thin and weak she knew the child was doomed. *Dios mío, Rosalinda!*

With the realization came a choking nausea so wretched that Anna missed her foothold, so painful that she failed to recover the misstep. Her hands clawed desperately in an attempt to slow her fall. Though her nails tore against rock, she plunged down the face and struck the trail below.

Her knees buckled with the impact, and the left side of her head slammed against a rock near the cliff's base. Pain exploded, and streaks of light slashed across her vision. Before she had a chance to wonder how badly she'd been hurt, the lights dissolved into the blackest night she'd ever known.

# Chapter Eight

The tapping at the door was far gentler than the hammering inside Lucy's chest. Judge Cameron had returned—or she supposed that she must call him Ward now, since they were man and wife.

Wife ... she was his wife, so what else could she do except allow him into his bedroom? *Their* bedroom, God help her, where he'd expect to touch her in a few short minutes, just beneath the pristine, lace-trimmed sheets. He'd expect a bloodstain on those sheets come morning. A bloodstain from a wife he had deflowered.

Dear God, she'd have to tell him before he found out on his own.

She called to him, but her voice, so arrogant before, refused to rise above a frightened squeak. Thank goodness he could not have heard it, she thought as she rose from the bed.

She smoothed her snow-white nightgown and fussed with it in the hope it wouldn't cling to the small prominence of her growing belly. With a sigh she trudged across the room with all the enthusiasm of a prisoner marching to the noose.

Her bridegroom tapped once more. She thought she heard impatience in the rhythm. After turning the key, she cracked the door and peered at him.

He smiled warmly, no doubt mistaking her reluctance for mere shyness.

"Come now, Lucy. This is what you wanted, isn't it?" Slowly he pushed the door until the gap was wide enough for him to step inside. He wore a robe in deference to her request that they not undress in the same room—not yet.

Dizziness weakened her knees once more as Ward Cameron turned the key to lock them in—together. She tottered toward a delicate cane-bottom chair and lowered herself onto it.

Cameron knelt beside her, instantly solicitous. "You look so pale, Mrs. Cameron."

She stared at him, heart racing, knowing her charade was at its end.

He took her hand, so gently, then kissed her trembling fingers. "Shall I have Elena draw a bath for you?"

Lucy stared into his face, almost too shocked for speech. "E-Elena? But—but I asked her to leave—"

"I assumed that with the wedding, your emotions might be running somewhat high. I thought that perhaps you might reconsider. Of course, I regard it as a household matter, so the final decision will be yours. But I will miss her *cuernitos*."

Lucy simmered at the thought of what he'd really miss. Did he think her blind to miss the surreptitious looks that passed between him and his housekeeper? Or perhaps it wasn't that at all. Perhaps Lucy's own experience—her guilt—with David had heightened her awareness of forbidden looks and furtive touches.

When she swallowed, she felt as if she were choking

down a pint of gravel. She took a deep breath, trying to steel herself for what she must say next.

But Cameron, apparently convinced she'd acquiesce, had gone back to kissing her fingers. As her thoughts roamed back to David, her stomach churned in protest. Almost involuntarily she pulled her hand away.

"My dear," the judge said, "please don't be frightened. I will be as careful, as gentle as I can."

Ah, but that's the shame of it, thought Lucy, for with David, there had been no gentleness at all. Only pent-up longing that flared brighter every time they were alone. Brighter, hotter, until it burned them both.

Despite her vow to put him from her mind, she wondered where David was now, on her wedding night? She'd heard a rumor that he had run off to join the navy, or perhaps the crew of a merchant vessel. She hoped it was true, that he was off in distant lands, leading foreign girls astray. That he'd run far enough to escape her father's retribution.

She couldn't help wondering how he'd feel about what she was doing, how he'd react to the idea of Judge Cameron playing papa to his bastard. Probably with gratitude and perhaps a smug grin at pulling off such a coup against one of her father's cronies.

It wasn't as if David would have married her even if she would have settled for someone of his station. She told herself it didn't matter, that the only thing that mattered was the brief memory of flame. A memory to warm her while she lay awake nights beside the judge in his cold bed.

Ward reached for her once more, forcing her to focus on the present. She stood, her hands writhing like twin serpents to avoid his. Time enough later to endure his touch, if he'd still have her. Now it was time to learn if her gambit had succeeded. Or if he'd cast her out, or even worse.

She lifted her chin and shrugged on her pride as if it were a coat of armor, or a shroud to hide her fear. "I am touched by your concern, Ward, but I must speak with you first."

He sat down on the bed's edge without inviting her to do the same. It was just as well. She didn't want to sit now, particularly not on the bed with him. If she needed to run, she wanted some distance between them at the outset. It was not out of the question that he might strike her. Worthington or not, she was his wife, and they were in wild territory. No one would likely question his right to discipline her.

Her gaze flicked to the lock, the key still in it. She doubted she would be quick enough to turn it to escape him.

"Tell me—what is it?" he asked.

Cameron leveled his sternest gaze on her, one Lucy suspected he normally reserved for ruffians and horse thieves.

Would he truly hurt her? She hesitated, so frightened she could scarcely breathe.

He shook his head and frowned. "I've been waiting since our engagement for the other shoe to drop. Tell me, please, what *is* it with you? Do you have fits or asthma? An uncontrollable desire to drink little bottles of some expensive patent cure?"

Her jaw dropped in surprise, though she knew how foolish she must look. It had never occurred to her that he'd suspected. But of course, now that she thought of it, their rapid engagement and her eagerness to come west must have made him wary. It could only have been his desire for her father's favor that kept him to the course.

"No, no," she stammered. "No abnormality, I assure you. It's only that—I'm—I'm pregnant."

He stared at her for a long, long while, his expression so blank, she could not decide whether bluster or a running start would be most beneficial. Finally he did the last thing, the *very* last thing, she expected.

He laughed. A deep roar of a laugh, as if he'd just heard a splendid jest. "Only pregnant? *Only* pregnant? How could I have been so stupid not to think of that? Your father—he truly took me for a fool."

She shook her head emphatically and chose words meant to minimize her guilt. "My father doesn't know. He knows how the assistant coachman—abused his trust—but he has no idea what came of the—the seduction."

She saw the rage snuff out whatever trace of humor she'd detected in his eyes. God help her now.

"You little slut," he hissed between clenched jaws. "So you spread your legs for a mere servant? I'd thought you more intelligent than that."

A fierce blush heated her face, but anger flooded past it. She refused to let him speak to her this way. "I may have married you, but I'm a Worthington and always will be. My father will be grateful—very grateful—to his son-in-law. The Worthington name will open doors to you, doors forever closed without his blessing. Surely you must have known there'd be a price."

He stood, towering over her so there was no chance of escape. With every word his index finger poked her shoulder painfully. "I should drag you right back to your father—in the Capitol—with a big red bow around your neck. I should tell him exactly what you've done, you scheming little tramp."

At least he hadn't throttled her. Still, she wondered, would he do as he had threatened? Would the shame of raising her bastard outweigh greed and ambition? And what, then, would her father do? Send her off into the countryside to live with Aunt Penelope to bear her child in shame and secrecy? Or would he disown her, leaving her no way to support herself, much less an infant?

Her child. She felt resentment churning inside her at

this tiny creature that had taken root inside her body, at the upheaval it had already created in her life. She knew, of course, that it was wrong to hate it, that she and David had been the ones at fault.

But neither her anger nor her guilt made any difference, so she waited in silence to hear the sentence Judge Ward Cameron would pronounce.

Finally he spoke again, his voice cold and harsh. "I won't take you back there. I won't because I deserve a judgeship in the civilized world, far more than those dolts who had the good fortune to be born into a family name. I deserve it, Lucy, and some other things as well. First of all, your cooperation. Anytime that I require it, you *will* satisfy my needs. Whatever I desire."

Her pretense of humility shattered against the outrageousness of his demand. "You prove yourself a man of exquisitely low character with such—with such—"

He grasped her upper arms with bruising firmness. "You needn't play the blushing bride with me. If you didn't mind flipping up your skirts for a mere servant, anything your husband asks should be well within reason. Anything at all."

Her retort caught in her throat, choked by fear of this huge man. Her brief encounter with David left her unsure of what Cameron might have in mind. Would he use his sex to punish? Did he mean to harm her or do something that might make her lose the baby? She felt the blood drain from her face as she wondered if such a thing were possible and how much it might hurt.

Relentlessly he continued without loosening his grip. "Secondly I require that Elena remain here. You have no power to dismiss her. And finally you will confess that we were married in secret this winter during my visit. Today's ceremony served only to appease your father. *No one* must question that this child is my own."

She wanted to argue, wanted to protest that one simply

could not treat a Worthington this way. But his big hands on her arms were too real, and the East Coast and her father were much too far away.

He must have taken her silence for agreement, for he pushed her down onto the bed. Opening his robe, he uncovered his arousal just before he spoke again.

"I believe that we'll get started on that first condition now."

---

Cold. The cabin felt so cold. Anna shivered, wondering if the ashes, too, had cooled, or if she might find glowing embers to help her resurrect the fire.

When she tried to move, the left side of her head flared so painfully she thought she might vomit. Her eyes watered with the hurt, making the stars above her swirl.

Stars? *Santa Maria*, she wasn't home at all. She was— her head throbbed, and the memory submerged into her groan.

A soft cry caught her ears.

"Notion?" Her voice sounded fuzzy as the silvery trunks of aspens in the fog.

The dog's form emerged awkwardly from shadow. In the moonlight she saw the bandage on his right front leg.

She hugged the animal close and dug her fingers into his warm fur. As she did, memories slid out of the darkness: Hamby waiting at her cabin, Señor Delgado's blood staining the snow, Notion's attack, and her desperate escape. She'd come to this outcrop to try to see where Hamby and his men went. She recalled dimly the hazy smoke rising from her cabin's chimney and her decision to climb down and ride for help.

She could remember nothing more, but her position at the base of the steep cliff face told her what had happened. Using the big dog to help support her, she stood cautiously.

As she did, her vision dimmed, so she leaned against

the rocky wall. Her torn nails, her right wrist, and her hip throbbed, though not as intensely as her head. She took a few experimental steps. Despite her various aches, she didn't think anything felt broken. For that blessing, at least, she could be grateful.

She sat against a larger boulder and rubbed her arms against the cold. How long had she been lying there unconscious? Were Hamby and his men still in her cabin? Peering up the rock face, she decided she was too unsteady to climb to the top again. She would have to take a chance that the outlaws remained at her home in the canyon below, drinking her small supply of whiskey and eating the remainder of her meager food stores. She grimaced at the thought and hoped that Padre Joaquín was tougher than shoe leather.

At first her stiff muscles and her throbbing skull slowed her descent. Gradually however, it grew easier to move, and her stomach no longer roiled with each step. Soon she would reach the bottom of the rock formation, where she'd hidden the horse that would take her to Quinn and whatever chance of safety he might offer.

Quinn could feel his mount's exhaustion in its trembling, could hear it in its breath. Never before had he driven an animal so hard, despite the deepness of the shadows cast by moon and starlight, despite the danger of the treacherous, broken land.

The gray moved swiftly, willingly, as if it sensed his reason for such haste. But speed and darkness were at odds, and the horse stumbled several times. The last occasion nearly unseated Quinn and finally brought him to his senses.

He checked the animal's pace, at last realizing that either horse or rider—perhaps both—would die if he did not. And his death would avail Anna nothing. If he lived to reach her, and if she were still alive, there might yet be a chance to save her. And if not . . .

A red wall of rage and hatred rose up at the thought. God help Hamby and the rest of those murdering bastards if she weren't, for he would make them suffer for each hurt they'd caused her.

Another image overrode his fury. Anna, gentle Anna, whose touch healed and whose heart still grieved for all they'd taken from her years ago. Anna should never have to suffer so again.

It was only then Quinn realized that he loved her, that perhaps he'd loved her from the start. The knowledge lodged like a sliver of the sun inside his heart, illuminating all of his dark years of hatred.

The horse's hoofbeats thrummed a rhythm to remembered words: *My only love sprung from my only hate! Too early seen unknown, and known too late!*

Shakespeare's words from Anna's lips, and none more painful than the last ones. *Too late . . . too late . . .*

Dear God, he couldn't be too late. Against all reason, terror prompted him to once more urge his mount to gallop.


The woman moved real quietly, so quietly that at first Black Eagle took her for an animal or maybe one of his own people traveling by night. But despite her agility, the moonlight must have fooled her eyes. He heard the sharp intake of her breath, the extra steps as she recovered from a stumble.

If he hadn't been shivering with the damned cold, he'd have slept right through the faint sounds. She might have crept right past him, taken back Ned's horse and maybe his as well. Could have even slit his throat if that was what she wanted. Once again he felt something like respect. This woman seemed to think the way he thought. Smart, for her to wait until the hour was at its darkest. Smart, for her to hide up here at all.

More coyote than rabbit, with her brains and stealth. He almost hoped she wouldn't scream. Almost hoped for something just beyond the edge of his imagination, something that might be shared between a man and woman who thought so much alike.

Black Eagle spat at the idea. She might move like a coyote, but any bitch would howl when she was cut. He could almost feel his fingers streak his face with bloody war paint, could almost hear his war whoops mingling with her screams.

He rolled slowly toward the soft sounds of her progress. Pushing himself to his feet, he dropped both quilt and blanket atop the saddle he'd been using for a pillow.

His fingers stroked the well-worn handle of his knife. He would have liked to use the knife, but some instinct warned him instead that he would need to keep more distance between himself and the woman he pursued. So he left it in its sheath and instead pulled out his pistol. Maybe, if things worked out right, he wouldn't have to kill her right away. The shade cast by a large juniper concealed him, and he crouched behind a fringe of some thorny horror that snagged his pants and pricked his skin.

Now that she'd recovered her footing, the woman padded quietly as a bobcat on the gravel. He stood stock-still as she approached.

He stared at her as she came nearer, fascinated by the silhouetted forms of female legs. Shaded by the wide brim of her hat, her face remained indistinct, but her slender legs tormented. Picturing the pale flesh beneath the denim, he felt his own skin beading with sweat despite the chilly air.

He sure as hell wasn't sharing *that* with Ned and Hop. His growing hardness pushed painfully against his jeans, making it difficult to remain still. Too difficult. Unable to wait another moment, he threw back the hammer of his pistol and stepped out to cut her off.

Or tried to. The barbs of the thorny bush fastened like tiny fangs on both his pant legs. Glancing behind himself, he hissed an oath, then lurched ahead until the threads popped loose.

In that fraction of a second he lost sight of her.

"Goddamm it!" he swore, louder now that the damage had been done. He paused and peered into the darkness until he saw a mass of juniper limbs waving despite the absence of a breeze. Regretfully he gave up on his plans for restraint, then raised his pistol and fired half a dozen shots into the tree.

Anna screamed as fragrant chips of wood exploded all around her. A branch struck by a bullet rebounded to slap across her eyes. Another caught the strap of her canteen and tore it from her shoulder. Tears streaming, she stumbled away from shots that cracked like thunderbolts. The sound echoed in the darkness, making it impossible for her to tell how many guns were being fired.

Nearly blinded by her stinging eyes, she barked a shin on a knobby stump and slammed down hard on hands and knees. Terror sent her scrambling, then running in the only direction open to her, toward the path she had just descended, and upward on that isle of rock where she would be marooned.

Quinn dismounted and gave the weary gray a pat. The horse's foam-soaked hide steamed in the chill night air, and the animal was blowing hard. Like it or not, he had no choice but to walk the animal these final miles. The gelding had clearly given all it had.

Perhaps, Quinn thought, this way would serve him best.

If Hamby and his men were inside Anna's cabin—the idea bore down on him like a hawk on a jackrabbit—they would surely hear him charging into the clearing on horseback. Instead, he would have to force himself to stealth, to tie the horse nearby while he crept forward to size up the situation.

*Size up the situation,* he repeated mentally. *Think like a lawman if you can.*

If he couldn't, if he let himself be overwhelmed by the flashes of Anna's terror as she'd spoken of what Hamby and his men had done to her before, he'd be dead before he ever got inside.

As they walked, the gelding's breathing grew less labored, and its lathered hide began to dry. By the time they reached the little creek, the horse had cooled enough for Quinn to allow it a long drink. Still clutching the reins, Quinn, too, drank the sweet water from his cupped hands. He felt the cool liquid traveling down his throat into his empty stomach.

As he walked the horse toward the clearing, he tried to steel himself against what he might find. The scalps swinging in Ned Hamby's fist arced through his memory, then the burned bodies of a pair of trappers he and Max had found not long before he'd left for Yuma. Jesus, he'd nearly managed to forget that stench, a charred yet sweet odor that left him doubting he'd ever again enjoy the smell of roasting pork.

Quinn's hands were shaking so hard, he couldn't tie the horse's reins. In the end he gave up and whipped one around a low limb. Likely the exhausted animal would stay put for a while. After giving it a pat, he started walking once again. Somehow he had enough presence of mind to shift his approach to stay downwind of the corral, in the hopes the outlaws' horses wouldn't grow restive as he came near.

The dark hulk of the cabin lay along the clearing's edge

like a strangely angled rock or a hole carved from the moonlight. He stared hard to discern the thin ribbons of light visible around the edges of the tightly shuttered windows. The scent of wood smoke told him there was a fire in the hearth.

Like all the fires he'd shared there with Anna. He whispered a prayer—his first in many years—that she slept warm and safe before it, that Hamby and his men hadn't come for her at all.

He imagined Anna, nude beneath a blanket, her breaths so smooth and even, her rest unruffled by dreams. The thought was so real, so compelling, he hurried toward the door, desperate beyond reason to confirm his fervent hope.

Something jabbed his leg beside the knee. He jumped away, then looked down and recognized a carved cross. A cross that he felt absolutely certain was his daughter's grave. He knew it as surely as if he had laid her there himself.

His daughter. Rosalinda. A chill swept up his backbone to prickle at his scalp, and he hesitated.

And in that moment's pause he saw the body. Lying half hidden by deep shadow, the old man's unnatural position assured Quinn he must be dead. To be sure, Quinn took a few steps closer, close enough to see that someone had cut a bloody swath of scalp.

Hamby! Before he could react, gunfire cracked through the brittle silence from somewhere closer to the canyon's mouth. Shot after shot, until Quinn couldn't tell reports from echoes.

*Anna!* His heart thumped wildly. Could those shots mean—

The cabin door creaked, and Quinn ducked around the corner. His ears strained to listen to the muffled voice.

"Yeah, thought I heard it too. Black Eagle musta got

her after all. Don't reckon that stupid slut's doin' much shootin' without her rifle."

Rough male laughter from both inside and at the doorway. The door clunked shut, leaving Quinn outside.

He used his jacket's sleeve to wipe his forehead. He was sweating nearly as much as his mount had been after the long gallop.

Anna wasn't here at all. And the men inside her cabin thought she'd been shot.

Quinn stalked back through the darkness toward his borrowed horse. Those bastards had better pray that Anna wasn't dead, he swore. Because if any one of them had killed her, he was coming back to tear those men apart with his bare hands.

Quinn swung aboard the gelding gently. Though it grunted as he nudged its sides, it moved forward without hesitation. Still, Quinn couldn't help wondering how much farther and how fast the animal could travel. If he were pursued now, the results would be disastrous.

That meant he would have to find and take the outlaws' horses. It would be a risk, for if the men inside were to hear him, they would come out shooting. If they were even all in the cabin. He tried to discount the possibility that a guard might be posted near the horses, waiting to kill anyone who came too near.

Surely not. If a compatriot had been nearby, wouldn't the voice at the door have called out to him?

He skirted around the clearing's edge, still trying to stay downwind from the corral, where he guessed the horses must be waiting. Though no horse gave away his presence, a shaggy, spotted billy goat baaed him a challenge, lowering its head as if it meant to charge Quinn's mount.

His heartbeat racing, Quinn glanced back toward the cabin, but the door remained closed. A covered window faced him. He wished he could be certain no one was peering through a crack and readying a weapon.

A dark shape nickered nervously from inside the corral. A single horse, still saddled, paced the enclosure. Quinn had to dismount to move the timbers that formed the gate. Despite his apprehension, he spoke soothingly as he approached the animal. He caught up its reins and dodged a kick as he tightened the cinch around its belly.

Half expecting bullets to slam into him at any moment, Quinn climbed aboard the animal. Riding out of the enclosure, he took up the gray's reins. He didn't mean to lose or ruin the Cortez family's only horse.

One final time he glanced toward Anna's cabin. Then, with a whispered prayer for safety, he urged his new mount forward in what he hoped was the direction of the shots.

Anna's pursuer hadn't paused a moment. Instead, he crashed through brush mere steps behind her as she ran.

*En el nombre de Dios,* she *must* not look back! Though small stones clattered, dislodged by his feet, though his breaths sounded like steam escaping a train's engine, she *must* not turn around!

*Eyes to the trail,* she warned herself as she scrambled ever upward. If she looked back for a moment, she would twist an ankle, tumble down, and he would fall upon her like a ravening wolf on a lame foal.

Something snarled, not unlike the wolf that rampaged through her imagination. The steps behind her faltered.

"Take that, you goddamn cur!" the man roared.

A deep thunk was followed almost instantly by what Anna recognized as Notion's cries of pain. High-pitched yelps that went on and on, bringing tears to Anna's eyes. And then the crying ceased abruptly amid the heavy sounds of hard blows on flesh and bone.

*Santa Maria,* the brute was killing her dog! She whirled around, fury overriding panic, and grabbed the nearest thing she could hurl. By sheer chance it was a stout chunk of ironwood, as heavy as its namesake.

"Why don't *you* take that, you murdering beast!" Anna's aim was true; the outlaw shouted as the rocklike wood thudded off his elbow. To her immense relief, the dim figure of the dog slunk away into the shadows.

The man pulled his gun once more, and Anna realized she had squandered the costly moments Notion's attack had bought her. The outlaw was going to shoot her down now because she'd turned around. But the hammer of his pistol clacked on an empty chamber, and she realized he hadn't yet reloaded from his earlier attempts. As he paused to remedy the problem, she raced uphill once more.

Like a cornered bobcat she climbed higher despite the certain knowledge that there was no way to come down past him. Instinct drove her upward, even compelling her to climb the nearly sheer face of the cliff. The cliff where she had fallen earlier and knocked herself unconscious. The cliff where a single bullet could send her hurtling to her death.

More nails tore, and injured muscles strained as she heaved her body upward, wondering all the while if she would feel the pain or hear the gunshot first. A cry, more animal than Notion's, rose in her throat, a choked sound too primitive for words. All thought fell away from her body's desperate struggle. She felt separated from herself, as if she were witnessing the action from a distant window.

She reached the outcrop's top, then peered down over a large rock perched on the cliff's lip to see if her pursuer followed. A puff of dust erupted beside her face, a bullet striking stone. The sharp crack of the gunfire failed to penetrate her mind's haze, but still her body acted. She pulled herself back up, then stared at the rock's base. Scooting back, she braced herself against an even larger boulder. With both feet planted against the smaller rock, she pushed, struggling to make it wobble, tip it over.

Pain finally penetrated: the bruised strain at her right hip, the old pull at her right knee. Ignoring it, she continued pressing hard with her boot soles until the rock at last tumbled over the cliff's edge.

For several minutes she sat trembling, not daring to move lest the small sounds of her shifting cover others from below. She'd heard no scream, no noises save the heavy cracks of rock on rock. Nothing at all to make her think her boulder had struck its mark. Yet neither did she hear the heavy huffing of a winded man climbing near the cliff's edge. At long last her mind worked well enough to press her hand into service. She took up a fist-sized stone, thinking to smash it into his head when its dark silhouette rose on her horizon.

If she could force herself to move so close to him. If she could somehow manage to do more than just recoil. Once more terror and exhaustion leached away her strength. She felt herself eroding, as if she were a tiny island crumbling into an angry river. An island formed of sand.

She almost wished he would hurry so she wouldn't have to fear his coming anymore. She almost wished she had the courage to leap headfirst from the outcrop's other side, where the fall was closer to a hundred feet than twenty, where afterward, she'd need never fear again.

But he didn't hurry, didn't come at all, and she hadn't fought so hard to save her life to fling it away into the canyon. Could she have killed him with the boulder? Could she at least have knocked him down?

Fatigue settled deep into her bones. *Dios mío,* she had never been so tired. She thought of crawling to the cliff's edge on her belly, of peering down into a pitch-black void. Trembling took her like a drunkard's palsied shakes. If she leaned over the edge, would he see her? Would her shape show black against the star-filled sky? She could picture his hand shooting up over the edge to grab her, his vicious face snarling just a hairsbreadth from her own.

The bottom seemed to drop out of her belly, and she folded her arms around her knees, too numbed by fear to move.

Quinn never would have found the draw without that second round of shots. The second set that must have meant Anna had lived beyond the first ones—otherwise why would anyone keep shooting? That second set that might have killed her despite the distance he had covered, the desperation in each stride.

The echoes of the gunshots led him close enough to discern two more horses' muttered greetings, close enough to hear their restless, shifting hooves. The reports, higher in elevation, convinced him it was safe to investigate more closely, to hunt for anything that might help him save Anna.

Even in the moonlight he recognized his mare, Titania, standing beside a bareback bay. He spared her only a quick glance as he dragged down the pack the roan horse he had stolen carried behind its saddle. He rummaged through loose bullets, spilled tobacco, and a reeking wad of cloth he took to be a spare shirt. Another packet held a few strips of dried meat and the crumbling remnants of what might be johnnycake. Nothing there that he could use.

Turning his attention to Titania, he ignored the bedroll and dug through the nearest saddlebag. His fingers quickly identified the familiar star shape of his badge. After tucking it into his pocket, Quinn continued his search.

His own spare cinch for the saddle remained, along with a sweat-stiffened old bandanna and a coil of rope. As expected, his money was long gone, but another absence troubled him far more. The bowie knife he'd carried for so many years was missing. He swore in frustration. Couldn't those thieving bastards have left a single weapon? Even having a knife would have been better than charging uphill completely unarmed.

Stepping around the mare, he tried the other saddlebag. He threw back the flap and dug his hand in, then pulled it out as if he'd grasped a fistful of hot coals. A few hairs from the object caught between his fingers, and it fell into a patch of moonlight on the rocky soil.

Titania stamped and fidgeted as if she shared Quinn's horror. Unwilling to believe what he feared he had found, Quinn stared at the black mass—and knew for certain he *had* touched a scalp. A child's scalp, judging from the size and the fineness of the hair. Perhaps the same one that had caused him to be shot.

"Sweet Jesus," he said softly, and he removed the saddlebags that once had been his own. A cursory inspection showed the one he'd reached into was stuffed with varied hair. All human, and not all of it Indian, by the variety of color and texture.

With a grunt he threw the leather saddlebags into the brush. He could have, maybe should have kept them, but he didn't think he could touch them after finding Hamby's grisly souvenirs.

A flash of Anna's wheat-gold hair shot through his mind like summer lightning. He'd be damned if he let that hair, her beautiful blond hair, end up stuffed in some outlaw's saddlebag like a profane trophy.

Turning away from both the horses, he rushed uphill to face her attacker. He was scared—more scared than he had ever been before. Yet his lack of a weapon had no more power to stop him than the fading illumination of the setting silver moon.

# Chapter Nine

Thirst began to penetrate the thick cocoon of Anna's fear. Thirst and the long span of darkness and the near silence of the cold spring night. Because of her parched mouth, she strained to listen even harder.

From somewhere far away she heard a faint howl, and then another. Coyotes, she decided, singing lamentations for their prey. Nearby, atop the rocky outcrop, something rustled in the sparse grasses. Mice, perhaps, out nibbling on the tender new shoots, hoping nighttime's dearth of snakes would offset the possibility of owls.

She tried not to think about her dented canteen tangled in the branches of the manzanita far below, tried not to remember the cool, sweet water it contained. But thoughts of that moisture stole into her consciousness until she no longer could ignore them. Sooner or later she must climb down and go back to look for the canteen.

Below her the night breathed through the treetops, its exhalations scented by the mountains and the spring. So very, very quiet for such a deadly night. The canyon had been sleeping for such a long time. Did that mean her pursuer was dead or gone away?

If she were only cold, she could bear to wait until first light to find out. If she were only frightened, she would outlast the darkness in spite of the knowledge that her attacker might well bring back others to help him hunt her down. But her exertion and the dryness made all her layers feel like the papery skin of onions, or of chaff about to lift off in the canyon breeze.

She must find out if her enemy remained there, waiting stealthy as a cougar for its prey to forget the danger, so it could pounce and kill. Her fingertips and wrist throbbed as she began to crawl toward the cliff's edge. Her injured hip and bad knee added their protests. Ignoring the pain, Anna whispered a prayer for courage, then forced herself to continue.

Below her, at the base, something large disturbed the brush, then sent a small rock clattering against another.

Though her heart was pounding wildly, she did not shrink back. "It's just Notion, frightening you again," she whispered.

But it wasn't, for the dark shape moving below her stood upright, then walked into the outcrop's shadowed lee. Where she could not clearly see it. Where it might be climbing even now!

Anna swallowed back a scream and groped desperately around her. There had to be something, anything, she might use to protect herself. Scraping at the rocky surface, she dislodged a number of stones, the biggest one no larger than her fist. Grabbing it, she raised her arm and listened for a sound to guide her aim. She might have only one chance at this. She needed it to count.

A sound floated up toward her, a softly whispered "Anna?"

Even though she recognized the voice, she barely caught herself in time to keep from hurling down the rock.

A wave of relief flooded over her, washing her with weakness. For several moments, she could not speak to answer.

"Anna?" Quinn tried again, tentative yet hopeful.

"You came back for me . . ." she whispered, then raised her voice enough so he would hear. "Ryan. You came back."

She couldn't be sure if he heard her, for her attention was diverted to a second tall, dark shape. Emerging from the deepest shadow, it staggered forward, far too close to the place where she had heard Quinn's voice. Anna screamed a warning.

As if in answer, the dark shape launched itself toward Quinn with a blood-freezing, almost inhuman cry. Before Anna knew what she was doing, she had hurled the rock in the direction of the screech.

The sounds of fighting followed, the thuds and grunts and curses. Despite terror and her injuries, Anna found herself scrabbling down the rock face as quickly as she could.

Only when she reached the bottom could she see what was happening. Her attacker was now slashing wildly at Quinn with a long and wicked knife. The outlaw lurched drunkenly, as if he were injured. Not far from his left foot, the thin light of the setting moon gleamed coldly from a pistol. Had he somehow dropped it, or had Quinn knocked it from his hand? It scarcely mattered. All that mattered now was getting to it before his flashing blade struck flesh or he managed to retrieve it.

Perhaps the outlaw didn't see the gun, for he lunged toward Quinn with the knife. Quinn ducked beneath his swinging arm and came up in a blur of motion.

Anna meant to grab the pistol, meant to bring it up and stop this, but it was as if a solid wall rose up before her. She'd lost sight of the flashing blade, but she could almost hear it slicing through the air, could almost feel it gouging flesh.

Her flesh . . . just as Hamby's knife had six years before.

She couldn't see this outlaw's weapon, but she *did* see Ned Hamby's. She remembered it—every inch of it—as it plunged into her belly.

*Sing somethin' pretty, Annie Faith. Sing for us, you stinkin' bitch!*

Her knees buckled unexpectedly, and she fell, her right hand just a few feet from the man's forgotten gun. All she saw above her was the dark blur of the two men's struggle. She recognized Quinn's cry of pain and felt something hot and liquid spatter her face.

Quinn's blood.

Without conscious decision her hand shot forward, grasped the gun. She raised it, shaking like a flame fanned by the wind, forced herself to pull back the pistol's heavy hammer.

But she was too late. Too late, for at that very instant both men tripped over her and went sprawling. Anna twisted her body away from their kicks and tried to extricate herself.

By the time she succeeded, the fight was over. In the darkness she saw one man raise himself to an awkward sitting position over the still body of the other.

She would have given all that she had left for a single ray of sunlight so she could see which man had lived.


Though hours had passed, Lucy lay awake, her nude body cool and exposed atop the covers. She couldn't bring herself to rouse him, to risk waking the man who slept beneath the quilt, snoring animal contentment. From the wreckage of her dignity she'd gleaned a fragile calm, but somehow she felt as if she mustn't move, lest it would crack and fall away. Like the thin blue of a robin's eggshell, it would expose the naked hatchling that writhed beneath the surface. Better that facade of perfection than the desperate clamoring within.

She wanted so much to go home. *Please stop. You're not a child anymore.*

She needed to see the brick buildings lining Main Street, to feel the soft green grass beneath her slippers, to hear the gentle strains of chamber music played at a dinner party. *That life is lost to you. You've no choice but to fashion a new life from what is left.*

She told that to herself as firmly as Miss Rathbone ever would have. Yet Lucy would have killed to once more pass by David on her way inside the house, to feel the way his fingertips "accidentally" grazed her thigh.

*"Deepest apologies, Miss Worthington." His voice was never sorry.*

*"One might well apologize," she'd told him as her gaze latched boldly onto his, "if one's aim is so far off."*

Oh, what a shameless coquette she'd been then, and what a naive little fool! Why couldn't she turn back the months and tell Miss Rathbone just how bold the coachman's assistant had been growing? Why couldn't she hint to her father that she'd love to play the hostess for him when he returned to Washington? Why couldn't she— *Useless. Nothing could be more useless than weeping over what had gone before.*

Except she wasn't weeping. She was far too Worthington for that.

She turned her chin just enough to glimpse the dim form of Ward Cameron. Her gorge rose as she thought of what he'd done. True, he hadn't beaten her, even after the grievous sin that she'd confessed. But she almost wished he had, for she could have stood against a beating, could have thrown her chin out in defiance, could have skewered him with righteous anger for all time.

What he had done to her had been worse.

He'd utterly ignored her stoic surrender, ignored the

stillness of her body, the disengagement of her soul, as if those were considerations unworthy of his notice. Instead, he'd behaved as though she were some thing provided for his amusement. He'd plunged into her with as little consideration as a milkmaid churning butter. When she cried out and jerked with the pain of his sudden intrusion, he laughed deep in his throat.

"I knew you'd like it, Lucy. I knew you wanted me. You might have been born a Worthington, but you're just a little slut at heart."

Lucy covered her face with both hands, hating Ward Cameron with an intensity beyond anything she'd ever felt before. And when the loathing bled into her shame and grief for all she'd lost, then and only then did Lucy finally give way to quiet sobs.

Without understanding where the knowledge came from, Quinn somehow felt the tautness of Anna's body, the swirling confusion in her mind. Perhaps it was only the barrel of the pistol shaking in the moonlight, aimed despite its quaver at the center of his chest. Or perhaps the knowledge was coded into the death rattle of the man who lay limp at his feet, his own knife jutting from his throat. Maybe instead it was something in the canyon itself that warned that if he moved too quickly or spoke too abruptly, her tension would explode into a single fatal shot.

So he kept his voice soft, as soft as if he were coaxing his mare to allow him to remove a painful stone from her hoof. As soft as when he was a child, confessing boyish sins to Father Donnelly, back before he'd had too many sins to share.

"Anna . . . Anna, it's all right."

"Quinn!" The pistol clattered to the rocky soil, and she launched herself into his arms.

But he paid scant attention to the sound. How could he, when she crushed her body close against his, so close that she might have been trying to press her way into him? He felt the length of her, from her knees up to her twining arms, and his body drank in every inch of contact like a tree's roots in a shower after months of drought. She trembled like a heavy rain on pine boughs, and her voice, too, shook.

"I thought—I thought you were him—I didn't know—I almost—almost pulled the trig—"

He silenced her with his lips, his mouth, with his own quivering hands, that stroked her hair, her back, that dropped to glide along her sides, then skim her slender waist and the slight flare of her hips. In his relief he turned loose all the years of hating as if they were a host of penned wild doves. But like doves, they wheeled about and fluttered back to roost in a flurry of white wings that beat a single question: *What are you doing with this woman?*

Yet still, his mouth consumed hers, his hands stroked her voraciously. He remembered what she'd said to him: *Ryan. You came back.* Remembered how the hoofbeats thrummed him into misery when he thought he would be too late to save her. Remembered the pain-bright realization that he loved her, that some ember of his love had long glowed hot beneath the thick white ash of all that happened. And he knew he couldn't let her go, couldn't let her fade back into this canyon, like an echo, dwindling . . . dimming. Like an echo of her old songs, fading out.

Still, he pulled away from her, for he wanted to try to see her in the darkness. He needed to look into the face he thought he'd lost.

"Did he hurt you?" Quinn asked quickly.

"Not him—I hurt myself. Fell climbing down this cliff the last time, but I'll be all right. I'll be all right now. But you—there was blood. Did he cut you?"

Quinn felt bruised, not cut. He shook his head. "I don't think so."

She squeezed his hand tightly, held it, and then asked, "What made you come back?"

"I ran into the Cortez family leaving with everything they could haul out on one horse. Señora Cortez told me Hamby's men had made them tell where you were—"

"*Dios mío!* Were they injured? Little Juan—"

"The boy? No. Not injured but badly frightened, all of them. They gave me their horse to find you."

"Their only horse . . ."

She leaned back into his arms, and her breath warmed his ear. Warmed it and sent little sparks of pleasure dancing down his spine. Sparks that ignited fires within him that only she could quench.

"We'll take the gelding back to them," he offered, "and get as far from here as possible."

Her body, so pliant just moments before, went rigid in an instant. "No. No, we can't leave those *bandidos* here."

"*Bandidos?* Hamby and his boys? Anna, they're holed up in your cabin, and they're armed. Don't you understand? It's over—at least until I can come back with help. I told you it wasn't safe for you to be here. You have to go with me now."

She jerked away from him and shook her head emphatically. "No. I thought I could do it, but I won't leave those killers in my home—I can't. I can't leave them there with her."

Alarm surged through Quinn's veins. "With *her?* They have somebody? Did they abduct a woman?"

She didn't answer, didn't move. Night breezes fanned her hair, which had by now escaped its braid completely. Quinn shivered with a chill borne on both her words and the cool wind.

Once more knowledge seemed to flow out of the darkness to take form, solidify inside him.

"With *her* . . ." he repeated, his voice not much louder than the wind's. "You mean with Rosalinda, don't you? Anna . . . Rosalinda's gone."

"She isn't. Not to me. She's in this canyon, Ryan. Can't you feel her too?"

Quinn hesitated. If he were anywhere but there, on any other night, he might have laughed at her. Or, more likely, he would have felt pity. For a woman who'd let isolation warp her thinking, who'd let a lost child live again inside her soul.

But like her, he stood near a pinnacle within these red-rock canyon walls. And like her, he'd felt something, something that had warned him to hesitate back near the cabin, when he'd bumped into a cross that marked a tiny grave. Something that had warned him that Anna didn't recognize him when she held the pistol pointed toward his chest. Something that convinced him that she spoke of leaving Rosalinda even though the child's death was long ago.

So he didn't laugh or argue. Instead, he tried to reason with her as if what she'd said were sane. "They can't hurt her anymore, but they *will* hurt you. Rosalinda wouldn't want that, would she?"

Anna pressed her fingers to her temples and rubbed as if she were in pain. "I can't let them take her from me again. I have to find a way to make them leave."

She must be hurt worse than she'd admitted. She was talking like a madwoman. Quinn became even more determined to get her out of there to safety.

"What do you suggest?" he asked impatiently. "That we tap on the door and ask them politely to go home? Don't you know what they'd do to us? Don't you remember what they've done?"

"I remember now. I remember all of it. Each word and every hurt. I won't forget again. I'm going to take this gun, and I *will* make them go, or I will kill them."

Quinn reached down to take up the pistol she'd dropped

and tucked it into his own belt. "Like hell you will. You're just one woman. Let me come back here with a posse, and we'll take care of this."

"They'll be long gone by then. You know it. And then I'll have to stay away."

"They won't get far. We have their horses." He only hoped they had them all. There might well be other outlaws searching for Anna in other parts of the canyon. But he kept his fears muzzled, for they'd do nothing to persuade her.

"No, Ryan. This stops tonight."

Quinn felt his temper rising. Why couldn't she let him do his job? There had to be some way to convince her she couldn't win against the desperados. "What happened to your rifle, Anna? How did they get that away?"

"I—I started to remember . . ." Her voice faltered. "I—I couldn't . . . I couldn't think . . ."

"So what makes you believe you'll do a better job this time? You're hurt, exhausted, hungry—I'm taking you to my house."

"I'm *not* going," she insisted, her shoulders square, her stance defiant. "I told you, I can't."

"I'm not giving you this gun."

She grabbed for the pistol, so swiftly that he barely had time to react. But Quinn had been a lawman for six years and before that both a gambler and a fighter. With reflexes honed by experience, he drew the gun—and pointed it at her—in an instant.

Notion limped out of the shadows, growling deeply.

"You wouldn't shoot me," Anna said. She sounded confident of that.

The big dog crouched as if to leap. Quinn pointed the gun at him instead.

"Maybe not. But I'd shoot him to save your life."

*"Tonto obstinado!"*

"I'll assume that wasn't complimentary."

"Notion, sit," Anna ordered, then spoke again to Quinn. "How can you do this?"

The dog glanced, as if confused, from Quinn to Anna, then whined before complying. Still, Quinn heard the low rumble of a growl warning him that any sudden moves might cost him a dog bite.

Quinn's aim didn't waver. During his weeks in Anna's cabin he'd come to feel affection toward the yellow cur, but he hadn't lied. No matter what the cost, he couldn't allow Anna to throw away her life.

"I won't forgive you for this, Ryan," she swore.

His heart ached with her words. He felt like an outlaw himself, forcing her to leave there, threatening to kill old Notion. How could he explain to her his desire to get her clear of this place, his need to keep her safe?

The words eluded him, so he settled for terse orders. "Use your belt to lead the dog. I don't want him coming up behind me. We're climbing down to get the horses. Then we're going to ride out of this canyon, find a safe place where we can rest awhile."

When she turned to comply, the setting moon's light streaked along a tear trail on her cheek. He wanted more than anything to take her in his arms, to comfort her, but he sensed that if he touched her, she would fight him. Then he'd really have to shoot her dog to keep from getting torn apart.

And if he took that desperate step, he knew there would be no way in all the world he would ever fulfill his newfound need to find the words to win her love.

# Chapter Ten

*Near Cañon de Sangre de Cristo*
*April 8, 1884*

Quinn led three other horses tied in one long line. The Cortez family's gray and the dead outlaw's bay gelding trailed along behind the white-flecked roan that Anna rode. The four horses clattered from the canyon's mouth and began the uphill trek toward the plateau above.

Anna scarcely noted the gnarled trees and rocks that marked the landscape. Instead, as she rode the gelding, her head bobbed. Yet she did not doze; she grieved.

For so very long she had lived alone. Alone with the breezes trailing through the canyon, scented by the juniper and piñon that grew along its ridges. Alone with the stark beauty of the red rock that hemmed her wounded spirit, sheltered her against the memories of the woman she'd once been. Alone with a presence she had always felt was Rosalinda.

Señora Valdez had disagreed.

"Have you never wondered why the Navajo come here whenever they're allowed to wander, why the Old Ones dwelled here in their caves? This *cañoncito* is no home for ghosts, but it *is* a sacred place. Though laws and papers say I own it, one might as well say it owns me. Just as it claims you, my *hija*, you, my daughter too."

"But I feel my child here," Anna had protested. She had whispered her next words, half afraid the old woman would judge her as mad as she'd first judged herself. "Sometimes I even hear her crying, crying like she did before she died."

Anna's eyes teared, remembering the conversation. Remembering what Señora told her next.

"This is not your child, but the force I have sought all my days. The Navajo call it something other, but to me it is *el don*, the curing power. I have seen you draw upon it to heal others. I used it years ago to restore your torn and broken body. Will you not allow this canyon to heal your heart as well?"

"But, Señora, the baby's crying. I can hear her where the music used to be. . . ."

"Perhaps someone made *un trabajo* against you. This is a sickness of the spirit and not your child's lost soul. She has gone with God already, as do all those innocents who perish. She has returned to *Dios*."

But Anna knew the curing woman had been wrong. Though she accepted many of the old woman's teachings, she didn't believe that anyone had put a spiritual curse on her. Hamby's assault, brutal as it was, had been direct in nature. She knew, too, that Rosalinda hadn't left her for that last and longest journey, for she often felt the presence of the child.

At least until Quinn had forced her from the canyon. Ryan, the one man in all the world she'd thought might believe her. The one man in the world she'd thought it might be possible to love.

To think she'd almost wanted him. She glared at Ryan's back as it swayed on his mount before her. She wished she had something more substantial to throw at him than *mal de ojo*. But she would have to settle for her best approximation of the evil eye, for the scoundrel had tied both her hands behind her with some scratchy rope he'd found inside a saddlebag.

Foolish to try to cast a curse whose existence she'd never admitted. How Señora would have laughed at her for that!

"*Mal de ojo* is always caused by wanting," the old woman had told her. "A woman admires a babe that is not hers, or she looks on a handsome priest. If she does not touch this person to release the wanting, the child, the man, will soon fall sick with fever."

Anna glared again at Ryan. Angry as she was, she refused to touch him even if he sputtered into flame before her eyes.

His tan shirt had lightened with the dawn, yet it grew no more distinct. Anna wondered if the thin clouds were at fault or her vision. Since yesterday her only sleep had come in the form of unconsciousness when she had fallen. The drink she'd taken from the canteen Ryan had helped her recover had only served to inflame both her hunger and her thirst. She needed food, more water, and rest to help her marshal her defenses against her one-time lover.

And then she would make him pay for what he'd done. She would find some way to escape with a weapon, some way to return to her canyon, to her home.

Ahead of her Quinn's form tilted, and she wondered if her eyes were playing tricks on her once more. But Quinn caught the saddle horn and righted himself, then shook his head as if to clear it.

"We have to find a place to rest soon."

"I have a fine cabin some miles back," Anna said, focusing more sarcasm into every syllable.

He turned toward her, and despite the fuzziness of her

vision, she would swear she saw deep lines of sorrow on his handsome face. Or perhaps his own hunger and exhaustion had worked against his strength as it had hers. As furious as she was at his behavior, she still remembered how recently he'd been shot down, left for dead at her front door.

A stab of pain jagged through her skull, reminding her of her own injury. Or maybe it was only the remembered horror of seeing him so cold, so still, as pallid as a corpse.

He scarcely looked much better now, with his unshaven jaw and the way he leaned in the saddle.

"We need to sleep. You look like hell," he muttered.

"Funny. I was thinking that you probably feel like hell yourself."

Notion whined, his right front paw held aloft. Now unleashed, he'd been struggling on three legs to trail their horses.

"We're not the only ones who need rest," Quinn said.

"So now you're concerned about his welfare. A few hours ago you said you'd shoot him—just before you tied me on this sorry excuse for a horse." She nodded toward the roan, who'd bitten her leg as Quinn had helped her mount it.

"I'm sorry, Anna. Threatening Notion and tying you were the only ways I could think of to make you see reason."

"There are many types of reason, far more than those you acknowledge. I *will* return to Rosalinda. I will not let them win this time."

"And I told you I won't allow it."

She glared once more at the former gambler, then decided it was time to call his bluff. "Then I hope you have bullets enough for both the dog and me."

"And I hope you have sharp teeth to chew your way through those ropes."

"You'll have to untie me sometime."

"Lord, I hope not." Quinn's smile was as lopsided as his posture. "I'd sooner turn loose a mad bobcat."

She scowled, but scowling did nothing to ease her body's needs. Finally she offered, "I know a place where we can go. The Rodríguez rancho is not so far from here. They'll shelter us until we're rested, and I can check their babe as well."

"Which way do we ride?"

"I'm not going as a prisoner. Untie me, and I'll lead the way."

Quinn's eyes narrowed. "How do I know you won't take off?"

"On this nag? Your mare could catch him in an instant. Besides, you have the gun. I may believe in spirits, but I'm not insane."

He urged his horse a few steps nearer, near enough that he could reach out and touch her if he wished. As if her thoughts prompted the motion, he moved to do just that. But his hand stopped before it reached her cheek. He sighed and let it drop to rest on his right knee.

"I don't think you're insane," he said, "just upset and confused. Anna, I want you to understand. Last night I nearly rode this gray into the ground, scared to death I'd find you murdered. I knew then . . . my feelings for you have changed completely. Promise me you won't leave, and I will untie you."

She saw how much it cost him to peel away the layer of charm he showed the world, to reveal so much to her. He tried to plaster over his admission with a lopsided grin, but anxiety showed through as he waited for her answer.

He could wait till hell froze over. She wasn't about to sit there and declare undying love to a man who'd tied her in the saddle.

"I won't run," she told him. And she didn't plan to, at least until she was well rested and fed.

Quinn sighed, no doubt disappointed that she'd chosen

to ignore his admission. True to his word nonetheless, he leaned forward and worked to loosen the knots binding her wrists. Her mount made the task more difficult by kicking at his mare, who snapped in retaliation. The roan gelding arched its back in what Anna suspected was preparation for a round of bucking.

As soon as she and her mount were free, Anna took the reins, which had been tied behind the roan's neck, and moved the horse away from the mare. They were in bad enough shape without allowing one horse to lame another. Too, the action took her out of range of Ryan's touch. Like his mare, she felt inclined to snap.

Yet she could not forget the truth in his voice. She could almost feel the desperation of his night ride, his growing fear for her. The sun rose higher behind the silver veil of clouds, illuminating the rock-strewn plateau, illuminating the reasons for his actions too.

But the flesh around her wrists had chafed, and the memory of the pistol leveled at her dog chilled her blood. His terror offered only explanations, not excuses. If fear could cast him in the role of brute, it was better that she know now, before she allowed his other charms to worm their way into her heart.

As if to pay a penance, Quinn dismounted and scooped up Notion in his arms. Anna wasn't sure how he managed, but somehow he mounted the mare and draped the injured dog across his thighs. Notion must have trusted him, for his tongue lolled and his tail wagged, sure signs of canine pleasure.

The sun had nearly reached its zenith when the villa came into view. Unlike the rest of the sparse collection of cabins that dotted the surrounding area, the Rodriguez home boasted several rooms of cream-colored adobe, which kept it cool in summer and warm during the winter months. In the distance, knots of cattle grazed serenely among the tender shoots of spring. A collection of more roughly built sheds spread across the area, and a trio of brown and white paint horses watched intently from a spacious corral. From its gate, a vaquero emerged, a saddle tossed over one broad shoulder. Anna recognized him as Esteban, the Rodríguezes' sole hired hand.

The young man smiled broadly, displaying both a thick mustache and the wide gap between his front teeth. He waved Anna a greeting. *"Curandera,"* he called cheerfully, "you come a day too late."

Despite his smile, alarm jolted Anna. Had she been right from the start when she'd believed the infant sickly? Had Catalina's daughter died so soon?

"They have all gone to take the little señorita to be christened by the priest in Copper Ridge," Esteban continued as they rode nearer. "But what's this? Are you injured?"

Just as Quinn had earlier, Anna found herself listing to one side with weakness. Only she lacked the strength to pull herself upright.

Quinn dismounted quickly and set the dog down, then hurried to catch her as she slid out of the saddle. Her vision grayed, and for a time she knew no more.

"You can tell him he's killed Papa! That's what you can tell him!"

Lucy stared in disbelief at the stranger who was shouting past Elena at the door. She'd never before seen a grown man crying as this man was weeping now. If he was truly a grown man. She couldn't be certain, but he looked even younger than her twenty years.

Mesmerized, Lucy stood immobile in the doorway of the parlor, where she'd been having tea with Miss Rathbone. She could hear the older woman's footsteps behind her, and she knew without looking that Miss Rathbone had put on her sternest bulldog glare.

Elena put her hands up as if to ward off the young man's emotion.

"His Honor sees visitors by appointment only." Elena's smooth, accented words gave no hint of welcome. "I will leave for him a message if you wish."

"Cameron, are you in there? It's Horace Singletary! Are you there?" he shouted past the woman. "Do you hear me? Papa's dead, you bastard! Do you know what that means? It means I won't rest until the truth's out!"

From behind his thin-framed glasses, his gaze came to rest on Lucy, and in the space of a moment his expression changed from fury to embarrassment. But in that fraction of a second that fell between the two, Lucy thought she recognized a flash of interest.

In the silence that followed, she imagined she could hear the beating of her heart. She revised her estimate. He was indeed a man, rather a handsome one despite his reddened eyes. His back straightened, and he took an audible breath.

"I—I do apologize . . ." His gaze flicked to take in both Miss Rathbone and Elena, then returned to Lucy once again. "I—I'm sorry for my outburst. It's—it's just that Papa has passed on."

"I will leave your message for the judge," Elena repeated coldly, and she began to close the door.

"Please don't do that," Lucy heard herself saying, though she could not imagine why. Didn't she have enough problems of her own without burdening herself with those of others? But there was something in the young man's face that so compelled her, as if he were a mirror reflecting her own misery.

Before she realized what she was doing, she'd stepped forward and grasped the door's edge just above the knob.

"You're upset," she said consolingly. "You must come in and take some tea."

Elena stepped back, her gaze accusing. "His Honor will not like this."

Lucy turned to face her. "I am the mistress of this house now, and Judge Cameron is not home. So you'll have to wait until he comes back to tattle."

The dark features hardened into fury. With a snort of disgust Elena turned on her heel and muttered something about making the judge's favorite chicken soup for lunch. Then she disappeared into the kitchen in a flurry of skirts.

The young man at the doorway flushed and tugged his collar. "It's not right that I should come inside when you're alone."

But something in his gaze convinced her he wouldn't mind being alone with her at all. She shook her head, berating herself for her wild imaginings. He had lost his father, for heaven's sake. His mind could hardly conjure thoughts of romance, particularly not with the wife of a man he clearly hated.

"Nonsense," she replied, offering her hand. "I'm not alone at all. Miss Rathbone's here. We were just having a good-bye tea in the parlor. Come inside; tell me all about your father. Perhaps there's something I can do to help."

He touched her hand; it felt to her as if a spark leapt from his fingertips to hers. Surely he had sensed it too. Or else why had he drawn away so quickly?

"I don't think this is a good idea," he told her. "There are arrangements I must see to. But I do hope you'll forgive my outburst. It was never meant for ladies' ears. And I won't forget your kindness either, Miss—I mean Mrs. Cameron."

"It's Lucy. I insist."

He bowed stiffly at the waist. "Good-bye, then, Lucy. I hope 'His Honor' appreciates what a lady he has wed."

He left then, and she watched him mount his horse and ride away.

Lucy turned toward an odd, wheezing sound. Miss Rathbone was holding a kerchief to her eyes.

"You're ill?" Lucy asked. It seemed no more likely than the moon dropping from the heavens or the endless prairie suddenly overgrown with trees. She'd always thought Miss Rathbone more a force of nature than a person who might grow sick or even die.

But when Miss Rathbone moved her kerchief, Lucy saw a most amazing sight, the woman's teeth. Small and sharp-looking, they appeared to smile, even to laugh. Such a thing was not to be imagined!

"So he wonders if Judge Cameron realizes what a 'lady' he has wed?" Miss Rathbone said, retreating toward her own room, presumably to pack. Her laughter and her words receded down the hall. "So do I, dear Lucy. So do I."

Lucy felt heat rising to her face as her eyes narrowed with fury. "I hope highwaymen beset your stagecoach!" she muttered. Somehow that didn't seem enough, so she imagined Miss Rathbone other hardships: the Harvey Houses boarded up, leaving the passengers to suffer vermin-ridden biscuits, rail cars crowded with uncouth Westerners, wild Indians forcing the train off the tracks.

When those scenarios failed to cheer her, Lucy consoled herself by remembering Horace Singletary's eyes. Beyond the rims of his glasses and redness of his fresh grief, they were very blue.

So very blue. Like David's.

Esteban's English wasn't a whole lot better than Quinn's Spanish, but by using simple words and gestures, Quinn explained that they were fleeing outlaws who had attacked Anna's cabin. They needed food and rest to recover.

The vaquero helped Quinn carry Anna to the house and insisted that she take the only bedroom. As Esteban pulled back a blanket woven with bright bands of color, Quinn laid her gently in the bed and loosened the top buttons of her shirt. As he did, she groaned and shifted restlessly. Still, Quinn reasoned, she'd feel better after resting, so the pair left her alone.

Esteban raided Señora Rodriguez's larder for tortillas and smoked sausage that he called chorizo, then left to rob the rancho's hens of eggs. The two men worked together to cook a hearty breakfast, though Quinn's part mainly consisted of helping to light the cast-iron cookstove fire.

As he gulped the reheated coffee the cowboy offered, Quinn hoped the thick brew would revive him. He concentrated on keeping his eyes open until Esteban removed the skillet from the heat.

As Esteban had before him, Quinn scooped scrambled eggs and fried chorizo into a flat, round tortilla. Then he drizzled the red sauce the Mexican used and rolled up the concoction. Half of the mixture fell out of the tortilla's back end as he bit into it, but he wasn't sorry. The heat from the red sauce was so blistering that all he tasted was the pain. He grabbed his mug of coffee but hesitated, his gaze sweeping the kitchen for something cool to ease the heat.

Esteban's laughter rattled the plates in the señora's china cabinet. He set down Quinn's portion for the dog, who bolted it down too quickly to even taste it, much less suffer burns. Once the cowhand recovered from his mirth, he wrapped another burrito, as he called it, and passed it to Quinn.

"Not so *caliente* this time," he promised. The tips of his thick black mustache still quivered with the effort of poorly restrained humor.

Quinn noticed there was no red sauce on this one, so he tried the roll-up, more cautiously than before. Now that the throbbing of his wounded taste buds had diminished, he relished the combination of the flat but tender bread, mellow eggs, and slightly spicy bits of seasoned sausage. His stomach had not been happier in days.

Anna staggered into the kitchen, her eyes bleary with fatigue. Her loose hair was tousled, reminding Quinn of times when he had bedded her, so long ago.

"Weren't you going to invite me to breakfast?" She turned her coolest gaze on him. "Or don't you feed your prisoners?"

Quinn flinched, wishing he could take back what he'd told her about the way he'd felt. Remembering her fainting spell, he tried to console himself by imagining she would forget his declaration. It wasn't that his feelings had changed one iota. His timing, on the other hand, had left a great deal to be desired.

Turning her attention from him, Anna conversed with Esteban in swift, torrential Spanish, words that blended until they became as indistinct as water. Although he busied himself rolling another burrito, Quinn hated being left out of the conversation. For all he knew, Anna was telling the ranch hand her own one-sided story of how she'd been bound and forced to leave the canyon. The two of them might be plotting against him while he sat there, eating.

Esteban's smile faltered, and he quickly crossed himself. Anna, too, looked grim. But the vaquero never glanced his way, let alone glared or made a move toward the gun stuck into his belt. And Quinn pulled Hamby's name out of the flood of Spanish, so he imagined Anna was describing the outlaw and his crimes.

For several more minutes Anna and Esteban conversed. Then the cowhand packed some food into a leather satchel and called, *"Adios."*

There. Finally Quinn could pick out one word he understood. He impressed himself by stringing together a pair. *"Adios* and *gracias!"*

The door closed, and Anna turned her gaze on him and switched to English. "He's seen what Hamby and his men can do. He was hired to help protect the rancho, but he's riding after the Rodriguez family to be certain they're all right. He insists we make ourselves at home for as long as necessary. These people are not only my patients, they're my friends. If they were here, they'd tell me what is theirs is mine."

"Good. I can't wait to settle into a soft bed with real linens."

Anna's expression hardened. "Esteban suggested you'd be comfortable in his bunk. The shed's just down the path."

He remembered his panicked ride to find her, his terror at the thought she would be dead. He didn't mean to settle for a bunkhouse, didn't think he could survive so far from her. "Anna, I'm so tired, I swear you wouldn't have to worry. Besides, it's not as if we haven't been sleeping in the same room for weeks."

"Then, there was no choice." She skewered him with a gaze as cold and hard as steel. "Now I prefer to share the room with Notion."

She turned and poured fresh water into the washbowl to clean her hands.

Quinn fixed her a burrito and slathered on enough hot sauce to melt the snowcaps off the mountains to the north. When she turned around, he pushed the plate toward her.

She rewarded him with a stiff nod, and for a moment he felt guilty about his childish retaliation. But the moment passed, and he watched eagerly as she bit into the tortilla.

She didn't even break a sweat. Instead, after a bite or two, she reached for the small clay pot and added to the inferno.

He supposed that when a woman had hellfire running through her veins, she didn't mind it so much in her mouth.

* * *

The moment Quinn left to find his borrowed bunk, Anna shoved half a plain tortilla into her mouth. She had long before discovered that gulping water only intensified the burning, and she didn't want to imagine—much less suffer—anything hotter than this fire.

She wiped tears from her eyes. *Madre de Dios,* she had forgotten just how spicy the Rodriguez family made their salsa! After living in the area so long, Anna had learned to enjoy food seasoned with the fruit of the chili. But her taste buds were Yankee born and bred; she'd never been able to tolerate anything so hot.

Curse Ryan for his mischief—and curse her stubbornness as well. She'd heaped on more torment just to prove that she was tougher—the same foolish machismo she had long disdained in men.

Grateful that the heat was abating, she drank a cup of cooling coffee, all the while fighting a smile that tugged the corners of her mouth. She'd seen Quinn watching her, trying to appear nonchalant while waiting for her to erupt like a volcano, for her eyes to overflow. She gave in to temptation and grinned, absurdly pleased with her performance. Maybe a touch of machismo wasn't so bad after all.

She must be giddy with exhaustion, she thought as she struggled to her feet. Exhaustion and relief, despite the fact that the outlaws might have other horses, that they could find Quinn and her at any time.

But she could think only of hauling her stiff body into a clean bed and sleeping for a while. She couldn't wrap her mind around the possibility that resting now might be a dangerous mistake.

* * *

Anna stood before the chamber set that rested on the mirrored stand. She watched herself brush out her tangled hair, then begin unbuttoning her torn and soiled shirt with a right hand that no longer throbbed with pain. Yet her brain pulsed a reminder of how Quinn had last loosened these buttons, how his warm fingertips had touched what lay beneath. Her breasts ached at the memory, unleashing a flood of others. How his lips had followed errant fingers, kissing at her neck, her hardened nipples. A long-extinguished fire flared to life inside her, heating her body with desire for a man she'd robbed and wronged six years before.

A man just a few short steps away in a bunkhouse, as if he were her hired hand. She groaned in frustration, banishing temptation. She was merely tired, that was all. So very, very tired.

Her soiled shirt fell to the wood floor. She dipped a fresh white cloth into the cool water, wrung it, used it to wash the dirt from her arms, her back, her breasts.... The mirror showed dark bruises scattered like constellations in reverse.

She pulled off her boots and socks, then unbuttoned the dusty jeans and slid them down. To continue washing off the stain of Hamby's touch.

She shuddered, thinking of the outlaw, somehow sensing that eyes were on her now. She glanced into the window, saw the silhouette behind her of a man—the upper half of a tall man framed by the window. The filmy curtains blew around him like a shroud.

Spinning rapidly, she stooped to snatch up her clothing, to try to cover her nude body.

"Too late, bitch," he said, climbing through the open window. One brown eye stared at her; the other angled sideways. "I've seen everything I want."

He was on her then; she saw the bright blade flashing.

His hand tightened around her throat, choking back her screams.

Her screams that came from somewhere, fighting past sleep's barrier.

She fought wildly, fists slamming into his chest, his face. She was struggling on . . . the bed? He pinned her hands down, shouting past her terror.

"Anna! Anna! It's just me! Stop fighting—please, stop fighting!"

Quivering with terror, her scream changed to a sob. The sheets were drenched with sweat, as they always were after one of her nightmares. At last she recognized the handsome face above her—Quinn's. Her flailing limbs grew still.

She saw the swelling smudge beneath his left eye. "I hit you?"

He released her shoulders and nodded, then sat against a pillow he propped up on the headboard. "I came when I heard you screaming. You didn't know me. Your eyes were open, but you were seeing—something else."

She sat up and leaned her head against his bare chest. She wanted him to hold her, to help her stop her trembling, to make the fear recede.

"I'm sorry that I hurt you," she whispered, conscious for the first time of the thinness of the nightgown she had borrowed once she'd washed. Conscious of the difference in the shadows of the room, the late afternoon sunlight slanting through the open window. She must have slept for hours before she'd dreamed.

"What did you see, Anna?"

She shook her head against him. His few coarse chest hairs tickled against her chin, but otherwise he felt so warm, so solid. She never wanted him to let her go.

"I don't want to talk about it. I just want it to go away."

He stroked her hair as if she were a small child, then

softly kissed the top of her head. She arched her neck back slowly, until his kisses fell upon her mouth.

His strength flowed into her, skin to skin and lips to lips. A strength so gentle that it soothed her body's shaking, so natural that it felt like coming home.

He broke off the kiss first, though he held her so close, she felt his words fan warmth against her cheek. "I want you, Anna. I have always wanted you, but never more than I do now."

She stroked the stubble of his cheek. "This won't change anything between us. It won't change what's past."

"But *we've* changed so much. We're not who we were then. What happened was another life, another woman. You're so much more than she was."

"It still hurts, just the same. Too many reminders, too many regrets." She turned to lean her back against his chest.

"What I regret is letting you go back to the cabin, not admitting to myself—or you—the way I feel. I could have lost you, Anna. For a while I thought I had. It was dark when I rode back, but I could see you. I could see them killing you inside my mind."

Fear prickled up her neck, and she shuddered at the echo of her nightmare in his words.

He wrapped his arms around her, held her. "I realized then, I love you. What I saw and loved of Annie Faith was only her potential, the woman she was destined to become."

" 'My only love sprung from my only hate,' " she quoted, her voice trembling as it had with the nightmare.

"But this time," he continued, reaching forward, his hands settling gently on her breasts, "this time it's not too late."

Her head rolled back and she leaned against him, enjoying the fire his touch provoked. The way he cupped her breasts, the way his thumbs stroked her nipples. She ached with need for him and longing. Longing to possess and be possessed.

He rolled her over, pinioning her gently on the bed, and she could not stop his kisses, could not stop herself from kissing back, her mouth opening as if to drink him in.

That served only to inflame him, and his lips trailed moist kisses down to her neckline, which he pulled down to expose her breasts. She felt the heat of his mouth sucking, and her body arched, wild with its want.

He paused to pull off his clothing, and in those moments she peeled away her borrowed gown. When he returned to her, she touched him. Her hands remembered all the things he'd taught her long before. Her heart remembered the long-forgotten joy of pleasing him.

And as she caressed him, his fingers and his lips did not forget her either. He consumed her with his kisses, stroked the source of all her heat. Then he pulled his body above her and satisfied the craving he had been meant to fill. Again, again, he thrust deep inside her. Her hips arched toward a rhythm that both felt but neither heard. Faster, like the hoofbeats of the swiftest racehorse, the pounding of their hearts.

Faster, until it roared into full flame that brought a rush of heat, a cataclysmic light. . . . She heard him cry out with it, and she smiled, feeling powerful and overpowered all at once. Feeling complete for the first time in all her life.

That was when she realized she had abandoned her reserve. That secret place she'd fled to while a man was using her. Sometimes she had felt things—as the Quinn of old had moved her—but this time she'd been present, equally involved. Risking her heart, not just her body.

The thought frightened her so deeply, she wanted to retreat. To go back to her safety, back to the canyon where both heart and soul belonged.

*April 9, 1884*

Quinn watched Anna ride ahead of him and wondered what he'd done to cause her to withdraw into herself. Ever since yesterday, when they'd made love, she'd barely spoken a score of words to him.

It could not have been the physical act that distanced her, not when she had given herself so eagerly. Nor could it have been the fear that that was all he'd wanted. In an attempt to reassure her, he'd told her half a dozen times how much he loved her, how he would never let her go. But that did nothing to thaw the barrier he'd felt rise up between them, nothing to explain her wall of ice.

When they set out that morning, Anna had claimed the half-breed's dark bay gelding, a scrawny but less temperamental mount than the roan she'd ridden the previous day. When they'd found the Cortez family walking among the scattered white-barked aspens, her reticence dissolved into another flood of Spanish conversation, hugs, and shared tears. From outside the circle of their friendship he'd suggested that they give the couple the roan gelding as well as their gray horse.

Anna's nod was quick, her smile fleeting. He'd thought his offer might touch her, but now, hours later, her silence was complete.

He jogged his mare past a thicket of stunted live oak to catch up with Anna's bay horse. Unlike the tall aspens of two hours before, the forest of the chaparral grew no taller than a man on horseback. He disliked it, knowing how easily it could harbor dangerous surprises. The thought of animal predators scarcely concerned him, but the human type was often on his mind.

"We'll need to make camp soon," he said. "We have a long ride tomorrow if we're to get home by nightfall."

She turned her head toward him, and he wished she'd take her hat off so he could see her eyes.

"Your home, not mine." Her words floated soft and sparse between them, like the seed of milkweed or suspended notes from an old song.

Like her words, the day was fading softly toward its close.

"Home is not a place. It's with a person or the people you love best." Why couldn't she see that? Why couldn't she come with him and be happy?

The late afternoon sunlight slanted between a pair of gnarled trees to light her face, to touch her eyes at last. But it availed him nothing, for her expression showed him only pain.

"Ryan . . . Quinn. I can't give back what you deserve."

"I've told you, I love you. You give me everything already."

"You know that isn't true. I can't. I'm too afraid."

"Afraid of me?" he asked her.

"Afraid of everything. Afraid if I give you my trust, my heart, you'll break it. Afraid of Hamby and his men. Afraid . . . afraid." Her eyes rounded abruptly, as if another nightmare gripped her, as if she saw—and felt and heard—things far beyond his reach.

"What is it?" he asked as the horses walked.

"I'd forgotten—I'd forgotten what he said," she whispered as if she spoke only to herself.

"Anna, answer me."

"When Hamby tried to hurt me, he said that Cameron—Judge Cameron—wants me dead."

"Cameron? But why? Why after all this time?"

She shook her head. "I don't know. I'll admit it makes no sense."

"How would he even know you're alive?"

"I can't imagine. Wait. Could he have read the papers for the change of ownership?"

"What change?"

Twenty yards ahead, Notion barked, sending a startled jackrabbit bounding past their horses. Titania whinnied in fear and danced to one side, but Quinn quickly calmed her. The bay laid back his ears and snorted but otherwise ignored the chase. Notion, still limping slightly, drew up short, sat on his haunches, and whined once, as if a show of frustration might make his prey turn itself in.

"This looks like a good spot to make camp." Quinn motioned toward a bald hillock partly ringed by an arroyo. Several deeper pockets in the gully held water for the horses and themselves. If they camped on the hillock, they could see above the undersized trees, so no pursuers could surprise them.

Anna nodded, then dismounted. As they unsaddled their horses, she continued with her explanation. "Señora Valdez left her land to me. Eduardo Rodríguez—Catalina's husband—filed papers for me witnessing the fact that she had died and transferring the land into my name. He said he took them to the county clerk of Agua Fresca. Isn't that in Copper Ridge?"

He nodded. "What was it she left you?"

"Her husband's Mexican land grant, the whole of Cañon de Sangre de Cristo and a bit of the surrounding area."

"Didn't you worry that the judge or the sheriff of Mud Wasp would still be looking for you?"

She shook her head. "Not really. Annie Faith was left for dead. Who was to know she'd turn up again years later as Anna Bennett? And who's to care about some remote land grant that this Bennett woman owned? The canyon's beautiful, but what's it good for?"

*What's it good for?* The phrase brought back a snatch of conversation he'd overheard while he was waiting to talk to the judge one morning about six weeks before. The assayer was just leaving, telling Cameron, "You see a worthless wilderness, and you wonder what's it good for, 'cept as spawnin' grounds for redskins and a coupla sorry Mexican ranchos. Then all a sudden like, it's a place that turns men into kings. It's a modern miracle, it's that."

The two had laughed, and afterward Judge Cameron emphasized that Quinn was paid to see to law and order only within the bounds of Copper Ridge. He'd spewed out some legal nonsense regarding jurisdictions, but Quinn didn't pay it much heed. He'd ceased to care much about anything since he had learned his family died.

The memory of those black years fell upon him like a shroud, but he shrugged aside the dark and forced his mind to focus on the conversation he was having now.

He used a curved pick to clean his mare's hooves. "Cameron must have somehow found out who you are, or he would have never sent Hamby after you this late."

"But how?"

He frowned at her, hating to bring up the possibility. "Wanted posters? They would give your name and alias."

"But I never—" she began, then stopped abruptly.

"Never drugged and robbed anybody besides me?" He let go of Titania's near foreleg, and she stamped on his big toe. Stifling a yelp, he watched for Anna's reaction to his question and moved on to the next hoof.

Her back stiffened, and her voice grew defiant. "Back in Virginia City. I hired on to be a singer, but he tried to force me to be a whore!"

"Where else, Anna?"

"That was all, I swear it."

"Anna?"

Her eyes narrowed at the skepticism in his voice.

He shrugged. "I told you, what you did then doesn't matter. It was all so long ago, you won't be prosecuted."

"I did what I had to to survive."

"Honey, I did things I'm not proud of either."

"But you did none of them to me."

"You've also saved me, in more ways than I can put into words. I've forgiven you for what happened back in Mud Wasp. Why can't you forgive yourself?"

She didn't answer but instead reached for the hoof pick and cleaned her mount's hooves as well.

Ryan continued with his theory. "What if there were something in your canyon Cameron wanted? There's a lot of copper mined now in these parts."

She shrugged. "Seems like awfully far to go for copper."

"It might be high-grade enough to make it worthwhile. Or maybe we're talking about silver, even gold. I may have heard a part of something—Cameron talking with the assayer." He shook his head. "But it might have been nothing, just a pair of greedy bastards jawing. Happens in saloons all over every day."

She nodded mute agreement, then hobbled the horse so he could graze without getting far away. Afterward she went to her pack and pulled out a pair of blankets that she had borrowed for bedding. After shaking out the first, she kicked aside a few stones and laid it down.

The sun nestled between a pair of distant hills, its descent painting the sky scarlet and coral with a smudge of indigo. She sat on the blanket and stared up at it, away from him.

He was hungry, and he knew that he should start a fire so they could cook. But instead, he walked closer, by her side, just so he could watch her looking. Just so he could see the cool light bathe her face, the colors paint her eyes.

"It's so beautiful," she whispered, still staring heavenward. "I've seen just a slice from inside the canyon, but out here it's boundless, isn't it? There's so much, it's almost frightening. It's just another thing that scares me."

She was rubbing her bruised wrist, and he sat down beside her to take over the task. And the two of them just sat there, watching as the day receded. Watching as the first bright stars emerged.

# Chapter Eleven

*Copper Ridge*
*April 10, 1884*

That stupid bastard, Horace Singletary, must not want to live much longer than his papa. Sitting behind his big black walnut desk, Ward Cameron crumpled up the telegram, his fury escalating with the pounding of his heart.

So Singletary had wired the office of the United States marshal, requesting an investigation, had he? Too damned bad he didn't realize the marshal's deputy, Norris Foster, who'd received the message, was Cameron's associate in another mining venture down near Tucson. The mine might have played out early and cost them both a pretty penny, but a bond of greed had formed between the two entrepreneurs. No way was Foster going to begrudge Cameron his chance to earn a buck now—particularly not with Singletary helping him earn his old partner's gratitude, perhaps even a cut.

Foster's assistance might cost him dearly, but Cameron

## CANYON SONG

was still grateful for the warning, among other things. Foster added a cryptic line about delaying things a bit. That must mean that he had "lost" Singletary's first request.

But in the end that wouldn't matter. Knowing young Horace, he would bury the marshal's office in telegrams until he had his inquiry. And then what? Cameron couldn't hope to buy off the district marshal too.

That wasn't all of it either. He'd heard from Elena about how Horace had shown up on his doorstep, shouting threats. And just how graciously his new bride had greeted the young man.

He wondered what the hell Lucy thought she was doing? If she talked privately with Singletary, he could fill her head with his suspicions. She could leave her new husband then, crying to her father about what a brute he'd been. If that happened, their marriage would last only long enough to give her bastard his name.

Senator Worthington would be furious when Lucy hinted at mistreatment at his hands. She'd no doubt offer her father the very lie that Cameron had suggested, that they'd secretly married during his earlier visit east, to explain the early birth. And Worthington would use Cameron's alleged crimes as an excuse to completely cut him off. Without any favors, forevermore, amen.

They'd laugh at him back east, the senator and all his old schoolmates. And the U.S. marshal might turn up enough evidence to have him indicted on a host of charges. If that happened, he'd lose his fine house, even Elena. His life, in essence, would completely go to hell.

His problems had only one solution, one surprisingly appealing and easily arranged. One so gratifying that he wondered why he hadn't thought of it months before, when the upstart clerk had just begun to bare his teeth.

Horace Singletary must join his father. Cameron only hoped it would be soon enough.

* * *

"I want to make *un trabajo* against a man-thief," Elena hissed. Again and again she wadded her lace handkerchief into a tiny sphere and prayed that the old man would cast a potent spell.

The *curandero* stared at her intently. Difficult to imagine what he thought of her request, peering at her as he did with those cloudy eyes. Blind eyes, and yet they saw things Elena never could. Their gaze took in the spiritual if not the physical world.

For Elena's comfort, he lit several candles to dispel the evening gloom. Despite his sightlessness and swollen knuckles, he handled the matches expertly.

Waiting for his answer, she felt as if the walls and ceilings of the narrow shack were closing in on her. From the rafters, both the scents and forms of dried bunches of herbs hung heavy: sweet basil and vervain, oregano and borage. There were others she couldn't name, most harmless, but at least one her mother had warned her long ago would kill goats or sheep, even cattle, if they grazed on it.

"Who is this woman you would make a spell against?" the healer asked.

"A stranger who would take the one that I love, *Tío*." The *curandero* liked it when younger people called him Uncle, though they were not related. Perhaps the affectionate name would keep him from asking questions she did not wish to answer regarding Miss Lucinda Worthington.

"The *Americana*, is it?"

How could she have thought she could hide anything from him? "For a blind man, you see all too clearly."

"Have I not told you, your judge will never wed you? For you the future holds another path. Embrace it, and not a man who shows you no respect."

She leapt to her feet, suddenly realizing his source of

information. "My mother has been coming here to tell her tales!"

He smiled, his lips crinkling around mostly toothless gums. "Patients often come for help with their disobedient children. Many a conjure have I held over you, and many a pastry has your mother baked in payment. Tell me, do you cook as well as she?"

Forgetting for a moment that he could not see her, Elena scowled at the bone-thin old man. "You will grow fat on my problems if you will help me with the eastern bride."

He coughed harshly. Then his head swiveled on his corded neck. "Not for a barrel of *cuernitos* will I do this. Can you not see the evil in this man you say you love?"

*Evil?* No, she *would* not see it. She could recognize only what he could give her. A way to have things no other man she knew could provide. A way to live inside the fine home she deserved.

She had earned that life. When the judge had come to her, she had learned to be a woman, a woman who could pleasure him as no one had before. Had he not told her that? Had he not whispered other sweet things and given her fine gifts?

Tears welled in her eyes, blurring shelves filled with bottles of blessed water, candles, and ground roots. Tears that told her that this eastern woman must have somehow bewitched Elena's lover into marriage, for she refused to believe all they'd had had been a lie.

If her judge truly loved this stranger, wouldn't he have allowed her to send Elena away? Instead, he'd come to her in secret just after the wedding and asked her to stay, kissing Elena in the manner of a man whose heart was filled with love.

And then he'd left her to couple with his new wife. She wiped away angry tears with the wadded handkerchief.

"If you are not my friend, you cannot be my uncle either," she told the old man.

She turned on her heel to leave, and the knot of hair behind her head caught in a bunch of drying herbs. Reaching up, she realized it was the deadly plant.

She glanced nervously at the old man. Would he somehow see her? Sometimes he seemed to know so much. But how much of his apparent sight was based on gossip?

If she missed this chance, she might not have another. She imagined indignity after indignity heaped on her by this bride. Orders to clean the house in *her* way, to cook her tasteless recipes, and after a while to tend her babies, those she would make with the judge.

*No!* She could not bear to think of it! The thought was like a blade thrust through her heart.

As Elena reached up to disentangle her chignon, she snapped off a section of the plant. Pushing it into a pocket of her skirt, she walked out before she had a chance to lose her nerve.

Later, in the judge's kitchen, she pulled out the brittle stem and feathery dried leaves of the weed that sometimes grew along the water's edges. She'd been so frightened in the *curandero*'s shack, she'd taken quite a bit.

Enough to kill a bull, at least.

Enough, then, to put a man-thief in the ground, where she belonged.

Anna vividly remembered the last time she'd ridden into Copper Ridge. Hands tied behind her, eyes downcast, she'd taken in very little of the town. Still, she recalled some sort of main street bordered by the usual cantinas, a blacksmith shop, a general store. Besides that, she remembered only a host of blurred faces watching from the street. Some tossed off rude comments; several children had thrown rocks. One stone struck her shoulder, and that had stung, but not as much as coming here a prisoner. She would have been kept in the Mud Wasp jail instead, but Sheriff Baker had no intention of housing a female prisoner for a month until the circuit judge came through. His wife, who fed the small jail's inhabitants, had taken one look at Anna in her violet silk dress before declaring she must go immediately.

The idea had taken little prompting. Baker had been so eager to brag to Cameron about capturing her, to turn over the gold she'd carried. He'd reminded Anna of a shaggy terrier she'd once had as a child in the years before her father turned her world inside out. After learning that a stick she retrieved would bring words of praise and petting, the dog brought her pillows, an uprooted fern from the solarium, even, once, Grandmother's cane. Grandmother had thumped the animal's behind on several occasions before the animal learned that objects fetched had different outcomes.

But Judge Cameron had praised Baker effusively this time, particularly when he hefted the bag of stolen gold to test its weight. She could almost envision the lawman's wagging tail. She wondered how he would have reacted to learn that less than a day later, she was given to Ned Hamby, taken far from here, then knifed and left to die. Or was Sheriff Baker in on it as well?

It hardly mattered now, six years later, in a place she'd be considered a fugitive if she were recognized. That was why Anna and Quinn had waited until nightfall to ride down the town's main street, why she'd covered her distinctive blond hair with a long scarf, which she'd wrapped around her neck like the Mexican women wore their rebozos.

Though she had hated giving up her practical denim pants and button shirt, she'd changed before they'd come to town. She donned a loose white *blusa* and full dark blue skirt borrowed, like the scarf, from Catalina. A wool serape completed the disguise and offered warmth. Wearing men's clothing in a town the size of Copper Ridge would provoke too much curiosity, and with her figure, it was unlikely that she would be taken for a man.

Still, stealth and a safe distance gave them the best chance to safely reach the small adobe house that Ryan rented. There was no disguising Anna's fair skin or her steel-blue eyes. And this far west, the rumor of a strange white woman would spread through the town like the flu. Likely the few married white women would descend upon Quinn's doorstep, bearing curiosity and casseroles. The results would be disastrous if—or when—Judge Cameron found out.

Their luck held. As they wended their way down side streets, Quinn gestured toward the largest building in the town. Cool moonlight lit the Catholic church's adobe exterior from without; the light of dozens of candles burning in the windows gave a contradictory impression of the warmth and the community within. The very facets of religion that Anna had so long shunned.

"Holy Thursday evening mass. Most of the law-abiding folks will be in church now, or their beds." Quinn's quiet explanation drifted just above the wisps of emanating hymn.

For a moment her heart yearned to join the gathering inside, to lend her voice to Latin hymns she suddenly remembered. Long ago, hadn't she read of churches offering lost souls sanctuary? But on the Arizona frontier, the only redemption available came behind bars in one of the territory's hellish prisons, or, worse yet, coiled in the end of a hemp noose.

The gallows stood, a grim reminder, not far from the church. Between the two lay a graveyard fenced in iron spikes. Crosses rose up in the moonlight along with clumps of wilted flowers. Beyond that graveyard lay another, excluded from enclosure. The markers there were mostly toppled, but Anna knew the area nonetheless. The final resting place of suicides, of whores, of outlaws, of men who'd been cut down from the gallows. As in life, the respectable kept addresses separate from the sinful, depriving them of the pleasures of decent company.

Anna shivered, suspecting that weed-infested plot—or one just like it—would be her final resting place. With no known relations and her criminal background, she could look forward to an eternity planted beside the likes of Hamby and his ilk. The thought almost made her want to commit some crime heinous enough to deserve the fate.

As they rounded a corner, she tried to brush aside her morbid thoughts. But she recognized the staunch rectangle of the Copper Ridge's jail ahead. Her memories of it did little to elevate her mood.

Quinn reined his mount once more so they would not pass the building. Glancing toward the darkened windows, he said, "Either Max is back at the saloons again, or we don't have any paying customers tonight."

She swallowed hard with the reminder that he was a lawman now, the kind of man who thumbed through wanted posters, who locked up criminals. Like her. She filled her lungs with cool night air, which soon hissed out through clenched teeth. He'd said he'd forgiven her; he'd claimed he understood.

And loved her.

She began to tremble, remembering how his face had burned with hatred just a few short weeks before, imagining their lovemaking and his sweet words all a ruse. Was that it? Was it all some clever plan to lure her there, where he could hold her in his jail, maybe even watch her swing from those gallows so conveniently nearby?

She blinked back tears and cursed herself for her suspicions. Stupid, to believe he could have orchestrated everything just to arrest her. Ludicrous, to think that he would have bothered riding back to rescue her from Hamby if all he'd wanted was to see her dead himself.

Shaking off her misgivings, Anna straightened in the saddle just as Quinn pulled his horse to a stop in front of a small adobe house.

"Home," he told her in a voice that suggested he was glad to see it. Home for him would mean a change of clothes, decent food, and probably another weapon, not to mention a bed both soft and clean.

Its proximity to the jail disturbed her, though she supposed that it made sense.

"Get down. I'll take you inside. Then I'll walk the horses back to the livery stable. I imagine Stan Roberts—the fella who boards Titania for me—has been wondering where I've been."

He had friends there, of course. She wouldn't be the only one for him to count on now. Perhaps he'd talk about her to them. But friends could be loose with others' secrets, just as they so often compromised their own.

Titania nickered restlessly, no doubt impatient for a meal of grain and hay. Quinn tied her, along with the bay, onto the porch rail. Anna was grateful when he helped her from the saddle, for the wide and unaccustomed skirt caught on the horn when she tried to dismount.

They stepped up onto the porch, and Quinn unlocked the door, then ushered her inside the darkened room. At her hesitation he whispered sharply, "Get in there before someone sees you."

She acquiesced, hating the near blackness that lay beyond the moonlit rectangle from the door. Only Quinn's presence convinced her to take a few steps farther.

Until she heard the unmistakable sounds of a gun cocking and whiskey-roughened words: "Stop right there—before I kill you both."

\* \* \*

Quinn stiffened at the voice's hard edge. Startled as he was, he nearly missed recognizing the familiar Texas accent.

"Max?" he called, irritated by the scare. "Max Wilson? What the hell are you doing, skulking around my house in the dark?"

*"Quinn?"* Max sounded even more surprised than he. "That's you, Quinn?"

"Exactly who were you expecting?"

"Wait a—wait just one danged minute so I can light this lamp."

A match flared and for just a moment lit Max Wilson's freckled face. In full sunlight his skin looked like a wildcat's, the freckles blending into mottled coppery spots.

The match traveled downward to light a kerosene lamp on the table. He replaced the globe, then turned up the wick to increase the light. The house's interior looked about the same as always, housing an oak table with a pair of chairs, a small stove, and few mismatched furnishings, including an iron-framed bed in the corner. A rumpled bed, as if his deputy had been asleep there.

Mindful of prying eyes, Quinn closed the door behind him. Anna glanced uneasily toward the blocked exit and backed a step closer so that her shoulder blades leaned against his chest. He imagined that she'd bolt and run with little provocation.

"Will you lookee here?" Max asked, staring at both Quinn and Anna. "You've come back from the dead."

Quinn could feel her trembling. He laid his hand gently on her shoulder.

"What are you talking about?" he asked Max.

As Max laid his gun on the table, his brown eyes gazed at Quinn. "Judge Cameron said he had it on good authority you was dead. Said the town charter called for me to take your place, no election or nothin.' Then Mrs. Harris said that now I'm sheriff, I could rent this place, get out of that flea-bitten boardinghouse for good. I only just moved in. Hadn't even gotten a chance to sleep here yet."

"Good," Quinn muttered, hoping Max hadn't yet found the money and extra gun he kept hidden beneath one of the floorboards.

Cameron must have been talking to his boys, Quinn realized, since he had it on such "good authority" that he'd need a new sheriff. But he didn't mention that to Max. Instead, he explained. "One of Hamby's gang shot me near the canyons west of here, then left me for dead."

"You got shot?" Max asked.

Quinn nodded. "In the shoulder. This woman saved my life."

Max jerked a nod at her, then went on with his questions. "How would Cameron know about you bein' shot?"

"You haven't been paying much attention, have you, Max?" Quinn asked. "You've seen the way he runs his district."

"I suppose he has his sources." After hesitating for a moment he frowned. "Guess this means back to the boardinghouse for me. Don't get me wrong, Quinn, I'm mighty glad to see you back and in one piece. It's just that—it's just that I was thinkin' how a woman might take a shine to marryin' a fella with a neat little place like this."

"I thought you were through with women."

Max shrugged, then smiled at Anna, his wavy red hair a tousled nest. "I s'pose I might say the same of you." He stuck out a thick-fingered hand. "Max Wilson, ma'am. Pleased to meetcha."

Anna hesitated, then accepted the handshake. "Miranda Flynn. It's good to meet you too."

She hadn't missed a beat, as if the skill of lying, once mastered, was easy to resume. Clearly she'd decided not to so quickly entrust Max with her tale, but then, Quinn had always known that Anna was no fool.

Max wasn't a bad fellow, but he rarely thought beyond the surface. To him a deputy's salary and a warm, dry bed were reason enough to go along with Cameron's rules. Or almost enough, as Quinn had discovered after the fiasco with Max's runaway mail order bride. The humiliation and loneliness had driven him back to the bottle. Even now, months later, Quinn still smelled the whiskey on his breath. But that was the way it always was with Max, a stretch of months or even years before some setback sent him careening off the wagon. Quinn had heard he'd been fired several times from other deputy's positions during his lapses. No, Quinn wasn't about to trust their safety to anyone who could be bought with a bottle or a swirl of petticoats.

He needed a story, then, and quickly. He wished he'd imagined this possibility earlier so he could have thought of one, or, better yet, consulted Anna. Clearly this was her area of expertise.

Settling for the first lie he could think of, Quinn said, "Miranda, honey, you have to get used to your new name. Miranda Ryan, from now on. Max, you surprised me being in here. I should have introduced you to my wife."

"You—your *wife?*" Max stammered, and Quinn could have sworn he saw his deputy go green as he appraised Anna anew. Despite the disguise of the scarf and serape, she was clearly beautiful.

He felt Anna's body tense. His lie must have surprised her too.

Quinn nodded, warming to his story. "Swung through Mud Wasp on the way here and got hitched. Miranda was widowed by, uh—Joe Flynn, a rancher."

"Never heard of him."

Anna recovered enough to be of help. "We were just

getting started when—when the outlaws came. I—I still can't bear to speak of it."

She turned to face Quinn before laying her face on his shoulder, where she expertly feigned tears. Or maybe they were real. He had no idea how she felt about the idea of posing as his wife.

Nails scratched at the door, and Notion whined to join them. Quinn let the dog inside before he raised a ruckus. Once in, the animal sat beside his mistress and nosed her hand for a pat.

"If you don't mind, Max, Mrs. Ryan and I would like some privacy."

"I imagine so." He started gathering his clothes and personal items. "Dang, Quinn, that's a hell of a black eye."

He glanced at Anna, who busily studied some spot near the ceiling. Then for Max's benefit he shrugged. "Fell off my horse when I was shot. It's looking better now."

Seeming to accept that, Max continued. "Folks is sure gonna be surprised to hear that you got married."

Once again Anna added to their story before he could think of what to say. "Please, Max. I—I haven't been a widow long, and I'm a little worried about what Joe's people might say if they hear before I tell them. Do you think it would be too much to ask for you to wait a bit before you mention me to anybody?"

"We'd be much obliged," Quinn added, grateful for her quick thinking.

Max's gaze slid uneasily from one of them to the other, then settled on Anna for several silent beats.

Anna flashed Max a dazzling smile. "I hate putting you to all this trouble. I'll tell you what. As soon as we're settled in, I insist you come for dinner. I'll even bake my specialty, apple pie, to celebrate."

Max grinned back at her. "I'll look forward to it, ma'am, and until you give the word, my lips are sealed."

Quinn shook Max's hand before he left. The door closed and they heard him step off the porch.

"That ought to buy us maybe two days' silence," Quinn said, *"if* we're lucky."

"Two days will have to be enough for this charade, then," Anna told him, "because I've never baked an apple pie in all my life."

---

The typewriter was the only thing of value that remained with Horace. Tomorrow he would have to sell the horse and saddle to settle up accounts with the doctor and the undertaker, but still, he refused to part with the gleaming black contraption. Plenty of times he'd been tempted to trade the Remington to buy more blankets or perhaps a better stove, comforts to help ease his father's passing. But neither buffalo robes nor the finest radiator would have kept Papa alive, and now Horace was glad to have the machine's noisy plinking keys for company. Glad especially to have the gift of seeing Papa's story neatly typed.

Horace reread the pages by the light of a kerosene lamp. He should put it out and save the last few drops of fuel. Behind him the moon had risen high in the single dirt-grimed window, and he needed desperately to sleep. But fatigue had pushed him past the point of caring whether the kerosene ran out now or the next time he needed light. Instead, the article he'd spent his evening writing held his full attention.

Despite the chill of the bunkhouse, a measure of internal warmth expanded as he read his work. He knew it was good. Well-written, clear, and utterly damning, his account of the acts that had driven Papa to his grave would ruin Cameron once it was set in print. For although the U.S. marshal had ignored his telegram, the editor of the *Territorial Gazette* had not. Instead, he'd offered Horace his first freelance assignment and the hint that he might be inclined to permanently hire such an "intrepid young reporter."

Horace didn't feel intrepid; he felt sick. Sick with grief for Papa, whose husk lay sheltered only by a thin-walled coffin in the cold, cold ground. Sick with anger at Cameron and with himself, for waiting until it was too late to fight in earnest. But mostly sick with fatigue, which made him feel so brittle that he might snap to pieces like loose fingers of tree bark.

He would post his article right away, before his anger faded. Now he could be honest with himself at least. He had to do it before his fear awakened, before he found some excuse to go on as he had. Keeping to his safe and stagnant job as county clerk, living the bare bones of a life from Cameron's scrap heap.

A shadow played across the paper from something framed by the ill-fitting window. He turned his head enough to catch movement in the corner of his eye. But thick dirt hazed the figure, and he was left with nothing but an impression of its bulk.

A horse. It could be his horse, escaped from its broken-down enclosure and hungry for an extra measure of grain.

After putting out the lamp he grabbed a jacket and headed for the door. If his mare ran off, he'd have the devil's own time catching her without another horse to ride. Best to lure her now with the dregs of the remaining oats before she gave up and grazed elsewhere.

He lifted the latch to go outside, but strange sounds stopped him. First a scraping, then loud crackling just outside the old bunkhouse's only door. In a moment he smelled smoke, and he realized a fire was burning just outside. He cracked open the door, where flames blazed high and hungry, curling right up past the lintel toward the roof. As he slammed the door against the heat and smoke, his mind struggled to make sense of what was happening, to process the barrel that had been shoved against the door and lit, to comprehend the fact that someone *meant* to do this; someone meant for him to die. Before he could react, to shout or run toward the window to escape, the glass exploded inward and some fiery missile landed near his feet. As it shattered, liquid flame splashed across the floor and licked his pant legs, caught and fed upon the blankets on his bed. And on the pile of papers next to his typewriter.

"No!" He couldn't let the story burn, couldn't let it go! He reached for the papers, only to see them curling, blackening, with thin, glowing ribbons at the outsides. Gone—destroyed, as he would be if he did not get out right then—and if he burned, Papa's story, like the papers, would crumble into ash.

Grabbing up the typewriter, he held it to his chest and faced the window. The curtains his sister had sewn in a pathetic bid to add cheer blazed brilliantly. He sucked in a breath and choked on thick, kerosene-rich smoke. Choked and coughed until his watering eyes refused to open, until he dropped the typewriter and crashed down on his hands and knees.

He must get up and out that window! He had to climb outside to the fresh air! Black splotches filled his vision, even though his eyes remained closed tight. Still coughing, he struggled to regain his feet. Oh, God. Were the men who'd set this fire still out there? No choice but to climb through and find out.

As he grabbed the bottom of the broken window, jagged glass teeth sliced his fingers. Ignoring pain and pumping blood, he pulled himself through the opening, praying he was not escaping into the sights of waiting guns.

"You look different in your friend's clothes."

Anna jumped at the sound of Quinn's voice. She'd been sitting on the bed, pulling off her boots, her mind swirling with misgivings. She wanted to be home in the canyon, where she could wear her own clothes and speak only in soft Spanish to those who came to her for peace.

"Sorry, didn't mean to spook you," he apologized, then turned back to his kitchen rummaging.

"I feel different too. Except for these," she answered, nodding toward the boots, which lacked the slightest hint of femininity. "They're out of place, like me."

Quinn shook his head, frustrated. "Damn, Max could at least have left us some food."

"Are you trying to pretend you cook?"

He shrugged. "Usually I eat at the boardinghouse, but I was hoping Max planned to try his hand."

Giving up the search, he walked over and stared at her where she was sitting. Her stomach fluttered, and the hairs on the back of her neck rose, as if her body recognized the danger in his gaze.

She knew that look, and she should stop this. Stop this before it became too hard to say good-bye.

"You don't *look* out of place," he said. Reaching down, he fingered the scarf's edge, then let it slide off her hair. "You belong here, in my bed, with me."

Her heart pounded at his nearness, thundered at his touch. She struggled to keep her words steady and her voice strong. "I doubt that Cameron would see it that way, if what you think is right."

He shrugged. "Maybe we should find a new bed then, in a new town. Let Max keep his promotion."

"You would run away from your responsibilities?" Just like her father had always run away from his. It must be the gambler in them, always imagining the next town offered better odds. Disappointment seeped through her bones. She had so hoped he'd changed. But at least it kept her from wanting him so badly, from falling into the same trap she'd fallen into the last time she had trusted too much.

Quinn shook his head and pulled a star-shaped piece of metal from his shirt pocket.

"Cameron rigged my first election. I'm almost sure of it. Otherwise who'd have voted for a hard-luck card cheat?" As he spoke, he turned the item over in his hands. "But when I won, I took an oath. I didn't give it much thought at first. I listened to Cameron, and I collected my pay, trying to save money to help my family back east."

Each time he flipped the silver badge, it winked reflected light.

Anna said nothing, but her stomach tightened with dread. Something bad was coming. She heard it in his words, saw it in the grim set of his jaw, the swift metallic flashes. Her breaths came quick and shallow, and she wanted more than anything for him to stop. But she knew he had to finish just as she couldn't have stopped telling him about the child they had made.

Quinn sat beside her on the mattress. "When I found out they were dead, the money didn't matter anymore."

He must have seen the question, the horror in her eyes, for he elaborated.

"They burned—my mother, sisters, and my uncle, in a tenement fire in New York." One of his hands closed around the badge; the other came to rest on her knee.

*Burned,* she thought, for the first time completely understanding what she'd done to him.

"I'm sorry," she whispered. Useless words that offered nothing. There had to be something better she could say. "I'm so very sorry. I never meant to hurt—"

"Shhh." He put a finger to her lips. "It was my fault for not taking care of things before then. I can see that now. And bad luck too. You didn't set that fire."

"But I—" Her vision swam with tears.

"You're a different woman now, and I've changed too. Hating you, even hating Cameron, couldn't solve things. Hating only emptied me, except . . ." His palm flattened, and he looked down at the badge. "Except this helped a little. I've started to see the meaning in that oath I took. I promised to uphold the law. But not Ward Cameron's version. I was wrong to turn a blind eye toward what he did, but I was too dead inside to care. A dying child brought me back—a dying child and you. Now I see the real law behind those fancy court words. It's what protects the people from savages like Hamby and his boys."

*Santa Maria,* she'd misjudged him badly. Her heart swelled with both hope and fear. Fear that her feelings were entangling her, binding her to him. "Then you won't run?"

"Depends on what you mean by that, Anna. I mean to leave this town once I'm done, but I won't run from Hamby. I won't rest until that sick bastard's in the ground."

Another fear grew inside her, and she gripped the hand that held the badge. "At first all I wanted was to get those men out of my canyon so I could go back home," she admitted. "But I'm afraid now. They've killed so many people. Before, they almost killed you. If you go back, maybe they'll finish what they started."

*And I don't want you to die.* The thought echoed her words, but she could not speak them aloud. Not without making him promises she didn't want to give.

"I'll take Max and a posse. They won't catch me unaware this time."

She nodded, fighting the temptation to beg him not to go. Quinn had to take care of these outlaws just as she had to use her healing gift. She could almost hear Señora Valdez's whispered admonition, *Let him be who he must . . .*

But she didn't have to like it, and she refused to simply wait.

"I'm going with you, then."

"You're staying here, in this house, safe and out of sight."

She shook her head, refusing to relent. "There is no

safe. Your deputy could be talking to Cameron now. If you'd trusted him, you would have told him more."

"He's not going to talk with Cameron this late. And I'll get Max out of town tomorrow, before he has the chance. You're better off here."

"But you can't be sure about Max, can you? Besides, you need a guide. If Hamby and his men have left my cabin, I can show you the places where they'd go. I know the canyon."

"You didn't listen to me back there before, and it could have cost your life. I don't want to have to worry about tying you to some horse to keep you safe."

"Ryan, you keep forgetting. I'm not your responsibility."

He used his thumb to stroke her hand. The caress sent pleasure rippling through her, quieting her fears and reminding her of other touches, other times. Times she didn't want to think about right now.

"Too late, Anna." Quinn lifted her fingers to his lips and kissed them one by one. His stubbly whiskers tickled her fingertips. "Of course I'm responsible for you. I already told Max we were married. You trying to make a liar out of me?"

"I'm years too late for that."

"Aren't you just the pot that called the kettle black? You're a gifted bluffer, Anna. You missed your calling at the gaming tables."

She knew he was joking, but still, a familiar pang jabbed through her. "My father was the gambler of the family. It didn't serve him well."

He put the badge down on the table and then stroked her cheek. "Tell me."

His voice was quiet, just a whisper louder than the thudding of her heart. She stared into his eyes. If he could explain to her about his family, if he could forgive her, she could manage this.

"After Mother died when I was five, he started wagering.

To help him relax, he told Grandmother. He used to leave me with her, sometimes for days on end. Then he stopped coming back at all." The old hurt throbbed now in earnest, but somehow she sensed that telling him would help.

"How could he leave after you'd just lost your mother?"

"I wondered that a lot of years myself," she told him. "But after Grandmother died, he finally came back. I was fifteen then, my head so full of silly dreams. I was going to be a star, and I was happy. Father *did* love me, no matter what Grandmother said. He'd come back for me after all."

She shook her head, remembering how foolish she had been. "But I wasn't what he wanted. His dead mother's money drew him back. He gambled it away: her bank accounts, her furniture and jewelry, and finally her house. We started running afterward, but every time he earned a little, some two-bit cardsharp would appear to convince him that this time he had a chance."

Quinn grimaced, and she wondered if he was thinking of all the times he'd used those very words.

"Father was a charmer, but he was a weak man too. When he couldn't outrun his creditors any longer, he stepped off a bed into a noose. I found him . . ." She closed her eyes against the images of nine years past. "I found him . . . hanging. . . This time he wasn't ever coming back."

She still recalled it vividly: the rope's grim creak as it stretched tight over the attic beam in that filthy boardinghouse, the slow swing of his socked feet before her eyes, her utter inability to look up to see the rest . . . She closed her eyes as if she might squeeze back those memories.

Quinn held her tight against him. "Is that what you're afraid of, that if I leave I won't return?"

She bobbed her head, bumping his shoulder with her chin. "I'm afraid that if I want you to come back too much . . . it won't happen, or if you do come, it will turn out all wrong anyway."

"Why would you think that? I am not your father, Anna. I love you so much."

"But after all that happened, after what I did—"

"I've asked you before. Why can't you forgive yourself?"

*Accept it,* something whispered. *Accept forgiveness and move on.* She sighed. "How am I ever going to stop apologizing?"

"Maybe we'll just have to think of some way to keep you quiet when you do."

He kissed her then, and so fast, her darkness lifted as if he'd lit a wick. She let him prise her jaws apart with the gentlest flicking of his tongue. A fire settled in her mouth as they kissed, sending hot spark showers cascading down her breasts and farther still, to that place that deepest craved his warmth . . . his touch . . . his length.

He tugged at the deep neckline of the *blusa*, loosening it until his mouth and tongue could soothe the aching tightness of her nipples. She moaned with relief and let him push her back onto the pillows. His left hand cupped a breast, but the other soon breached the skirt's hemline. His fingers danced along the sensitive flesh inside her knee.

"You should wear your friend's clothes more often," Quinn whispered.

"Why? You'll just—try—to charm me out—of them." Gasps broke Anna's voice as his right hand swept ever higher. She closed her eyes, caught up in a delirious swirl of sensation.

Quinn gave each breast a last moist kiss before she felt a swish of unfamiliar skirts around her legs. Her eyelids shot open when his stubbled cheek brushed the inside of her thigh.

*"Dios mío!"* Anna cried. "What are you doing down there, Ryan?"

"Why don't you lie back and see?" came the shrouded answer.

She could swear she heard the lazy smile in his voice.

Anna wanted to tell him he must stop, wanted to say that if he continued, their inevitable parting would rend both their hearts to shreds.

But instead, she traced the progress of his whiskered kisses to that place beyond which she lost all control. And soon, instead of worrying about their parting, she counted the long, sweet moments until their bodies slid together, until he filled her physically the way his presence filled her heart.

# Chapter Twelve

*Copper Ridge*
*April 11, 1884*

Judge Cameron checked his pocket watch and took a *cuernito* from the plate Elena offered. Ignoring her, he spoke instead to his new wife. "I'm sorry I won't be available to drive you to the station, but Elena's cousin, Manuel, is a fine, honest young man. I've left him the phaeton and the team."

Lucy could barely look him in the eye. Once again last night he had come upon her like an ancient plague. Once again he managed to convince himself she enjoyed his crude intrusions.

"I'm due to try a couple of cases in Broken Fork. Nothing that should take too long—maybe four days with the travel. Roy Hadley's riding there with me this morning. He wants to look at a prime bull out at the Ortíz hacienda—and he's pretty handy with a rifle in case any road agents or Indians turn up."

Did he delude himself to think she cared? Did he truly imagine this a marriage, or was he only goading his former mistress to remind her of her place? Lucy forced a nod to end his explanations, then flinched when he kissed her on the cheek.

Elena, who lingered in the kitchen doorway, watched intently. She stepped forward and handed him a packet, and Lucy noticed how their gazes locked.

She didn't give two hoots. As far as she was concerned, Ward Cameron could take his unwanted attentions to the woman's bedroom as long as he left her in peace.

Cameron nodded curtly to Miss Rathbone before leaving.

The older woman checked the watch pinned to her bosom once again, as she had already a dozen times or more.

"Shouldn't we be going now?" Miss Rathbone asked, a hint of a quaver in her voice.

She didn't look so much like a bulldog as she fidgeted with the clasp on her reticule and smoothed her sensible brown skirt. Lucy thought the uncharacteristic display of nervousness made Miss Rathbone seem almost likable. Too bad she'd chosen her final morning there to affect some semblance of humanity.

At first Lucy had been just as eager to see the last of her disdainful warden as Miss Rathbone was to leave. Yet now she felt surprising sadness at the loss of the only familiar person in her life. She imagined the woman going back to Connecticut to resume the management of the Worthington home, a home that Lucy had forever put beyond her in a few moments of pleasure. A wave of loneliness nearly swamped her.

"It's more than two hours until the stage is due," Lucy said. "Have something to eat. Heaven knows the next time you'll have decent food."

She gestured toward the plate Elena had just set on the

table. On it an assortment of dainties steamed enticingly. Perhaps in an effort to buy some sort of peace with Lucy, Elena had offered to try some of her American recipes. Though Lucy was grateful for the Mexican woman's efforts, Elena's attempts had so far proved quite wretched. Delicious as the pastries smelled, Lucy decided that for the sake of her delicate stomach she would wait until Elena's skills improved.

Miss Rathbone, however, sank onto a chair's edge and murmured, "Yes, I suppose if I've learned anything from our adventure out here, it's to eat food when it's offered." She recovered her old form enough to smite Elena with a delightfully disdainful glare. "Almost *any* food, prepared by any sort of person."

Lucy smiled as Elena bit her lip and disappeared into the kitchen. In her wake Spanish words ricocheted like bullets.

"You don't suppose she's swearing, do you?" Lucy asked.

"It would be unthinkable. Those must be prayers of gratitude for the opportunity to serve a Worthington. I've uttered quite a few myself."

Miss Rathbone bit into the pastry, giving Lucy no clue as to whether or not her words had been in jest. Miss Rathbone, joking? This trip had truly brought out the most unexpected qualities.

Lucy poured the two of them a cup of tea.

"So how was today's experiment?" she asked, gesturing toward the plate.

Miss Rathbone took a nibble from a second pastry. "A bit better than the last. But still, there's an off note. Perhaps she substituted something for the baking powder. I understand it's not always available in these wild places."

Lucy saw the woman's jaw twitch violently. Miss Rathbone's nerves must be more sensitive than she'd expected. Lucy was about to ask if she was quite all right, when Miss

Rathbone's whole head jerked. The older woman's hands shot toward her stomach, and they, too, appeared to spasm uncontrollably.

Alarmed, Lucy jumped to her feet. "Miss Rathbone?"

Foam dripped from Miss Rathbone's mouth, which opened in a silent scream. She fell forward, sloshing steaming liquid from the teacup, then rolled out of her chair onto the floor. Her body convulsed violently, and the dining room filled with the acrid odor of her vomit.

"Elena!" Lucy screamed. "Elena, I need help!"

Though the smell made her want to retch as well, Lucy dropped to her knees and turned Miss Rathbone's head to one side to keep her from choking. But Miss Rathbone continued to flail and thrash so violently that Lucy's efforts mattered little.

"Elena! Elena, come in here!" Lucy's throat strained with her shouting, but still Elena did not come.

Leaving Miss Rathbone for the moment, Lucy went to find her. Elena had left the kitchen, but perhaps Manuel would be outside, since he was to drive them a bit later. Lucy ran down the back steps and to the carriage house.

"Thank God!" she exclaimed on seeing the young, dark-featured man brushing the red-brown flank of one of the sorrel horses. "We must have a doctor here at once! Miss Rathbone is having terrible fits!"

He nodded rapidly, *"Sí,* Señora. I will try to find him quickly."

Without bothering to throw a saddle on the gelding's back, he leapt aboard and grasped the animal's mane. As the horse's swift hoofbeats receded quickly, Lucy rushed back into the dining room.

She found Elena stooping beside Miss Rathbone. The older woman lay completely still. Elena turned to look up at Lucy, her expression fathomless.

"She was having fits. I called you," Lucy quickly explained.

"She suffers no more. She is dead." Elena's voice betrayed not a glimmer of emotion.

Lucy stared, disbelieving. "She—she can't be. She's never been sick a day. We were just sitting here and talking. No, I don't believe . . ."

Elena stood as Lucy knelt and shook Miss Rathbone. The older woman's eyes stared, looking as shocked as Lucy felt. Her body moved a bit as Lucy tried to rouse her, but otherwise she lay completely still.

"No!" Lucy cried again, and she laid her head on the woman's chest. But nothing gave the faintest evidence of life, not a heartbeat nor a breath. At last Lucy had no choice but to admit that Elena had been right.

And then she noticed the crumbled pastry beside Miss Rathbone's hand. The pastry that had tasted a bit off. The pastry from a basket that Lucy had not touched.

She thought about Ward Cameron, leaving that morning, eating a *cuernito*, not one of Elena's fresh-baked dainties. Before that morning Elena had been eager to present to him her new creations first.

*Elena.* Lucy lifted her head and then her gaze, which she allowed to travel to Elena's face.

The raven-haired young woman watched expectantly, and Lucy decided there was only one way to be sure.

"Unh!" Grabbing her midsection, Lucy bent sharply at the waist. She fell beside Miss Rathbone and struggled to imitate the woman's jerking motions.

Looking up, she saw Elena. The Mexican woman watched impassively, appearing not at all surprised. The next time she glanced that way, Elena had vanished.

Lucy lay still at last and silent. From the kitchen she heard the sounds of a woman's singing. And though the Spanish lyrics mystified her, the melody was gay.

* * *

Even on Papa's worst days Horace Singletary hadn't felt so low. He'd held on to his anger and his honor even when Judge Cameron hinted that letting go of both could prove quite profitable.

Yet in the wake of the fiery attempt on his life, the illusion of honor had melted away. With his eyebrows singed, his hands bloody, and the greater part of his shirt burned away, Horace had fled his bunkhouse home. After hiding in some bushes for an hour or two, he'd caught his mare, which had been turned loose. He saddled her, using items from the unburned tack shed, and rode for town. Once there he'd taken the first steps toward his new path.

He'd broken into Francis Knowlton's general store and stolen what he needed. The thought of the theft made his blistered face burn with shame. Someday, when this was over, he swore he'd repay Knowlton. Someday, if he lived . . .

Huddled behind a clump of scraggly trees, he fumbled to load ammunition into the new rifle. It had been years since he'd last handled a gun, but back when Papa still had the ranch, he'd insisted that both his children learn how to shoot. Horace especially had been pushed to dispatch coyotes and the occasional rattlesnake. Too bad he'd been back east in college when the real predators arrived.

Funny thing was, he'd always been so squeamish about killing. Yet now he meant to use this stolen gun to kill a man, to lie in wait and ambush him as he left town on the way to try the cases scheduled in Broken Fork. Horace remembered hearing something about a couple of fellows accused of getting drunk and shooting up a local brothel. A soiled dove had been clipped by a bullet and later died.

Horace tied his mare behind a rock outcrop, then checked to be certain she could not be seen from the bend in the only road leading north from town. Then he found a thick clump of undergrowth to shield himself.

If Cameron were going to keep his schedule, he ought to come by soon. And when he did, Horace was going to stop this predator at last.

"Didn't seem right, Ryan turning up alive—dragging home a woman and sayin' that they're hitched," Max told the judge.

Max had ridden hard to catch Judge Cameron. His long-legged dun horse was already sweating despite the morning's chilly air. Max was sweating too. That morning Quinn had rousted him out of bed. Quinn insisted they were going after Hamby and his boys, and that this was something Cameron didn't need to know about.

Max had had to do some smooth talking to buy himself an hour, supposedly for breakfast. He'd been lucky enough to catch the judge as he was riding out of town. Max didn't want Cameron going anywhere until he shared what Quinn said, and what he'd realized too.

"Quinn Ryan's come back?" Judge Cameron turned in the saddle of his elegant palomino stallion. The horse pranced nervously, as if it scented either a rainstorm or a mare.

Max nodded. "And he's mad as hell at Hamby. Says he's gonna bring those boys in one way or the other. Tells me I got to help."

Cameron shook his head, then shrugged. "One can't shoot a man like Ryan and expect him to do nothing. Ned Hamby will no doubt get what he deserves."

The judge didn't look too sorry, even though Max knew Ned sometimes took care of his unpleasantness.

Pulling a gold pocket watch from his coat, Cameron checked the time. "I'm late to meet Hadley. Oh, yes. What was there about a woman?"

"He brought back this pretty blonde—says he's married her. She looked damned familiar though, and their story didn't sound quite right."

The judge flipped the watch cover closed. He seemed to have lost interest in the time. "Blonde, you said?"

Max nodded. "Yes sir—a damn good-looking blonde. The kind of woman a man don't forget so easy. But it was her voice that really did it. Back when I was deputy in Broken Fork, I had to ride through Mud Wasp one day, and I don't mind tellin' you how dry that trail was that summer—"

"Yes, yes." Cameron waved a hand impatiently. "We all know how parched your throat gets."

Max paused, seething, then decided his story was too good to withhold. "I stopped at this saloon to have myself a drink or two, and that's where I heard this girl. She was singin' like a regular canary. Never heard anything so fine. I asked around, wanted to see what a little visit with a woman like that might set me back. They said Annie Faith didn't hold truck with that sort of goings-on."

A grim smile rippled Cameron's thick mustache.

"Yes, sir, Annie Faith," Max repeated. "She was somethin' special though, so I went ahead and asked her myself while she was takin' a break. Offered her more money than I'd pay for ten turns with one of our Blue Streak whores. She turned me down flat. Didn't even pause to pretend like she might think it over. Sort of riled me. Later on I remember hearing how she disappeared after a charge of robbery."

Max poked his own temple. "I don't have a half-bad memory for a pickled Texan. Won't Ryan be surprised to find out he hitched up with a wanted woman?"

Cameron shook his head. "I daresay he knows already."

"He knows? But why—"

"Quinn Ryan was the gambler Annie robbed."

Max felt his mouth drop open. With an effort he moved

it enough to speak. "Then—then what the hell's he think he's doing?"

Judge Cameron glanced sharply at Max. "I believe a lawman with your acumen deserves to be a sheriff, maybe even a U.S. marshal at some time in the future."

"A marshal—" Had the judge been drinking? Weren't they just talking about Quinn? Recovering from his surprise, he added, "but the president appoints those fellas."

"Who the hell do you think appointed me? My father-in-law is a United States senator from the state of Connecticut. I assure you, Wilson, my name is well known to Chester Arthur."

Max whistled. "Well, I'll be. I always figured you was a man goin' places."

"And I can take you with me, Max. If only . . ."

Max leaned forward. He could already picture himself sporting that U.S. marshal's badge, a woman on his arm even prettier than Annie Faith. Yes sir. He'd figured early that with Cameron he'd hitched his wagon to a star. He might hit the bottle now and again, but Max Wilson was no fool.

"There are certain entanglements," Cameron continued. "This blond woman, for instance."

"I don't care what Quinn says. I'm bringin' her in."

"Maybe I don't want her captured," Cameron told him. "Maybe I need her to disappear instead."

"To disappear," he echoed. Was the judge suggesting what he imagined?

"Perhaps you could hang back a bit while Quinn goes after Hamby. Perhaps you could double back and find this Annie Faith."

"And then?" Max wanted everything spelled out. What he'd have to do and what he'd get. Cameron could be slippery with his promises, and he'd lost out a few times on the judge's insinuations.

Cameron looked annoyed, as if Max weren't smart—or

sober—enough to take his meaning. "Take her somewhere private. Tell her you know who she is, and she'll go with you. Who knows? She may even offer you her favors in order to secure your silence. But she can't ever come back—and the body can't be found."

"And I'll get to stay sheriff?"

Cameron nodded solemnly. "And so much more."

Max nudged his gelding a step closer, then reached out to shake the hand of the man who knew the president. After a moment's hesitation Cameron shook it. Then the judge's stallion backed away.

"What about Quinn Ryan?" Max asked.

"Just stay out of his way. I'll take care of him myself."

The rifle's barrel shook despite the support of the V formed by two stout branches. Through a screen of leaves Horace watched Cameron wheel around his horse, then urge it northward at a ground-eating lope. Horace eased his finger's pressure on the rifle's trigger and watched the deputy.

Max lingered for a moment, staring after the judge, before he turned his mount toward town.

Horace sighed at his own failure. Certainly he couldn't have shot Cameron with the deputy sheriff right there. Nor could he miss the chance to listen to the incriminating conversation between the two. But even if Cameron had been alone, even if no murder had been plotted, he couldn't say with any certainty that he would have pulled the trigger.

As much as he hated to admit it, he wasn't the sort of man cut out to ambush anyone, even someone as deserving as Ward Cameron. Or maybe the approach was right, only he had the weapon wrong. Instead of using the stolen Winchester to destroy the judge, perhaps Cameron's conversation would do as well.

Clearly this woman, Annie Faith, knew something. Something Judge Cameron was eager to conceal. If Horace could find her before Max Wilson did, he could warn her. Perhaps then she'd be willing to speak out, to hammer yet another nail into the coffin of Cameron's corrupt reign.

Quinn nudged open his front door and carried in a crate containing flour, lard, coffee, beans, and bacon. Thankfully Max hadn't found the money he had hidden at the house, money he had needed for supplies. His healing shoulder ached a reminder that he hadn't yet recovered from his bullet wound, so he quickly set the box on the table.

"We're going to need a packhorse if you keep bringing food," Anna said. She sat on the bed, where she braided her hair with quick, deft movements. He noticed she'd put on her jeans again, although she'd apparently brushed them to remove much of the dirt.

"The only packhorse I'll need will be to haul Hamby—or his carcass—back to town. Most of these supplies are for you while I'm gone. I don't want you going out."

She raised her eyebrows in mock horror. "Not even to use the privy?"

"You can dump the pot at night."

When her nose wrinkled, he continued speaking, not wanting to give her a chance to protest. "If you're recognized, we both know what might happen."

"There's no *might* about it. Cameron would have me killed. That's not the main reason I'm coming with you, but it's a good one."

He shook his head. "I thought we settled this last night."

"We did. You need a guide and I need to go home."

"Why can't this be your home, Anna?" Unable to keep his distance, he stepped closer and reached down to touch her face.

She stood before his fingertips grazed flesh, then flipped the completed braid over her shoulder. The serape slung over one arm, she took up her hat, which she'd stowed safely with her other things. Yet she didn't move back. Instead, she stared into his eyes so intently that he couldn't look away—could barely blink for fear of breaking a contact that felt as warm as summer sunshine.

Quinn measured the span of time she looked at him by the throbbing beat of his pulse in his ears. He'd never before told a woman how much he wanted her, never before even desired to be with one forever. It felt as if he'd cracked open his chest and handed her his heart, a heart he couldn't be completely certain she desired.

She smiled and stepped into his arms. As he pulled her closer, he felt his lungs fill with air, though he hadn't been aware he'd been holding his breath.

"There are people in the canyon who depend on me," she whispered. "You have forgiven the unforgivable. You have even offered love. I will always love you for what you've given me. But you must see that Copper Ridge does nothing but bind me to an ugly past. The canyon is my present. The canyon—and Rosalinda—are my future."

He shook his head. "You're wrong. You want to go back there only to lick your wounds some more. You talk about a future, but what do you do there except relive the past? Relive our daughter's death . . . You're stuck there, Anna, stuck in a place that keeps you bleeding."

At that moment he could almost see the canyon walls, their red rock named for Christ's blood. Red rock that lay so vividly behind every stand of juniper, every grove of white-barked aspen. Red rock that jutted upward toward the crisp blue of the Arizona sky. Was he telling her the truth? Did those walls imprison her spirit? Or were his reasons selfish excuses to try to keep her for himself?

But selfish or not, he did want her, so he quoted, " 'What's gone and what's past help should be past grief.' "

*"The Winter's Tale,"* she supplied, her eyes shimmering with tears. "But Shakespeare never gave birth, never suckled a child at his breast. There is no moving past what I feel in that canyon. I'm leaving, with or without you. You must have been confused last night. Making love to me is different from making up my mind."

He pulled at her shirt, pulled it up and gestured toward the scar across her belly. "It was a bad wound, but it didn't kill you. So don't bury yourself there. Stay out in the world, with me. We don't have to live in Copper Ridge. There are a thousand other places we could go. I'll even take you to San Francisco. I remember, long ago, how you said you'd like to see it."

She spun away from him toward the door. For a moment he thought she might walk out and leave him, but she drew her back ramrod straight and seemed to gather strength. "I'm going with you, Ryan."

"You are the most exasperating woman. I'm not going to argue with you on this."

"Good." She favored him with a glance over one rigid shoulder. "That will save us both some time, and you can't very well tie me up for weeks while you're off hunting outlaws. So where's this posse you've assembled meeting?"

"Ah, the posse . . ." Quinn fumed at the way she'd so deftly turned the conversation—and at her reminder of that morning's failure. He'd gone out scouting for help, stirring up considerable excitement over his "resurrection." He'd received four invitations for drinks, two for dinner, and one for a "free sample" from Liliana, who was hanging out the upstairs window of the Blue Streak. Her breasts, which appeared in imminent danger of escaping her low-cut bodice, further enlivened the crowd that gathered. But despite the festival atmosphere, Quinn couldn't convince a single man to help him bring in Hamby. There were plenty of well-wishers and quite a few hearty claps on his sore shoulder, but every able-bodied male in the vicinity suddenly remembered somewhere else he had to be. Quinn even had to threaten to fire Max to make him come along. Sometimes being on the side of right was damned humiliating.

Anna quirked a smile. "I'll be your posse, then."

"Oh, hell. Why not? At least then I can keep an eye on you, and you ignore orders just about as well as Max. I think he's still mad about the house. Thought it was his ticket to matrimonial bliss."

"So he's not coming either?"

"Oh, he's coming. Practically at gunpoint, I might add."

"Good. If he stayed, sooner or later he'd mention me, and rumor might get around to Cameron."

"That rumor wouldn't have to exert itself at all. Max is always slobbering at the judge's heels, trying to catch some crumbs." Quinn shook his head in disgust.

Max met them at the livery stable, where he was securing saddlebags on a rangy dun gelding already damp with sweat. The deputy regarded Anna's jean-clad legs with a poorly disguised mixture of lusty interest and disapproval.

"You ain't thinking of bringing her along?" Max asked.

"If you're addressing me," Anna replied, "my head is up here. And if you aren't, I wonder why not. I answer for myself."

A red flush formed a background for Max's coppery freckles. His gaze swung abruptly toward familiar territory—Quinn.

"You can't be serious," Max complained. "Way I heard you talkin', this is a manhunt, not a honeymoon."

Before Quinn could reply, the redheaded man turned what he probably considered his most charming smile back on Anna.

"Ma'am, you don't understand," Max explained. "This may seem glamorous, but it's hot, dirty, dangerous work. There's rattlesnakes, bad grub, and badder outlaws out there. It ain't fitting for pretty little ladies. You stay home and work on some of those apple pies, 'cause I aim to eat my fill once we're back."

Quinn noted the rising color in Anna's face and sighed. Some men seemed bent on self-destruction.

"In case you've forgotten, I've just come from the trail, and I've recently experienced ample evidence of what outlaws can do," Anna said. "And since this may well be as close as you ever get to a real honeymoon, you may as well enjoy it."

Max winced, then his eyes narrowed. "All right, *Mrs. Ryan*. You just come along, then. I'll be riding right behind you."

---

Elena's heart thundered in her chest at the sight of Manuel leading the old *curandero* through the front door.

"The señora say she have fits. Very bad ones." Manuel caught Elena's eye as she stood in the kitchen doorway.

"Where? Where is Señorita Rathbone?" he demanded.

Her throat felt too tight to speak. How could he have brought the *curandero* here? Would the old man guess?

"Why did you bring him? She will want an American, the doctor," Elena managed to say.

"The doctor ride halfway to Apache County to set a broken leg. But the señora say she need help right away. Now where?"

Elena gestured toward the dining room, where both her rival and the ugly old woman lay past help. Desperately she tried to think of some convincing story to tell the *curandero*. But she could no more think than she could control her shaking.

Manuel and the old man hurried past her. Tío Viejo knelt beside the body of the mean-faced woman and began to search for signs of life.

"Where is Señora Worthington?" Manuel asked.

Alarm shot through Elena's body as she realized Lucy

was not where she had fallen. Could the *gringa* have revived enough to crawl elsewhere to die? Surely the dose that killed Señorita Rathbone would be enough to finish such a small, frail woman. Elena pushed past the healer.

"She was here—I swear it!"

"Then, where is she now?" Manuel demanded. Elena could swear she saw suspicion in his eyes. Manuel was her cousin, the son of Mama's sister. Working here as he did, he had no doubt reported her behavior to the family. Just as many others had, he'd tried to persuade her that the judge would bring her only grief. How much did he guess now? And would family ties keep him from public accusations?

The *curandero* sighed over the body, then bowed his head in prayer. Respectfully he passed his hand over the staring brown eyes. The motion closed the lids as if by magic. Then he turned his own gaze, just as blind, toward Elena. His clouded pupils might not see her face, but she felt sure they saw to the core of her—and judged her.

No! He might suspect, but how could he be certain? Once more she tried to convince herself that Tío Viejo might be as cunning as an old coyote, but his knowledge was sparked by loose talk, not enchantment.

Still, her heart's blood crackled with sudden ice when he rose to his feet and pointed directly to her.

Several moments later his voice dropped into low, commanding tones, tones she could not imagine disobeying. "You must tell us. What have you done with the other *gringa*—murderess?"

From the shelter of the carriage house Lucy peered at the two men entering the house. Urgent snatches of Spanish drifted her way from their conversation.

Spanish. That meant they were Elena's people, not hers.

Possibly friends or relatives. In any case, it seemed clear the stoop-shouldered old Mexican was no true doctor.

Wait. Hadn't the judge called Manuel Elena's cousin? A cold prickle of dread swept over her scalp. Could it be possible the two of them were in league? Dare she go inside, shrieking accusations?

Dear God, she had to get away from there, had to find people who wouldn't talk around her in their foreign tongue, who wouldn't plot to take her life. The house was too isolated to escape to town on foot. Though her few experiences on horseback had been long ago and with a sidesaddle, Lucy could see she had no other choice except to ride. She peered at the two horses tied carelessly to a hitching post outside the carriage house. Cautiously she stole forward, wondering which one she should take. Both were blowing and sweating from a gallop, but neither seemed in much distress. On closer examination she realized the taller animal to her left was not a horse at all. Its long ears and dark gray coloring marked it as a mule. Normally she would never consider riding such a humble mount, but at least the mule was saddled. Manuel had left too quickly to properly equip the sorrel horse.

Since she had no idea how to saddle the horse, she untied the mule's reins and led it a short distance away. But how to get on board? Its back looked so very high, and before when she had ridden, there had always been a coachman—or sweetly leering David—to assist her getting up. Her petticoats, too, would be a hindrance, much more difficult than her stylish equestrian attire at home. In the end the mule laid back its ears and shuffled backward in tight circles while she clambered aboard it as if she were a small boy attacking a large tree. But somehow she ended up facing the correct direction.

Emboldened by her success and eager to get away, she dug in her heels the way she'd seen a cowboy do during the trip west. The mule brayed loudly and shot off like a bullet—away from Copper Ridge and help.

The more Ned thought about it, the surer he felt. Black Eagle must have caught the blond woman and spirited her back to Copper Ridge. Judge Cameron wouldn't give a good goddamn who brought her. He'd pay—and the conniving half-breed would pocket the whole bounty.

Ned slammed his fist into the cabin door in frustration. Hop, lounging beside the fire, looked up at him and grinned.

"What the hell do you think is so funny? It's your share that half-breed made off with too, not to mention your horse." And probably his Ginger too, which Black Eagle would take from the woman.

Hop brushed his hair out of his eyes, and Ned watched the younger man's resentment flicker into life. "Just thinking how you was gonna pop your stitches whacking at that door. But don't you fret. I aim to settle up accounts with our old partner too."

Ned glanced down toward the uneven row of stitches Hop had sewn into his forearm. Fortunately the dark thread had held. Luckier still, his wounds looked to be healing. He'd half expected hydrophobia, the way that dog tore into him. He was stitched in half a dozen places, from jaw to wrist to lower leg.

Despite his injuries, however, Black Eagle's treachery rankled him more. If he ever caught up with the half-breed, he'd tear into the bastard with a viciousness that would put the blond slut's cur to shame.

Hop pulled a legged skillet of cornbread off the hearth and used a finger to test its doneness. Yanking back his hand, he stuck one finger in his mouth, then blew on it to cool it. Steam rose enticingly from the skillet to mingle with the scent of the young goat they'd roasted.

"We've been in worse fixes. Leastways we got better food here and a cleaner cabin," Hop said. "Thought we'd lay up here until you're feelin' better."

Ned knew Hop was right, knew they'd never catch Black Eagle on foot. He'd even admit that he could use a little healing time. But something about this canyon, in particular this *place* in the canyon, gave him a premonition of disaster. He wanted badly to be gone.

He swore under his breath. He'd been so close to leaving this godforsaken territory, he could taste it. So close to collecting Cameron's money and returning to Texas a success.

Once again queasiness rippled in his stomach. Something felt so wrong. Though nothing of the sort had ever troubled him before, he saw a fleeting vision of his mama, slowly dying. Dying without ever seeing him again.

Christ! He'd waited long enough. With or without Cameron's money, he'd get to see Mama one way or another. Even if he had to kill his way back home.

Horace rode a half-mile back from the trio he followed. He'd watched Max Wilson leave town with Quinn Ryan and an attractive blonde wearing dark blue trousers. At the sight of the woman, Horace wondered what had gone wrong with Max's plan. Surely this was the same woman he was meant to turn back toward town to kill. Just as surely she would not be safe here either, with the ambitious deputy so close at hand.

He decided just to follow for a time. He wished he could trail the group more closely without being detected. But as they rode out of town, the vegetation thinned in some areas, making it impossible to observe unseen from a lesser distance. Maybe during a meal break or after the group made camp that night, Max would step away from camp to take care of privy needs. Then Horace could ride in and have a talk with Ryan and the woman.

Behind him a scream distracted his attention. Horace turned to see a dark gray blur approaching. The mule bucked and plunged in an obvious attempt to rid itself of the petite woman astride it. Her petticoats flashed white with each kick, but somehow she managed to cling to the beast's back.

Before he stopped to consider consequences, Horace urged his mare toward the animal. As soon as he was close enough, he leaned forward to grasp the mule's headstall and then catch up the dangling reins. Though the leather strained against his bandaged fingers, he held tight.

Once the beast had settled, he stared in surprise at its rider. Though her long, dark brown tresses had unwound into a disheveled mass and the shoulder of her bodice drooped beneath a split seam, he recognized her immediately. Lucy—Cameron's wife, and she was clearly in a state, her face unnaturally pallid, her deep brown eyes wide and full of tears.

Had the judge somehow harmed her? Did this mule, which surely was not one of Cameron's fine beasts, mean she had tried to run away? Remembering her kindness, he almost hoped so, God forgive him. Such a woman was far too fine to be bound to any man as cruel as Cameron.

"Are you hurt?" he asked quickly.

"I—I—no." She was shaking hard. Even her words trembled. "But—but she tried to kill me. She killed Miss Rathbone—murdered her, I'm sure."

*"She?* Who, Lucy? What are you talking about?"

Haltingly, with many tears, she recounted what had happened: her suspicions regarding the judge's beautiful young housekeeper, the animosity that grew between them, Elena's new recipes, and the events surrounding the death of Agnes Rathbone, the woman who'd accompanied her from Connecticut.

Horace believed every word. Rumors of the judge's improper relationship with the Mexican woman had long been fodder for town gossip. And clearly Lucy was far too distraught to be lying.

He glanced back up the trail, mindful that ahead of him, Max Wilson plotted to kill another woman. But he could not leave Lucy in such need either. *Then take her*, something whispered. *Take the judge's bride.*

Why not? Hadn't Cameron taken Papa—and so much more as well.

He looked at Lucy, who was nervously trying to re-pin her fallen hair, and once more he felt the attraction he'd experienced when he'd first met her, almost painful in its intensity. But wanting her did not make stealing her all right.

He cleared his throat and forced himself to ask the question his conscience demanded. "Do you want me—do you want me to take you to your husband?"

"No! Mr. Singletary, I hope never to spend another day—or especially a *night* in the presence of Judge Ward Cameron. Please, can you help me?"

Relief flooded over him. But he must tell her the truth. "Call me Horace, please. Men came to kill me last night, men I believe were sent by your husband. A woman is a target too. She's leaving town right now. I was following her in hopes of warning her, when I heard you scream. The sheriff is with her, and I know him to be a good man. You can come with me, or we can try to find someone else to help you."

"Someone else might not believe me, or maybe they won't care what happens to a stranger. Please, just take me far from here. I want to go with you." Her dark eyes brimmed with more tears. "I need you . . . Horace."

* * *

Fine weather made folks careless, Ned had observed on more than one occasion, and today was the finest he had seen in many months. As the haze of gun smoke lifted, brilliant sunshine warmed an azure sky and fresh spring leaves nodded in a gentle breeze. From the spreading pool near his feet, the sharp, almost metallic scent of blood burned in his nostrils, making him feel strong and alive.

Fortunately the same could not be said of the two men he'd just shot down.

Judging from their equipment, the pair of them were miners. They'd come knocking at the door, seeking the healing woman who lived there, probably to tend the balding man's bandaged knee. Their surprise at finding Ned and Hop instead had been so great that Ned had little trouble plugging both before Hop's revolver cleared leather.

He couldn't help feeling smug that he had been so quick despite his injuries. He felt even better when he stepped out of the doorway and saw the dead men's mounts. A pair of tough-looking saddle horses had been turned out in the corral, along with a swaybacked pinto packhorse.

"That's what you get for enjoyin' a fine day too much to be careful," he told the two dead men.

"You gonna give these fellas Indian haircuts?" Hop asked.

Ned considered, and toed the larger corpse. It rolled easily, and the man's black curls bobbed with the movement. "Maybe just this one. Ain't got a scalp like this one."

"You ain't got any now," Hop reminded him. "Not since that woman stole your horse."

Ned grimaced at the reminder. His collection had been tucked inside a saddlebag. "I'll get 'em back—both my Ginger and my collection, with a couple other scalps besides. I mean to get that blond bitch's, and Black Eagle's gonna regret ever teachin' me his heathen trick. And after we fix them, I'm goin' home."

"You mean to leave today?" Hop asked. " 'Cause if we're gonna stay awhile, we'd best drag off these bodies and that old man's before they get to stinkin'."

Ned walked back to near the doorway, where both miners lay, their limbs splayed haphazardly. A string of jet-black beads dropped from the pocket of the man he'd planned to scalp. Stooping carefully on account of his stitches, Ned hooked a finger beneath the beads and pulled them toward him. A rosary carved from onyx felt very warm in his hand, almost too hot to hold. Far too hot to be explained by the dead man's dissipating heat.

Ned dropped the rosary and backed up, once more troubled by the sense of *wrongness* in this place, the feeling that he should leave there right away.

Hop stepped forward and began searching the bodies for more valuables. When he saw that Ned wasn't joining in and had not retrieved the beads, he scooped them up and stuffed them into his own trouser pocket. Only the black cross remained visible, jutting upside down out of the opening.

"Let's say we give all these fellas a nice, warm send off," Hamby suggested, nodding toward the cabin. "If she had visitors both today and yesterday, there'll probably be more. We've been lucky so far. But it don't seem likely all of 'em will be this easy—'specially if folks start noticing disappearances."

Hop grinned, glancing at the little cabin. "Always liked a bonfire. We used to have 'em back home to celebrate. Let's clean out what we want and drag in these fellas. Then I'll light her up."

"You do that, Hop," Ned told him. Truth was, the sooner they were shed of this place, the better he would like it.

* * *

They might not be really married, but they sure as hell behaved like sweethearts, Max Wilson observed. He watched Quinn trot his mare closer to the bay that Annie Faith rode, watched him lean closer so the two could speak in quiet voices. At the sight Max's stomach churned with jealousy.

She called herself Miranda, called herself a widow. Both claims might be possible. Perhaps she'd shucked the saloon life to marry some rancher with good prospects. Single white women being in such short supply, some men in the territory even married whores.

Not that this woman was much better. Any female who sang in such places was hardly virtuous, and this one had proven it with the crimes of robbery and escape. The robbery of Quinn Ryan. Max shook his head, wondering how the man could be fool enough to fall under her spell twice.

Annie Faith leaned closer to Quinn and laughed, a musical sound that reminded Max once more of her glorious voice. He found himself remembering how beautiful she had looked singing in her brilliant silk attire, and he grew hard with resurrected want.

Maybe it wasn't so surprising that Quinn had succumbed once more to her charms. Even knowing all he did, Max wouldn't hesitate a moment if fate awarded him a chance to enjoy her.

He thought once more of the judge's words. *Who knows? She may even offer you her favors in order to secure your silence.*

The thought made him groan with desire. All he had to do was figure a way to lose Quinn for a while. Then he'd treat this Annie Faith to one fine honeymoon before she met her Maker.

# Chapter Thirteen

Ward Cameron's first reaction to seeing Manuel galloping the sorrel toward him was to swear at the condition of the horse. The gelding's sides heaved heavily, and foamy sweat lathered its flank.

"Christ almighty, you're ruining an eight-hundred-dollar carriage horse!" But even as Cameron shouted, he noticed the horror in the young man's black eyes, along with the fact that he hadn't taken time to put a saddle on his mount's back.

Roy Hadley, the big, rawboned rancher who'd been riding with him, held up one hand. "Wait, Ward. Hear him out."

Manuel pulled the sorrel to a stop. "You must come back home now, señor! There has been a killing!"

Max Wilson had acted faster than he'd imagined possible, so Cameron's expression of surprise was not completely contrived.

"In Copper Ridge?" he asked, hoping to elicit further details.

"In your own casa, Señor Cameron."

In his own house? That made no sense. Why would Max take Anna to The Pines to kill her? Had the fool no brains at all?

"Who was murdered?" Hadley asked.

"The woman who come here with your new señora—the one who never smile!"

This time, when Cameron's jaw dropped, his shock was genuine. Miss Rathbone? "But who—why? I thought you'd put her on the stage by now."

*"El curandero* say she eat the poison—the poison that *mi prima,* my own cousin, take from him."

*"Elena?* Horse shit! Elena would do no such thing!" Ward argued.

Heedless of his outburst, Manuel pressed on. "Your wife—we can no find her."

*Elena!* Oh, dear God! Cameron knew how much the surly Bostonian Rathbone bitch annoyed her—just as she irritated everyone—but he couldn't imagine Elena doing anything to harm her on the day of her departure. But Lucy was another matter.

Then he remembered Elena's angry words as clearly as if she'd just shouted them. *If you do not send Señorita Holy White Daughter of the senator and her complaining duenna from this house this instant, I swear to you I kill them both—and maybe you as well!*

His mistress's temper was no less fiery than her passion; he'd imagined her outrage would pass. He'd certainly never believed that she had ever truly expected him to marry *her* instead. Why, it would be unthinkable!

A wave of nausea made his bowels feel weak and watery. Dammit to hell! How would he ever explain this to the senator? A dew of sweat popped out on his forehead, and he could almost hear his grand political career shattering beneath the weight of Manuel's news.

"I'm sure we'll find your wife." Hadley placed a reassuring hand on Cameron's elbow, then turned his horse around.

Cameron followed, glad to have with him the big rancher, a man who owed him favors beyond counting. Today, the judge realized, might turn out to be a good one for calling in some of his markers, for God alone knew what kind of mess awaited him at home.

Though the air had warmed considerably, Lucy's trembling only increased as Horace told his tale. Her mule, now tractable enough, walked quietly alongside his horse across a rugged landscape, beneath the bluest sky that she had ever seen.

"Dear God. I'm so sorry for what he did to your family and all the others. I never imagined I'd married such a monster," Lucy said. Her stomach roiled with the thought that legally at least, she belonged to the foul man.

Horace shook his head. "He must have mistreated you as well, or you would have asked to go to him for help."

Lucy laid a palm across the gentle swell of her midsection. "He was horrible—but—but it's not as though I didn't deserve it."

"I don't believe it. What could anyone like you ever have done to merit his abuse?" Horace asked.

At that moment Lucy saw something so precious in his blue-eyed gaze, something she hadn't realized how badly she missed. Trust. She felt absolutely certain that no matter what she told him, he'd believe her. Months ago she had thrown away that luxury for the pleasure of a moment— and sown herself a harvest of shame and misery. It occurred to her that she might tell him anything and he'd believe her.

Instead of tempting her, that knowledge freed her and made her want to share the truth. All of it. All the things she'd held inside her for so long rose like gorge.

She cast her eyes downward, too embarrassed to look him in the eye as she spoke. "I'm going to have a baby,

Horace. I came here because the judge was my only chance to salvage something from my ruin."

"Oh, Lucy ..." He sounded comforting rather than judgmental.

She continued, for the relief of telling outweighed the pain. "I made such terrible mistakes. I flirted outlandishly with our assistant coachman, a young man known for his affairs. He said things to me, things so wicked and exciting—even more so because I knew how improper such a relationship would be. I was a virgin, but I was no victim. At the time I truly wanted him."

Her face burned with shame, and she imagined how red her fair skin must appear. But it hardly mattered. All that was important was the telling—all of it.

"It happened only once, and we were caught," Lucy explained. "The young man fled before my father could have him punished. I'm certain that he never gave my plight another thought."

"So was it your father's idea to marry you to Cameron?"

"Oh, yes. 'A perfect solution,' he told me. 'Why, the man practically worships at my feet. He'd give anything to ally himself with Worthingtons,' " Lucy explained. "Besides, the judge was visiting from the Arizona Territory, too remote a place for him to have heard the rumors of my disgrace. Father arranged it all so deftly."

"Did he know you were in a—er—delicate condition?"

"Of course not. At first I didn't know myself. And once I did, I only prayed to marry quickly enough that Ward Cameron wouldn't guess."

"But Cameron does know, doesn't he?"

She nodded and squeezed her eyes shut at the horror of the memory of their wedding night, just days before. "I told him just after we were married. He—he was beastly. Oh, God, the way he used me . . ."

Her voice—and her composure—dissolved into deep sobs. She lifted her hands to hide her face.

Horace pulled his horse to a stop and dismounted, then helped her down from the mule when it paused to chew a patch of grass. Then he held her, his hands stroking her hair and back as one might comfort a small child.

When she recovered, she felt a sudden rush of shame at her tears—so weak and unseemly, as her father might have told her. "I shouldn't do this," she muttered. "He had every right. I'd tricked him into marriage—and I am his wife."

Horace pulled her closer. "We'll have to see what we can do about that."

"There's nothing—nothing I can do. I have no money, no place to go. I should have stayed my course."

"And gone back to Elena? You were right before. It's very possible that no one would believe your accusations, and then she would kill you."

Lucy stared up into his face. "Perhaps that's what I deserve. I was proud and wanton, and I was dishonorable to marry under false pretenses."

"You made mistakes, but you married Cameron and came to a new land to protect your child. In that act there is great honor."

He might believe that, but Lucy knew she'd been thinking only of how to save her own miserable existence. Motherly emotions hadn't figured into it at all, only a base desire to survive.

Horace reached under her chin with gentle fingers and turned her face upward, toward his. "And I will help you, Lucy. I swear it on my father's grave."

"Shoulda done this at night," Hop said, staring at the dancing flames and the dark, smoky column rising above the canyon walls. "Fire this pretty's wasted on a day this bright."

"Better toss in that old Mexican too," Ned answered.

Unlike Hop, who always took a special delight in fire, he didn't give a damn about watching the flames dance, but whenever possible he liked to get rid of bodies. Despite Cameron's influence, someone would likely come after him if he left behind too many corpses.

They walked to the side of the cabin opposite the corral and feed shed to find the old man's body.

"Wasn't it right here?" Hop asked, gesturing toward a patch of flattened dried leaves.

Ned looked around. "Somethin' musta drug it off."

"A bear?" Hop's head swung rapidly from side to side, lifting his lank red-brown hair in oily clumps. Hop had a special dread of bears. He'd told the story several times about how a grizzly in the Sierras tore apart his pap.

"Could be." Ned shrugged. The more likely culprit would be coyotes or perhaps a cougar, but it never hurt to remind Hop that despite the killings, rapes, and burnings, he wasn't far off bein' a snot-nosed kid.

Hop peered intently at the ground, his gun drawn and at the ready. Backing away from where the body had lain, he said, "But I don't see no tracks."

Wood cracked, and Hop screamed suddenly. Before Ned could figure what was happening, Hop fell backward on the fallen needles and half-rotted leaves that blanketed the ground.

Ned saw the jagged piece of wood sticking up, sharp as a blade, out of the soil. Several drops of blood, beaded near its tip, ran down the side.

Hop howled with pain, grasping his deeply punctured lower leg. The onyx rosary had snaked its way out of his pocket. Beside the jet-black cross lay another, this one larger and of wood.

"A grave marker," Hamby said, and a chill gripped him despite the bright heat of the fire crackling nearby. Hop had stepped on and broke off a wood grave marker. And it had bitten back.

"Forget the old man," Ned suggested. "Let's get your leg bound up to stop the bleeding. Then we're getting out of here."

For once Hop didn't argue. Instead, he struggled to his feet and hobbled toward where the horses waited.

Neither of them bothered to pick up the string of onyx beads, far blacker than a night sky, far warmer than their hearts.

---

Ward Cameron arrived home to a scene right out of Bedlam. Coming in from the bright sunshine, it took his eyes several moments to adjust to the dining room's dim light. But even in those seconds he could hear Elena wailing hoarsely, alternating between fits of begging, cursing, and denials. As his vision cleared, he saw her, bound hand and foot to a straight-backed chair and screaming at an old man at her right. Beside her, the thin old Mexican sat impassively, completely heedless of both her pleas and the still figure lying on the floor.

Cameron remembered seeing the old blind Mexican a few times on the streets of Copper Ridge. Ward thought he was some sort of medicine man, the kind that ignorant have-nots substituted for real doctors. From the sounds of Elena and the old man's complete stillness, he might well have added deafness to his deficits.

Walking past the pair, Cameron approached the woman lying on his Persian rug, her shoes sticking out from beneath the blanket that had been draped over her body.

"Is that—is that your wife?" Hadley asked, standing behind him. He held a blue bandanna to his mouth to block the dreadful stench.

For one horrifying moment Cameron wondered if it could be. His world careened as he once more imagined himself trying to delicately word the telegram he would have to send the senator, her father. But he quickly realized the shape beneath the blanket must be Miss Rathbone, for both the figure and the feet were far too large to be those of his delicate bride.

"Where is Mrs. Cameron?" he asked the two Mexicans sternly.

Elena stopped screaming and blinked at him, as if only then noticing he'd come into the room. She renewed her pleas more loudly, only this time she addressed him instead of the old man.

"I did not do this thing!" Elena's voice, raw from shrieking, hissed in places, making her difficult to understand. "Manuel and Tío Viejo make a terrible mistake! It was *her*, Señor, the one you bring here to destroy our happiness! Anyone could see how much she hated that old woman! Please!"

Thankfully after that her words became inaudible save for a few screamed snatches now and then. Seeing Elena's state, he didn't credit her accusation one bit. Lucy was as arrogant a schemer to ever come his way, but she was not a murderess.

He spoke to the old man. "Where is my wife? Tell me!"

It felt disconcerting, waiting for the old Mexican to answer. Whenever Cameron's gaze leapt to Elena, Ward saw her jaw still working and her eyes gleaming bright with madness. Her thick black hair, which he'd caressed so many times, cascaded wildly to her waist. She resembled more a witch than the woman who had for two years given him such exquisite bed-sport.

The old man might be blind, but his expression brimmed with a depth of understanding. At last he turned his clouded gaze toward Cameron. Gesturing toward Elena, he said sternly, "She never would have come to this if you had not humiliated her with this *gringa*. She has been always far too proud for her own good."

"Goddammit!" Cameron roared. "I've asked you twice,

where's Lucy? Tell me now, before I throw you in the hoosegow!"

"Where she is I cannot say, but when I thought to find this poor broken child's mother, I found my mule gone. Perhaps your new bride seeks help. Or perhaps she merely runs. Perhaps, even, from you."

"Old man, I have been appointed by the president of these United States to stand in judgment! Do not presume to judge my marriage or my soul!"

The impertinent old son of a bitch dared laugh at him, at *him*, a man who had ordered men hung, whether or not they deserved it.

"As you wish, Señor," the Mexican said calmly. "I now leave your judgment to *Dios*, who judges all of us, even your *compadre, el presidente* Señor Arthur."

Furious, Cameron stormed toward the front door. He bumped into Manuel, who'd just come in from tying up the horses.

"Take care of this mess," he said, gesturing toward the dining room. "Have the undertaker put the old woman in the cheapest box he can build—nobody here knows her. And for God's sake, keep Elena locked up until I can get back."

He turned to Hadley. "Coming with me, Roy?"

The rancher nodded firmly. One thing Cameron appreciated about Hadley, he remembered who'd settled that water rights problem he'd been having with some dirt-poor sheep farmers. Cameron could have set both Hadley and his hired gun swinging for the way they'd shot up those stupid mutton punchers. Now he'd do whatever was needed to help Cameron find Lucy and bring her back here, where she belonged.

Whether or not his young wife wanted to return.

\* \* \*

"Can I talk to you in private?" Max asked.

Quinn glanced back toward his deputy and noticed how he shifted in the saddle, the way he always did when something was bothering him. About half the time it meant he wanted to see if Quinn brought whiskey.

With the slightest lift of the reins he slowed Titania. Anna said, "Notion and I will ride up ahead a bit."

"Don't get too far away," Quinn said. After her bay horse topped a hillock, he said to Max, "Sorry, but I didn't bring a flask this time."

Max shook his head. "It's not that. It's—on that last rise I happened to look behind us. I saw riders following."

"You think Carl Stark and One-Arm Ramsey decided they weren't too busy to join us?" Stark and Ramsey always offered handshakes—though Ramsey's was left-handed—and drinks to their success, but as folks around here put it, both were about as useful as tits on a boar hog.

Max's grin looked forced. "You've always been a dreamer, Quinn."

Taking his cue from Max's expression, Quinn grew more somber. "How many, do you think?"

Max shook his head. "I'm not sure. Four, five, maybe more. Couldn't tell for certain, and couldn't recognize anybody that far away."

"Damn," Quinn said. "It's getting close to time to make camp, and we can't risk anybody sneaking up on us after dark. Could you at least tell whether they were Indians?"

Last he'd heard, Geronimo and his Apache raiders were somewhere in Mexico, but keeping track of anybody in the vast, mostly unpopulated territory was guesswork at best.

"Looked like white men from their tack and clothing." Max squirmed in his seat once more.

Quinn squelched the temptation to ask whether he'd been visiting those infested harlots again lately.

He wondered if Hamby could possibly have rejoined with

other members of his gang and ridden there so quickly. He wished he could rule out the idea.

"Maybe we'd better find them before they find us," Quinn suggested.

"Outnumbered the way we are, I don't think we oughta march right in."

Quinn nodded. "I agree. Let's go ahead and make camp like always, just in case they're watching."

"Then you can slip back and check them out," Max finished quickly.

Quinn couldn't help noticing how Max, as usual, suggested hanging back to let Quinn do the checking so he could stay at camp. He'd probably pester Anna about what she was going to make for dinner. Suppressing a grin, Quinn imagined several variations on how she might respond to Max's "instruction." On the whole Max might be safer eyeballing desperados.

"Let's catch up with Miranda, then, and find a likely camp," Quinn said.

When they reunited, Quinn spoke quietly to Anna about the plan.

"I don't want you to go alone," she protested. "If it's really Hamby and his boys—"

"One man can go back without being spotted. Two would make an easier target, especially if someone's already watching us."

"Ask Max to go this time," she pleaded. "You're still wounded, in case you've forgotten."

"I hate to cast aspersions on my deputy, but he'd make more noise than a Bowery wake—and believe me, that's saying something."

"I don't like it," Anna said. "What if I borrowed Max's gun and came with you?"

Quinn held up an index finger. "Only one of us, and if you'll remember, I've been doing this a long time. It's probably just a group of cowboys heading to their rancho.

But just in case we need to leave in a hurry, don't unpack anything we can't afford to leave behind."

Within a half an hour they stopped at a site scarred with the black ash of a previous campfire, the same bald hillock where he and Anna had stayed before. All three dismounted, and Anna retrieved a sack of fine dry bark and other tinder she'd collected along the way. She began preparing it to start their evening fire.

Trying to appear casual, Quinn scanned the horizon. Already a stain of salmon to their west presaged a magnificent sunset. Something large and tan moved, something nearly as large as their horses.

"Look at that." He pointed out the huge animal for Anna. It was browsing on the leaves of a stunted live oak, partially hidden among the shrublike trees that marked the chaparral.

"An elk." She sounded awed. "She's beautiful."

The elk lifted its head, and Quinn thought of a few men he knew who hunted the animals in autumn, when the bulls had massive racks of antlers. When one hunter got lucky, half the town shared in the bounty.

"Jesus, look at all that fresh meat." Max started to pull his rifle from its scabbard.

"No!" Anna argued. "We can't use that much. Besides, she's near to calving. Can't you see?"

Max looked about to argue, but Quinn interrupted.

"You forgetting about those fellas behind us?" he asked. "We don't want to make anybody nervous shooting."

The elk's ears twitched in their direction, and it bounded off with a flash of white tail.

Notion, finally catching sight of the fleeing animal, barked and rushed after it.

Quinn smiled at Anna. "If he comes back dragging that thing by a hoof, you and Max cook me up a nice steak while I'm gone."

Ignoring the jest, Anna hugged him. "Be careful, Ryan—Quinn."

Quinn nodded, not missing her use of his first name.

"I'll be back as quick as I can. Try to act like you're preparing to stay the night, but be ready to move fast—just in case," he warned.

She nodded, then cast one last worried look at him before going back to start the evening fire.

He stopped behind Max, who'd lifted a stirrup to make some adjustment to his saddle.

Lowering his voice, Quinn said, "You hear shots, don't come after me. Just get her out of here. You understand me?"

Max peered over his shoulder. "You really care about her, don't you?"

Something in his voice skirted disbelief. Quinn realized Max and Anna hadn't exactly hit it off, but for the first time he wondered if this was something more than his deputy's jealousy.

"I love her," Quinn said simply. Later he'd have a serious talk with Max, try to settle down his feelings. But now wasn't the time.

Dismissing this concern, Quinn turned to leave. Notion, returning from his chase, tried to follow.

"Could you tie him up someplace?" he called to Anna. "He might bark if he sees strangers, and I don't want to get caught unawares."

Anna found a rope and tied the dog to the base of a sturdy piñon tree.

Quinn kissed her cheek and once more reassured her that he would be back soon. Then he started downhill, threading his way between thick clumps of evergreens that might well conceal the unknown men who traveled in their wake.

* * *

Anna stared at Max's back for some time before asking, "You didn't really see any riders, did you?"

Max turned slowly. "What makes you say that?"

"You were about to shoot before, and now you're loosening the cinch on your horse's saddle. Those are not the actions of a man concerned about the possibility of pursuit."

In contrast with his red hair, Max's brows had bleached blond in the sun. Still, she saw them rise, saw the color deepen behind his myriad freckles.

"If you're so damned sharp, then tell me what I'm up to," Max challenged, and as he did so, he eased back the right tail of his jacket, exposing the butt of a revolver.

Anna's heart beat like a dove's wings against the cruel bars of a cage. Had he seen through her story? Clearly this was not how a man spoke to the wife of his superior. Yet, with an effort, she strained the fear out of her voice. "I'd say you were trying to get rid of Quinn so you could put me in my place."

*Or try to.* She hoped desperately that that was all. She'd offended him that morning, and he meant to tell her his version of how a proper woman ought to act.

"I'd say you're very wrong," he answered, shattering her hopes. "Maybe I just wanted to hear you sing again. Do you still sing—Annie Faith?"

He knew! *Dios mío!* He knew all of it! He'd sent Quinn away so he could arrest her! Unconsciously Anna took a backward step. As if that one step could remove her from the crimes she'd committed years before.

He advanced on her and reached out with his left hand to stroke her cheek. His right palm rested on the gun butt.

She flinched as if his touch burned like a brand. "What is it you want?"

He looked her over thoroughly, his gaze so slow and

licentious that she wished she could bathe. "What you should have sold me years ago. But you were too good back then, like you was some sort of saloon star. Guess you don't mind giving it to Quinn though, when you ain't stealin' from him."

She wasn't going to cry. She wasn't going to beg him. Blinking back a haze that threatened to form tears, she tried to talk her way out of this. "Quinn will be back soon. We can both explain."

"When Quinn gets back, we won't be here. We're gonna take a little walk, then take care of things for my friend, Judge Cameron. Now, move." He gestured in a direction that would take them far from Quinn's path.

"Quinn will kill you if he finds out you hurt me."

"Then we'll just have to make sure he don't." His gun was out now, pointed toward her. "Go, before I get impatient."

Her mouth went dry, and her knees grew so weak, she wasn't certain they'd support her. Notion strained against his rope, his panting sounding choked. Her breathing felt no easier.

Somehow, though, she forced her feet in the direction the elk had taken. As she walked among the lengthening shadows of the stunted trees, she noticed how the hard-packed sand refused to take her footprints. She wondered if Max would try to hide her so Quinn would never find her body. How would he explain her sudden absence?

She had little doubt he meant to kill her once he had taken what he wanted. If she were merely a lone woman with a criminal past, he could rape her and then bring her back to town for justice. No one would credit—much less care about—her claims of abuse, and she knew beyond the slightest doubt that Cameron would hang her quickly to keep her from exposing his illegal actions. But she hadn't lied when she claimed that Quinn would kill Max. She knew it as well as she knew her real name.

Suddenly a deeper terror slashed through her fear. Max meant to kill Quinn too! That must be why he didn't fear him! She stumbled with the force of it and grasped a clump of prickly juniper to keep herself upright.

Deliberately she snapped the branch. Behind her, not fifty yards away, she heard Notion whining. The dog was little used to being left behind.

Stubborn tears welled once more in her eyes. If Quinn didn't loose him soon to find her, she'd be leaving both of them for good.

It didn't take Quinn long to find them. The man and woman were talking so intently that they didn't even notice him until he stepped out in front of their mounts.

"Easy," he said softly, not wishing to startle the horse, the mule, or the pair astride them. But Quinn had no fear for himself, for he knew Horace Singletary slightly from Copper Ridge.

"Sheriff Ryan!" Horace said, sounding relieved to see him. "Just the man I rode out here to see."

"You were following us?" Quinn asked.

It was hard to believe Max mistook these two for a half dozen or so men. He hadn't noticed the smell of liquor on his deputy's breath today. Again he thought how something about Max's behavior didn't quite sit right with him. They'd have to talk as soon as possible.

"There's been a murder!" the woman blurted out.

For the first time Quinn focused his attention on her. A pretty, petite woman, her brown eyes glittered bright with purpose. Her dark brown hair might be disheveled, but her clothes appeared to be of far finer stuff than the calicos most white women around there wore.

"Who's been killed?" he asked quickly.

"Miss Rathbone, my chaperone. She accompanied me

here on my trip west to marry the judge. Since the wedding's over, she was to leave for home today."

Cameron had gotten married? He pitied the poor girl.

"Why didn't you go to your husband for help? Is he away?"

She nodded rapidly. "He left for Broken Fork this morning for a trial. And then Miss Rathbone was poisoned!"

"Poisoned? Are you sure? Who would want to hurt this lady?"

"Elena—the judge's housekeeper. She's been—involved with Mr. Cameron, and she meant to kill me. But I ran when I realized—"

"Please, Lucy," Horace interrupted, using his bandaged hand to gently still her fluttering arms. "I know this is important, but there's something else I must speak with Mr. Ryan about first. I came here for another urgent reason, Sheriff. Where's the woman who was with you? I think her name is Annie Faith."

Ryan felt fear grip his guts. How would Horace Singletary know Anna at all, much less by that name?

"You left her alone with your deputy?" Horace continued, obviously upset.

The fear tightened its hold, and he asked, "Why?"

"I overheard Max talking with Cameron this morning. He means to kill her, Quinn."

Involuntarily Quinn's head turned toward the bald hillock. He was too far away to see it through the maze of trees, but he strained his ears to try to hear raised voices or the barking of the dog.

In the fading light a few branches stirred with the light breeze. The only sounds that carried were those of birds and insects, crying to the bright orange half-disk of the setting sun.

Quinn didn't stop to ask Horace for proof of what he said or details. Instinctively the story fell in place with his misgivings. Somehow Cameron must have learned Anna was in town and bribed Max to solve his problems. Once Anna was killed, would Max murder him too, to keep his place as sheriff and reclaim his little house? Sweet Jesus, was he being betrayed for a dented tin star and a leaky roof?

Ignoring Horace and Cameron's wife, Quinn spun on his heel and started uphill at a dead run.

"That's far enough," Max told her. "Now turn around."

She did so slowly. Above them she saw the first faint stars of evening. Must they also be her last? Hating her weakness, she tried to will the flow of strength into her limbs so she would not simply crumple at his feet.

"You don't even remember, do you?" Max's mouth curled into a sneer. "You turned your damn nose up at my money like it wasn't worth a thing."

A rush of temper loosened Anna's tongue. "Don't pretend you'd think better of me if I were a soiled dove! No, I don't remember you, but I've met a hundred men like you. I've seen the marks you leave on those poor women. I've heard the way you speak of them as if they're something less than human. If I'd slept with you then, you'd be calling me a whore and feeling even more entitled."

Despite his raised revolver, she stepped closer. Why not tell him exactly how she felt? He meant to murder her anyway, and if she had to join her daughter, she'd just as soon cross over without first suffering the pain of rape.

For a split second a fleeting image of Ned Hamby's face froze her feet and stopped her. But this was not the outlaw. This bastard was paid to uphold the law!

"Take off your clothes—now," Max ordered, cocking back the hammer on his pistol.

The thought that he would demand this, then kill both her and Quinn, made Anna so angry that whatever control she had left burned off in a flash. She thought of how ineffectual she'd been against Ned Hamby. This time she had no gun to drop, no surge of song to flood her mind with bitter memories. If she had to die there, she might as well do something more useful than emptying her stomach at his feet.

With a shout of outrage she sprang at Max. Her left wrist thrust beneath the barrel and forced it slightly upward.

Almost against her ear the shot exploded. She felt the heat of burning powder, and she fought toward Max's face. Clawing for his eyes, she continued screaming more out of fury than in the hope that Quinn would hear her in time to be of help.

Though he outweighed Anna by some fifty pounds, Max fell back against her onslaught. Desperately trying to save his eyes, he tried to shield them with his forearms. The revolver made a poor defense, but he couldn't put it to better use without risking his vision.

Anna didn't dare relent. She didn't dare let him escape to shoot her. Though she'd never fought before, she wasn't hampered by the same rules that most men respected. Here survival was the only rule—and the chance of saving Quinn's life too. She gouged with her short nails, tore at Max's hair, then slammed the heel of her hand into his teeth.

Drawn by the gunshot, Quinn rushed toward the pair. As he pounded closer, Max, who'd been scrabbling backward to put distance between himself and Anna, fell heavily, tripped by a twisted stump.

Anna tottered but kept her balance, then kicked hard at something. Reaching her side, Quinn saw that it had been Max's revolver, which now lay out of reach.

Max struggled toward his feet, his face barely recognizable, a scarlet mask crosshatched with deep gouges. He didn't seem to see Quinn, probably couldn't see much at all for all the bleeding near his eyes. He howled in pain and anger and swung his arms in the direction where he guessed Anna stood.

Panting hard, Anna leapt out of reach.

Quinn cocked his revolver and warned his deputy. "Don't move or I'll shoot."

God, how he would love to shoot! His pulse whooshed in his ears, nearly drowning out everything but his relief—and growing rage. The barrel of his pistol shook, and he chastised himself for his lack of professional composure. But how could he possibly remain detached, when his own damned deputy had tried to hurt, probably even kill, Anna?

"The bitch attacked me!" Max screamed. "God, my eye! She got my eye!"

Quinn switched his gun to his left hand and used the right to punch him in the jaw. Max lost his newfound footing and landed on his rear.

"Are you hurt?" Quinn asked Anna over Max's wailing.

She looked surprised, then put her hand to her left ear. Cupping it, she asked, "What did you say?"

"Shut up, Max, or I'll put out your other eye," Quinn ordered, rubbing his knuckles. When the deputy's shouts subsided into moaning, he repeated his question.

Anna nodded. "I'll be fine. It's just that he shot so close to this ear, I can't hear out of it."

Quinn looked at his deputy. In an attempt to calm her, he offered a weak jest. "It's almost biblical. An eye for an ear."

Anna's smile was feeble. "You're the king of misquotes, Ryan."

"You're listening to *her?*" Max screamed, using his sleeve to wipe his bloody face. "She's a wanted woman—and a lunatic as well."

He wiggled a front tooth and saw it come out in his hand. "Look at this! She knocked out my goddamn tooth!"

"He was going to 'take care of me' for Cameron," Anna told Quinn, "after he raped me first."

"You son of a bitch!" Quinn holstered his gun and reached for Max's collar. He raised his fist to strike, but Anna's protest stopped him.

"Don't!" she shouted, and grasped his wrist with both hands. He glanced at her face. Though it was pale with fear, no bruises marred her features. If not for that detail, he knew he would have beaten Max into the ground.

He let go of his deputy, who once more sat down hard. A moment later two riders appeared. Anna glanced up at them, then looked to Quinn.

Quinn explained to her. "This is Horace Singletary. He came to warn me about Max. He overheard him talking with Cameron this morning."

The woman aboard the mule winced at the sight of Max's face. "Did you do that?" she asked Quinn.

"I wish I could take credit. Allow me to introduce our not-so-helpless damsel in distress. This is Anna." Deliberately he didn't mention her last name. "Anna, this is Mrs. Cameron."

"Lucy," the young woman corrected Quinn as she slid off the mule. "Are you quite all right, Anna?"

"Lucy *Cameron?*" Anna's color dropped another shade. "You're married to the judge?"

Lucy glanced toward Horace before answering. "Not for long, I hope."

Quinn retrieved Max's gun.

"I ought to shoot you with this," he told his former deputy. He yanked the star off Max's vest, beneath his jacket, and tossed it away. "You're a damned disgrace."

Max wriggled loose another tooth and spat a mouthful of blood. "And you're a crazy man to hook up with this thieving hellcat!"

"Get back to camp," Quinn told him, "before I set her loose on you again."

* * *

Quinn poked at the fire, not to accomplish anything but because he needed to do something with his hands. Probably he ought to start something cooking for the group that had now swollen to five, but Max's betrayal left him unsettled, and Horace's appearance raised the specter of regret.

Amazingly Anna knelt nearby, cleaning the very wounds she'd given to Max Wilson. The latter had his hands and feet tied and a look so sour, it would likely curdle milk. But at least he'd ceased his cursing in light of Quinn's offer to knock him out cold if he didn't quiet down.

Cameron's wife moved stiffly toward Anna and offered to take over.

"I wouldn't expect you'd want to help him after what he tried to do," she said.

"I'm a healer," Anna told her. "It's not my job to judge worth, only to tend the wounded."

That was what he was when he'd been brought to her, Quinn thought morosely. The wounded. He was glad she hadn't tried to judge his worth. Looking at Horace, he found it a bit lacking.

"I'm sorry," he told the clerk, who was standing near the fire, polishing his glasses with a handkerchief.

"For what?" the younger man responded.

"For not doing any more." Quinn sighed. "You did a fine thing today, riding out to warn me about Max. You may have saved both Anna's life and mine. I'm not sure whether I deserve the favor, but I thank you."

Horace stood in silence, his blue eyes forming a question that he did not voice.

Quinn continued. "Your father asked for help when outlaws started running off his herds. Hell, he didn't just ask, he begged for it. I rode to the ranch to check on things a few times, but of course by that time the raiders were long gone. Couldn't raise much interest in a posse, and the judge kept hammering home the point that I was paid to keep the town safe, not run all over the territory hunting rustlers. So I went back to dragging drunks out of saloons at closing time and arresting petty thieves."

"Wasn't that your job?" Horace asked him.

"I should have done more for him. You were still away at school, and I suspected his old friends had been warned off. But I turned a blind eye, didn't ask too many questions. Cameron had enough on me to make that difficult."

Horace put his glasses back on, but Quinn could still see how the eyes behind them watered.

"A lot of folks have been hurt by Cameron," Horace said quietly. "My question isn't what you did before. It's what will you do now."

"I'm going after Hamby, for starters," Quinn promised.

"And I'm going after Cameron. Will you help?"

Quinn stood and offered his hand. "In every way I can."

Horace accepted, and the two shook over his promise. He might have failed Horace's father, but Quinn swore he would help this Singletary.

No matter what the cost.

After she finished cleaning the scratches on the face of the deputy who had attacked her, the tall blonde stood, holding the bloody rag she'd used.

Remembering her own panic after Elena's attempt upon her life, Lucy wondered at this woman, who seemed so self-possessed. How could she separate crime from criminal to help the very man who'd meant to harm her? And how could she, as a woman perhaps no more than five years Lucy's senior, call herself a healer and dress in men's attire?

This territory was full of even stranger things than she'd imagined. But instead of being repelled by the differences between herself and this odd woman, Lucy wondered if some magic of the land had worked upon her, if the ruggedness of rock had somehow added mettle, if the endless bowl of blue sky had widened her perspective.

"I need to walk down to the arroyo so I can rinse this cloth," the blond woman explained.

"I'd like to stretch my legs too. May I come with you, Annie Faith?"

"It's Anna, please.

"We'll be right back," Anna told Sheriff Ryan and Horace, who remained deep in conversation near the fire.

The two women walked down to one of the pockets of water that lay along a crevice near the hillock's base. By then stars reflected on the small pool's surface. Above them warm yellow light danced between the men.

When Anna knelt to rinse the rag, Lucy could hear one of her knees pop. Ignoring it, the healer glanced up at her.

"How far along are you?" she asked.

Shock resonated through Lucy's core. If this stranger could see her condition, there was no hope of keeping it a secret any longer. Everyone she met would know; everyone would judge her.

"How?" Lucy began. "How can you . . . ?"

"The way you walk," Anna explained. "A woman balances herself differently as a child grows."

Lucy shook her head, and once more she felt panic welling up inside her as well as unreasoning anger with herself, with David, even with the unborn babe. "Everything's been out of balance ever since it started, about four months ago. And now—now—I don't know—"

"Shhh . . . A little while ago Quinn told me about what happened back in Copper Ridge. Lucy, an attempt was made on your life too. I remember . . . the first time it happened to me . . . when I was carrying a daughter, just as you are."

"A—a daughter?" Was there no limit to this woman's knowledge?

From the distance an eerie cry rose, a wild sound from a wild creature Lucy could not name. As the echo died away, Anna did not explain how she had formed this last opinion.

"Your daughter," she said instead in a voice as soft as the reflected starlight. "Your daughter is your gift, just as mine was."

"My baby—my daughter," Lucy said, accepting, "is illegitimate."

"Ridiculous," Anna admonished. "Every child is legitimate. Sin can't be handed down through generations. Each of us has the chance to commit our own. As you committed yours . . . and I committed mine."

"This baby is my punishment!" A rush of anger burned her face.

Anna chuckled without a trace of humor. "I'm not God, Lucy, but I'd say marrying Judge Ward Cameron is punishment enough for one lifetime. Loving your daughter, I swear to you, will be your reward—if you can let it. Cherish her for every day you have her."

A lump formed in Lucy's throat, and though she was genuinely curious about the woman, she could not bring herself to ask where Anna's child was now. For she had heard enough in the woman's voice to guess her daughter died.

Lucy took a deep breath—and felt movement, a quickening inside her. The first stirrings of a new life, the first stirrings of new hope.

# Chapter Fourteen

*Near Copper Ridge*
*April 12, 1884*

Cameron was the first to spot them, his wife riding a mule in the company of two men. To his utter shock, one of them was Horace Singletary. He'd been told that the bastard burned the night before last!

Had Lucy run to that weasel when she was frightened? He'd ignored Elena's tale of how his wife had "encouraged" the young man after he'd come ranting to The Pines. Elena might say anything, as jealous as she was.

Deep in the pit of his stomach, something burned at the thought of Elena, with her wild eyes and her hoarse shrieks. He felt as if he'd swallowed a live coal.

But before he had time to wonder if Elena had been right about his wife and the young clerk, yet another shock assailed him. Max Wilson was the second man, and he'd been tied onto his horse, which Singletary was now leading.

Cameron mainly recognized Wilson from his clothing.

His face looked as if it had gone a few rounds with an irate bobcat.

"That your wife?" Hadley had ridden up beside him and also stared down at the trio.

None of the riders appeared to see them, as they were partially hidden by the shadow of a taller live oak tree.

Cameron nodded.

"What do you make of this, then?" Hadley asked.

"Nothing good," Cameron said as his mind fumbled to piece together what had happened. Whatever Horace had told Lucy would surely be enough to end their marriage, especially considering its inauspicious start.

The thought of Lucy squalling home to Daddy Worthington was bad enough that Cameron thought of killing both Horace and Lucy. Ward wondered if maybe somehow he and Hadley could "find" the bodies and pin the murders on Elena.

But Max's presence and the ropes that bound him complicated things a great deal. It meant that somehow or other Quinn Ryan must have figured out what his deputy was up to. It also meant that Ryan, Singletary, and Lucy had all talked. For all Cameron knew, Ryan might have Anna with him too.

And all of them would know enough to ruin everything.

Hadley clapped a hand to Cameron's shoulder. "I remember what I owe you, friend. You need anything, just ask."

Cameron's mind raced as he thought of the ruination of all he'd worked to build. They could send him clear back to newspaper-covered walls and nothing in his belly. Hell, they could do worse. They could pack him off to Yuma for his crimes. Trapped among the men he'd sent there, he wouldn't last long enough to break a sweat in the intense heat of the desert prison.

The three riders moved in the direction of Copper Ridge until they passed out of sight.

"Can you make sure those three don't get back to Copper Ridge?"

"You want me to kill the county clerk, the deputy, and your own *wife*? Hell's bells, man, I don't mind payin' back what's due, but that's an awful lot of interest, don't you think?"

Cameron nodded stiffly. Hadley might have done some questionable things to defend his water from the sheep lovers, but he was a prosperous family man with too much to lose to get his hands this dirty. "Hell with that, then. Forget I asked. I'll figure out a way to straighten up that mess when I get back. There's just one thing I really need for you to do."

"Sure." Hadley looked relieved that he hadn't pushed harder.

"You still have that gunslinger on your payroll?"

"A man has to watch both his cattle and his water out here if his ranch is gonna last."

Cameron put a hand up. "I understand that. What I want is for you to send him into Copper Ridge to see if there's anyone holed up in Ryan's house. Anyone at all. If there is, there needs to be an accident. Or at the very least a permanent disappearance."

This was more Hadley's style. Send someone else, a hired gun, to do the actual killing. And if Anna Bennett had been hidden there, that would be one less complication.

Hadley backed his horse away a few steps, then turned its head toward town. "All right, Cameron. But you mark me 'paid in full.' You hear?"

"You could have hung," Ward reminded him coolly, thinking of the band of Mormons that had been found dead on his range.

Hadley's blue eyes burned with defiance. "And so could you. You comin' back to town now?"

Cameron shook his head. "Not yet. I have another thing to settle first."

*Cañon de Sangre de Cristo*

"This way," Anna advised, pointing out a cleft of red rock to their left. "If we ride down into the canyon on the main trail, there are too many places where we might be ambushed."

Quinn glanced upward to the sheer and narrow walls. A shaft of sunlight slipped between the building gray clouds and into the same slot where they would have to ride their horses single file. His expression looked dubious, but after a moment he relented. "If you say so."

Anna had never thought much before about the closeness, but his misgivings made her feel hemmed in by her safe haven, even the wider canyon opening. Or perhaps it wasn't Quinn at all. Perhaps leaving the canyon for a few days had somehow changed her outlook. The air she'd breathed had swept across the land unbounded; the skies she saw formed a great bowl, not a strip.

Glancing once more at the wide expanse above, she urged her mount into the slim corridor that would lead her home once more. Her horse's hooves echoed loudly against the windswept rock. Startled by the change in tone and volume, the bay snorted and rose on its rear legs.

"It's all right," Anna reassured him, but her voice rebounded off the smooth walls.

The gelding shuffled, bumping rock, and whinnied shrilly in its fear.

"Hold it," Anna warned Quinn. After much coaxing, she backed the bay out of the channel.

"Maybe he'll follow if I go first," Quinn suggested. But Titania, as if spooked by the gelding's fear, pranced and sidestepped. Despite Quinn's reassurances she steadfastly refused to enter the narrow passageway.

"I don't understand it. Canto never seemed to mind," Anna complained. But Canto had been so old that few things stirred his blood. She grimaced, remembering how he had started just before the cougar had attacked. She should have realized then that something was amiss.

She dismounted and made one last attempt to lead the bay in, but the horse planted his feet as stubbornly as any mule.

"I suppose it's the main trail after all," Anna said. "But mind the caves up on the east side. Anyone could hide there."

"You're such a comfort," Quinn said.

She remounted and they rode forward together, both knowing that trouble—in the form of a gun barrel—could await them from behind any of a thousand trees or rocks.

Lucy shifted in the saddle. Although she'd felt pummeled by the rough buffeting of the stage into Copper Ridge, she had never suffered a fraction of the discomfort that riding this mule caused. She had ridden before from time to time—wearing an elegant equitation outfit and sitting upon a proper sidesaddle. However, her earlier outings had merely been brief jaunts designed for the healthful exposure to fresh air and sunshine, and always she had ridden the smoothest and gentlest of mounts.

She was likely the first Worthington to ever sit on so disagreeable a creature as this mule. It stank, for one thing, and whenever Horace helped her mount it, it tried to kick at her. Instead of a feather touch with her heels, she had to "kick hard enough to show it you mean business," as Horace advised her. Since she'd left without her gloves, her hands were chapped and red from hauling on the reins. That discomfort dimmed, though, compared to her sore thighs and bottom.

"I'll make a muleskinner of you yet," Horace called from his horse. "He's starting to respect you now. Your arms won't have to work so hard."

If only the same could be said of all her body parts. She

was too miserable to return his smile, but even so, his compliment felt good. Though she'd never admit such a thing aloud, she felt a little proud of her escape and the way she was now managing her rough mount. The Lucy of four months ago never could have done it.

Glancing at Max Wilson, who appeared to be dozing in his saddle, she felt the spark of satisfaction doused. She might have fled Elena and kept her seat on the mule, but her troubles were still far from over. Partially because of the deputy, she would have to go with Horace to Copper Ridge once more.

"We'll be glad to take him back to Stan," Horace had told Quinn Ryan that morning. "That's the least I can do, after your loan."

"No," Quinn had answered earnestly. "That was the least *I* could do. Tell Stan to be sure he's locked up good and tight until I get back to see to charges. It'd be best to keep this quiet too, so the judge doesn't catch wind of it and turn him loose."

Horace agreed. Later he explained to Lucy that Stan, the owner of the livery stable, was a friend of Sheriff Ryan's and a decent man.

The idea of riding back to Copper Ridge deeply frightened Lucy. If she encountered that murderess Elena, she would doubtless expire on the spot from terror. The sheriff had promised to thoroughly investigate Miss Rathbone's death as soon as he returned to town, but until that happened, Elena could be anywhere.

However, both Quinn Ryan and Horace persuaded Lucy that it would be unwise in these parts to continue riding the "borrowed" mule. Even as the judge's wife, she'd have difficulty escaping punishment if the owner pressed theft charges.

"Don't worry," Horace reassured her as if he sensed her distress. "I promised I would help you—and I will. We'll keep clear of The Pines. After we return the mule, we'll buy another horse and some supplies with the money Sheriff Ryan lent me." He patted his chest pocket, where the sheriff's cash remained. "Then we'll get away from Copper Ridge."

"To where?" Lucy asked him quietly.

"To Tucson, where the *Territorial Gazette* is located. I'm not only going to give them Cameron's story, I'm going to write my way into a job as a reporter."

The determination sparkling in his blue eyes made her believe he'd succeed. "Aren't you worried the judge will find some way to stay in power? He could ruin you."

"He already has once—and I've survived. But you heard what Miss Bennett told us last night. Between my testimony and hers, Cameron will lose his judgeship—and probably his freedom."

Lucy pressed a palm against her forehead. She felt dizzy with the implications. "I still can't believe I married such a man. I'll need to send a telegram to Father as soon as possible."

"How do you think he'll react?"

"He'll say Cameron was a fool for 'getting himself caught.' And I daresay he'll somehow think I'm guilty of ruining both the marriage and the judge. He'll doubtless arrange for a divorce—perhaps even an annulment, given the circumstances. And he'll send money enough to bring me home. He wouldn't want it said he'd stranded me in some territorial outpost surrounded by Mexicans and heathens. At least, that's how he would put it."

"And once you go home, then what will he do?"

"By then he'll see that I'm with child. My father is a man of legion flaws, but he does know how to count months. He'll realize immediately whose baby this must be. I'll be sent away to my aunt's for my confinement. And then—" Her voice hitched with the thought. "Then he'll take her away from me, to—to allow some 'proper family' to raise her.

Anna's words flooded back into her consciousness. *Loving your daughter, I swear to you, will be your reward—if you can let it.*

Placing her palm on the small prominence of her belly, Lucy remembered the fluttering she'd felt inside and the strong surge of hope that had stirred with it. Maybe this country was broadening her expanses too, changing her future into a form that could be shaped with enough will and courage.

She looked up into Horace's blue eyes. "I can't let Father take her from me. I won't go back home."

Horace Singletary, Lucy Cameron, Quinn Ryan, Anna Bennett. They all knew enough to ruin him, thought Cameron. He racked his brain for ideas about what he could do, but the only thought that he could conjure was *Cut your losses and get out.*

Jesus, he would have to. He thought about the spreading web of others who might be enticed to testify against him. Max Wilson, Hadley, even the three men he'd coerced into burning Singletary's bunkhouse.

But he knew from experience that retribution in the territory could be slow. Especially with no local lawman to arrest him. If Quinn Ryan never returned to Copper Ridge and if Anna Bennett turned up dead, he might just be able to slide through his claim. Then he could sell it and get out before a trial took place.

Couldn't he?

His forehead beaded with sweat despite the protection of a thickening layer of gray clouds. Goddammit, he would make this work. He was going to have to. He could run—could leave the country. Unlike others, he had not been born with a good name. He had built his, and he could build another.

In Canada. They'd expect him to head for Mexico, since

it was so much closer. But he'd had enough of deserts; he wanted to see green. In Canada he'd know the language. He could start again there as long as he had money.

Without it he might as well ride straight for Yuma. Without it he might as well be dead.

The rest might all be lost, but he could still have money. As long as Quinn Ryan and Anna Bennett were both dead.

---

As the sky dimmed and the light rain increased, Horace wondered where they would stay that night. Lucy had camped out the previous night without complaint, though he imagined she'd never before even considered sleeping out of doors on the hard ground, protected only by a borrowed blanket. Another night in the open, in the rain, and close to town, seemed out of the question.

At least the weather kept the streets deserted.

But not the livery stable. Stan Roberts fed the horses every evening around this time, and horses' stomachs didn't care about the weather. Horace was thankful, for he was eager to part ways with his sullen prisoner. He tied his buckskin mare outside the livery stable and helped Lucy dismount.

While she rubbed her back, he began untying the rope that bound Max's ankles together beneath the belly of his horse.

Stan Roberts stepped through the wide double doors, a feed bucket in each huge hand. Stan had always had a way with horses. Horace's papa had once said Stan's secret was his size; the animals knew that if it came down to it, the brawny man could throw a draft horse. Though Stan's hair had long since grayed, he retained most of his muscle, yet as far as Horace knew, he saved his brawn for tossing bales instead of livestock.

Stan put down the buckets, ignoring the hungry nickers of two horses in their small corrals. Folding his thick arms, he watched the scene at his business's front door with an expression of concern. The fact that he'd also just lifted Judge Cameron's wife off a mule that neither owned merely added to the strangeness of the circumstances.

"Understand you had trouble, but I thought you might still come to sell me that mare of yours today," he said at length to Horace.

"I got a little busy, Stan. Didn't get to it," Horace said by way of explanation. He nodded toward Max, who glared fiercely in response. "The sheriff asked me to have you lock him in a cell. He'll be back in a few days to take care of the charges."

"Quinn wants me to lock *him* up?" he asked, squinting toward Max's scratched and swollen face. "You sure he didn't say to fetch the doctor?"

"If you know what's good for you, you'll do just that." Max's voice had soured during all the sullen hours of their ride. "Ryan's making one hell of a mistake. No need for you to get sucked in as well."

"You been hitting the cactus juice again, Max? I warned you it would likely cost your job," Stan said. "I'll make you some coffee thick enough to sober you."

"He tried to kill a woman," Horace said.

Max raised his voice, as if doing so would drown out the accusation. "Don't listen to him! How long you think this pissant place will last if you mess with the judge?"

"A woman?" Stan's expression darkened with disapproval. He glanced quickly at Lucy, then back to Max once more. "You tried to kill a *woman*, Max?"

"Goddammit!" Max roared. "She ain't no lady! She's a thief, a criminal, a whore!"

"How dare you say such things!" Lucy interrupted, suddenly indignant. "After all she did to help y—"

But her protests were drowned out as Stan grasped Max by his shirt and lifted him, one-armed, against the stable wall. His head and shoulders thudded against wood, and a quick check showed his booted feet hung several inches from the ground.

"You apologize to the lady right this instant!" Stan Roberts thundered.

"B-but I d-didn't mean h-her!" Max choked out.

Another thud. This one shook the livery wall. A startled horse inside whinnied in fright.

"I don't give a—" Again he glanced at Lucy, then quickly amended his words. "I don't *care* at all. Your mama taught you better than to talk like that in front of ladies!"

"You stupid son of a—" Max began to say. He never got the chance to finish.

*Bam!* This time Max's head bounced back, then sagged.

Stan Roberts kept him from falling long enough to check his breathing. Then he hoisted the unconscious man over one broad shoulder.

He tipped his hat to Lucy. "My apologies, ma'am. He wasn't brought up that way, I assure you. I'll go lock him up now, and I'll make sure he's fed until Quinn gets back to sort this out."

After Stan walked toward the jail, Lucy turned to Horace. "Those men are related, aren't they?"

Horace nodded. "Stan's his stepfather. Married Lena Wilson a few years after Max's father passed away. He treasured the woman."

"She's gone?"

"She died a few months before I left for college."

"Sheriff Ryan trusted him to lock up his own stepson?"

Horace nodded. "You see the kind of man he is. Quinn's spent enough time with him to know that Stan would do the same thing even if Max were his natural son."

"Because doing it was right . . ."

She lapsed into quiet thoughtfulness.

Horace gestured toward the stable. "Come in out of the rain."

She followed him inside the wide double doorway, where they waited until Stan returned.

He removed his hat as he spoke to Lucy. "There's been talk around town about what's become of you, ma'am. Manuel Santiago's been looking high and low."

"I . . . I see," Lucy said, her voice brimming with caution.

"So what's the talk?" Horace asked.

"Manuel claims Elena went clean out of her mind. There's a dead woman out at The Pines who needs explaining, and Manuel was afraid that maybe his cousin did something to you. But when the old man's mule turned up missing, he thought maybe you'd run off."

Lucy bobbed her head. "I had to. I—I'm a stranger here. I didn't know if anyone would believe me. And I knew Manuel and Elena were related."

"Manuel is as honest as they come. He wouldn't have liked it any better than I liked locking up my stepson, but he would have seen to it that she faced justice all the same."

"Would have?" Lucy echoed. "What does that mean?"

Horace stepped closer, noticing how pale her face had gone. She looked as if she might faint at any moment.

"Elena Santiago won't be buried inside the fence there in the churchyard. The padre is a stickler about allowing suicides on hallowed ground."

Horace heard the sharp intake of Lucy's breath, and he prepared to catch her. But she did not waver.

"Elena . . . Elena killed herself?"

"Slit her own throat with a kitchen knife." He shuddered as if the image had elicited a chill. "But it might as well have been a murder, too, is what folks think. I'm sorry to say this of your husband, but Ward Cameron broke that girl's heart—and her mind too."

Lucy drew herself to her full height, which couldn't have been more than five feet. "Forgive me if I sound uncharitable, but I can't much sympathize with her. She poisoned the woman who helped raise me, and she meant to take my life as well. As for my *husband*, I hope when he takes his place with her in hell, she's saved him a warm spot."

Stan looked stunned for a moment, but he quickly scraped together his manners once again. "Perfectly understandable, ma'am. More and more folks are starting to share your opinion on the judge. No offense, I hope."

"None taken," she said crisply.

Horace thought it might be wise to change the subject. "Whose mule did you say Lucy borrowed? We'll need to take it back."

"I've trimmed that animal's hooves a time or two. It's Tío Viejo's—at least that's what the Mexicans call him. Means 'old uncle,' I think. Never heard him called by any other name. He does some fair doctoring for a blind man, I've heard tell, but not the kind you'd get back east."

"Then we'll go see him." Horace stuck his hand out. "Thanks for being here."

Stan took his hand—and held it. Their size difference was much too great to fight, so Horace waited, knowing that the stable owner had something more to say.

"There's talk about you too, Horace. Town's a-buzzin' like a nest of stirred-up rattlers. Might be best if you stay out of sight. The gossip's turned against 'His Honor,' but he's still got plenty on his payroll, if you take my meaning."

"You know about my house?"

"I know."

"And they don't think I died there?"

Roberts shook his head. "I helped search through the rubble myself, and I was happy not to find you. What with both you and Mrs. Cameron disappearing so close, there's those that think you might have run off together. If they see the two of you, the wags'll likely pop their eyes out."

"I thank you for your concern, but I'm past worrying about my reputation," Lucy told him.

"Maybe you care more about his life," Stan added bluntly. "That sort of talk could get him killed."

Lucy's gaze swung toward Horace. "Of course. I'm sorry. I was thinking only of myself. Maybe we should separate."

Horace took her hand. "Is that what you want, Lucy?"

She hesitated for a moment, and in that narrow span he felt his heart stop beating. Then she shook her head emphatically.

Until then he hadn't realized how completely some part of him had claimed her, even though she was married to his greatest enemy.

Lucy's gaze flicked toward Roberts and then returned to him. "You said you would help me. I'm not going to let you get away so easily." Her voice dropped then so he could barely hear it. "And it sounds as if you could use a friend yourself."

But her dark eyes bespoke an offer more than friendship, an offer nothing in the world could convince him to refuse.

---

Often, fires smolder for days after they have burned. Though the blaze that had burned Anna's cabin may have been set hours earlier or perhaps even the night they left the canyon, the breeze yet lifted puffs of smoke, and the charred smell still burned his nostrils.

Quinn shuddered, reminded briefly of the carbonized dead trappers he and Max had found, then more strongly of the burned-out Navajo hogan. He could almost see Ned Hamby grinning, those small, blood-clumped scalps still swinging in his fist.

*Once I pick the nits off, scrape the hair, and stretch 'em, might make a decent pair of winter moccasins, I 'magine.*

A wave of nausea nearly choked him, and icy prickles climbed his back and neck. Thinking of the sick mementos he'd found stuffed in the saddlebag, his own scalp tingled.

Despite the gunshot he had suffered, he felt fortunate to still have it on his head.

Anna dismounted the bay and dropped the reins without bothering to tie her horse. Quinn slid down from his mare and wrapped both animals' reins around small trees upwind from the drifting puffs of gray.

Afterward he circled the entire cabin in search of prints that might help him determine which way the outlaws had gone when they left. The hoofprints he found disturbed him. How had Hamby's men been resupplied with mounts so soon? At first he thought his earlier suspicion about the presence of other members of the band in the area had been correct. But he found only two distinct sets of tracks, both equine, leading away toward the canyon entrance. Either the men had doubled up to ride together, or—

His gaze fell to the blackened timbers. Had someone else come to see Anna? Had those bastards killed again, then burned the proof?

The smoking remnants remained too hot to search for answers. And the most recent pile of horse manure he found wasn't fresh enough to suggest that Hamby—and the answers—remained close enough to either pose a threat or overtake that night.

Putting those chores behind him, he watched the stiff way Anna stood before the smoldering wreckage of her belongings. He wanted to go to her, to comfort her for what she'd lost, but somehow, interrupting her felt wrong. Once more, as he looked on, he felt a prickling sensation. His skin erupted into gooseflesh, though waves of heat still rolled off the coals. But instead of horror, the impression this time felt eerily consoling. Moments later his hesitation lifted, and he began walking toward Anna, yet he could not honestly say his own mind moved his feet.

If Anna heard his steps, she ignored them, though he stood so close to her that he could hear her breaths. A few minutes before, the sun had slid beneath the layer of the clouds beyond the western red-rock wall. Its absence gave over this part of the canyon to the early evening gloom. He thought of all the years she had spent here, cast into the premature dusk of this shadowed land, burying herself within this deep rock tomb. For that, more than her burned cabin, he wanted to hold her, to weep with her for all their wasted time.

Yet nothing in her posture indicated she was grieving. Light enough remained to see that her shoulders did not tremble, her body did not shake. The sounds of her breathing, although rapid, betrayed no quiet sobbing. Perhaps, he thought, she was too shocked to cry.

Notion snuffed frantically, trotting from one heap to another, as if he wondered where his home had gone.

A spattering of raindrops fell. Despite the quiet sounds of the creek's flow and the breezes playing among treetops, Quinn heard the water hiss against the still-hot coals.

He reached out for Anna, but before his hand met her shoulder, she turned to face him. Her smoky blue-gray eyes were glimmering with unshed tears, but they were bright, so bright.

"She's still here," Anna told him, her voice betraying no surprise that he'd moved so close. "Can't you feel her?"

This time, instead of fighting the idea, he let the chill ripple over him, *into him*. He felt no fear, though nothing in his Catholic upbringing had prepared him for such a possibility.

"I *do* feel something," he admitted, "and I believe you when you say it's her. *Rosalinda.*"

The name tasted of honey, reminding him of her mother's voice. Reaching out, he pulled Anna against him. Their mouths moved together; their lips touched in the most delicate of kisses.

Only then did Anna shudder, as if that kiss unlocked some gate. In a moment he felt her tears against his face— or perhaps it was only the increasing rain. She pulled back enough to whisper in his ear. "They couldn't take her from me this time, so they took everything else."

And they had. The small outbuildings, too, had been burned, even the timbers of the corral now smoldered, and no trace of Anna's goats or chickens remained. Except for what she carried, she had nothing left.

She pulled down the brim of her hat, which had been knocked askew as they had kissed. She used the back of her hand to wipe away the dampness on her cheek.

Relief surged through Quinn's system. Nothing now remained to tie her to this place.

"I want to marry you," he told her. His words were followed quickly by a forewarning of disaster. Instead of coming out the way he meant it, his offer sounded selfish, like that of a boy who wouldn't mind the thought of winning by default.

Anna's expression, shadowed by the wide brim of her leather hat, was difficult to read. But there was no mistaking the anger in her words. "Damn you, Ryan! Do you think I want your pity? Just because I love you doesn't mean that I don't want my life back! Can't you feel it? Rosalinda needs me here!"

It was the only time he could remember her swearing, at least in English. He felt fairly certain she had cursed him in Spanish many times.

She had pulled away, so he stepped closer. Close enough to touch her—but he didn't. Mad as she was, he didn't want to end up looking like his deputy.

"I'm sorry," Quinn offered. "That didn't come out the way I wanted it to sound. I . . . I love you so much, Anna. I have this awful sense of how many years we wasted, how much grief we both went through alone. I don't want that anymore. I want you . . . but only if you want me too. If you don't want to marry me, I'll help you get started elsewhere. Somewhere you'll never have to see my face again."

He stared at her and prayed for all he was worth that she wouldn't call his bluff.

She shook her head, flinging raindrops from her hat's brim into his face. "You're still a gambler, aren't you, Ryan?"

He tried to look wounded, in the hope that she'd have mercy. It didn't help a bit.

"Come on," she said, flipping the brim of his hat with her thumb. "This rain is setting in, and we'll get soaked. I know a place where we can hole up for the night."


*"Bienvenidos,"* said the old man who showed them into the shack. "I have been expecting both of you."

Even in the dim light Lucy saw the clouding of his ancient eyes, but even so, she would swear he really knew her.

"Come inside, Señora Cameron," Tío Viejo said, confirming her suspicion. "And bring your friend as well."

If not for Horace's presence, she didn't think she could have forced herself to go inside the shabby dwelling. As it was, she hesitated.

"Go in," Horace told her quietly, "before someone sees us from the street."

Horace offered his hand to the old man and introduced himself and Lucy despite the fact that the old man behaved as if he already knew them both.

Apparently not seeing the outstretched hand, Tío Viejo groped for several cowhide-covered stools.

"Please sit down," he offered, then took his own advice. "I knew you would come here. I told Manuel already you were safe somewhere and hiding. A frightful thing, what happened with Elena. Who can blame you for borrowing an old man's mule?"

"I'm sorry all the same," Lucy apologized as she sank

carefully onto a seat. "I was afraid you would think that he'd been stolen."

Tío Viejo waved off her words. "Bah! You are no mule thief. Only a frightened girl. I tell you what. For my part in this, I give you Paquito."

"For your part?" Lucy echoed, confused on several counts.

The old man nodded, then sighed heavily. "Elena stole the poison from my home. She confess to me she use it in her baking. Many things I cannot see, but I know others. But *Dios* did not see fit to warn me just how troubled that lost child had become. Or maybe I just close my eyes and hope. For that, forgive me, *por favor.*"

"It wasn't your fault," Lucy insisted. "But what do you mean, you give me—what did you call it?—Paquito. What is that?"

Tío Viejo's laugh was thin and brittle—and ended in a spasmodic coughing. Recovering, he said, "Paquito is my mule. So no one can ever say you stole it, I make him *un regalo*, a gift."

"Oh! Thank you, but I can't accept such a gener—"

"Bah!" he interrupted with that same wave of dismissal. "I am far too old to ride about on such an animal. He is too much to care for for a dying man."

"Surely you aren't dying!" She didn't know why the thought should so upset her. She had only just met him. And besides, he was a Mexican, a man who lived in a cramped shack filled with drying roots and branches, a man who smelled as though he hadn't bathed in a long while. She was shocked to realize that none of that mattered any longer. All that mattered were his generous spirit and the kindness in his wrinkled face.

He smiled as if he knew the ways that she had changed. "I welcome this long night, my daughter. The day has been so tiring. Just take good care of Paquito."

She didn't quite know what to say. She sensed that

despite its willful ugliness, that mule was the finest gift she'd ever received.

"Thank you." Not the right words exactly, but they seemed to suffice.

"Now you can ride him home," the old man said.

"Home? But home is too far. It's in . . ." Where *was* her home? She'd meant to say Connecticut. Now she wasn't sure.

This time Tío Viejo found Horace's hand. With his other hand he reached for Lucy's. She let the old man join her hand with Horace's, and once again she felt something powerful pass between them, something she hadn't fully recognized before.

"You both will know it when you reach it," said the old man, "but only by journeying together can you find your place."

Horace squeezed her hand and stared at her intently. "I think you're wrong," he told the old man. "When I look at her I see it. It's reflected in her eyes."

He moved so much closer, he shared the vision with her in a kiss so sweet, it sealed their future.

Though the day's warmth had ebbed as the sun met the horizon, Ward Cameron once more mopped sweat from his forehead. Rain pattered off his hat brim, adding to his damp discomfort. Glancing at the low clouds, he wondered if there was anywhere he might spend the night to shelter from the rain.

He had to admit that riding alone after Quinn and Anna Bennett had been a mistake, the result of panic and not clearheaded logic. He'd easily followed their horses' tracks as far as the canyon's entrance, but afterward the trail faded and then vanished onto windswept rock.

He had ridden for hours more, believing this to be the same canyon he meant to claim and then mine for its silver. But nowhere did he find a trace of Quinn or Anna or any other person. Too frustrated to continue, he yanked his horse's reins and swore in the fading echo of its footsteps.

Mammoth walls towered above him, their jagged ridges unmoved by his fiercest oaths, their smooth red planes indifferent to influence. Not far away a small stream tumbled cheerily over round gray rocks.

His stallion pricked its ears eagerly toward the gurgling water. Cameron rode the palomino closer, then dismounted, reasoning that both horse and rider could profit from a drink. And in his case, time to think as well, about what he would do now, since he had lost the pair he'd trailed.

Doubt crept up Cameron's arms, colder even than the water he drank from his cupped hands. Again he considered simply riding out of there and heading north for Canada and a new beginning. But going now meant that he would start with nothing, less than nothing since he would no longer be able to resort to practicing the law.

At that moment his thoughts were interrupted by a glimpse of riders in the distance. Keeping very still so as to attract no notice, Cameron watched them. He could make out two, but at this distance he couldn't tell for certain whether it was the sheriff with a woman or someone else.

He cautioned himself that out here he might even come upon Ned Hamby. The thought caused more sweat to bead on his upper lip and forehead. Hamby in his office, in *his* territory, was one matter, but this place was the outlaw's own domain, where a judge might be robbed and murdered just as easily as an Indian squaw. No, it wouldn't do to meet Hamby here alone.

So with that in mind Cameron decided he would follow carefully to try to identify the riders, and if they proved to be his quarry, to find a place to ambush them without risking his own hide.

*Cañon de Sangre de Cristo*
*April 13, 1884, Easter Sunday*

Anna held her infant daughter against her shoulder and gently stroked her tiny back. "Shhh . . ." she urged, "don't cry now," though the child had been still for hours.

In the bright October moonlight she walked beside the stream with Rosalinda, where dried leaves whispered with her passage and the music of the water offered its soothing sound. Anna wished that she could sing too, wished she could remember the words to any lullaby, to any song at all. She thought she recalled a snatch of melody, but when she tried to hum it, the notes spun apart like leaves carried downstream by the swift but shallow flow.

She'd risen from the chair where she'd held vigil to come here, risen in the darkness so she would not have to face Señora Valdez, with her sad and knowing gaze. Risen so she could walk with Rosalinda's tiny, cooling form pressed close against her aching bosom, so she could be a mother for a little while more.

Then it occurred to her, she could be. She could hold on for as long as it was needed. Not by Rosalinda, who needed nothing further. But as long as Anna needed, as long as she stayed there.

She kissed the little forehead, then tucked her daughter's lamb's-wool blanket more snugly about her. If she blurred her eyes just so, Anna could pretend her daughter was still sleeping . . . for a little while more.

Yet even within dreams the seasons change too swiftly. This time her arms were empty as she walked along the stream while it was frozen, in the bright glare of winter sun upon the drifted snow. Her feet punched holes into the icy crust, and the deep chill radiated up both of her legs. Yet Anna felt warmed by something, a breath of a mild October breeze, remembered moonlight from a solemn autumn night. It enshrouded her, made her feel protected as a babe herself.

As Anna began to rouse, the dream began to ebb. Still, within those last few fleeting moments, she longed to walk again beside that stream, even though, since the coming of Quinn Ryan, the lonely canyon bottom had at last been touched by spring.

Anna's eyes slid open, and for just a moment the light fooled her into thinking day had dawned. Instead, the three-quarter moon's illumination had flooded the shallow cave where she and Quinn lay sleeping. Still tired from a long day in the saddle, she wiped away the tears left over from her dream. Then she pulled her bedroll closer to Quinn's and spooned her body against his before sinking back to sleep.

Ned had decided they should hole up in the caves a spell, to give Hop's wounded leg a chance to mend. The cabin would have been a damn sight more comfortable, but he wasn't sorry Hop had set the fire. Those caves had always worked on his nerves, but his worst misgivings were nothing compared to the way he'd felt in that clearing by the cabin.

Ned shuddered. No, he wasn't sorry they had burned the place. He wouldn't have spent another night down there for all the judge's gold.

He nudged Hop with his foot. "You hear them horses? They sound restless."

Hop mumbled something inaudible in reply.

Ned kicked harder. "You oughta go check on 'em." He didn't like the thought of climbing down to where they'd tied the animals.

Instead of waking, Hop just curled away from him and snored.

"Goddammit! Can't count on you boys for a thing." He'd forgotten for a moment that Hop was his last man.

He heard another nicker and the stamp of hooves. The horses didn't sound alarmed, but something had disturbed them.

Ned moved cautiously to the cave's opening. Though the moon had dipped low, its bluish light yet illuminated the craggy bowl of the canyon bottom. But clumps of brush and shadow hid the horses. He wished like hell he could see them. He hadn't killed two men just to have some thieving Indians steal the horses or some hungry predator run them off.

After pulling on his boots, Ned buckled on his holster and checked his Navy Colt to be certain each chamber held a bullet. Last of all he tucked his sheathed knife into his belt. With or without Hop's assistance he intended to make whatever was down there pay the price for his interrupted sleep.

*"My only love sprung from my only hate . . ."*

Anna barely recognized her own voice as it talked her out of sleep.

"Whaaa?" Quinn, lying nearby on the cave floor, stirred, but barely, before drifting off again.

She leaned forward to brush her lips across his stubbled cheek.

"It's all right," she whispered softly. And it was, for Shakespeare's line was followed by more words. Lyrics slid out of the darkness, a thousand luminous snatches, each one caught and woven on a loom of melody.

Her mind brimmed with her lost music. She could again sing if she but chose to, any song she wished. Each one in

English and to its final verse. And all the joy rushed back to her, that first pure joy of singing, not of being heard.

But the only notes that filled the night were those of the nocturnal insects and a solitary howl not far away. Anna's songs slashed along the crimson ribbon of her scar, filling her with emotions too raw to give voice. Not only ecstasy, but deep grief, for she felt utterly certain that with the restoration of her music, there had come an awful void.

No longer could she hear her daughter's weak cries, no matter how she strained her memory. Though she still recalled that moonlit walk beside the autumn stream, she could not place herself there, to feel the bare weight of the cooling body, to see the rounded outline of her baby's pallid cheek.

For better or for worse, Rosalinda's time was done here. And Anna felt just as bereft as if she'd lost her child again.

Too bereft for tears. She moved to the cave's entrance and sat inside an oval of silvery light cast by the setting moon. Miserable, she barely noticed that the sky was growing lighter to the east.

As if he sensed her mood, Notion rose from the corner he'd been warming and stretched stiffly. He joined her and then lay with his broad head on her knee.

As she rubbed the loose skin behind his neck, something large stirred on the hill below her. She heard the horses mutter nervously.

The dog's ears perked in the direction of the noises.

Thinking of the howl she'd heard before, Anna whispered, "What do you think, Notion? Coyotes?"

At the mention of coyotes Notion growled and bounded down the hill. Anna decided she should go and check as well.

She glanced toward Quinn and decided there was no need to disturb him. She and Notion had chased a lot of coyotes in their endless, futile quest to save her chickens.

**Besides,** she reasoned, she'd have Max Wilson's revolver with her. It would more than likely take just one shot to run off the hairy villains.

Then she could return to Quinn and devise a more pleasant method to end his night's rest.

Before Anna, Quinn had never proposed marriage to a woman. As his mind replayed the way he'd bungled this attempt, he decided his inexperience definitely showed. Or maybe that wasn't the problem. He imagined men with better timing had to suffer through it only once.

And it was a form of suffering, wondering if she'd ever have him. Wondering how he'd go back to living on his own if she did not. Would he ever be able to move past Anna? Would he someday find another woman to fill the empty years?

He turned restlessly, knowing even in his sleep that he wanted no one else. Knowing that somehow he had to make Anna see . . .

He sat up. To hell with sleeping if he had to worry in his dreams. He had to talk to Anna, to convince her that even if he had to stay with her in this canyon, no one else would ever do for him.

Looking through the cave's mouth, he saw that the sinking moon was dimming in the lightening predawn sky. His heart thudded painfully as he realized Anna was no longer with him. She had left during the night. Left him without even a good-bye. His hands searched the still-dark corners so swiftly that his fingers stubbed against cold stone. But he felt no more than he saw, except—

He breathed again when he realized her blanket remained, as well as her canteen and saddle pack. Little as she had now, she would never leave those necessities.

But then, where had she gone? Even if she'd simply left to check the horses or attend the needs of nature, she should have let him know. Predators roamed this canyon, perhaps human ones as well. Although they'd seen no signs along the rocky trail, it was possible Hamby and his boys remained nearby.

At least she'd taken Notion. He did a quick search and determined she had Max's gun as well. Instead of going after her and maybe getting shot, he'd sit and wait for a few moments, and she would come right back.

Except the moments stacked up on each other like a deck of playing cards. And none of them brought Anna back where he could hold her safe and close.

# Chapter Fifteen

Ned damn near jumped out of his skin when loud barking erupted. He leapt atop a rock and jerked his head, all the time expecting the blond bitch's cur to finish tearing him to shreds.

Something streaked past, swift and silvery. Then another streak. Coyotes, he realized. But he scarcely had time to feel relief before the huge gold dog, too, raced by him.

He drew his gun but too late. Though he peered intently, the animals seemed to disappear in the poor light. Within seconds the dog's deep-throated barks, too, faded.

Ned's heart felt like it would explode inside his chest, and for half a minute he crouched atop the rock in an attempt to slow his breathing.

And then he saw the woman trotting in the same direction her dog had run.

"Notion?" she called but not too loudly, as if she feared that someone else might hear.

She was so intent on the fading barks that she never saw him slide behind her, never heard him until he leapt and brought her down. She slammed into the ground beneath his weight. Slammed so hard, she did not scream.

"You shoulda left here, you stupid slut. Shoulda left and never come on back," Ned hissed. But she did not respond, and her body's utter limpness convinced him he had somehow knocked her unconscious, maybe even broke her neck and killed her.

"Goddammit!" he swore. He didn't want her dead, at least not yet. Now she couldn't scream or fight him, couldn't do a thing to make him hard.

"Bitch!" Yanking back her head, he screamed frustration in her ear, wanting her so badly, yet unable to perform.

At least he had his knife. Drawing it, he slashed at her forehead—just before he heard an outraged shout.

Quinn couldn't wait another moment. He started downhill from the cave just as somewhere nearby Notion's loud barks broke the predawn stillness.

As Quinn raced toward the sound, he realized they were quickly fading, as if the dog were chasing something fast. His heart pounding, Quinn prayed the animal was only trailing a jackrabbit. He wanted so desperately to believe it that he imagined himself shouting at the mongrel for scaring him half out of his mind. Reaching further, he imagined Anna laughing at his panic.

Then he came to the narrow clearing, and those hopes were snuffed out like a candle flame at bedtime. He stopped dead still, his mind unable to conceive that what he saw was anything but a nightmare. Ned Hamby, knee planted atop Anna's back, holding up her hair and—God help him—it was real—Hamby was scalping her dead body!

His pain and shock exploded in a single exclamation. "NO!"

* * *

Pain brought Anna back, the bright pain that arced across her forehead. Ignoring the weight pressed against her spine, she reached to touch it, and she gasped at the streaming wetness and the flap of skin and hair. Her eyes rolled in her skull at the realization she'd been scalped—or near enough to cost her life.

Nausea choked her. If she didn't bleed to death, she would die of infection unless help came for her—and soon.

Stupid, to think she would have time to bleed out. The knee pressed against her back meant that whoever had done this was still there. She froze in horror, expecting the knife to finish hacking at her scalp at any moment, then expecting whatever death her attacker had in store.

"Hold it right there, mister!" Someone—not the man on her back—shouted. He sounded young but mean.

"Get off her!"

She instantly recognized Quinn Ryan's voice, enraged and terrified at once.

The man atop her laughed. "Don't make no nevermind to me. She's dead already. Just the way you're gonna be. Now throw your gun down 'fore Hop blows your damned head off."

*Reina del cielo*, it was Hamby! How in God's name had he caught her unawares? Once again his voice rendered her helpless. She couldn't fight against him if she tried, especially not with her strength spurting out of her forehead.

"Goddamn," the young man—apparently Hop—swore. "Didn't I kill you once already?"

"You're going to wish you had," Quinn growled.

She wished she could see him. One last glimpse of his face was all she asked.

The weight lifted from her back; Hamby rose and took

a few steps forward. Dimly she could see him put away his knife and draw his gun.

"You're in a hell of a spot to be threatening anybody," Ned told Quinn. "Now toss the goddamned gun before Hop and I both plug you."

Apparently Quinn did not comply.

"Now, you stubborn bastard!" Hamby screamed.

They were going to shoot him down, Anna realized. They were going to kill him while she bled to death. Already the edges of her vision were growing gray and hazy. Unconsciousness pulled at her like the moon tugging the tides.

*Why couldn't I tell him I would marry him? Why couldn't I move on?*

She'd been so intent on living in the past, on holding on to Rosalinda's memory, she hadn't been able to look forward to a future with her lover at her side. Yet tonight that last remnant of her daughter had gone home. Or maybe the old woman had been right. Rosalinda had never really been here. Perhaps, instead, Quinn Ryan had healed what Señora Valdez called her "sickness of the spirit."

Why had it taken her so long to listen to what the curing woman told her? Why had she waited until the moment of her death? Both of their deaths.

She shifted slightly, and her hip ground into something hard and painful. It was the revolver she had taken with her from the cave! Incredibly Hamby hadn't found it.

She heard a thunk—Quinn throwing down his pistol.

"On your knees!" screamed Hamby.

Could she force herself to use the gun beneath her hip? Her arms felt heavy as lead, and she recalled her failure with the rifle. But this time Quinn's life hung in the balance, not just her own. If she was going to die, she'd do it giving him a chance.

By focusing on Quinn's need, she managed to drag out the pistol. But when she raised it, she could see nothing for the blood that poured into her eyes.

God help her, she was as likely to shoot Quinn as to save him! And even if she didn't, Hop, the second man, stood somewhere out of sight. When she opened fire, would he kill Quinn? In an attempt to clear her vision she used her left wrist to try to wipe away the blood.

The pain exploding through her forehead was so severe that her hand unconsciously clenched, the index finger squeezing off a shot. And then all hell broke loose.

Gunfire seemed to erupt from everywhere at once. She was surprised to realize she was still shooting, shooting at every blast she heard.

She lost consciousness before she could determine what, if anything, she'd hit.


As Quinn dropped, he felt the wind of a bullet pass by his neck. Almost in the same instant he heard the boy behind him scream in agony.

Quinn slammed hard onto his sore shoulder and rolled toward the spot where he'd tossed his gun moments before. As he reached for it, he saw Hamby drop his aim, and he knew the gunman's second shot would not miss him.

But that bullet never came. Out of the corner of his eye Quinn saw the muzzle flash from Anna's revolver. A fraction of an instant later the sound of the gunshot exploded—as did Ned Hamby's left temple.

The bullet passed completely through the outlaw's skull. As he swayed on his feet for one final moment, his right temple erupted in a waterfall of gore.

Leaping to his feet, Quinn forgot everything but Anna. He raced toward her, his heart sinking at the sight. Her head had flopped to one side. With the first ruddy light of dawn, her face, which had appeared masked in obsidian, now looked wet and scarlet. If he didn't help her quickly, she would bleed to death.

Dropping to his knees, he reached down to touch her.

Behind him he heard a gun's click and a familiar voice. "Leave her be and get up."

*Cameron.* But what in God's name would he be doing here? Slowly Quinn turned toward the judge.

"She'll die if we don't help her."

The bastard shrugged, though his pistol pointed steadily at Quinn's heart.

"She's a criminal, a horse thief," Cameron told him. "Don't you remember? We hang them when we can."

"She's not the thief here, Cameron. We both know it."

The judge's thick mustache twitched, and his eyes brightened. "Perhaps not. Perhaps she's instead an unfortunate young woman, scalped by Navajo squatters. Her death could convince the army to clean them out of this canyon for me so my mine will be safe."

"You know the Navajo are innocent. Hamby did this."

Cameron shook his head. His smile seemed to radiate cold, as if his teeth were chunks of ice. "Your services will no longer be required, Quinn. I've found a more tractable sheriff. A whore and a bottle will be more effective than my threats against you ever were—"

"It took you this long to figure that you catch more flies with honey than with vinegar?" Quinn asked. Anything to keep Cameron talking. Maybe then he'd have a chance to think of something, anything, to get himself and Anna out of this alive.

The noise of a gunshot made both Quinn and Cameron duck for cover. Hop, apparently not dead of his injury, had fired on them both.

"Help me, you sorry bastards!" the boy screamed, his plea nearly incoherent. "Quit your jawin' and come help! It hurts so bad!"

He fired again, as if to force the issue.

Cameron, distracted for the moment, recovered just in time to see Quinn grab the gun from Anna's hand.

The judge would have shot first, except a bullet from

Hop's gun at that moment struck his lower left leg. His shout of pain and fury was cut short when Quinn shot him through the chest.

There was a sound of gurgling, and the judge spent his last breath. Hop, too, grew silent, as if he'd passed out or even died.

Shaking, Quinn crawled toward Anna. In the area around them, three men lay dead or dying, but as far as he was concerned, justice had been served. But what justice would there be—and what life for him remained—if the woman he loved were now dead too?

# Chapter Sixteen

*Cañon de Sangre de Cristo*
*April 14, 1884*

Anna's first consciousness was of Quinn Ryan's voice beside her. Too exhausted to open her eyes, she rested, listening.

"I meant what I said before. I want you to be my wife." Quinn paused. "Hell, that's not romantic. Sounds like I'm issuing an order to my deputy."

"How 'bout this?" he continued. Apparently he spoke to himself, for the only other sound she heard was that of pine boughs in the distance, stirred by a crisp breeze.

Anna heard movement, and she peeked from beneath her lashes to watch him get down on his knees.

She couldn't tell for certain, but the light looked strange, fragmented. Where were they? she wondered. She didn't ask though. As her strength returned, it felt more pleasant to listen to Quinn's rambling monologue.

"I love you, Anna. Will you marry me?" he asked. Apparently not satisfied, he tried again. "Would you do me the honor of becoming my wife?"

His words so completely lacked his usual cocky self-assurance that he sounded like a boy. As if to underscore the point, impatience rumbled to the surface.

"Dammit, will you wake up, Anna, so I can get this humiliation over with? I messed this up the last time, and I'll probably mess it up again—but I want you. I want you, darling. Wake up!"

Anna's pretense of sleep erupted into helpless laughter. Laughter that shook her shoulders and made her head ache. Still, she couldn't help herself. With Quinn she never could.

"That's what—" She tried to catch her breath but had to start anew. "That's what I've always liked about you, Ryan. You make me laugh."

Opening her eyes, she took in the rounded framework of hide-covered sticks that gave them shelter. In an instant she realized they were inside a Navajo hogan and she was lying on thick sheepskins, nude but for a blanket. But that hardly mattered as compared to the swift play of emotion in Quinn's eyes.

He pulled her into his embrace and rocked her. "Sweet Jesus, Anna, I was so afraid you'd never wake up. An old Navajo woman and a child brought me here. The old woman stitched your forehead—"

"How'd she do?" Anna asked, feeling the bandage. Thankfully the swelling beneath it seemed minimal.

"I checked earlier. It looks fine. I think it's healing well. She made you drink something and then put on some kind of medicine. I have to admit I was a little disappointed."

"Disappointed?"

The Ryan grin she knew so well reemerged. "Yeah. I was hoping to put on a goat-turd poultice like you did to me. After she tended you, the woman and the little girl disappeared."

"They disappeared?"

"Must have just walked off. Didn't even say a word. I don't know if they would have understood me, but I wanted to thank them just the same."

That fit with what she knew about the Navajo of the canyon. They'd experienced enough unpleasantness with Americans to make them wary.

"What about the others?" she asked. "Hamby and—"

"Dead, all of them. Even Ward Cameron. Did you know he was here?"

She shook her head, careful of the soreness. "What happened to my clothes, Quinn?"

"It's awfully quiet around here. A man needs some entertainment."

She slapped at his arm.

"You were so sticky with blood, I decided to try to clean you up a little," he explained.

"A likely story."

Quinn looked at her, and once again the humor faded from his eyes. In its place she saw the strain of worry and of want.

Despite the tenderness of her wound, she wanted nothing more than to reassure him there was no need to worry anymore. Gently, tentatively, her mouth sought his for a kiss.

He responded in an instant, deepening the kiss with all the emotion he'd held in check while she lay ill. It was a kiss that bared all his desires, a kiss that did not falter in the struggle to find words.

Her own passion flared in answer, and she eagerly accepted the questing of his tongue, the blazing sensation of his fingertips stroking the warm flesh beneath her blanket. Her nipples hardened with his teasing, and she felt that she must have him soon or die.

She drew strength from his caresses, strength enough to begin unbuttoning his shirt.

Pausing, he tried to help her, but she pushed his hands aside.

"You undressed me while I was sleeping." She gazed boldly into his eyes. "Now I'm rested, and I'm ready for my turn."

Working with deliberate, excruciating slowness, she loosened each button, moving steadily downward. She paused to kiss each inch of chest that she exposed and to listen to his gasps of pleasure.

"Oh, dear," she said as the two sides of the shirt parted at last. "It seems I'm out of buttons."

She put her thumb and a forefinger on a new one at his waist, the first of several that secured his trousers.

"Perhaps these will do as well," she suggested, her honeyed voice all innocence.

To her utter shock, he rolled away.

"Lord, Anna. I hope I don't spend my whole life regretting this, but this isn't what I want."

She glanced down but did not point out the evidence that suggested he was lying. Instead, heart pounding, she waited for him to explain.

"I don't want this to have to last me through a thousand lonely nights. I need this to be forever. I want you to be my wife. If you're going to stay alone in this canyon, I won't—I can't." He shook his head, then filled his eyes with her. "You're the most beautiful, amazing woman I have ever known. I know I'm going to regret this, Anna, but I have to tell you to stop."

"No, you don't," she told him, offering a smile. "You don't. This *is* forever, Ryan, because the Bard was wrong in our case. For us, as long as there is love, it's not too late."

He looked as stunned as she had felt just moments before. "Then, you'll—"

She nodded. "I'll marry you, Quinn. We'll work to straighten out things so you can do your job in Copper

Ridge. I'm sure the town can always use a midwife, enough so people won't worry about what happened years ago. We can ride out here once a month or so to see those homesteaders who need me. I don't care if Cameron found a vein of pure gold in my canyon. There's not going to be a mine here. I can't let greed drive the Navajo from their hogans or the ranchers from their spreads."

Careful so as not to hurt her, he kissed the top of her blond head. "I have all the gold that I need here, enough to last forever."

She kissed him deeply, her fingers making short work of the final buttons. And as the spring winds whispered through the red-rock canyon, Anna made each caress a promise, each kiss a sacred vow.

# ABOUT THE AUTHOR

Gwyneth Atlee lives in The Woodlands, Texas, with her husband, son, and a retired racing greyhound. Gwyneth is the author of *Touched by Fire* and *Night Winds* as well as the upcoming *Against the Odds* and *Trust to Chance*.

She loves hearing from readers; write to her at P.O. Box 131342, The Woodlands, Texas 77393-1342 or via e-mail at gwynethatlee@usa.net.

Learn more about her upcoming releases and read excerpts from them at http://atlee.cjb.net on the Web.

# Enjoy *Savage Destiny*
## A Romantic Series from
# Rosanne Bittner

___#1: Sweet Prairie Passion**     $5.99US/$6.99CAN
        0-8217-5342-8

___#2: Ride the Free Wind Passion**   $5.99US/$6.99CAN
        0-8217-5343-6

___#3: River of Love**            $5.99US/$6.99CAN
        0-8217-5344-4

___#4: Embrace the Wild Land**    $5.99US/$7.50CAN
        0-8217-5413-0

___#7: Eagle's Song**             $5.99US/$6.99CAN
        0-8217-5326-6

Call toll free **1-888-345-BOOK** to order by phone or use this coupon to order by mail.
Name _____
Address _____
City _____ State _____ Zip _____
Please send me the books I have checked above.
I am enclosing                                  $_____
Plus postage and handling*                      $_____
Sales tax (in New York and Tennessee)           $_____
Total amount enclosed                           $_____
*Add $2.50 for the first book and $.50 for each additional book.
Send check or money order (no cash or CODs) to:
**Kensington Publishing Corp., 850 Third Avenue, New York, NY 10022**
Prices and Numbers subject to change without notice.
All orders subject to availability.
Check out our website at **www.kensingtonbooks.com**

# Put a Little Romance in Your Life With
# Rosanne Bittner

| | | |
|---|---|---|
| \_\_Caress | 0-8217-3791-0 | $5.99US/$6.99CAN |
| \_\_Full Circle | 0-8217-4711-8 | $5.99US/$6.99CAN |
| \_\_Shameless | 0-8217-4056-3 | $5.99US/$6.99CAN |
| \_\_Unforgettable | 0-8217-5830-6 | $5.99US/$7.50CAN |
| \_\_Texas Embrace | 0-8217-5625-7 | $5.99US/$7.50CAN |
| \_\_Texas Passions | 0-8217-6166-8 | $5.99US/$7.50CAN |
| \_\_Until Tomorrow | 0-8217-5064-X | $5.99US/$6.99CAN |
| \_\_Love Me Tomorrow | 0-8217-5818-7 | $5.99US/$7.50CAN |

Call toll free **1-888-345-BOOK** to order by phone or use this coupon to order by mail.

Name_____
Address_____
City_____ State_____ Zip_____

Please send me the books I have checked above.
I am enclosing                                           $_____
Plus postage and handling*                               $_____
Sales tax (in New York and Tennessee)                    $_____
Total amount enclosed                                    $_____

*Add $2.50 for the first book and $.50 for each additional book.
Send check or money order (no cash or CODs) to:
**Kensington Publishing Corp., 850 Third Avenue, New York, NY 10022**
Prices and Numbers subject to change without notice.
All orders subject to availability.
Check out our website at **www.kensingtonbooks.com**

# Thrilling Romance from
# Meryl Sawyer

__Half Moon Bay__ $6.50US/$8.00CAN
0-8217-6144-7

__The Hideaway__ $5.99US/$7.50CAN
0-8217-5780-6

__Tempting Fate__ $6.50US/$8.00CAN
0-8217-5858-6

__Unforgettable__ $6.50US/$8.00CAN
0-8217-5564-1

---

Call toll free **1-888-345-BOOK** to order by phone or use this coupon to order by mail.
Name _____
Address _____
City _____ State _____ Zip _____
Please send me the books I have checked above.
I am enclosing $_____
Plus postage and handling* $_____
Sales tax (in New York and Tennessee) $_____
Total amount enclosed $_____
*Add $2.50 for the first book and $.50 for each additional book.
Send check or money order (no cash or CODs) to:
**Kensington Publishing Corp., 850 Third Avenue, New York, NY 10022**
Prices and Numbers subject to change without notice.
All orders subject to availability.
Check out our website at **www.kensingtonbooks.com**